Mediterranean
MEN
Unleashed

Jacqueline
BAIRD

Melanie
MILBURNE

Natalie
RIVERS

Harlequin (UK) policy is to use papers that are natural
and renewable products and made from wood grown in
forests. The logging and manufacturing processes conform to
legal environmental regulations of the country of origin.

Printed and bound in Spain
by Blackprint CPI, Barcelona

MILLS &
BOON

Mills & Boon, an imprint of Harlequin (UK) Limited, Eton House, 18-24 Paradise Road, Richmond, Surrey TW9 1SR

MEDITERRANEAN MEN UNLEASHED
© Harlequin Enterprises II B.V./S.à.r.l. 2012

The publisher acknowledges the copyright holders of the individual works as follows:

The Billionaire's Blackmailed Bride © Jacqueline Baird 2008
The Venadicci Marriage Vengeance © Melanie Milburne 2009
The Blackmail Baby © Natalie Rivers 2009

ISBN: 978 0 263 90203 7

010-0912

… al, renewable
… n sustainable
LONDON BOROUGH OF WANDSWORTH … nform to the
… in.

LONDON BOROUGH OF WANDSWORTH	
9030 00002 7508 6	
Askews & Holts	23-Aug-2012
AF ROM	£6.99

Experience the fiery revenge of these
Mediterranean males!

Mediterranean
MEN
Unleashed

Three sinfully seductive stories from
favourite authors Jacqueline Baird,
Melanie Milburne and Natalie Rivers!

The Billionaire's Blackmailed Bride

Jacqueline
BAIRD

Jacqueline Baird began writing as a hobby, when her family objected to the smell of her oil painting, and immediately became hooked on the romantic genre. She loves travelling and worked her way around the world from Europe to the Americas and Australia, returning to marry her teenage sweetheart. She lives in Ponteland, Northumbria, the county of her birth, and has two sons.

CHAPTER ONE

'I STILL can't believe you chose this for me,' Emily Fairfax said with a shake of her head as she sat down opposite her older brother Tom and his wife Helen at their table in the vast ballroom of the deluxe London hotel. 'I feel terribly conspicuous.' Embarrassment coloured her face almost as red as the outfit she was wearing.

'Oh, lighten up, Emily. You look great.' Tom grinned at her. 'This is a costume ball for Dad's favourite charity, The Children of Africa's Guardian Angel Project; he would have appreciated the Devil and Angels theme. Dad had a great sense of humour. Remember Mum's fortieth when he insisted everyone dress as Knights and Squires? I think he would have seen the funny side…'

'All too well. Most of the women ended up looking like young boys, dressed in doublet and hose. I wondered at the time if Dad had secret gay tendencies,' she quipped and then turned her sparkling blue gaze on her sister-in-law, a petite gamine-faced brunette. 'But this is different, Helen. There is nothing funny about being squeezed into a red latex suit that is a couple of sizes too small. What on earth were you thinking of when you ordered it?' she demanded, and saw the mischief dancing in Helen's brown eyes and her lips twisted in a wry smile.

Tom and Helen had met at university and had married two

years ago at the age of twenty-three. They were now the proud parents of a one-year-old daughter, who had been born the week before Tom and Emily's father had died suddenly of a massive heart attack. The child was named Sara after their mother, who had died three years earlier after a long battle with cancer.

'I don't know what you are complaining about. You look fine, and I went to a lot of trouble to get that costume in the right size. At four and a half months pregnant I am actually the same bust measurement as you and I tried it on to make sure it would fit,' Helen said with a grin.

'Did it never occur to you that you're five feet nothing and I am five nine—that it would have to go a little further on me?' Emily groaned. 'You damn near broke my neck pulling the hood over my head. It is still aching.' She slipped a hand beneath the heavy fall of her hair and rubbed the nape of her neck to emphasize the point.

'Don't blame me. If you had come back to London yesterday as you were supposed to, you would have had time to get your own costume. But instead you spent another day on site and only arrived a couple of hours before the event. Plus it is April Fool's Day,' she said with an impish grin. 'And be fair— I did cut the hood off and twist it into a braid so you could wear the horns as a head band.' She burst out laughing.

Emily bit her lip to fight down the answering grin that threatened. She had totally forgotten it was the first of April, and Helen was right—she should have returned from Santorini yesterday instead of flying into London this evening. She really had no one to blame but herself, but she wasn't going to let her beloved sister-in-law off too easy.

'Anyone with a grain of common sense would have ordered an angel costume for me. The same as yours, I might add. It is only logical that the women dress as angels and the men as devils. Like my idiot brother T—'

'Excuse me.' A deep, slightly accented voice cut into Emily's good-natured tirade. 'Hello, Tom, nice to see you again.'

'Anton, glad you and your friends could make it.'

Emily looked over at her brother as he greeted the new arrivals he had invited to make up their table of eight.

She glanced up at the man who had so rudely interrupted her. His back was turned to her and he was pulling out a chair for his companion, a stunning brunette who naturally was dressed like an angel in a diaphanous gold and white fabric that seemed to reveal a lot more flesh than Emily imagined any self-respecting angel would reveal.

At least her outfit covered her from neck to toe, she consoled herself, though she had been forced to undo the front zip a few inches to prevent the damn thing crushing her chest so tightly she could barely breathe. It wasn't her usual style, that was for sure, but it didn't really faze her. She knew she had a decent enough body, she just wasn't used to displaying it quite so dramatically.

'Allow me to introduce my friend Eloise,' the deep voice continued as the brunette sent a social smile around the table, 'and my right-hand man, Max.'

Emily glanced at the middle-aged burly man and smiled in welcome as he took his seat at the table next to Helen. Then the stranger turned to her.

'Emily, isn't it? Tom has told me a lot about you. It is a real pleasure to finally meet you. I am Anton Diaz.' A large strong hand was held out and she politely put her hand in his, while her mind busily wondered how Tom knew the man, and why her brother would have mentioned her to him.

Then suddenly her mind went blank as a bizarre sensation a bit like an electric eel snaking up her arm had her skin breaking out in goose-bumps under the latex. Hastily she pulled her hand free and slowly looked up.

Emily had a long way to go… He had to be at least six feet four, she reckoned, and then her curious blue gaze collided with deep brown eyes and she simply stared…

The man was like a sleek black panther: poised, powerful and predatory.

She grimaced inwardly at the fanciful notion, really not her usual style.

The introductions moved on and Emily supposed she had made the right response, though she could not be sure. Her mouth felt dry and she had trouble tearing her fascinated gaze away from the tall, striking man.

He was dressed all in black. A black silk-knit roll-necked sweater outlined the impressive musculature of his broad chest. A short black cloak covered his wide shoulders and flowed down like bats' wings to broad cuffs around strong wrists, set off by tailored black trousers. He should have looked ridiculous in costume like the majority of the people present. Instead, if ever a man looked like a devil it was this one…

Dark and dangerous, she thought, her heart inexplicably tightening in her chest, and for a moment she had difficulty breathing that had nothing to do with the latex suit she wore.

His straight black hair worn slightly longer than was fashionable was swept casually back off his broad forehead. Distinctive arched brows framed deep-set almost black eyes, high cheekbones, a large hawklike nose and a wide sensuous mouth completed the picture. As she stared his lips parted to reveal even white teeth. He was smiling down at her. She lifted her eyes to his and even in her stunned state she recognized the humour did not entirely mask the cool remoteness of his dark gaze.

The man was not conventionally handsome, his features too large and harshly chiselled for classic male beauty.

Brutally handsome…was a better description.

There was something insulting about the way his dark eyes slid casually down to her cleavage and lingered for a long moment. But even as she recognized his insolent masculine appraisal for what it was her skin prickled with shocking awareness. The breath caught in her throat and she gave a shaky inward sigh of relief when he casually pulled out the chair next to hers, and lowered his long length into it.

It could be worse, Emily told herself, at least with Anton Diaz seated at her side, she did not have to face him.

Instinctively she recognized he was a man who was supremely confident in his masculinity and totally aware of his effect on the opposite sex, and discreetly she crossed her arms over her suddenly hardening nipples. A sophisticated charmer with an aura of ruthless power about him that would intimidate anybody, man or woman, she concluded. Not her type at all…

Even so, there was no escaping the fact he was an incredibly sexy man, as her body's unexpected response confirmed.

'I could not help overhearing your comment, Emily. Shame on you, your chauvinism is showing.' The devil spoke in a deep, dark, mocking voice that made her hackles rise.

'What do you mean, Mr Diaz?' she asked him with cool politeness, flicking him a sidelong glance, and was once again captured by the intensity of his dark eyes.

'In today's world of equality between the sexes isn't it rather politically incorrect to assume all the women should dress as angels and the men as devils? And, given the very striking outfit you are wearing, just a little hypocritical,' he drawled mockingly.

'He has got you there,' Helen piped up and everyone laughed.

Everyone but Emily.

'My costume was my sister-in-law's choice, not mine. She has a warped sense of humour,' she explained, forcing a smile to her lips. 'And I see you are dressed as a devil, rather upholding my theory. Though you do seem to have forgotten the horns,' she prompted smoothly.

'No, I didn't forget. I never forget anything,' he asserted, his dark eyes holding hers with an intimacy that made her pulse race and she could do nothing about the pink that tinged her cheeks. 'I am supposed to be an angel, admittedly a dark angel, but an angel nevertheless.'

Emily saw what he meant, her blue eyes sweeping over him. It was the perfect costume for him. Unrelenting black and somehow threatening… She glimpsed a darkening in his deep-set eyes and something more. Anger… Why? She had no idea, and in an attempt to control her overheated imagination and body she looked somewhere past his left shoulder. She took a deep steadying breath, but for a long moment was incapable of making a response. No man had ever had such a startling effect on her in her life, and she had met plenty, and been attracted to a few, but never quite like this.

She was a twenty-four-year-old freelance marine archaeologist and had spent the last two years since qualifying gaining experience in her field. She had been on a few seagoing explorations. Her colleagues were mostly men, explorers, divers and fellow archaeologists with the skills needed to search and map out underwater wrecks and artifacts. Yet never once had she felt the sudden heat, the stomach-churning excitement that this man aroused in her with one look.

Get a grip, girl, she told herself. He was with his very beautiful girlfriend and, while Emily considered herself passably attractive, she was no competition for the lovely Eloise.

What was she thinking of?

At twenty-one, after a disastrous engagement that had ended abruptly after three days when she had found her fiancé in bed with her flatmate at university, she had sworn off men.

Nigel had been an accountant in her father's firm. A man she had fallen in love with at sixteen, a man who had kissed her at her eighteenth birthday party and declared he felt the same, a man who had offered her comfort and support when her mother was ill and died, a man whose proposal she had accepted shortly after. A man who, when she had confronted him in bed with her flatmate, had actually admitted the affair had been going on for a year. Her flatmate, her supposed friend, twisted the knife by telling her she was a fool. Nigel's interest in Emily had only ever been for her money and connections.

Which was a laugh. Admittedly the family home was probably worth millions in today's market, but they lived in it, had done for generations. The business earned the shareholders a decent dividend each year but not a fortune by any means, but at the time she had felt utterly betrayed. She would no more compete for a man than fly to the moon, and, to be honest, over the intervening years, she had never felt the need. Which was probably why she had never since had a long-term relationship? she thought wryly.

'Yes, of course, I see it now, a silly mistake on my part,' she finally responded.

'You're forgiven,' he said with a smile that took her breath away all over again.

But at that moment the last two guests making up the table arrived and Emily smiled with relief. It was her aunt Lisa, her father's older sister, and her husband, James Browning, who was also the Chairman of the Board of Fairfax Engineering since her dad's death. She felt the light brush of Anton's shoulder against hers as, like a perfect gentleman, he stood up until Lisa was seated, and she determinedly ignored it.

Her equilibrium thankfully restored…

James took the seat on the other side of Emily. 'Aunt Lisa, Uncle James, it's good to see you,' she offered, her wayward emotions firmly under control.

But it was the *sotto voce* comment that Anton Diaz made among the flurry of introduction as he sat back down that threw her off balance yet again. 'But if a devil is more to your liking I'm sure something can be arranged.'

Her mouth open, her face scarlet, she stared at Anton. One dark brow rose in sardonic query, before he turned to respond to Eloise's rather loud request for champagne.

Was she hearing things? Had he actually made such a blatantly flirtatious comment or had she imagined what he said?

She did not know…and she did not know whether to feel angry or flattered as dinner was served. Emily's emotions stayed in pretty much the same state of flux until it was over; she was intensely aware of the man at her side.

The conversation was sociable, and when the meal ended and the band began to play Emily could not help watching Anton and Eloise as they took to the dance floor. Both Latin in looks, they made a striking couple and the way Eloise curved into her partner's body, her arms firmly clasped around his neck, left no one in any doubt of the intimacy of their relationship.

Emily turned to James and asked what she had been dying to ask all evening. Who exactly was Anton Diaz?

According to her uncle, Anton Diaz was the founder of a private equity business that made massive profits out of buying, restructuring and then selling on great chunks of worldwide businesses. It made him a man of enormous influence and power. It had also made him extremely rich. He was revered worldwide as a financial genius, with a fortune to match. His nationality was hazy, his name was hispanic, yet some considered him Greek because he spoke the language like a native. Rumours about him abounded. Her aunt Lisa offered the most colourful speculation that his grandmother had been the madam of a high-class brothel in Peru, and her daughter had been a wealthy Greek's mistress for years and Anton Diaz was the result of the affair.

Her aunt also informed her archly that he owned a magnificent villa on a Greek island, a vast estate in Peru, a luxurious apartment in New York and another in Sydney. Recently he had acquired a prestigious office block in London with a stunning penthouse at the top, and there were probably more. Plus the parties he held on his huge luxury yacht were legendary.

James attempted to steer the conversation back to less gossipy ground by continuing that he knew Anton was multilingual because he had heard him employ at least four languages when they had first met at a European conference a couple of months ago. Since then they had become business acquaintances and friends of a sort, hence Tom inviting Anton and his party to join them tonight. In fact, Anton Diaz's expert advice had been instrumental in them deciding to diversify and expand Fairfax Engineering, James informed her in an almost reverential tone.

It was news to Emily that the firm needed revising or expanding, but she had no time to dwell on that revelation as her aunt chimed in again. Apparently Anton was a confirmed bachelor and as famous for the women he had bedded as he was for his financial skills. His countless affairs were apparently well documented by the press, actresses and models featuring prominently.

Emily believed her uncle and aunt and in a sense felt relieved. Her earlier reaction to Anton Diaz had been normal under the circumstances. The man exuded a raw animal magnetism that probably affected every woman he met the same way, and if his press was to be believed he took full advantage of the fact. He was not the type of man any self-respecting woman would want to get involved with.

After her one disastrous relationship Emily had very firm ideas on the type of man she eventually wanted to marry. She wanted a like-minded man she could trust. Certainly not a womanizing, globe-trotting billionaire, plus she was in no hurry to marry—she enjoyed her work far too much to think of curtailing her career for any man for years yet.

Draining her coffee-cup, she smiled at James and Lisa affectionately as they decided to dance. Then looking around the table, she saw only the burly Max was left.

Emily was naturally a happy, confident girl with a successful career and a growing name in her field of expertise. She was also a realist and never let anything she could not change bother her for long. She was a firm believer in making the best of any situation. Neither the blatantly sexy costume she wore nor her strange reaction to the indomitable Anton Diaz was going to prevent her enjoying the evening.

'So, Max, would you like to dance?' she asked with a broad smile. She watched him blink, then grin and leap to his feet with alacrity.

'It will be my pleasure,' he said as he pulled out her chair. His brown eyes widened as she rose to her feet, sweeping over the length of her body with unconcealed admiration. 'You are a very lovely lady, señorita,' he said, taking her hand and leading her to the dance floor.

Max was about an inch taller than Emily, and quite a lot wider, but for a heavy man he was a very good dancer and surprisingly light on his feet. Emily relaxed in his hold and began to have fun.

* * *

Anton Diaz allowed a small satisfied smile to curve his hard mouth. True, the man he had really wanted to meet, Charles Fairfax, had died a year ago. But his family and firm still existed, and would do just as well for his purpose.

He glanced around the glittering throng. London's social élite letting their hair down in a costume ball in aid of African children, and apparently a favoured charity of the Fairfax family. The bitter irony of it did not escape him and for a moment his black eyes glinted with an unholy light.

Last December when his mother, as if sensing the end was near, had finally told him the truth about the death of his sister Suki twenty-six years ago it had given him one hell of a shock. Actually Suki had been his half-sister, but as a child he had never thought of her like that. To him she had been his older sister who took care of him.

He had believed Suki died in a car accident, tragic but unavoidable. But apparently she had deliberately driven her car off a cliff and left a note for his mother that she had immediately destroyed.

Suki had committed suicide because she had been convinced it was due to her family name and her illegitimacy that her lover, Charles Fairfax, had left her and married someone else. Then his mother had made him promise never to be ashamed of his name or his heritage.

Bitterness and bile rose in his throat just thinking about it now. He had named his company in memory of Suki, but the name had an added poignancy now. The letter he had discovered among his mother's papers after her death had confirmed she had told him the truth and more, and he had vowed on his mother's grave to avenge the insult to his sister no matter how long it took.

He was not a fan of costume parties and usually avoided them like the plague, but on this occasion he had an ulterior motive for accepting the invitation to share a table with the Fairfax family.

A deep frown marred his broad brow. Never in his hugely successful career had he ever had any trouble taking over any company he wanted and Fairfax Engineering should have been an easy acquisition. His first idea had been a hostile takeover bid and then the destruction of the company, but on studying the firm's set-up he was reluctantly forced to the conclusion that plan would not work.

The problem was the company was privately owned by family members and a small portion was diverted into a share scheme for the workforce. Also unfortunately for him it was well run and profitable. It had originally been based on the ownership of a coalmine, but a previous Fairfax had had the foresight to expand into engineering. Now that coalmining was virtually defunct in Britain the firm had found a niche market building a specific type of earth-moving equipment that was used in most countries in Europe.

With a few discreet enquiries it had become obvious none of the principal shareholders was prepared to sell even at a very generous price, and, while not giving up on a buyout, he had been obliged to adopt another strategy.

He had planned to persuade the company it would be in their best interest to expand into America and China, with his expert advice and generous financial backing, of course. Then when they had overextended themselves financially he could step in and pull the rug from under them and take the firm, in the process virtually bankrupting the Fairfax family. With that in mind he had deliberately made the acquaintance of the chairman of the board, and the MD, Tom, the son of Charles Fairfax.

The only downside to his strategy was it was taking him a hell of a lot longer than he had anticipated to grind the Fairfax name into the dust. Three months of manoeuvring and, while he was closer to attaining his goal, he wasn't there yet. The problem was the son and uncle that ran the business were both competent but very conservative businessmen and, again unfortunately for Anton, neither of them appeared to be particularly greedy or the type to take unnecessary risks.

But why would they be? he thought cynically. The company was over a hundred and sixty years old and they had never had to fight to make a living or to be accepted by their peers.

'Anton, darling, what are you thinking?'

He disliked the question, though he had heard it often enough and experience had taught him where women were concerned it was best ignored or answered with a white lie. Exasperated, he looked down at the woman in his arms. 'The latest figure on the Dow Jones—nothing that would interest you.'

'My figure is the only one you should be thinking of,' she responded with a pout, plastering herself to him.

'Save the flirting for your husband. I'm immune,' he said bluntly. Eloise was very beautiful, but she did nothing for him except remind him of his sister. That was why he had helped her out of a bad situation twelve years ago in Lima when her manager at the time had signed her up for what was undeniably a porn movie. He got her out of the contract and found her a reputable manager and they had been friends ever since. She was married to a close friend of his and yet given the chance she wasn't above trying to seduce him.

He supposed it was his own fault in a way because once, a decade ago, he had succumbed to her charms one night, though he had very quickly realized he had made a big mistake. Their friendship had survived, and now it was a game she played whenever they met, and he could not entirely blame her. He should have got tough with her long since.

Eloise was her husband's responsibility now. He had to stop pandering to her constant whims this time to hold her hand while she auditioned for a lead in a West End musical. Actually it had been no hardship because he was staying in London a lot more than he had at first anticipated. He had Fairfax Engineering firmly in his sights… He almost felt sorry for the son and daughter; they were young and no competition for him.

He thought of the report he had got from the investigator some months ago. The only photo of the daughter was of a woman standing on a deserted beach with the ocean behind her, wearing a baseball cap that masked her eyes, an oversized shirt and combat trousers. There had been no point of reference to say if she was tall or short, fat or thin.

He had been surprised when he saw her seated at the table. The photo had not done her justice. A ridiculous horned headband held back a shinning mane of blonde hair that fell smooth as silk down past her shoulder blades. Whether the colour was natural or dyed he didn't know, but it looked good. She had the peaches and cream complexion of a stereotypical English rose with magnificent big blue eyes, a full-lipped wide mouth and her breasts looked just about perfect. As for the rest he could not tell, average height maybe. But as a connoisseur of women he would reserve judgement until he saw her standing up. She could quite possibly have a big behind and short stumpy legs. Not that it concerned him; he wasn't going there. The fact she was a Fairfax was a huge turn-off; he wouldn't touch her if she were the last woman in the world.

Charles Fairfax had married the Honourable Sara Deveral in what had been the society wedding of the year twenty-six years ago. His wife had borne him a son nine months later, Tom, and a daughter, Emily, a year after that. The perfect family…

Emily Fairfax had led a charmed life. She had the best of everything. A loving family, a good education, a career of sorts as a freelance archaeologist, and she moved in London society with a confidence that was bred in the bone. The likes of Charles Fairfax were big on breeding, and the thought brought back the bitter resentment that had simmered within him since the death of his mother.

'I don't believe it.' Eloise tilted back her head and Anton glanced down at her. 'Max is actually dancing the tango...'

Anton was diverted from his sombre thoughts and followed his partner's gaze, his dark eyes widening in shock and something more as they settled on his Head of Security and erstwhile body-guard, though Max, at fifty, was more of a friend than anything else. He hadn't registered the band was playing the tango.

When Anton had a woman in his arms he held her close and naturally moved to the rhythm of the music, the steps not important. But Max was old school and was dancing the tango with all the passion and arrogance of a real aficionado. Incredibly his partner was with him every step of the way.

His eyes narrowed, absorbing the picture she presented. Emily Fairfax was stunning, and the only reason Anton had thought she was average height was instantly apparent. She had fantastically long legs in proportion to her height, a round tight behind, narrow waist and high firm breasts. The red suit was glued to her like a second skin leaving absolutely nothing to the imagination and as Max swung her around Anton doubted there was a man in the room who wasn't watching her. Her blonde hair swung around her shoulders in a shimmering cloud as she moved. And what a mover... An instant pleasurable though inconvenient sensation stirred in Anton's loins.

'Don't they look ridiculous?' Eloise tugged on his neck. 'No one dances like that these days.'

'What…? Yes…' he lied, for once less than his suave self, while silently conceding the pair looked superb, and the majority of people on the floor had stopped to watch. Max dipped Emily low over his arm, her hair touching the floor as the music drew to a close. Anton saw Emily grin as Max lifted her upright and then burst out laughing as the applause echoed around the ballroom.

The woman was not afraid of making an exhibition of herself, and, given the fire and passion in the way she danced, she was definitely no innocent. Such passion could not be confined solely to the dance floor; he recalled that she had been engaged once, according to the report he had read, and there had probably been quite a few men since.

Suddenly, having decided he would not touch her if she were the last woman on earth, Anton was imagining her long, lithesome naked body under his, and it took all his self-control to rein in his rampant libido—something that hadn't happened to him in years.

Deep in thought, he frowned as he led Eloise back to the table. He had set out to destroy Fairfax Engineering, everything Charles Fairfax owned, but he had to concede it was going to take him some time. But now an alternative scenario, a way to hedge his bet on gaining control of the company, formed in his Machiavellian mind. The solution he reached had a perfect poetic justice to it that made his firm lips twist in a brief, decidedly sinister smile.

Marriage had never appealed to him before, but he was thirty-seven, an ideal time to take a wife and produce an heir to inherit his fortune. He bred horses in Peru, and at least physically Emily Fairfax was good breeding stock, he assessed sardonically. As for her morals, he wasn't bothered about the past men in her life, with what he had on her family, she would dance to his tune and disruption to his life would be minimal. He frowned again; maybe Emily Fairfax had a man in her life now. Not that he was afraid of competition—he never had any trouble getting any woman he wanted. With his incredible wealth his problem was the reverse: fighting them off. And Emily had no partner with her tonight, which left him a clear field.

'Thank you, Max.' Emily was still smiling as her dancing partner held out her chair for her. 'I really enjoyed that,' she said as she sat down.

'It is good to see the fortune the parents spent on sending us both to dancing classes wasn't completely wasted,' Tom said, grinning as he and Helen sat down.

'The lessons were certainly wasted on you,' Helen quipped. 'I don't think my feet will ever recover.'

Lisa piped up with, 'Join the club—after forty years of marriage and countless attempts at dancing James still has two left feet.'

Emily laughed at the friendly banter between her family and friends, unaware that the other couple had returned to the table.

CHAPTER TWO

IT WAS a shock when into the cheerful atmosphere Anton Diaz laid a hand on Emily's arm and asked her for the next dance.

She wanted to refuse, but, glancing at Max, she saw he had taken Eloise's hand and was obviously going to dance with her. The hostile look the other woman gave Anton said louder than words she wasn't delighted at the change of partner.

'Go on, Emily,' Tom encouraged. 'You know you love dancing.' He grinned. 'And if our wives are to be believed James and I are useless. Anton is your only chance.'

'Thanks, brother.' Emily snorted and reluctantly accepted and rose to her feet.

Anton gave her a wry smile. 'Your brother lacks a little subtlety,' he drawled as if he knew exactly what she was thinking. 'But I am not complaining if it gets you in my arms.'

Then, rather than taking her arm, he placed his own very firmly around her waist, his strong hand curving over her hipbone as he urged her towards the dance floor. His touch was much too personal and his great body much too close for Emily's comfort and it only got worse...

As soon as they reached the dance floor he turned her to face him, his arm tightening around her waist as he drew her closer, and at that moment the band began playing a dreamy ballad. She stiffened in his hold, determined to resist a sudden inexplicable desire to collapse against him as he took her hand and linked his fingers with hers and cradled it against his broad chest.

'You surprised me, Emily,' he said, his dark eyes seeking hers. 'You dance the tango superbly—I was quite envious of Max,' he admitted. 'Though to be honest, dancing is not one of my talents. I could not tango to save my life. I am more a shuffle-to-the-music man,' he said with a self-effacing grin that lightened his saturnine features, making him look somewhat approachable. 'So I hope you won't be disappointed,' he concluded with a querying arch of one black brow.

Disappointed… It was a rare occurrence for Emily to dance with a man she had literally to look up to and it turned out to be frighteningly seductive. He fitted her perfectly and, enveloped in his arms, the black cloak enfolding her created an added intimacy. Disappointment was not an emotion troubling Emily, though a host of others were. With his long leg subtly easing between hers as he turned her slowly to the romantic music, her pulse raced, her heart pounded and every nerve end in her body was screaming with tension as she battled to retain control of her wayward body. The damn latex suit was no help; it simply emphasized every brush of his muscular body against hers. And she seriously doubted Anton Diaz had ever disappointed a woman in his life. Certainly not the lovely Eloise, and the thought cooled her helpless reaction to him enough for her to respond.

'Oh, I think not,' she said with blunt honesty. She knew she was reasonably attractive and she had been hit on by many men over the years, but since her failed engagement she had learnt to put men off with no trouble. 'I also think, Mr Diaz, a man of your wealth and power is perfectly well aware of his talents and exploits them quite ruthlessly for his own ends.' Anton might make her heart beat faster—her and the rest of the female population—but she had no intention of falling for his charm. 'As I'm sure the tabloids and your friend Eloise could confirm,' she ended dryly.

'Ah, Emily, you have been listening to gossip. What was it? I was brought up in a brothel surrounded by willing women,' he mocked. 'Sorry to disappoint, but it is not true, though my grandmother did own one,' he admitted, 'and it is a poor reflection on the male of the species that she made rather a lot of money. Enough to send her daughter to the best school in the country and on to a finishing school in Switzerland.'

Emily's blue eyes widened in surprise at his blunt revelations, her tension forgotten as she listened intrigued as he continued.

'When she was in Europe she met and fell in love with a Greek man who was unfortunately married with children. But he was decent enough to set her up in a house in Corinth where I was born. Their affair lasted for years, he died when I was twelve and my mother decided to return to Peru.'

'That is so sad. Your poor mother, you poor boy,' she murmured. Totally absorbed in his story, she compassionately squeezed his hand.

'I might have guessed you would feel sorry for me.' His dark head bent and his lips brushed her brow. 'Ah, Emily, you are so naive and so misguided. As a wealthy man's mistress my mother was never poor in the monetary sense and neither was I.' He looked into her big blue eyes, his own gleaming with cynical amusement. 'I hate to disillusion you, but your sympathy is wasted on me.'

'So why did you tell me all that?' she asked, puzzled. He did not strike her as the sort of man who would bare his soul to a relative stranger.

'Maybe because it got you to relax in my arms.' He smiled.

'Was it all lies?' she shot back, her body stiffening again, this time in anger.

'Not all…I actually am a bastard.' He grinned, the hand at her waist stroking slowly up her back, drawing her closer still. And she involuntarily trembled in his hold. 'And as you so rightly said,' he drawled softly, 'I use all the talents I have to get what I want. And I want you, Emily Fairfax.'

Stunned by his outrageous comment, she stared up into his night-black eyes, and saw the desire he made no attempt to hide. 'You devious devil,' she exclaimed.

'Angel,' he amended, his dark head dipping, his warm breath tickling her ear as he urged her hard against him, making her intimately aware of his aroused state. 'And the way you tremble in my arms I know you want me. The attraction between us was instant and electric so don't pretend otherwise, Emily,' he commanded, and straightened up.

'You're unbelievable,' she gasped. Though she could not deny the trembling, or the attraction, she had no intention of succumbing to such blatant seduction. 'Coming on to me when you have the beautiful Eloise with—'

He cut her off. 'Eloise is a very old friend, nothing more I can assure you, and so could her husband,' he said, his dark eyes holding hers, a wicked gleam in their ebony depths. 'She is quite a famous television star in Latin America, but she has ambitions to be famous worldwide. Which is why she is over here to discuss the possibility of starring in a musical production in the West End next year. She is going back to her husband tomorrow so you have nothing to be jealous about.'

'Jealous. Are you crazy? I don't even know you,' Emily spluttered.

'That is soon remedied. I will call you tomorrow and arrange a time for our dinner date,' he declared, and stopped dancing, his hands sliding to span her waist, and hold her still. 'But now I think we'd better get back to the table, before people start to gossip. The music has ended.'

Emily had not noticed, and, embarrassed, she followed him like a lamb to slaughter, she realized later…much later…

'For heaven's sake, Emily, will you stop devouring that disgusting fry-up—it is turning my stomach—and listen to me,' Helen declared. 'You have to put the poor man out of his misery and have dinner with him. He has sent you roses every single day and the housekeeper is fed up with taking his phone calls. The house is overflowing with blooms and in my pregnant state I might very well get hay fever.'

Emily popped the last bit of fried egg into her mouth, chewed, then grinned at her sister-in-law. 'You know the solution—I told you to throw the flowers away. I'm not interested.'

'Liar—the woman is not born who would not fancy Anton Diaz. Your trouble is you're afraid to get involved after the hateful Nigel. You haven't dated any man for more than a couple of weeks in years.'

'*Moi*?' Emily quipped, placing a hand on her heart. 'I am not afraid of anyone, but I know a devil when I see one, and Anton Diaz is not the kind of man any sensible woman would ever get involved with.'

'Forget the sensible, and live a little. You're at home for the next few months and your research at the museum does not take more than a couple of days a week. It is spring, when a young woman's fancy turns to love.'

'A young man's fancy, you mean, and Anton Diaz is no young man,' Emily responded dryly.

'So what if he is a dozen or more years older than you? You

have plenty of spare time and a wild passionate affair with an experienced man would do you the world of good.'

'I don't think so, and I have no time right now. I am going to view another apartment today,' Emily said, hoping to change the subject, because the subject of Anton Diaz had taken up a great deal of her waking thoughts since the night she had met him. His phone calls she had refused after the first day as just the sound of his deep accented voice made her temperature rise and her whole body blush; the daily roses she could do nothing about.

'Oh, for heaven's sake, Emily, forget about buying an apartment. It's a stupid idea. This is your family home, has been for generations since the first Fairfax made his fortune as a coal baron in the nineteenth century, and it is big enough for all of us and half a dozen more.'

Helen rolled her eyes around the spacious breakfast room of the ten-bedroomed double-fronted Georgian house in the heart of Kensington. 'I would hate it if you left and you would hate living on your own. Admit it. And you might as well admit you fancy Anton Diaz something rotten. I have seen the way you try not to blush every time his name is mentioned. You can't fool me.'

Emily groaned. 'Your trouble is, Helen, you know me far too well.' She rose to her feet and smiled wryly down at her sister-in-law. 'I am still going to look at the apartment, though. After all, if I am going to have a wild, passionate affair I will need a place of my own. I'm sure you wouldn't appreciate my bringing a lover back here where your gorgeous child might see and hear more than she should.' She grinned.

'You're going to do it—you're going out with the man?'

'Maybe if Anton calls again and asks me out I will accept. Satisfied?'

'You will accept what?' Tom demanded as he walked into the room, with his daughter in his arms.

'Emily is going out with Anton Diaz,' Helen declared.

'Is that wise, sis?' he asked Emily, his blue eyes serious as they rested on her. 'He is a hell of a lot older than you. Are you sure you know what you are doing? Don't get me wrong, he is a great guy and his business knowledge is second to none—his input and advice to Fairfax Engineering has been exceptional. But he is the type of man that makes other men want to lock up their wives and daughters. The man definitely lives in the fast lane and has a poor track record with women.'

'I don't believe it!' Emily exclaimed. 'Much as I love you two, you should work at coordinating your opinions and advice.' And, grinning, she walked out.

Fate, kismet, whatever it was, but as she entered the hall the telephone rang and she answered. Anton...

'You're a very hard lady to get hold of, Emily. But I like a challenge. Have dinner with me tonight?'

So, she did what she had wanted to do for days and said yes...

Emily viewed the apartment and decided against it. Then spent the rest of the morning at the museum, and the afternoon shopping for a new dress.

Emily smiled, happy with her reflection in the mirror, and, straightening her shoulders, she picked up her dark blue wrap and matching purse from the bed and left the room. She was nervous, butterflies were fluttering in her stomach, but none of her inner emotions showed as she opened the drawing-room door and walked in. Anton Diaz was picking her up at seven and it was ten to.

'Well, Helen, will I do?' She smiled at her sister-in-law reclining on a sofa, a glass of juice in her hand, and saw the embarrassed expression on her face just as a deep dark voice responded.

'You look beautiful, Emily.'

Emily turned her head, her eyes widening as Anton walked towards her from the far side of the room, Tom trailing in his wake.

'Thank you.' She accepted the compliment politely, but it was an effort. She had thought he looked dangerous dressed as a dark angel, but in a perfectly tailored light grey suit with a white shirt and silk tie he looked gorgeous. 'You're early,' she added, raising her eyes to his face. He had stopped barely a foot from her, and his dark gaze slid slowly over her from head to toe, then he lifted his eyes to hers and what she saw in the smouldering black depths made the breath catch in her throat.

For the second time in a week Anton Diaz could not control his instant arousal at the sight of a woman. He had seen a photo of Emily in baggy clothes, and seen her in a very sexy latex suit with her hair down. But the Emily who stood before him now was something else again. She was the personification of so-phisticated elegance.

Her blonde hair was swept up into a knot on top of her head, her make-up understated, but perfect. Her big blue eyes were accentuated even more by the clever use of cosmetics, her full lips a soft glossy rose. As for her gown, it was designer; he had bought enough over the years to know. Ice-blue to match her eyes, it was cut on the bias, the bodice, supported by slight straps, clung faithfully to her high firm breasts and subtly shaped her narrow waist and hips to flare ever so slightly a few inches from the hem that ended on her knees. Not too short to appear tacky, but short enough for a man to fantasize about slipping his hand beneath it.

'Beautiful does not do you justice—you look exquisite, Emily. I will be the envy of every man in the restaurant.' Reaching for a cashmere wrap that she held in her hand, he gently took it and slipped it over her shoulders. 'Shall we go?'

It was definitely going to be no hardship to bed the lovely Emily, the finer details of when and where were all he had to decide on, he thought as he battled to control his libido.

Amazingly, Tom Fairfax, despite his usual easygoing nature, had taken him to one side when he had arrived and told him quite seriously he expected Anton to behave himself with Emily and return her home at a reasonable hour. No one had attempted to tell him what to do in years, if ever, and he had been too stunned to reply when Emily had walked into the room.

He could understand the man's concern, but it simply reminded him that he had been unable to take care of his own sister, and the memory cooled his wayward body in an instant.

Emily was too flustered to do more than take the hand Anton offered her. She felt his hand tighten on hers, and caught a flicker of some strange emotion in his dark eyes, gone as he turned and said goodnight to Tom and Helen.

He opened the passenger door of a silver Bentley and ushered her inside. She watched as he walked around the bonnet and slid behind the wheel. He glanced at her, one brow arched enquiringly, and she realized she was staring like a besotted fool.

'Where are you taking me?' She blurted the first thing that came into her head.

He chuckled a deep dark sound. 'To dinner, Emily.' Slipping a hand around her neck, he tilted her face to his dark eyes dancing with amusement. 'But ultimately to my bed.'

His provocative statement had her lips parting in a shocked gasp, and Anton's mouth covered them, firm, warm and tender. Her lips tingled and trembled as his hand trailed around her throat, his fingers curving around her small chin to hold her firm as the tip of his tongue sought hers with an eroticism that ignited a sudden warmth deep inside her. Her eyes closed and her hands slid up to clasp his nape, her fingers trailing involuntarily into the silken blackness of his hair as he deepened the kiss, his tongue probing the moist interior of her mouth, and the slow-burning heat ignited into flame.

'Emily.' He raised his head, and lifted her hands from their death-like grip around his neck. 'Emily, we have to go.'

She looked dazedly up at him, then down at his hands holding hers. Had she really flung her arms around him and clung like a limpet? And suddenly the heat of arousal became the heat of embarrassment.

'What did you do that for?' she asked.

'I believe in getting the first kiss over with quickly, instead of wondering all evening, and to be blunt you have kept me waiting a week already.' He grinned.

'I'm surprised you persisted.' She grinned back, suddenly feeling wonderful, all her doubts and fears about Anton wiped out by his kiss.

'I surprised myself. I am of the W.C. Fields train of thought. If at first you don't succeed, try, try, and then give up—there is no point in being a damn fool about it. Usually two approaches with no response and I move on. But in your case I made an exception. You should be flattered.'

Emily chuckled. 'You are impossibly arrogant, Anton.'

'Yes, but you like me.' He grinned and started the car.

The restaurant was exclusive, the food superb and Anton the perfect dinner companion. His conversation was witty and gradually she relaxed. He told her he spent a lot of time travelling between his head office in New York, and the subsidiaries in Sydney, London and Athens, where he had an island villa within commuting distance by helicopter. But he tried to spend the winter months on his estate in Peru.

Without being aware of it, Emily was already half in love with him by the time he took her home.

'Admit it, Emily, you enjoyed yourself tonight,' Anton prompted as he stopped the car outside her home and turned to look at her. 'I am not quite the ogre you thought, hmm?' And he slid an arm around her shoulders.

'I concede you really are very civilized and, yes, I did enjoy myself.' The champagne she had consumed making her ever so slightly tipsy, she smiled up at him and added, 'But you are still arrogant.'

'Maybe, but will you allow me to take you out again tomorrow night?' he asked formally, but there was nothing formal about the sensual gleam in the black depths of the eyes that held hers as he drew her close.

'Yes,' she murmured, and watched in helpless anticipation as his dark head bent and his wide mouth covered hers.

The second kiss was even better than the first and she leant into him with bone-melting enthusiasm, her arms eagerly wrapping around his neck. She felt his great body tense, felt the brush of one hand against the fabric covering her breast as he deepened the kiss, his tongue searching her mouth with a skilful eroticism that sent shuddering sensations of pure pleasure coursing hotly through her slender body.

She inhaled the unique masculine scent of him, trembled with wild excitement at the pleasure of his kiss, a kiss so deep, so passionate, she never wanted to come up for air. When his fingers closed around the strap of her dress she quivered, but made no objection as he peeled the fabric down over her braless breasts.

He raised his head and she didn't understand his husky

words as he palmed her breast, his long fingers grazing over the rosy tip. Her whole body jerked and her head fell back as he lowered his head and his mouth closed over an exposed nipple. Fierce sensations lanced from her breasts to her loins, moisture pooling between her thighs. She groaned out loud as with tongue and teeth he teased her rigid nipples, until she was a quivering mass of heated sensations she had never experienced before, never believed existed until now.

She threaded her hands through his dark hair, and held him to her aching body, wanting more. She felt the gentle trail of his strong hand sliding beneath her skirt, stroking up the silken smoothness of her thigh, felt his long fingers trace the thin strip of lace between her legs. Involuntarily her legs parted and one long finger edged beneath her panties.

'My God!' Anton exclaimed, rearing back. 'What the hell am I doing?'

She stared up at him, her body sprawled back against the seat in total abandonment, her blue eyes glittering wildly and her pale skin flushed with the heat of arousal at the hands of a man for the first time in her twenty-four years. Quickly he smoothed her skirt down over her thighs and hauled her up in the seat, slipping the straps of her dress back over her shoulder, and placing her wrap carefully around her, folding it over her still-tingling breasts.

'That's better,' he said, his dark eyes suddenly shadowed.

Emily's body still pulsed with sensation, but slowly it dawned on her Anton was no way near as affected.

'Sorry, Emily, I never meant to take things so far in the car of all places.' He smoothed a few tendrils of hair from her brow. 'Damn it to hell, I promised your brother I would look after you.' He swore.

That did get through to Emily. 'You promised my brother…'

she exclaimed. 'You mean Tom had the nerve… I'll kill him.'
She could not believe her own brother, and her embarrassment
at her helpless capitulation to Anton was overtaken by her
anger at Tom. 'He seems to forget I am a grown woman and
perfectly able to look after myself.'

'I'm sure you are,' Anton agreed. 'But right now you better
get indoors, before I lose control completely,' he added with a
self-derisory grimace as he got out of the car and walked around
to open the passenger door. He slipped an arm around her waist
and led her to the imposing front door of her home. 'I won't
come in, I don't dare.' Dropping a swift kiss on the top of her
head, he added, 'I'll call you in the morning.' He waited as
Emily, her head in a whirl of chaotic emotions—embarrassment, anger and, most telling of all, frustration—found her
key, opened the door and walked in.

CHAPTER THREE

THE weeks that followed were like a fairy tale to Emily. She was head over heels in love with Anton Diaz. The love she had thought she had felt for Nigel was nothing compared to how Anton made her feel. There was no point in denying it. She only had to hear his deep, melodious accented voice to go weak at the knees, and when he touched her excitement buzzed through every nerve in her body. She wanted him in ways she had never dreamed of before, but now kept her hot and restless in bed at night.

Thinking about that first night now, four weeks later, as she sat in front of the dressing mirror applying her make-up, ignited a slow-burning heat in the pit of Emily's stomach. But then that was something that pretty much happened every time she thought of Anton these days. A secretive smile curved her full lips as she ran a brush through her hair and rose to her feet.

Anton had been in New York for almost a week, and she ached to see him again. In fact she ached for him, because for some reason there had been no repeat of that first steamy episode except in her head.

They had enjoyed themselves over a few dinners and a trip to the theatre. She had accompanied him on several high-profile social occasions that included his business acquaintances, and the one time they had attended a film première he had quite proudly confirmed to the waiting photographers that they were an item.

But it was their relationship on the sexual front that puzzled Emily. Innocent though she was, she knew deep in her heart she wanted him with every fibre of her being. Given his reputation, she knew the best she could hope for was an affair, and she had confidently expected to be invited to his London penthouse. Within a week of meeting him, she had prepared for their relationship to progress to the physical, but it had not advanced at all. On the contrary, Anton had never even suggested taking her to his apartment, and made a point of drawing back after a kiss or two, while she was left aching for more...

Still, perhaps after a six-day separation tomorrow night would be the night, she thought as she clipped the diamond studs in her ears and stood back to view her reflection. But first she had to get through tonight. A family party for her uncle Sir Clive Deveral's birthday.

Her mother's brother was a bachelor and it was a bit of a tradition that he dined with them all on his birthday before heading off later to his club and his old navy mates to reminisce and get drunk. She had made a determined effort to dress up for her uncle because she knew he really appreciated glamorous women.

He had told her so when, in his own bumbling way, he had tried to comfort her after her disastrous engagement. He had confided that years ago he had lost his fiancée to another man, but he had soon got over it; with so many glamorous women to choose from he preferred to play the field. Then realizing what he had said, he had exclaimed, 'Not that I mean you should play the field. Heaven forbid. I simply meant there are plenty more fish in the sea,' and made her laugh.

He was a real sweetie and Emily adored him. She had spent

many a school holiday at his home, Deveral Hall in Lincolnshire, or at his rather dilapidated villa in Corfu. When her childhood dreams of being a ballerina were dashed by her increasing height it was her uncle who had taught her never to waste time hankering after things that she could not change and move on. Then he had got her interested in archaeology and sailing and swimming in the warm waters off the Greek island and had been instrumental in her decision to be a marine archaeologist.

She smiled at her image in the mirror. The dress she wore was a strapless silver lamé that clung to every inch of her body like a second skin to end six inches above her knees. She had left her long hair loose and she was wearing ridiculously high-heeled diamanté sandals that showed off her legs to the max.

Emily was still smiling to herself as she walked down the stairs to join the family for pre-dinner drinks. Her uncle would love her outfit—he was always telling her that the latest generation of men on the Fairfax side of the family needed shocking out of their staid conservatism once in a while. For that reason he always turned up at any family dinner in a velvet dinner jacket and outrageous waistcoats. The rest of the family would probably have a fit.

She reached the bottom of the stairs and headed towards the sound of talk and laughter coming from the drawing room, and then turned again as the doorbell rang.

'I'll get it, Mindy,' she said as the flustered housekeeper popped out of the kitchen.

She opened the door and her mouth fell open with shock. 'Anton, what are you doing here? I thought you weren't due back until tomorrow.'

'Obviously I got back not a minute too soon.' His dark eyes glittered with some fierce emotion as they swept over her. 'You look unbelievable, though I find it hard to believe you dressed like that for an evening at home. Who is my competition?' he demanded, his dark eyes narrowing with anger on her face. Then without a word he hauled her into his arms and covered her mouth with his own in a hard possessive kiss that knocked the breath from her body.

When he finally allowed her to breathe again she looked up into his burning black eyes. 'What was that for?' she gasped.

'To remind you, you are mine. Now who is he?'

'You're jealous—you think I am going out with another man,' Emily prompted, ridiculously delighted, and, lifting a finger, she stroked the firm line of his jaw. 'You have no need to be, Anton. There is no other man, and we are having a birthday party for my uncle,' she explained, a broad smile curving her slightly swollen lips. 'Come and join us. You will make the dinner table up to an even number.' And she watched as what looked surprisingly like a blush stained his high cheekbones.

'What can I say?' He groaned, holding her away from him. 'Except I've missed you.' His eyes roamed hungrily over her and then, grabbing her arm, he urged her inside. 'I have to speak to Tom.'

'Why?'

'I want to marry you, and I need to ask his permission.'

'What?'

'You heard.' He folded her against his long body. 'Marry me, Emily. I can't wait any longer.'

Not the most romantic proposal in the world, but Emily's blue eyes filled with tears of happiness. Suddenly everything made sense. Anton, wonderful Anton, the man she loved with all her heart, the man she had been worrying would never take her to bed, actually wanted to marry her. Now his behaviour made magnificent sense. She had heard the rumours of his many mistresses, but with her he had behaved with admirable restraint because he wanted more, he wanted her to be his wife, he loved her.

'Yes, oh, yes,' she cried, and flung her arms around his neck.

'What is going on out here?'

Anton raised his eyes and looked at Tom over the top of Emily's head. He had shocked himself by proposing marriage so precipitously. He had had it all planned, the ring in his pocket, a romantic dinner, a skilful seduction; instead he had blurted it out in the doorway like an idiot. But hell! If ever a woman looked like sex on legs and ready to bed it was Emily tonight, he reasoned, so naturally he had to get in quick. And Emily had said yes, mission accomplished. Not that he had doubted for a moment she would say yes, and he refused to admit it was the thought of Emily seeing another man that was responsible for his hasty proposal. He straightened his broad shoulders and tightened his arm around Emily's waist.

'I have just asked Emily to marry me, Tom, and she has agreed. But we would like your blessing,' he said, once more in complete control.

'Is this true, Emily? Is Anton the man for you?' Tom asked quietly, his eyes on his sister.

'Oh, yes.'

'In that case you have my blessing.' Anton met his soon-to-be brother-in-law's eyes and saw the slight reservation in the blue depths. 'But you are a lot older than Emily.' For that, read *You have a reputation with women*, Anton understood instantly. 'And if you hurt her in any way you will have me to answer to.'

'I'll guard her with my life,' Anton declared, and he meant it, though not necessarily for the reason Tom Fairfax thought…

'Knowing Emily and given her career choice, I don't envy you,' Tom teased.

'Tom—please…' Emily groaned. 'You are going to put Anton off before I get the ring on my finger.'

'Never.' Anton glanced down at the woman by his side. 'As your husband I will support you every which way you want, Emily.'

'So stop making cow's eyes at her, and come and meet the rest of the family.' Tom grinned. 'We can make it a double celebration and you will have some idea of what you are getting into, my friend.'

Anton knew exactly what he was getting into, he had engineered the whole thing, so he was surprised that he actually felt something suspiciously like guilt as the introductions were made. Tom and Helen, he knew of course, and James and Lisa Browning. The Brownings' two adult sons and their wives seemed pleasant enough. Another aunt, Jane, was the younger sister of Sara Fairfax, a widow with twin sons about twenty. Then there was the birthday boy, Sir Clive Deveral, wearing a deep blue velvet dinner jacket, a ruffled yellow shirt and a brilliant scarlet waistcoat with a face to match.

Although he had seen all their names on the report his investigator had presented, meeting them in the flesh was a little disconcerting. As the dinner progressed he found it impossible to dislike them. Everyone without exception made him welcome and congratulated him on having won Emily's hand in marriage. The conversation was lively and funny and inevitably reminiscences of other family parties were laughed over. For the first time in years he wondered if there was something to be said for a large close-knit family.

'So what did you think of them?' Emily asked Anton, her arm linked in his as she walked him to the door at one in the morning.

'I think your uncle Clive is deliberately outrageous but a great character and the rest are all lovely just like you,' he murmured as he slipped his hand in his pocket and withdrew a small velvet box.

Emily stared in wonder and a happiness so profound she could not speak.

'I meant to do this over a romantic dinner for two.' His lips quirked at the corners in a wry smile as he opened the box. 'But events rather overtook us.' And grasping her hand, he raised it to his lips and pressed a soft kiss on the backs of her fingers, before sliding a magnificent sapphire and diamond ring onto her finger.

Tears of joy sparkled in Emily's eyes as she looked up into his darkly handsome face. 'It is beautiful. I love it and I love you,' she declared. Anton was everything she wanted, and the fact he had said in front of Tom he would support her in her career banished the faintest doubt, and she kissed him.

They were married quietly on a Wednesday a month later in the church adjacent to her uncle Clive's home, Deveral Hall. Uncle Clive considered Tom and Emily as close to his own children as he would ever get and was delighted to throw open his once elegant but now slightly shabby home for the occasion.

On a brilliant day in late May the old stone house glowed mellowly in the sun. Emily was a vision in white and Anton every inch the perfect groom, tall, dark and strikingly attractive. The fifty-odd guests, mostly family and friends of Emily, were all agreed it was a wonderful intimate wedding.

Anton stared down at his sleeping bride, a slow satisfied smile curving his firm lips, his dark eyes gleaming with triumph.

Emily Fairfax was his... His wife...Señora Diaz...or Mrs...whatever. He considered himself a citizen of the world, and it was only the Diaz that was important. He had applied for a passport weeks ago in her married name, and on production of the wedding certificate Max pulled a few strings and obtained the new passport and delivered it as they boarded the plane for Monte Carlo. Anton had accomplished what he had set out to do from the first time he had set eyes on her. He had married Charles Fairfax's daughter, the niece of a knight of the realm. Not that he cared about titles, but Charles Fairfax certainly had.

Anton's expression darkened. According to his mother, over twenty-six years ago Charles Fairfax had been on holiday in Greece and had seduced Anton's eighteen-year-old sister, Suki. Anton had been eleven at the time and attending boarding school so had known nothing about it. When his sister had died a few months later in a car accident he had been devastated, but it was only after his mother had died he had pieced together the full extent of Charles Fairfax's betrayal, from the letter addressed to Suki he had found among his mother's things.

Charles Fairfax had left Suki pregnant and returned to London. When she had contacted him about the child he had written back saying he did not believe the child was his. Then added he was well aware that Suki was the illegitimate daughter of a Frenchman, and that her mother was the daughter of a Peruvian brothel-keeper, and was now the mistress of a wealthy Greek and had yet another illegitimate child. With such a pedigree there was no way, even if he were free, which he was not, that the proud old name of Fairfax would ever be associated with the name Diaz.

Five months after Fairfax had left her, Suki had picked up a copy of *The Times* newspaper and read the announcement of the wedding of Charles Fairfax to Sir Clive Thomas Deveral's sister, Sara Deveral, and she had given up all hope and committed suicide. Killing herself and her unborn child.

Anton shook his head to dispel the dark memories. Today he had righted the wrong done to his family in a way he knew his mother would have appreciated. Emily Fairfax was now a Diaz, a very fitting revenge.

As for Emily, he glanced back at her sleeping form in the seat beside him. She really was exquisite; in fact, if he had met her without the past to consider, while he would not have married her, he would certainly have bedded her and kept her as his mistress until he tired of her. But looking at her now with her silken blonde hair falling loosely over one side of her face, her soft lips slightly pouted in sleep, he was glad he had.

Emily was intelligent, well educated with a career of sorts and she was not likely to interfere in how he ran his life. Certainly not after he told her why he had married her, and the thought made him pause. Somehow the revenge he had achieved did not give him quite as much pleasure as he had expected. The soul-corroding bitterness that had consumed him since his mother's death had faded slightly. Probably because of Emily—she really was delightful.

Her constant avowals of love, rather than irritating him, he was beginning to find quite addictive. He had known a few women, and he was realistic enough to recognize that, great sex aside, the biggest part of his attraction was his wealth. Personally he thought love was an excuse the female of the species, Emily included, used to justify having sex with a man. Wryly he amended that thought, with the exception of the three generations of females in his family who had imagined themselves in love and suffered for it.

His grandmother had been the daughter of a wealthy Spanish Peruvian rancher, a Señor Sebastian Emanuel Diaz. Her father had disowned her after she had disgraced the family by getting pregnant and running away to Lima with a ranch hand. They never married and he left her when their daughter was barely a year old. His own mother had repeated the same mistake twice over, first by falling in love with a Frenchman who had left her with a baby girl, and then with Anton's father, a Greek who was married, and she became his mistress. While not a complete tragedy, his mother had not made the wisest of choices. As for his sister—to kill herself for love didn't bear thinking about.

No, if love existed then it was a destructive emotion and not one Anton was prepared to embrace. He lusted after Emily, but he had no illusions about the female of the species. He knew his wealth and power were probably just as much an aphrodisiac to Emily as they had been to the countless other women he had known.

The wedding had gone perfectly and they were now on his private jet heading for the South of France to board his yacht anchored off Monaco.

His dark eyes narrowed as they roamed over her lovely face, serene in sleep. He noted the fantastic sweep of her lashes over her eyes, the sensuously curved passionate mouth, the slight curve of her breasts revealed between the lapels of the wild blue silk suit she wore, and his body tightened.

Pity he had not been able to remove the exquisite white wedding gown. The image of her as he had turned to watch her walk down the aisle would live in his mind for ever. Beautiful was an understatement; her sparkling blue eyes had met his and for a long moment he had not been able to breathe, such was her effect on him. Even now remembering made his heart beat faster and he fought the temptation to kiss her awake. He had waited this long, he could wait a little longer until they reached the comfort of his yacht. He did not want to rush what he had promised himself would be a long night of passion.

A light flashed in the gathering darkness, and he heard the sudden change in the engine noise; they would be landing soon. Good, he was getting impatient. He could not remember the last time he had waited so long for a woman, if ever…though it had all been part of his plan.

Emily was a passionate woman, and as an experienced man of the world and a skilful lover Anton had recognized that immediately. He had quickly decided his best policy was to give her just a taste of what she wanted and no more. To build up her frustration until she was so desperate to have him she would accept his proposal of marriage without a second thought. Which of course she had.

Anton shifted uncomfortably in his seat. The trouble was he had suffered just as much if not more from the enforced celibacy, as the stirring in his groin could testify. He had ended his last affair a month after his mother's death when the woman he was involved with at the time had started hinting at marriage now he was alone in the world. He grimaced painfully. He had never gone so long without sex since he was a teenager, but thankfully the wait would soon be over.

A slight frown creased his brow as, thinking back over the past few weeks, he suddenly realized every time he had stopped after a kiss or two Emily had looked at him with desire-dazed eyes, and yet she had made no attempt to seduce him, no attempt to touch him intimately. Not the usual reaction of a sexually sophisticated woman. In his experience they normally made their desire very clear. Odd…or maybe not so odd, he corrected cynically. She had probably been playing the same waiting game as he had to make sure of getting a ring on her finger…

'Anton.' A throaty murmur had his eyes flying back to her face.

'You're awake. Good.' He lowered his head to taste the soft

sweetness of her luscious mouth. 'We are landing soon,' he murmured, lifting his head, and, taking her hands in his, he folded them on her lap. 'Another half-hour and we will be on board the yacht.'

'It can't be too soon.' Emily smiled up at him, her brilliant blue eyes dazzling him. 'My love. My husband.'

'I agree, wife.' Anton smiled back. Yes, she was his wife, he had succeeded, he thought complacently as, with a sexy Emily firmly clasped to his side, he led her off the jet to the waiting helicopter.

His mother must be smiling down on him and that snobbish swine Charles Fairfax must be spinning in his grave, or burning in hell. He didn't care which. Because his daughter was now a Diaz, the name he thought not fit to be connected to Fairfax. A result all around…

His hand tightened possessively around her slender waist and in that moment he decided… Actually there was no pressing need to tell Emily what a two-timing dirty swine her father was, the real reason he had married her. It was enough for Anton to know he had kept the vow he had made on his mother's grave.

Emily staggered out of the helicopter into Anton's arms. He swung her off her feet and she wrapped her arms around his neck as, ducking his head under the still-swirling blades, he carried her to the stairs leading down from the helipad and into the body of the yacht. He didn't stop until he reached the main salon and lowered her slowly to her feet.

'Welcome aboard.' He grinned down at her and Emily registered the swell of his arousal as he dipped his head and kissed her.

She felt the earth move, or maybe it was just the yacht, but either way she flung her arms around Anton's neck again and clung.

'I want to make it to the bed at least,' she heard him groan, his hands roaming restlessly down her spine and over her bottom.

Emily shivered with excitement and, glancing around her in awe, she laughed out loud. 'This is huge!' she exclaimed, turning back to Anton, and saw his lips twitch. 'I have been on expeditions on ships half this size.'

'Emily—stop talking,' Anton commanded, his ego slightly deflated. His lips sought hers once again, and she closed her eyes in willing surrender as his tongue slipped between her softly parted lips in a long drugging kiss.

Finally when she was breathless he raised his head. 'I have waited too long for this.' He peeled off his jacket and hers as he walked her backwards in what she hoped was the direction of the master cabin.

She felt her breasts swell as his hand stroked one lace-covered breast, his thumb grazing the tip over the fine fabric, and her nipples tightened into hard pulsing points of pleasure. His mouth caught her soft gasp of delight, then moments later he nudged a door open with his shoulder.

She barely registered the bedroom; she had eyes for nothing but Anton.

Without a word he cupped her face and bent his dark head, covering her mouth with his at first tenderly. Then, as she opened her mouth to him, with a fast-growing passion that she returned with helpless fervour.

'Emily.' He said her name, and, lifting his head, he locked his dark eyes with hers, black with a hunger, a passion, that burned through to her bones. His hand slid around her back to dispense with her bra and stayed to hold her to him. For a long moment he simply stared and just his gaze on her naked breasts made her tremble with excitement.

'Exquisite,' he murmured throatily as he lowered his head

to trace the slender length of her neck with his mouth and suck on the rapidly beating pulse there. Then trail lower to her breast.

His tongue licked one pert nipple and the tightened tip engorged at his touch. She cried out as his teeth gently tugged, and her head fell back over his arm, her back arching in spontaneous response as she offered herself up to the incredible pleasure only Anton could arouse. He suckled first one and then the other with a skill that drove her crazy with need and had her writhing in his hold.

She felt her skirt slide to the floor, and suddenly he was swinging her up in his arms again and lowering her gently to the bed. She whimpered as he straightened up and looked down at her.

'You have no idea how much I want you,' he grated, his black eyes ablaze as he divested himself of his clothes in seconds.

She stared at the wide tanned shoulders, the muscular, slightly hair-roughened chest, the strong hips, the powerful thighs and long legs. Totally naked and fully aroused he was almost frightening in his masculine beauty, and nervously she crossed her arms over her throbbing breasts.

'Let me look at you,' he growled and, leaning over her, he grasped the top of her minuscule lace briefs. 'All of you.' He slid them down her long legs and dropped them. Then his hands curled around her ankles and slowly stroked up her long legs tracing the curve of her hips, the indentation of her waist. She was trembling all over by the time he reached for her wrists and, unfolding her arms from her chest, pinned her hands either side of her body.

'There is no need to pretend shyness,' he husked. 'You are exquisite, more than I ever dreamed of.'

Excitement arced through her like an electric charge, her blue eyes as bright as sapphires as his dark eyes dropped to her breasts and lingered before roaming over her from head to toe once more. Emily had thought she might be embarrassed naked for the first time before Anton, but instead she was wildly excited, her slender body reacting heatedly to his intense scrutiny.

'I can't take my eyes off you, Emily, my wife. And soon to be my wife in every way.' Taking protection from a bedside table, he lowered himself down beside her, his magnificent body sliding against her, flesh on flesh.

What followed was so outside anything Emily had ever imagined it was unreal. The odd time she had imagined the act of love she had thought it would be some magical meeting of heart, body and soul, sweet, tender love reaching a joyous climax. But the violent emotions flooding through her were nothing like that.

'You can touch me, Emily,' he murmured, his dark eyes gleaming down into hers as his mouth covered hers. She reached for him in an almost desperate haste, the masculine scent of him, the sleek slide of his skin against hers, the devouring passion of his mouth igniting a white-hot heat inside her.

With tentative hands she explored the width of his shoulders, the strong spine. She shuddered as his dark head lowered and found her pouting breasts once more. No longer tentative, but eager, she stroked up his back and raked her fingers through the black silken hair of his head, holding him to her. She groaned out loud as he lifted his head and moaned her delight as he found her mouth again. The sensuality of his kiss made her head spin and her body burn.

She closed her eyes and savoured the slight masculine scent of him, and wreathed helplessly as his hands slid down the length of her body caressing, stroking and finally settling between her parted thighs.

His long fingers found the moist, hot centre of her femininity and a low aching moan escaped her, and she wanted more, much more, her hips lifting, her whole body throbbing. She was helplessly in thrall to the wonder of his expertise and her own uninhibited response. She clutched desperately at him and looked up into his taut dark face, saw the black passion in his eyes and revelled in it.

Wild and wanton, she caught his hair and pulled his head back to her mouth. She was panting with frustration and an incredible need to feel all of his long, hard body over her, in her, joined with hers. She groaned as he paused to slip on protection and then kissed her. The sensuous pressure of his lips, the thrusting of his tongue mimicking the sexual act and the fire in her blood turned her whole body into a flame of pure sensation. He settled between her thighs, and she cried his name, burning with a fever for more. His hands on her hips tightened and she arched up as he thrust home.

Emily felt a stab of pain and winced. She saw the shock in his dark eyes as he stilled and began to withdraw. But she could not let him go, not now as the thick fullness of him made her inner muscles clench, and instinctively she locked her legs around his waist, slid her arms around his back. 'Please. Please, I want you. I love you.'

She heard the sharp intake of his breath, felt the heavy beating of his heart and the tension in every muscle of his body. Then he moved, slowly thrusting a little deeper, and then withdrawing and sliding deeper still.

Miraculously her silken sheath stretched to accommodate him, and Emily was lost to everything except the pure physical wonder of his possession. The indescribable sensations beating through her, the sleek skin beneath her fingers, and the heated scent of two bodies joined. The wonder as in seconds she matched the rhythm he set, driving her ever higher to some unknown destination she ached…was dying for.

Her nails dug deep into his satin-smooth skin as great waves of ecstasy rippled through her and then roared as he thrust hard and fast and she cried out as her body convulsed in exquisite rapture, and she was flung into a hot, mindless oblivion. She heard Anton groan, and she forced her eyes open and felt his great body buck and shudder with the force of his own release.

Loosely she wrapped her arms around him as he buried his head on her shoulder. The heavy pounding of his heart against hers and his weight were a solid reminder of the power and passion, the love he had given her. A soft smile curved her lips. Anton truly was her husband.

CHAPTER FOUR

EMILY had never imagined such ecstasy existed, and as the rippling aftermath of pleasure receded and her breathing steadied a beauteous smile curved her swollen lips. She savoured the weight of Anton lying over her, the heavy pounding of his heart against hers.

'I am too heavy,' he rasped.

'No, perfect,' she murmured and felt the warmth of Anton's breath against her throat as he rolled off her.

Her blue eyes misty, she watched him walk to the bathroom, and return moments later, his great body bronzed and glistening with beads of perspiration. 'Come back to bed.'

He lay down beside her, supporting himself on one elbow, his dark eyes searching hers. 'Anton.' She lifted a hand to brush the damp fall of hair from his brow. 'I never knew love could be so…' She was lost for words except to say, 'I love you.' She couldn't stop saying it. 'I love everything about you.' Her finger traced the line of his cheekbone, his strong chin shadowed with dark stubble. She sighed. He was so magnificent…so perfect…and incredibly she felt slow-building warmth once again in her slender body.

'Why didn't you tell me you were a virgin?' He shook his head, and her hand slipped to his broad shoulder, relishing the feel of his smooth skin beneath her fingers.

'Does it matter? We are truly married now,' she said, but her smile faded a little as she looked into his eyes. They were no longer gleaming with desire, but narrowed in angry puzzlement on her face.

'But you were engaged to be married once before. How could it be?'

Emily was surprised and intrigued. How did Anton know she had been engaged before? She was sure she had never told him, and without a second thought she asked him.

'Someone must have mentioned it,' he dismissed, and she had the oddest notion he was avoiding a direct answer. 'But that is not important; you should have told me I was your first.'

'Why? Would you have refused to make love to me if I had?' she teased, and stroked a slender finger down his chest. Slowly, sensually…

'Yes… No… But I could have been more careful if I had known.'

She lifted both her hands and ran her fingers through his black hair, holding his head firmly between her palms. Her blue eyes were sparkling with devilment. 'Well, you can be careful the next time.' And pulled his head down, wanting to kiss him.

She heard the husky rumble of his laugh and suddenly he turned, and in one fluid moment he pulled her on top of him. She wriggled a little, her legs parting to enclose his strong thighs, and heard his sharp intake of breath with feminine satisfaction.

'For an innocent I have a feeling you are going to be a very fast study,' he said with husky amusement in his tone.

'I hope so,' she quipped, and ran her hand over the soft curling hairs of his chest, her finger grazing a very male nipple. 'When does the next lesson begin?' she asked mischievously, resting her chin on his breastbone and looking up into his darkly handsome face.

His sensuous grin sent a delicious shiver the length of her spine. 'I think I have awakened a sleeping tigress, and the first thing you need to know is the male takes a little longer to recover than the female, though it is a known fact that with a little encouragement the waiting time can be reduced.'

'Like this, you mean,' she prompted softly, and dipped her head to brush his lips with hers, and then his throat, and finally her tongue slipped out to lick a hard male nipple. She loved the musky male taste of him; she could not get enough of him, revelling in the strong hard body beneath her. She trailed one hand down over his rock-hard diaphragm, her slender fingers tracing the slim line of black body hair down to the flat plane of his belly, and lower to explore his essential maleness, and very quickly the waiting was over.

Time had no meaning as they explored the hunger, the depths of passion and the exquisite tenderness of their love. They bathed and made love again, slept and made love again...

Emily yawned and opened her eyes to find Anton standing over her dressed in khaki shorts and a white polo shirt, and holding a coffee-cup in his hand. Sleepily she looked at him, a slow beautiful smile curving her full lips.

'You're up,' she murmured and her stomach gave a distinct rumble. 'What time is it?'

He grinned and placed the cup and saucer on the bedside table. 'One.' Then he bent his head to drop a swift kiss on her brow.

She frowned. 'It's the middle of the night. Come back to bed.'

'It is one on Thursday afternoon.'

'Oh, hell!' she exclaimed and stretched, then winced as muscles she never knew she had stung. 'I must get up.' She started to, then realized she was naked, and, finding the cotton coverlet, she tugged it over her body.

* * *

Anton winced guiltily with her, his dark eyes roaming over her lithe, shapely form. She looked so delectable, her blonde hair tousled around her beautiful face, her lips pink and swollen from his kisses, and the sheet barely covering her luscious breasts.

He had bedded some of the most stunning women in the world, but none came close to Emily. She was perfection incarnate, and he knew the image of her naked body, the wild passion they had shared, would be for ever etched in his brain. She had been a virgin, and he should have had more control, and he had *tried*.

After the second time, he had carried her to the bathroom and bathed her, but by the time he had got around to drying her he had lost control again, then he had given up counting. He had never known a woman like her in his life; she was all Eve, a temptress, and a siren with a body to drive a man out of his mind.

As he had expected from the first time he laid eyes on Emily, she was a sexy, passionate woman. She had gone up in flames as soon as he touched her. She had wreathed in his arms, and cried his name, cried out her love as he possessed her exquisite body, convulsing in orgasmic pleasure time after time.

What was even more amazing, with remarkable aptitude in no time at all she learnt just what buttons to press to make him equally helpless in the power of their passion. She was a naturally born sensualist…

The only thing he had not expected was that she would still be a virgin. The man she had been engaged to before must have been a eunuch or an absolute saint.

He found it incredible that he was her first lover. He had never made love to a virgin before. Innocence had never appealed to him, he preferred experienced women who knew the score, and yet he was stunned by the uniquely erotic experience. And if he was honest, in a totally chauvinistic way he felt an overwhelming masculine satisfaction and pride that she had given her virginity to him. She was his…only his…

He didn't believe in love, but there was something extremely beguiling in having a wildly sexy wife who did. He had intended revealing the true reason he had married her after spending one passionate night with her. But he had already virtually dismissed the idea on the plane over here, and now, having discovered how innocent she was, he would have to be the biggest fool in Christendom to disillusion her. Anton was no fool and he thanked his lucky stars he had kept his mouth shut about her father.

His body hardened just looking at her and his mouth tightened as he fought the temptation to join her in bed, captivated by her every movement as she reached for the cup he had left for her on the bedside table.

'Good idea, drink your coffee,' he finally answered, 'and join me in the salon when you are dressed.' He didn't trust himself to keep his hands off her, and she needed time to recover. 'The chef has prepared lunch and then I will give you a tour of the yacht and introduce you to the captain and crew.' Turning on his heel, he walked rather stiffly out of the cabin.

Emily drank the coffee and, sliding off the bed, headed for the shower. Washed and wearing only a towel, she glanced around the cabin and saw her suitcase standing by a wall of cupboards. She had never thought of unpacking it the night before. In a matter of minutes she unpacked her trousseau so carefully bought over the last few weeks. One exquisite evening gown, and a host of smart summer clothes, some stylish if slightly risqué lingerie and bikinis courtesy of Helen.

As she closed the lingerie drawer a secret smile curved her

lips at the thought of wearing them for Anton. She slipped on lace briefs and a matching bra, and a pair of white cotton shorts and a blue cotton top she had chosen to wear. She brushed her hair back off her face and fastened it with a slide. She didn't bother with make-up, just a sun screen; she was in a hurry to get back to her husband.

After lunch, Anton spent the next three hours giving Emily a tour of the yacht and introducing her to the captain and crew. The chief steward and the chef, he explained, arranged all the catering and the domestic running of the yacht. She wowed them all with her natural ease and grace, and her obvious interest in the mechanics of the yacht. Surprisingly for a woman she was quite knowledgeable about the workings of a ship.

While he appreciated her interest, after half an hour all he wanted to do was get her back into bed. Her fantastically long legs were displayed in all their glory by the shorts she was wearing and he could not keep his eyes off her. It hadn't escaped his notice neither could any other man around.

'So what do you think, Emily?' he asked as he leant against the ship's rail, and clasped his hands loosely around her waist, and drew her between his splayed legs.

'I think it is the ultimate boys' toy.' She looked up at him with such love and laughter in her eyes, inexplicably his heart tightened and his body followed suit. 'I have seen cruise liners smaller than this.' She shook her head in amazement. 'I am not surprised we are anchored offshore—there is probably not a berth big enough even in Monte Carlo.' She laughed. 'I knew you were wealthy, but I had no idea how rich.' She grinned up at him. 'A helipad, a swimming pool and a wicked-looking motor launch to take us ashore. It is unbelievable, I love it, and I love you.' And he felt the touch of her lips against his chin.

'Then that is all right,' Anton answered gruffly, swallowing a peculiar lump in his throat.

'But what I want to know is when are we sailing and where to? The captain, when I asked him, did not seem to know. Is our honeymoon going to be a mystery tour?' she demanded with a chuckle, and moved seductively between his thighs increasing the ever-present sensual awareness between them.

Her bare legs brushing his sent his temperature soaring and Anton hardened still further; he could not help himself. But her question reminded him of where they were and why, and he felt a bit selfish, not a feeling he was comfortable with. He tightened his hands on her waist and lightly urged her back, then dropped his hands from her far-too-tempting body.

He let his gaze rest on her lovely face; her luminous eyes revealed her every thought. She was so open, so affectionate and this was her honeymoon.

His black brows pleated in a frown as belatedly he realized his decision to use the long-standing arrangement he had made for his annual trip to the Formula One Monaco Grand Prix to double as a honeymoon no longer seemed quite so reasonable. Emily had probably been expecting a romantic out-of-the-way place and just the two of them. Whereas he, without a second thought given the reason he had married her, had decided to do what he always did at this time of year, confident that Emily would fit in with his plans.

His frown deepened. He had never had to consider a woman's feelings before. Every woman he had known in the past had been quite happy to pander to his every whim, and why not? He was an extremely wealthy man and a generous lover for as long as an affair lasted. He had made it clear from the outset he never had any intention of marrying them, all he had wanted was good sex. He didn't do romance, and he wasn't about to start now simply because he was married.

Married to the daughter of the man who destroyed his sister, he reminded himself. He had been in danger of forgetting that fact in the throes of what was basically nothing more than great sex, he reasoned. Straightening his broad shoulders, he told her the truth.

'There is no mystery; I stay here at the end of May every year for the motor racing. The Monaco Grand Prix is on Sunday. As a sponsor for one of the teams, I usually watch the race from the pits. Then there is an after-race party,' he explained, studying her reaction through narrowed eyes.

'Oh, I see.' Her blue eyes shaded and Anton knew she did not see at all. 'I never realized you were a racing-car enthusiast, though I suppose I should have guessed. Boys' toys again, hmm? Well, it will be another new experience, I suppose.' And her sensuous lips curled in a bewitching smile. 'At least I will have you to myself until Sunday.'

Frustration and the fact she was so damn reasonable angered Anton. That and the unfamiliar feeling of guilt that assailed him because he had not told her the half of it yet. For a brief moment he wondered if he could just order the captain to set sail immediately, but dismissed the notion.

Emily was his wife, his extraordinarily beautiful, incredible, sexy wife, but he changed his plans for no one, and he wasn't about to start now. He had his life organized exactly as he liked it, and although Emily had a career it was pretty flexible—she would quickly adjust and go where he led.

'Not exactly…' He paused. 'I don't use the yacht solely for my own pleasure; sometimes it is chartered out. It would not be financially viable otherwise. But also as a single man up until now,' he swiftly added, 'it has been a convenient way to repay hospitality rather than the more conventional house party.' He was prevaricating…not like him at all, and bluntly he told her, 'Anyway, it has become a bit of a tradition of mine to invite a few like-minded guests whose hospitality I have enjoyed in the past to join me on board for the Grand Prix weekend, and they usually stay until Monday.'

For a long moment Emily simply stared at her very new husband. He was standing, his long body taut, apparently unconcerned. But she caught a glimmer of uncertainty in the depths of his dark eyes, probably a first for him, and she hid a smile. Anton had it all. Wealth, power, and as a one-hundred-per-cent-virile male he was accustomed to doing exactly what he wanted to do without ever having to consider anyone else. Women had been falling over themselves to please him all his adult life, if rumours were to be believed. But he obviously had a lot to learn about marriage—they both did.

'Let me get this straight—you have invited guests on our honeymoon to watch motor racing. Yes?'

'Yes,' he said with a negligent shrug of his broad shoulder.

'A novel honeymoon.' Emily placed a slender hand on his chest. 'But, hey, I am all for tradition, and if this is a tradition of yours, why not? In fact it will be nice to meet some of your friends. So far I have only met business acquaintances—and Max, of course. He made a very good best man, and where is he, by the way?' she asked. 'He came on board with us last night.'

'He has gone ashore in the launch,' he said, avoiding her eyes. 'The guests are arriving this evening.'

Anton was obviously embarrassed, Emily thought, and, while she wasn't delighted at the idea of spending the weekend with strangers, she allowed her smile to break free.

'Don't look so serious, Anton. It's okay. We have only known each other a couple of months, but we have a lifetime together to get on the same wavelength.' Standing on tiptoe, she kissed his cheek.

'My mum told me she and my dad fell in love at first sight. They got engaged after four months and married two months after that. They had only ever lived with their parents until they married and it took time to adjust, especially as they were both virgins when they met. At least I have started off with a great lover even if you are dumb when it comes to arranging a honeymoon.'

Anton's eyes narrowed incredulously on her smiling face and he was not in the least amused, the mention of her father hitting a raw nerve.

'Dumb,' he repeated. She had the cheek to call him dumb. Was she for real?

He scowled down at her and noted the shimmering sensuality in her sparkling eyes, and he did not know if he wanted to shake her or kiss her… For a man who prided himself on his control, he did not like the ambivalent way she made him feel. She looked about seventeen dressed in white shorts and a blue tee shirt the colour of her eyes, and her hair pulled back in a slide, and her youthful appearance simply increased his unwelcome sense of guilt and anger.

'For God's sake, Emily, you are the only dumb one around here. You can't possibly believe that rubbish you are spouting. Your mother might have been a virgin, but your father certainly wasn't. Trust me, I know,' he declared with biting cynicism.

Emily's euphoric mood took a huge knock. She stumbled back a step, her blue eyes widening at the icy expression on his brutally handsome face. The lover of a few hours ago had gone and in his place was the man with the cold, remote eyes that she had seen on the night they first met.

'You knew my father?' she asked, feeling her way through

an atmosphere that was suddenly fraught with tension. 'You met him?'

'No, I never met him, but I didn't need to to know what a womanizer he was.'

Emily could not let his slur on her father pass.

'As you never met my father you can't possibly know that. But I do know that my mother never lied,' she argued in defence of her parents. She loved Anton, she had married him, but she was not going to let him walk all over her. It was bad enough she was going to share the first few days of her honeymoon with a group of strangers. 'You're not infallible, you know, and in this case you are wrong.'

Anton heard the belligerence in her voice, saw the defiance in her glittering blue eyes and was outraged that she was daring to argue with him. Very few people argued with him and nobody doubted his word. He could not quite believe his very new wife had the nerve to say he was wrong.

'Your mother must have been as naive as you,' he opined scathingly, 'if she believed Charles Fairfax was anything other than a womanizing swine and a snob to boot.' He was seething with anger and it made him say more than he intended. 'He probably only married her for her aristocratic connection.'

Without her giving it a second thought Emily's hand scythed through the air, but Anton's strong hand caught her wrist before she could make contact with his arrogant face.

'You little hellcat.' He twisted her hand behind her back and hauled her hard against his long body. 'You dare to lash out at me, because I have told you a few home truths about your sainted family.'

'At least I have one,' Emily spat, and was immediately disgusted with herself for what was a low blow. But somehow the passion Anton aroused in her sexually seemed to just as easily arouse her anger. She who was normally the most placid of women, and it shocked her.

She glanced up at him. He was looking at her with eyes as cold as the Arctic waste. Then abruptly he let go of her wrist and moved back as though he could not bear to touch her.

'And do you know why I have not, Emily?' he said with a sardonic arch of one black brow, and, not waiting for her to answer, he added, 'Because of your lech of a father.'

'You never knew my father, and yet you seem to dislike him,' she murmured. She knew it from the animosity in his tone, the tension in his body, and suddenly she was afraid.

His handsome face hardened. 'Dislike is too tame a word. I hate and despise the man, and I have every right to.'

Emily shook her head, trying to make sense of what was happening. She was too shocked to speak. How had they gone from a simmering sensual awareness to a senseless argument in minutes?

'Once I had an older sister, Suki, a beautiful gentle girl. She was eighteen, barely more than a child herself, when she met Charles Fairfax. He seduced her and left her pregnant with his child. Five months later, after learning Fairfax had married your mother, she committed suicide. Obviously he was seeing both of them at the same time.'

All the colour leached from Emily's face. This was no senseless argument, but deadly serious. She had never even known Anton had a sister. But there was no mistaking the absolute conviction in Anton's voice, and for him to have apparently held a grudge against her father for over a quarter of a century she found totally appalling. She could not believe what she was hearing, didn't want to.

'No, that cannot be true.' She murmured a denial. 'My father would never have betrayed my mother.'

'Believe me, it is,' he said harshly. 'Women who foolishly imagine they are in love are dangerous to themselves as well as to others. My mother never fully recovered from the loss of her daughter and I was kept in ignorance of the full facts for decades. As a boy of eleven I was told Suki had died in a tragic car accident. It was only when my mother was dying I discovered the real truth.'

Her blue eyes widened in horror as she recognized the latent anger in his black eyes, the brooding expression on his face, and knew he totally believed what he had just told her. And with the knowledge came pain, a pain that built and built as the full import of his words sank into her brain.

'When did your mother die?'

He frowned down at her. 'Does it matter? Last December.'

Oh, my God! Only six months ago. No wonder Anton was so angry, with the death of his mother, the pain of losing his sister must have hit him all over again. From that thought came another, deeply disturbing. Shortly after his mother's death Anton had made the acquaintance of her brother and uncle, and taken an interest in the Fairfax family and then in her. Coincidence—or something much worse, and a cold dread enveloped her.

Her eyes swept helplessly over him, the bold attractive face, the strong tanned throat revealed by the open neck of his polo shirt, the khaki shorts that hugged his lean hips ending mid-thigh and his long legs. Her heart squeezed as vivid images of his naked body flashed in her mind, the body she had worshipped last night. Anton, the man she loved, and had been certain loved her. But not any more…

CHAPTER FIVE

ANTON had shaken her world on its axis and Emily was no longer certain of anything. She could not bear to look at him.

Her mind spinning, she let her gaze roam over the view of the tiny principality. The sea as smooth as glass, the spectacular marina, the gleaming buildings were picture-postcard perfect, but wasted on her. She needed to think…

The sun was still shining but the warmth no longer seemed to touch her. Yesterday she had been a blushing bride confident in the love of her husband, but now… She let her mind wander back over the first time they had met, the sequence of events, the conversations, his proposal of marriage that had led to this moment, and belatedly she realized he had never actually said he loved her…

Not even last night in the heat of passion had the word love passed his lips.

Emily shivered as cold fingers seemed to grip her heart, the icy tendrils spreading slowly through every part of her. She was an intelligent woman, and suddenly her whirlwind courtship and fairy-tale marriage were falling apart before her eyes. Slowly she turned her head and allowed her gaze to rest on her husband's hard, expressionless face.

'Why did you marry me, Anton?'

'I decided it was time I took a wife and produced an heir. I chose you because I thought you were a beautiful, sensuous woman who would fit me perfectly.' He reached out a hand to her. 'And I was right,' he stated.

Emily batted his hand away. 'And the rest.' She stared up at him ashen-faced, horrified at the cynical practicality of his reasoning, but instinctively knowing there was more he was not telling her.

'I might be dumb. But I am not that dumb. You only came into contact with my family after the death of your mother, and I don't believe in coincidences. You might as well tell me the whole truth.' And, though her heart was shattering into a million pieces, bravely she added, 'Because it is becoming increasingly obvious you did not marry me for love.' She prayed he would contradict her, declare he loved her and it was all a horrible mistake.

'Why not?' Anton said with a shrug of his broad shoulders. 'You are now my wife—Mrs Emily Diaz, a name your father refused to acknowledge or be associated with, and it satisfies my sense of justice to know you have my name for the rest of your life.'

His dark eyes, a gleam of mocking triumph in their inky depths, clashed with her pained blue. 'As for love, I don't believe in it myself. Though women seem to have a desperate need to. What we shared last night and will continue to share is great sexual chemistry, not love.'

Tears blurred Emily's vision and fiercely she blinked them away. So this was what it felt like to crash and burn. All her hopes and dreams ground to dust in a few short minutes. For a short while, a very brief two months, Anton had been the man she loved. For an even briefer twenty-four hours she had been his wife. He had made love to her, and it had been the most amazing experience of her life and she had thought she was the luckiest woman in the world to be loved by him.

But it had not been love… He freely admitted it was simply sex, nothing more.

For Anton yesterday had been about sex and some misguided notion of retribution, not love, never love…

How could she have been such a blind idiot? She had known the first time she set eyes on him, he was dangerous. She had avoided going out with him for a week. She should have trusted her gut instinct about the man.

Her shimmering blue eyes swept over him, noted the arrogant certainty in his gaze. The Anton he had been when they had first got together, the man she had thought had refrained from making love to her because he respected her, bore no relationship to the Anton before her now. Cold and cynical, he was not the man she had fallen in love with.

She shook her head in disgust, nausea clawing at her stomach as she was forced to accept the man she thought she loved did not exist… 'I need the bathroom.'

'Wait.' He grasped her upper arm, halting her retreat. 'This does not change anything, Emily.'

'It does for me.' She looked at him. 'Let me go.' And she meant it in every sense of the word. 'I really do need the bathroom.'

Anton's mouth twisted. 'Of course.' He removed his hand from her arm, wondering why the hell he had told Emily about her father when not long ago he had been thanking his lucky stars he had kept his mouth shut.

But then from the minute he had watched her walk down the aisle he had not been his rational self. The woman had that effect on him. Last night he had lost control in bed, a first for him, and this afternoon he had lost his temper at the mention of her father. He was going weak in the head and it had to stop.

Honesty was supposed to be good for a marriage; he'd been honest, he reasoned arrogantly. It was Emily who was unreasonable.

'Arguing on the deck is not a great idea. We can talk later. After all, neither of us is going anywhere,' he said dismissively.

He would catch up on some work—he had let things slide a little in his pursuit of Emily and it would give her time to cool down. She said she loved him, and she certainly wanted him. Given his experience of her sex, she'd soon get over the shock of realizing her father had feet of clay after a few days in his bed.

Emily heard the threat in his words and glanced at him in disgust and walked away. Was he really so cold, so insensitive to believe for a second they could carry on as husband and wife now she knew why he had really married her?

Emily walked into the cabin and locked the door behind her. Blindly she headed for the bathroom, and was violently sick. She began to shake uncontrollably and, ripping off her clothes, she stepped into the shower. She turned the water on full, and only then did she give way to the tears. She cried until she could cry no more. Then slowly she straightened and, picking up the shampoo provided, she washed her hair, and then scrubbed every inch of her body, trying to scrub away the scent, the memory of Anton's touch from every pore of her skin. Trying to scrub away the pain, she had a hollow feeling that would be with her for the rest of her life...

She did not know the man she had married, had never known him. It was Nigel all over again, but worse, because she had been foolish enough to marry Anton. Nigel had wanted her for her supposed fortune and connections, and Anton—he had married her simply because her name was Fairfax. He had seduced her into marriage because he believed her father had seduced his sister. To fulfil a primitive need for revenge…no more or less…and she could not pretend otherwise.

The pain, the sense of betrayal were excruciating, but slowly as she finished washing, turned off the shower and wrapped a large towel around her naked body the pain was overtaken by a cold, numbing anger.

She thought of her parents, and, no matter what the arrogant Anton Diaz thought, she knew her father was incapable of doing what he had said. Her parents had loved each other, they had married in their twenties, and when her mother had died it had broken her father's heart. She firmly believed it was the stress of losing his wife that had helped cause the heart attack that had killed him far too young.

It was her mother who, when she was terminally ill, had constantly told Emily to embrace life to the full, and not to waste time dwelling on past failures or grudges—life was much too short. A theory her uncle Clive had first taught her when as a child of twelve she had had to accept she was never going to be a ballet dancer.

A trait that Emily had inherited from the Deveral side of her family.

So why was she even giving Anton's tragic tale a second thought? Where he had got it from she had no idea, and she cared even less. As for her marriage, as far as she was concerned it was over…

Five minutes later, dressed in casual drawstring linen trousers and a matching sleeveless top, Emily lifted her suitcase onto the bed and began to methodically pack the clothes she had unpacked only hours before.

She heard a knock on the door but ignored it.

She was immune to everything except the need to leave. She snapped the suitcase shut, and straightened up. Now all she needed was her travel bag and she was out of here.

'Just what the hell do you think you are doing?' a deep voice roared. And Emily spun round to see Anton striding towards her. 'How dare you lock me out?' he demanded. His black eyes leaping with fury, he grasped her shoulder. 'What the hell do you think you are playing at, woman?'

'I am not playing. I am leaving… The game is over,' she said, standing tall and proud. 'Your game,' she said bitterly.

Emily felt nothing for him. She was cocooned in a block of ice. The hands on her shoulders, the close proximity of his big body had no effect on her. Except to reinforce her determination to leave. It was bad enough she had made the mistake of marrying him. She was certainly not going to allow him to manhandle her.

Anton was furious. He had got no work done, he couldn't seem to concentrate, and finally he had given up and decided to smooth things over with Emily, only to find she had locked him out of their cabin. Not that it mattered—he had a masterkey. But his temper was at breaking-point.

'Over my dead body.'

'That would be my preference,' Emily tossed back.

She felt his great body tense and his hands fell from her shoulders. She watched his handsome face darken and for a second she thought she saw a flash of pain in his eyes, and for a moment she was ashamed of her hateful comment. She would not wish anybody dead. But Anton had the knack of making her say and feel things she did not want to.

'Well, I think I can safely say, barring accidents, you will not get your wish any time soon. Though for the foreseeable future it appears I must watch my back where you are concerned, my sweet loving wife, because I have no intention of letting you leave. Not now. Not ever.'

'You have no choice.' She tilted up her chin and drew on

every ounce of her pride to face him. 'As far as I am concerned the marriage is finished.'

Anton's dark eyes studied her.

He was furious at her defiance but he did not let it show. Because in a way he could understand her distress, her desire to lash back at him, though he had not appreciated her wishing him dead.

He didn't do emotions, other than over death and birth maybe. But Emily was an emotional, passionate woman, as she had proved spectacularly last night. She had been brought up on love and happy ever after. Hell, he could still hear her cries of love ringing in his ears when he had taken possession of her exquisite body. And he would again, he thought confidently. She just needed time to adjust to the reality of life as his wife.

'We always have a choice, Emily,' he murmured silkily, and, snaking an arm around her waist, he pulled her into the strength of his powerful body. 'Your choice is quite simple. You stay with me, your *husband*,' he emphasized, grasping her chin between his fingers and tilting her face up to his. 'You behave civilly as my wife and the perfect hostess I know you to be with our guests and you can continue to dabble at your career until you're pregnant with my child. Something that was implicit in the promise you made yesterday, I seem to recall.'

She stared at him. 'That was before I knew the truth. Now let me go.'

Her usual luminous blue eyes were impenetrable, her body rigid in his hold, and it made Anton want to pierce her icy control... Something he would never have imagined she was capable of.

'You have two choices. One, you stay with me. The other is you return to your brother's home, and his pregnant wife, and inform them you have left me.' He let his hand stroke down her throat, a finger resting on the pulse that beat wildly in her neck. Not such icy control as he had thought…

'Then you can explain that naturally, as I am deeply upset, I am severing all ties with your family,' he drawled with mocking sarcasm. 'Which unfortunately for Fairfax Engineering will mean an immediate repayment of the loans I forwarded some months ago for the expansion of the company.'

Then, like all good predators, he watched and waited for his victim to recognize her fate.

He saw the puzzled expression on her face, could almost see her mind assimilating what he had said, and knew the moment she realized. Anger flared in her wide blue eyes and flags of colour stained her cheeks. She twisted out of his hold and he let her, smiling inwardly. He knew she was not going anywhere…

Emily took a few steps back on legs that trembled. The numbness that had protected her since his shocking revelation about her father was fading fast and the effort to remain un-affected by his closeness had taken every bit of control she possessed. She was horribly conscious that just being held against him had made her traitorous body achingly aware of him and was furious at herself and him… She drew in a few deep steadying breaths and wrapped her arms defensively around her midriff, grittily determined to control her anger and the rest…

The silence lengthened.

She could feel Anton watching, waiting, and finally, when she was confident she could speak to him without tearing the lying rat's eyes out, she glanced across at him.

'And what exactly does that mean for Fairfax?' she asked in a cool little voice.

'An educated guess. The expansion will have to stop and they will be in deep financial trouble, and probably ripe for a hostile takeover.' He gave her a humourless smile. 'As I said before, the choice is yours, Emily.'

He didn't need to add a takeover by him. Emily figured that out for herself. 'You would do that…' she prompted, and saw his proud head incline slightly, the glimmer of triumph in his dark eyes, and she knew the answer.

'If I have to. I will do anything to keep you.'

A hysterical laugh rose in her throat and she choked it back. *He would do anything to keep her.* A few hours ago she would have been flattered by his words, now she was just sickened.

Suddenly her legs threatened to collapse beneath her, and abruptly she sat down on the bed, her hands clasped tightly in her lap, and stared up at him in sheer disbelief…

She shook her head and looked down at her hands, her gaze lingering on the gold band on her finger. What a travesty…

Slowly she reran the scenario of the future of their marriage Anton had painted in her head. It did not take a genius to work out he must have planned this all along. She also realized there was one glaring flaw in the choice he had given her as far as she was concerned.

'If what you say is true you can take the company any time, whether we are together or not,' she said slowly. 'And you freely admit you don't love me, or anyone else for that matter. We both know you can have any woman you want without much effort, and frequently do by all accounts.' Though picturing him in another woman's arms doing what he had done to her was like a knife to her heart. She paused for a moment, drawing on every bit of will-power she could before lifting her head and asking, 'So why on earth, Anton, would I stay with you?'

He stood towering over her, his expression unreadable. He was so close she imagined she felt the warmth of his body reaching out to her, and she trembled and despised herself for it.

Then he smiled—he actually smiled, all confident macho male, and she wanted to thump him. He sat down beside her, his great body angled towards her, and hastily she moved away, but banged against her damn suitcase and sent it tumbling to the floor.

'Steady, Emily.' He reached across her to put a restraining hand on her arm and she flinched at the contact. 'And though I am flattered you think I can have any woman I want, I want only you.'

Anton knew he had her. He had noted her tremble. His original assessment was right—in a few days she would forget this nonsense about leaving him. But he had to tread warily. Naturally she was upset and angry because he had forced her to face reality and accept he was not quite the Prince Charming she had imagined…but as human as the next man.

He had not got where he was today without being ruthless when it came to what he wanted. He never took an insult to his integrity without seeking retribution. Anything less was a sign of weakness, and no one could accuse him of that.

But he could do charming…

She was as skittish as the newborn foals he bred on his ranch in Peru and needed gentle handling. She would stay with him anyway, of that he was determined. But he would prefer her to stay with him willingly and what he wanted he always got.

'I regret arguing with you, but you have a knack of inflaming all my passions.' He grimaced. 'I never meant to tell you the truth about your father, but your rosy view of him spiked my temper and for that I apologize. So now can we put this argument behind us, and get on with our marriage? It is up to you, Emily, but I promise if you stay I will never harm your family firm in any way.' He reached for her hand, and he found he was grasping air as she shot off the bed at the speed of light, and spun around to stare down at him.

Surprise didn't cut it; he had been at his caring best, what more did she want? His mouth grim, Anton studied her. God, she was magnificent. Statuesque, her blue eyes blazing, her perfect breasts rising and falling in her agitation, her hands placed defiantly on her slender hips. He was aroused simply looking at her, and then she spoke, and his softly-softly approach flew out of the window.

'Are you mad? After today I would not believe a word you said if you swore it on a stack of bibles,' she yelled.

'Then trust this,' Anton snarled, his temper and frustration finally boiling over, and, catching her around the waist, he tumbled her onto the bed.

The breath left Emily's body and before she knew it she was flat on her back with Anton's long body pinning her to the bed.

For a moment she was too shocked to move, and then his mouth was crashing down on hers, and instantly her pulse rate surged and she was wildly, passionately angry. She fought like a woman possessed, she kicked out and he retaliated by pinning her legs between his heavy thighs. She bit his tongue, her hands tangled in his hair and pulled. He did the same.

'Hell—Emily—'

His voice was ragged and then his mouth slammed back down on hers. Still she tried to resist, but his big body pressed against her, his hand in her hair holding her firm, his other hand cupping her breast, kneading, igniting a different kind of passion.

His hand left her hair, and he shoved her top and bra up over her breasts, his mouth covering her already-straining nipples. Wild excitement ripped through her and all thought of resistance was blown away in the storm of passion engulfing her.

'You want me,' he rasped.

'Yes,' she groaned, her arms involuntarily wrapping around him. She didn't notice when he removed her trousers. She wanted him; he was right—she could not help herself.

His lips brushed her breast, her throat, her mouth, and her mouth twined with his in a desperate greedy kiss. Involuntarily her slender body arched up beneath him, and she gloried in the pressure of his surging masculine arousal. He moved sensually against her, and she moaned as his teeth and tongue found her aching nipples, teasing and tasting until she was wild with wanting. Anton's hands curved around her buttocks and her body jerked violently as he plunged to the hilt into the sleek, tight centre of her, the sensation so intense, she could barely breathe.

Hard and fast, he thrust repeatedly, and her body convulsed in an explosion of pleasure so exquisite she could only gasp as he plunged on to his own shuddering release.

She lay there, her eyes closed, exhausted and fighting for breath, the shuddering aftermath still pulsing inside her. She felt Anton roll off her and say her name. But she kept her eyes closed. She could not face him, a deep sense of shame and humiliation consuming her.

Knowing he did not love her and had an ulterior motive for marrying her… Nothing had stopped her melting like ice in the sun as soon as he had kissed her. In one passionate encounter he had turned her lifelong belief in love on its head. She felt his hand smoothing back her hair from her face, his fingers trace the curve of her mouth.

'Emily, look at me.'

Reluctantly she opened her eyes. He was leaning over her, determination in every angle of his brutally handsome face.

'No more pretence, Emily. You want me and I want you. You may already be carrying my child, so no more arguments. We are married and that is the way it is going to stay.'

She almost told him then…

Emily was a practical woman and she had started taking the pill a week after their first date as a precaution for the affair she had hoped would follow, marriage not on her mind at the time. Now she kept her secret. Why feed his colossal ego by letting him know how ridiculously eager she had been to go to bed with him?

'And I have no say in the matter.'

'No.' Anton's dark eyes swept over her, his lips curving in a brief satisfied smile as he straightened up, flexing his shoulders. 'Your body said it for you.'

He was so damned arrogant, Emily thought bitterly. He was standing at the foot of the bed, his shirt in place and zipping his shorts, and suddenly a fiery tide of red washed over her as she realized he had not even removed his clothing. Whereas she… She looked down… Oh, God… Hastily she tugged her bra and top down over her breasts. She was mortified and glanced wildly around for her trousers.

'Yours, I believe,' Anton drawled, a hint of amusement in his black eyes as he dropped her white trousers and briefs on her legs. 'Though you might like to change for dinner—our guests will be arriving soon.' And he strolled out of the cabin without a backward glance, while Emily fumed.

She leapt off the bed, and headed straight for the shower for the third time that day. She wasted no time, knowing Anton would be back to change.

Washed and wearing only bra and briefs, she unpacked her case yet again. She would allow Anton to think she agreed with him, until she could figure out a way to leave without harming her family.

She chose a short, black, thankfully crease-proof slip dress, and put it on. She slapped some moisturizer on her face, covered her lips in pink gloss and brushed her hair. She saw no reason in dressing up to the nines for Anton and his friends. They were not hers and never would be now. He had had the nerve to say earlier she could dabble with her career until the children arrived. The word 'dabble' said it all. So much for his promise to support her given on the night he proposed. He obviously had no respect for who or what she was. As for children... She hardened her heart against the image of a dark-haired beautiful baby, a replica of Anton, in her arms... Like all her foolish dreams of love, that was never going to happen now.

She slid her feet into black sandals, and exited the cabin. She needed some fresh air.

Emily walked to the seaward side of the yacht and, half hidden by a lifeboat, she leant against the rail to watch the thin crescent of the sun sink beneath the horizon in a last red blaze of glory. She stood for a long time, her mind swirling, trying to find a way out. She looked at the darkening night sky and felt as though the same darkness were wrapping its way around her heart and soul.

She would never do anything that might harm her brother and family. After today, her trust in Anton was totally shattered. How could she love a man she didn't trust? It wasn't possible. Yet when he had tumbled her on the bed her anger had been fierce but fleeting, she had welcomed his possession, and with bitter self-loathing she knew she would again. She was helpless to resist. She also knew she had no alternative but to go along with what he wanted. She was trapped...

CHAPTER SIX

EMILY heard the sound of raised voices and realized the launch must have arrived with the guests, but she didn't move, reluctant to go and face strangers with her emotions so raw.

A deep painful sigh escaped her. Short of discovering she had married a homicidal maniac, she must have had the worst first day of marriage in history. Still, it couldn't possibly get any worse, she told herself, and, taking a deep breath, she turned.

'Emily.' Anton was moving towards her. He was dressed in a lightweight beige suit, his shirt open at the neck, and his black hair slicked severely back from his brow, and she realized with a sick sense of shame he looked more gorgeous than ever to her tortured mind.

'I wondered where you were hiding,' he drawled sardonically. 'Our guests have arrived.' He took her arm and led her into the salon.

Emily was wrong: the day could get worse...

Seated on Anton's left, Emily glanced around the table. The dinner party from hell was a pretty fair assessment, she mused.

They were seven couples in all, a single young man and, with the inclusion of Max, sixteen around the dinner table in the sumptuous dining area of the yacht.

Anton at his eloquent best had introduced her as his wife, and she would have to have been an idiot not to notice the surprise and outright disbelief at his pronouncement. While in an aside to her he had warned her to behave impeccably in front of his guests…or else…

Else what? Emily wondered. He could not hurt her any more than he already had. The congratulations were gushing, but the looks she got from the six other women on board varied from genuine pleasure to curiosity to almost pitying and, from one, simply venomous.

She smiled and Anton kept the conversation going with very little help from her through five courses that she barely remembered eating. She was in shock.

Wouldn't you just know it? she mused. The first person she had seen was Eloise. Anton had introduced her to Eloise's Italian husband, Carlo Alviano, and his twenty-two-year-old son from a previous marriage, Gianni.

She raised her glass and took another sip of wine, and glanced around the table. Sally and Tim Harding she recognized from a business dinner she had attended in London with Anton. As for the other four couples, they seemed pleasant enough. One couple was Swiss, another French, and a rather nice middle-aged American couple, and the last pair were Greek. It was a truly international gathering of the seriously rich, and, from the designer dresses and jewellery on show, she wouldn't like to estimate how much their combined worth came to. Billions no doubt…

She glanced at the young man, Gianni, seated on her right. There was something familiar about him but she could not quite place him. She took another sip of wine, and let her gaze roam over him. He was classically handsome with perfect features and thick black curly hair. Maybe he was a model; perhaps she had seen a picture of him in a magazine.

'More wine?' the steward offered and Emily nodded. She knew she was probably drinking too much, but she was past caring and let her eyes stray to rest on Eloise, with a kind of morbid fascination.

Eloise was obviously Anton's type of woman.

She was wearing a red minidress, that barely covered her voluptuous breasts or her bum. She was seated on the right of Anton and had spent most of the meal trying to hold his attention, gossiping away to him about old times with much touching of his arm and anywhere else she could reach. As for her husband, Carlo, who was seated next to her, she virtually ignored him.

Why Carlo put up with her Emily could not fathom. A sophisticated, handsome man in his fifties, he was quite charming and owned a merchant bank. Maybe that was why Eloise had married him, she thought cynically.

She took another sip of her wine. And maybe Carlo didn't care so long as the sex was good... Maybe he was the same type of man as Anton—look at the reality of her marriage after one day—and she giggled, seeing the black humour in the situation.

'Oh, please, you must share the joke,' Eloise trilled, all fake smiles.

Emily glanced across at her, saw the spite in the other woman's eyes and said, 'It was nothing. Just a humorous thought.'

'Let us be the judge of that,' Eloise prompted. And for one moment Emily was tempted to tell her exactly what she had been thinking. But although she had consumed a little too much wine, it was far from enough for her to make a fool of herself.

'No,' she said and froze into immobility as Anton lifted a hand to her cheek and trailed his fingers down and around the nape of her neck, urging her head towards him.

'Some coffee or water maybe.' His gaze locked with hers and something moved in the dark depths of his eyes. 'You have had a couple of very full days, my darling, as I know,' he drawled, his finger pressing on the pulse that beat strongly in her throat.

Her eyes widened, and she barely controlled an involuntary shiver until he added, 'Any more wine and you will fall asleep.' And she realized that his show of affection was purely for the guests and to add insult to injury he had implied she was drunk…the swine.

She drew in a deep steadying breath. 'You're right as always, darling,' she mocked, and reached up to remove his hand from her neck, digging her nails into his wrist in the process. 'Coffee, thanks.'

Anton's eyes narrowed, promising retaliation, then he turned to beckon the steward and coffee was provided.

Hot and angry, Emily silently seethed. The atmosphere stank, there was no other word for it, and she wished she could go out on deck for some clean air. Better still dive overboard and swim to shore—it couldn't be more than half a mile…

'That's it,' she cried and slapped her hand on the table, making the glass and cutlery rattle.

'Gianni, I thought I knew you.' She turned to the young man at her side, the first genuine smile of the evening lighting her face. It had come to her out of the blue when she had thought of swimming.

'You were in the under-twenty-ones swimming team for Rome University at the European Universities' sports challenge held in Holland four years ago.'

'Yes, señora, I recognized you immediately, but I thought you did not remember me.'

'Oh, please call me Emily—you did before,' she reminded him. 'I watched you win in an amazing split-second finish in the fifteen hundred metres—you were fantastic, and we met at the party afterwards.'

'That's right, and I saw you win the two hundred metres with two seconds to spare. You were brilliant.'

'Thank you. That was one of my finer moments.' She preened and laughed and so did Gianni.

His father intervened. 'You two know each other.' And his handsome face was wreathed in smiles. 'What a happy coincidence.'

'Yes. And you must be very proud of your son. Did you see him win that race? It was such a close finish after such a long race. He was incredible,' Emily enthused.

'Regrettably, no. I was in South America at the time,' and Emily noticed his eyes stray to Eloise.

'Enough about swimming,' Eloise cut in. 'That is all the boy ever talks about, that and the bank, just like Carlo,' she said petulantly. 'It is so boring.'

'I found it rather enlightening,' Anton said. 'I never knew you were a champion swimmer, Emily.'

Emily caught the faintly sarcastic tone and a hint of anger in the dark eyes that met hers. 'Why should you?' She shrugged. 'You have only known me a couple of months, and anyway I am not any more.'

Suddenly she felt bone-tired. Only an idiot could be unaware of the undercurrent of tension beneath the surface of the supposedly friendly conversation all evening, and it had given her a horrendous headache. That and the appalling realization that all she had to look forward to were countless more such encounters with Anton and his friends had stretched her nerves to breaking-point.

Pushing back her chair, she stood up. 'Well, it has been a delightful evening meeting you all.' She cast a social smile around the table. 'But I am afraid I will have to call it a night. Please excuse me.' The men made to rise. 'No, please, Anton will keep you entertained.'

Anton placed an arm along the back of Emily's waist and she stiffened in shock—she had not realized he had risen with her.

'I will escort you to the cabin, Emily.' His tone was as smooth as silk, and then, raising his voice, he added for his guests' benefit. 'If you need anything ask the steward. I'll be back soon.'

'A champion swimmer. I'm impressed,' Anton declared as he stopped and opened their cabin door, and ushered her inside. 'You are full of surprises, Emily, but if there are any more on the horizon pass them by me first,' he drawled sardonically. 'I do not appreciate being made to look a fool in front of our guests, while you flirt and reminisce with another man.'

'You made to look a fool?' She shook her head and twisted out of his arm to cast him a look of utter disgust. 'I am the only fool around here, for being stupid enough to think I could ever love a man like you. A man who invites his mistress Eloise on his honeymoon.'

'Eloise is not—'

'Oh, please, you have had sex with her; it is in her eyes every time she looks at you. So don't bother denying it.'

'Once, a decade ago,' he snapped. 'Carlo is an old and valued friend of mine and I introduced them. I was best man at their wedding four years ago. Eloise is an old friend, nothing more.'

'You don't need to explain. I couldn't care less, though I am amazed her husband puts up with it—he seems like a really nice man. Whereas you have to be the most devious, arrogant snake of a man it has ever been my misfortune to meet. And if you imagine for one second making me stay with you will change how I think of you…it won't. Now go back to your guests, Anton. I have a headache and I am going to bed. Alone.'

Anton fought down the furious impulse to shut her smart

mouth with his own. 'Not alone, Emily,' he said with implacable softness and took her arm.

She struggled to break free, but he tightened his grip. 'You are my wife and sharing my bed—that is not negotiable.'

His dark brooding eyes held hers. He saw the anger, the pain she tried to hide in the blue depths, and surely not fear?

Shocked, he let go of her arm. He was a huge success at everything he did; women looked at him admiringly, hungrily, with adoration, wanting to please him, but never with fear. So how the hell had he managed to make his bride of one day actually look afraid of him?

'You look worn out. I'll get you some painkillers, and you can get some sleep.'

Hmm. Emily sighed her pleasure as a strong hand slowly massaged her breast. She settled back against a hard male body and arched her neck as firm lips caressed the slender length of her throat, a warm tongue lingering on the steadily beating pulse there. Her eyes half opened and fluttered closed as she gave herself up to the wondrous world of sensations engulfing her. Long fingers caressing, arousing her eager flesh, she was lost in a sensual dream, her heart beating with ever-increasing speed. She turned, restless heat spreading through every cell in her body, her hands curving over strong shoulders. His mouth was on hers, his muscular legs parting hers.

Her eyes flew open. It was no dream—it was Anton lying over her, the morning sun highlighting his blue-black hair, his dark molten eyes scorching through to her soul promising paradise and it was way too late to resist. She didn't want to resist. She wanted him, burned for him. She felt the velvet tip of him against her and raised her pelvis, pressing up to him.

'You want me?' Anton husked throatily.

'Yes, oh, yes,' she moaned.

His hands curved around her thighs, lifting her, and in a single powerful thrust he filled her. He thrust again harder and faster as her body caught his rhythm and they rode a tidal wave of sheer sensation. Emily climaxed in seconds with a convulsive pleasure so intense it blew her mind, and Anton followed, his great body jerking in explosive release.

Later when the tremors stopped Emily felt a wave of shame at her easy capitulation. She opened her eyes and lifted her hands to push at his chest; instead she found them gathered in one of his. He lifted his other hand and she felt him brush a few tendrils of hair from her forehead.

'You okay, Emily?'

'As okay as I will ever be as long as I am stuck with you.'

'Hell and damnation.' He swore. 'We had a fight yesterday. It is over, done with. The two people we were fighting over are dead—that is the reality. Now we move on.'

'The only place I want to move is out of here.' She couldn't help herself. He had cold-bloodedly deceived her, and he rubbed her up the wrong way with his blasted superior tone and his flaming arrogance.

'Your trouble is you can't admit that you want a man like me, can you?' he grated, bending his head and crushing her mouth under his. Then he pulled back to look into her eyes.

'You can't face reality, that is your problem; you want love and sweet nothings, a fairy tale, when anyone with any sense knows the love you imagine does not exist.'

He ran a hand through his rumpled hair, and swung his legs off the bed to sit looking down at her, totally unconscious of his nudity.

'Sexual chemistry brings a couple together, they marry and

after a year or two the lust is burned out, but usually there is a child to cement the union. For a man it is a natural instinct to protect the mother and child, and in most cases a moral duty that ensures a marriage lasts.'

Emily listened in growing amazement. 'Do you actually believe that?'

'Yes.' He stood up, stretching like a big, sated jungle beast, and turned to glance down at her. 'Mind you, from where I am standing I can't imagine ever not lusting after your naked body.' And he had the nerve to grin.

Emily grabbed the sheet and pulled it up over herself, blushing furiously. 'You are impossible.'

'Nothing is impossible if you try, Emily.' The amusement faded from his eyes. 'That is what marriage is all about,' he stated. 'Having realistic expectations.'

He was completely sure of himself, his powerful, virile body magnificently naked, and she could feel her insides melting just looking at him, and in that moment she realized she still loved him…always would…and it saddened and infuriated the hell out of her.

'And you're the expert? Don't make me laugh,' she snapped.

'I will certainly make you cry if you keep up this ridiculous fight. We can be civil to each other, the sex is great and we can have a good marriage, or you can turn it into a battlefield—it is up to you. I need a shower; you can join me, or make your mind up before I come back.'

There was only one answer, Emily realized.

Being civil and having sex… That was Anton's idea of a perfect marriage. She could do civil and sex, and a lot more. He had said he had not intended telling her what he thought of her father, but his temper had got the better of him. Well, maybe she could convince him he was wrong about her father.

Not now, not with a boatload of guests, but when they were finally alone.

He had said he would do anything to keep her. Maybe there was hope for their marriage, maybe he cared about her a lot more than he was prepared to admit…and pigs might fly…

The bottom line was, even if she proved her father had nothing to do with his sister, she could not escape the fact that was the main reason why Anton had married her.

Anton emerged from the bathroom and Emily hastily sat up in bed, dragging the cover up to her chin.

His only covering was a white towel slung precariously around his lean hips. And as she watched he moved to open one of the large wardrobes that covered one wall, withdrew something and turned.

'So what is it to be, Emily?' he asked, and discarded the towel, giving her a full-frontal view of his toned bronzed body, and stepped into a pair of Grigio Perla aqua shorts.

Emily recognized the brand because she had seen the James Bond movie that made them famous. On Anton they looked even better than the star of the movie. Fascinated by the sheer masculine perfection of his physique, she simply stared.

'I asked you a question.'

'What? Oh! Yes.' She was so mesmerized by the sight of him, she replied without thinking.

'Good,' was all he said as he pulled a polo shirt over his head. 'Make yourself decent. I'll send the chief steward in with your breakfast, and you can have a chat with him. He knows how the weekend works. It is a pretty casual affair, but if there is anything you want to change just tell him.'

Who was it said fascination is the very absence of thought, the denial of reasonable brain function? Emily wondered. She was so mesmerized by Anton she could not think rationally.

'I will see you on the pool deck when you are ready. Friday everyone tends to laze around until lunch. Then go ashore, the men to check out the cars and the women to shop. Later we all meet here to eat and then sail along to St Tropez for those who want to hit the Caves du Roy nightclub, a favourite among a few of our guests.'

He strolled over to the bed, and held out a credit card. 'Take this—you will need it later.'

She took the card and turned it over in her hand. Mrs Emily Diaz was the name inscribed.

She looked up. 'How did you get this so quickly?' she asked, no longer mesmerized but mad. Anton was so confident in his ability to get exactly what he wanted in life, including her, she realized bitterly.

'I arranged for the card to be forwarded here the day we married, as I did your passport,' Anton said, a hint of a satisfied smile quirking his wide mouth.

She affected a casual shrug. 'You're nothing if not thorough,' she said coolly. But inside she was seething with a mixture of emotions, from hate to love and, yes, lust, she admitted. But her overriding desire was to knock the smug look off his face.

'Thank you. But I don't need your money; I have enough of my own.'

'You won't for much longer if you insist on this confrontational attitude,' he drawled with a sardonic arch of one brow. 'Give it up, Emily. You're my wife—act like one. I'll expect you on deck in an hour to take care of our guests.'

The timely reminder of his hold over Fairfax Engineering knocked all the defiance out of her. 'Okay.'

She watched him walk out. He really was quite ruthless, and she had better not forget that. But if he thought she was going to be a meek little wife he was in for a rude awakening.

* * *

The number of gorgeous women lining the pit lane came as a shock to Emily. She would not have thought that so many women were keen on motor racing to bother coming for the time trials. She said as much to Max, and he gave her a grin.

'It is not the cars they are interested in, but the men—they are motor-racing groupies.' He chuckled. 'Pit Ponies.'

'Oh.' It had never occurred to her, but now she saw exactly what he meant. No wonder Anton was such a passionate fan of motor racing. Fast cars and fast women lined for his delectation, she thought scathingly.

Personally she hated the scene. The noise was horrendous, the choking smell of oil took her breath away, and she cast a baleful glance at Anton. He was standing by a low-slung racing car having an animated discussion about the engine with the chief mechanic. He looked almost boyish in his enthusiasm and at that moment, as if sensing her scrutiny, he turned, his dark eyes clashing with hers. He smiled and in a couple of lithe strides was beside her. 'So what do you think? Isn't this great?'

'Put it this way,' she said dryly, 'I can see now why they call it the pit. The place is full of men, noise, and stinks of oil and super-charged testosterone, and if it is all the same to you I think I'll go back to the yacht.'

He grimaced. 'You're right—it is probably not the place for a lady. Max will take you back, and I'll see you later.'

Back on the yacht, she heaved a sigh of relief when she learnt most of the guests had gone ashore. 'I'm going to change and have a swim,' she told Max and headed for the cabin.

She had spent yesterday being polite to their guests, and playing the perfect hostess. The nightclub in St Tropez had been a real eye-opener, all the beautiful people—she had recognized a famous American film star and a chart-topping singer to name just two. She had drunk champagne and smiled until her face ached and had hated every minute.

Then later when they had returned to the yacht she had vowed she would not respond to Anton. But when he had slid into bed naked and reached for her, her resolve had been strained to the limit. His kiss had been hungry, possessive, and passionate. She had tried to resist, her hands curling into fists at her side. But when he had lifted his head, and caught the strap of her flimsy nightgown and moved it down to palm her breast, a groan had escaped her.

'Give it up, Emily,' he said harshly. 'You know you want to.'

He was right, shaming but true…

Now with Anton on shore she felt not exactly relaxed, but at least in control for the first time in two days. Slipping into a shockingly brief black bikini, courtesy of Helen, she headed for the swimming pool. She lathered her body with sun lotion, and was wondering how to do her back when Gianni appeared, and did it for her.

Anton stepped out of the helicopter, and took the stairs two at a time to the lower deck. He was feeling great, fired up… His passion for motor racing had been fulfilled with a day in the pit watching the time trials for tomorrow's big race. The team he supported had pole position. He flexed his shoulders…and soon his other passion would be fulfilled with Emily.

She had appeared to accept his take on marriage without further argument, and yesterday she had proved to be a hit with their guests.

Last night had been incredible; his body stirred thinking about it. He had climbed into bed, taken her in his arms and kissed her. At first she had tried to play it cool, but within minutes she had gone up in flames just as she had every time before.

Yes, life was just about perfect… He needed a shower. Maybe Emily would be in the cabin. She wasn't and, ten minutes later, dressed in shorts and shirt, he walked out on deck looking for her. Carlo was leaning over the guard rail with Tim Harding and Max beside him, but there was no sign of Emily.

Anton strolled over. 'Hi, guys.' He leant against the railing next to him. 'Have you seen Emily around?'

Max pointed to a small yacht anchored about two hundred metres away. 'She is over there with Gianni. Apparently the boat belongs to friends of his and the pair of them decided to race each other across and back. They arrived there twenty minutes ago.'

The feel-good factor vanished. He felt as if he had been punched in the stomach and realized it was gut-wrenching fear. His impulse was to dive off after them, but he realized it was pointless, and then blind rage engulfed him and he turned on Max.

'You let my wife dive thirty feet off the bloody yacht,' he swore. 'Are you mad? You are supposed to be a bodyguard.'

He stilled, his chest tightening as he recognized the source of his rage. He felt an overwhelming need to protect Emily, something he had never felt for any other woman except his mother and sister.

'Sorry, boss, I couldn't stop them. They were balancing on the rail when I came out on deck. But you have nothing to worry about. Emily swims like a fish. In fact the three of us still can't decide which one won.'

'That is why we are waiting here to see them come back,' Carlo said. 'We have a little bet on the result.'

Anton could not believe his ears. 'Forget your damn bet. Nobody is swimming back. I am getting the launch.'

Carlo lifted a pair of binoculars to his eyes. 'Too late.'

Anton looked across just in time to see two figures dive into the sea.

He'd kill her; he'd shake her till her teeth rattled. He'd chain her to him… But first he needed her back safely. A boat could cut across her path, she might get cramp—the opportunity for disaster loomed huge in his mind and with bated breath he watched with Carlo and Max as the swimmers drew closer.

Reluctantly he had to admit Emily was superb. She glided through the water with barely a ripple, her long pale arms rising and falling in a perfect crawl, keeping a punishing speed. He watched as they approached the stern and saw Emily grab the ladder first.

'I won,' Emily cried, hanging onto the ladder with one hand and brushing the hair from her eyes. Gianni's arm came up and grasped her waist.

'OK—so it is one all.'

Breathless and grinning, they scrambled up onto the deck.

Anton stood transfixed. Emily, wearing the briefest of bikinis, stood glowing with life and vitality laughing with Gianni. Jealousy ripped through him and he had to battle the urge to rush across and shove the younger man overboard.

'Best of three. I'll race you tomorrow,' he heard Gianni say and his wife was totally oblivious of him as she responded.

'Right, you're on.'

Anton moved to grab Emily, but Carlo's hand on his arm stopped him. He looked up at him and said softly, 'So, my friend, now you know how it feels?'

'What do you mean?' Anton demanded.

'You know Emily and Gianni are just friends, as I know you and Eloise are just friends. But when you love a woman it doesn't always follow that you can easily accept her male friendships. Take my advice—don't make an issue out of their harmless fun.'

Carlo's words gave him pause for thought. Of course he did not love Emily. But he knew Carlo imagined he loved Eloise, and it had never occurred to him his friendship with Eloise might hurt Carlo.

Then again he wasn't Carlo, and Emily wasn't having fun with anyone but him...

'You will not be racing tomorrow, Emily.' He strode across and took her arm. 'And you, Gianni, will not encourage my wife to risk her life in such a damn-fool way.'

'Oh, don't be such an old fuddy-duddy,' Emily said, lifting her eyes to his. 'You have your motor racing. I prefer a more natural race.'

He felt every one of his thirty-seven years and he did not appreciate the reminder. His dark eyes narrowed on her beautiful face. 'Have you forgotten tomorrow we are all attending the Grand Prix? And Gianni is leaving on Monday so it is never going to happen,' he said bluntly.

'Oh, yes.' She turned away from him. 'Excuse me all, I need to shower and get ready for the party.' And he had to let her go, as Tim Harding asked him a question about the time trials.

Coloured lights strung from prow to stern lit up the great yacht. Dinner was a buffet as the original guests had been increased by about another thirty from shore. Apparently another tradition of her indomitable husband. She glanced across to where he stood surrounded by friends, mostly of the female variety. He was wearing a white shirt open at the neck and dark trousers, and looked devastatingly attractive. The dress code for the men appeared to be smart casual, actually designer casual, Emily amended, glancing around, but her eyes were helplessly drawn back to her husband.

As she watched he laughed down at the woman hanging on his arm, and Emily looked away. Anton was always going to be the centre of attention, the outstanding Alpha male, in what she quietly conceded was quite a gathering of such men. But then why not? Monaco was the playground of the rich and famous and never more so than this weekend.

'Hi, Emily.' She glanced at Gianni as he stopped beside her. 'May I say you look wicked,' he said with undisguised appreciation in his golden eyes. 'Mind you, I think you are wasted on this crowd. What say we do a bunk to my friend's yacht?'

But before she could respond Carlo appeared in front of them. 'Damn Eloise. That woman could shop for Peru,' he declared, exasperation in his tone. 'You do know she only arrived back ten minutes ago—the helicopter had to go and pick her up, hopelessly late as usual.' He snorted. 'She said it wouldn't take a minute to change.' And grasping a glass of champagne as a waiter walked by, he added, 'I will believe that when I see it.'

Gianni responded with, 'Here she comes now, Dad.'

Emily's mouth fell open in shock. The woman was wearing a white off-the-shoulder dress that revealed her breasts almost to the nipples—not that it mattered as the fabric was see-through, a silver belt was slung around her hips, and the rest of the garment barely covered her behind. Emily glanced up at Gianni and saw the slight tinge of embarrassment on his handsome young face and she felt for him.

'New dress?' Carlo demanded and Emily's attention returned to him. His eyes were popping out on stalks. He had obviously not seen it before, she surmised, and her lips twitched in the briefest of smiles. Not that there was much to see other than the fact the woman was also wearing a thong. Outrageous didn't even begin to describe it.

'No, darling.' Eloise pouted. 'You told me to hurry so I just flung this old thing on.' She preened, doing a twirl.

'She obviously missed,' Emily said under her breath to

Gianni. His golden eyes widened and he cracked up with laughter, as did Emily.

'Oh, Emily.' He flung an arm around her shoulder. 'You are priceless.' He offered between guffaws, 'And so right.'

Anton broke off mid-sentence in a rather serious discussion he was having with the Swiss banker, his attention diverted at the sound of Emily's uninhibited laughter. Her head was thrown back, revealing the long line of her throat and the upper curves of her breast; her blonde hair fell in a silken curtain almost to her waist. The dress she was wearing was red and strapless and faithfully followed every curve of her body to flare out at thigh level and end just above her knees. She looked drop-dead gorgeous and as he watched Gianni's arm went around her.

In a few lithe strides Anton was at her side. 'I am all for you enjoying yourself, Gianni,' he drawled, 'but not with my wife.'

He reached down and caught her hand as Gianni's arm fell from her shoulders.

Surprised, Emily raised laughing eyes to her husband's face and was struck by the deadly warning in the black depths of his, and looked away.

Gianni said nothing, but moved back a step; the look in Anton's eyes had said it all.

'I said be civil.' Anton slid a hand around the nape of her neck and tilted back her head so she had no choice but to look up at him. 'Not flirt with the guests and make a spectacle of yourself. What was so funny anyway?' He was jealous—not an emotion he had ever suffered from before—and he was fed up as he saw all expression drain from her face.

'You had to be there at the time to appreciate it,' she said, 'but I take your point and I am sorry. I will endeavour to be civil at all times.' And she smiled.

A perfect social smile that didn't reach her eyes.

He kept her by his side for the rest of the evening, and later in bed he utilized every bit of control and skill he possessed to drain every drop of response from her incredible body. Only when she lay exhausted and sated in his arms was he satisfied.

He gazed down at her. She had been helpless in the throes of passion as he had brought her to the knife-edge of pleasure time after time, and had held her there shuddering and writhing until finally he had possessed her completely and she had convulsed in wave after wave of excruciating delight.

Then he had started again.

She was his… He had exactly what he wanted. He frowned slightly. So what was niggling at the back of his mind? Surely not conscience… No—something else. It would come to him later, he assured himself before sleep overcame him.

The following night Emily stood in front of the floor-to-ceiling mirror in their cabin and studied her reflection. She was wearing the one floor-length gown she had packed and she grimaced. Blue shot through with silver, the halter neck left her shoulders and back bare down to her waist, and the plunging neck revealed more than a glimpse of cleavage. The rest clung to her body like a second skin. A side slit enabled her to move. When she had bought the dress it had been with her honeymoon in mind. For Anton's eyes only. Because she had loved him, even after their argument she had still harboured a lingering hope of convincing him he was wrong about her father, and making him care for her. Not any more. Once trust was destroyed there was no going back.

She had no illusions left regarding her arrogant husband. Last night he had taught her what an avid sensualist she was, and she had relished the lesson. He had driven her to the erotic height of pleasure and beyond until it had almost been pain. He was a magnificent lover.

Today she had had her relatively inexperienced opinion verified…

They had all gone to watch the Grand Prix at the home of a friend of Anton's. Settled on a long terrace overlooking the race with their guests and some more friends of the owner, Anton had asked if she minded if he went to the pits. She had bit her tongue on the caustic comment *he was the pits*. Deciding she still loved him had not lessened her feeling of betrayal. But deep inside she had still held a faint hope that their marriage might work and instead she said, 'Not at all.'

Bored out of her skull watching cars roar past at intervals, she drank a couple of glasses of champagne. And then went inside to stretch her legs. She was standing behind a huge column admiring a sculpture set in an alcove when she heard the click of heels on the marble floor and a cut-glass English voice mention her name.

'Emily Diaz has my sympathy. He is incredibly wealthy, a handsome devil, and great in the sack, as I know from personal experience. But, let's face it, the man is not marriage material. I mean, bringing her here for her honeymoon, with over a dozen guests for company—how crass is that? I couldn't believe it when we arrived. But then we never knew he had married. Heaven help the poor girl, is what I say. She seems a really nice woman, well bred by all accounts and far too good for him. I bet she has no idea that he has had affairs with at least two of us on board and probably more.'

Staying out of sight, Emily recognized the voice as the footsteps faded away. It was Sally, the wife of Tim Harding, and Emily's humiliation was complete. She had known about Eloise, but to discover another of his ex-lovers was on board was beyond belief.

That any man could be so incredibly insensitive as to invite one ex-lover on his honeymoon was the stuff of nightmares, but two… She had more or less accepted Anton's version of why Carlo and Eloise were guests…but not any more. This latest revelation was the last straw.

At that moment something finally died in Emily.

Thinking about the conversation now, Emily briskly turned away from the mirror, slipped her feet into silver stiletto sandals, and straightened up.

CHAPTER SEVEN

'You look incredible.'

Emily hadn't heard Anton enter, and turned slowly to face him. 'Thank you.' He was still wearing the same chinos and a polo shirt he had worn all day, and he was still grinning. The team he had sponsored had won, and the driver was now leading the world championship race and Anton had been in a celebratory mood ever since.

But then he won at everything, Emily thought sourly, but at least while he was celebrating on deck, with the other men on board, it had given her the chance to slip away.

'But a bit premature.' His hooded gaze raked over her with blatant masculine appreciation, and the eyes he lifted to hers were gleaming with a hot sensuality she could not fail to recognize as he stepped closer. 'I was hoping we could share a shower.'

'Too late.' She forced a smile, and cursed the curl of heat in her stomach his suggestion had ignited. 'I thought as this is your guests' last night, I should make an appearance at the cocktail hour, before we go ashore to the party, so if you will excuse me.' She moved to walk past him, but he caught her arm.

His lips curved in a wry smile. 'You're right, of course—the perfect hostess. I can wait, and I won't spoil your lip gloss.'

His head dipped and he brushed his lips against her brow. 'But I have something for you.'

She watched as he crossed to a small safe set in the wood-panelled wall of the cabin and withdrew a velvet-covered box.

'I meant to give you this on our wedding night,' he declared, moving to her side. 'But I was distracted.' And he opened the box to withdraw a sparkling diamond necklace. 'You might like to wear it tonight.'

Emily glanced at the necklace, and reached out to stop his hand as he would have slipped it around her neck, and took it from him.

'Thank you. It is beautiful.' She let the waterfall of diamonds run through her fingers, and slowly raised her eyes to his. 'But unfortunately it is not right for this gown.' She handed it back to him. 'I'll wear it some other time.'

It was a first for Anton, a woman rejecting his gift, not just any woman but his wife… How dared she? Grim-faced, he scanned Emily's exquisite features and slowly it dawned on him while he thought they had had a great day, his wife did not share his enthusiasm. He had given her a fortune in diamonds and yet she looked singularly unimpressed. No woman of his acquaintance would have dreamt of doing that—usually they fell over themselves in gratitude. But Emily had actually handed them back to him.

'If you say so.' He placed the necklace back in the box and returned it to the safe, and when he turned back Emily had fastened something around her neck, and was slipping a bracelet on her wrist.

Anton moved towards her and stopped. Her long blonde hair was swept back in a smooth knot on top of her head, the severity of the style emphasizing the perfect symmetry of her delicate features. The shimmering blue dress caressed her superb body like a lover's hand. The simple tie at the back of her neck left the shoulders bare and revealed the silken-smooth skin of her straight back almost to her waist. But it was the platinum chain with a heart-shaped diamond and sapphire-encrusted locket suspended between the creamy soft curves of her breasts that captured all his attention.

'Nice pendant.' He reached out and fingered the locket and wondered who had bought it for her. Maybe her ex-fiancé? Not that it mattered, he wasn't jealous…he was never jealous…he was just curious, he told himself.

'Yes, I like it,' she said and, stepping back, she added, 'and I have the bracelet to match.'

She held out her wrist for his approval. The heart motif was followed in a string of diamonds with smaller sapphire centres around her slender wrist.

'I have never seen you wear them before.' He wasn't going to ask her… But he did. 'Who gave them to you?'

Emily glanced up at him. So far Anton had got all his own way in this farce of a marriage, but not any more, and she took great delight in telling him.

'The locket was a present from my parents for my eighteenth birthday. And the bracelet was a present from my father on my twenty-first birthday. Beautiful, aren't they? And surprisingly they match the ring you bought me. Isn't that fortuitous?'

Anton frowned at the mention of her father, though, if he was honest, in a way he was relieved. 'Yes, very,' he agreed. Better a father than the ex-fiancé he had imagined.

She turned to leave, and he caught her wrist. 'Wait.'

'Was there something else?' Her eyes flicked over him.

'No, not really.' It was not like him to be so indecisive. But there was something… She was as exquisite as ever, as polite, but the blue eyes that met his no longer revealed her every thought. Instead, he realized, they looked cold, almost cynical…

He let go of her hand and she left.

Was he responsible for the change in Emily, her cynicism? he wondered for a moment. He shrugged his shoulders. No… In his experience all women were notoriously volatile; wrong time of the month, wrong clothes—anything could upset them. Problem resolved, he headed for the shower.

Emily looked around her. Not only did it make it easier for her to ignore Anton's hand resting lightly on her waist, it enabled her to study the glittering throng, or, if she was honest, the women.

Anton was at home in this crowd. He had introduced her to the winning owner of the team, and a host of other people whose names she didn't even try to remember. But all the time in the back of her mind was the nagging question if he could invite two of his ex-girlfriends to stay with them for the weekend, how many more of the women here had he slept with?

By Anton's own admission he had been attending the Monaco Grand Prix for years, and she had not forgotten what Max had told her about the 'Pit Ponies'. What a degrading nickname for female groupies, and what did it say about the men who used them? Her husband probably one.

'So, Emily, have you had enough?' Anton said softly. 'Want to go back to the yacht?' She felt the warmth of his breath against her ear and tensed.

His hand tightened on her waist and the warmth of his long body against hers was a temptation, a temptation she was determined to resist.

'No.' She looked up at his brutally handsome face. His dark eyes held a wealth of sensual knowledge that excited and shamed her.

'Actually, I would like to go to the casino,' she said sweetly. 'Carlo told me you usually all go after the party—it is another tradition of yours, apparently.' Along with bedding any beautiful female he fancied, she almost added…

Anton cursed Carlo under his breath, and, much as he ached to get Emily back in bed, he could not deny her the trip. He had already taken all the eye-rolling and ribbing he could stand from his motor-sport acquaintances when he had introduced her as his wife, when Emily had quite blithely told them this was his idea of a honeymoon. 'Yes, okay.'

Anton gritted his teeth as the roulette wheel spun again.

'Oh, my God!' Emily exclaimed as the white ball landed on her age, number twenty-four, on the roulette wheel. 'I've won again.'

The croupier gave her a broad smile and shoved a huge stack of chips towards her, and Anton wanted to shove him in the face.

'Yes, Emily,' he said, stopping her hand as she went to place another bet. 'But we have been here over three hours. The others left ages ago. You have won at least ten thousand, so don't push your luck.'

The euphoria of his team's win, his earlier good mood had totally evaporated and slowly he had begun to realize that Emily was delaying going back to the yacht. Trying to avoid going to bed with him. Well, not any more; she enjoyed sex with an appetite that matched his own, and he had waited long enough.

She cast him a look. 'Have I really? That rather proves the maxim—lucky at cards, unlucky in love.' And she gave him a brittle smile.

'Cut out the sarcasm. Collect your chips—we are leaving.'

He was angry. She had with very little persuasion been a willing bed partner after their original argument. She had agreed to continue their marriage in a civilized manner. He could not fault her—she had been perfectly polite to their

guests, if a bit sarcastic to him at times, which he could understand given her upset over her father and the honeymoon, he
silently conceded. But he wasn't a fool. Now there was definitely something else bugging her…

He was sure of it when they finally got back to their cabin
and he drew her into his arms.

She tried to pull away from him, but he merely tightened his
hold on her and looked down at her with smouldering eyes.

'I have waited all night for this,' he said, and bent his head
to take her mouth. But she averted her face and his lips
brushed her cheek.

'Do you mind, Anton, but it is four in the morning and after
the last few hectic days I am exhausted.' Her eyes avoided his,
and her body stiffened in his arms. 'Plus I need to be up in a
few hours—a couple of your guests are leaving early.'

'One kiss.' He grasped the nape of her neck and tipped back
her head; she closed her eyes, and parted her lips, and he
kissed her.

He kept on kissing her until she was melting in his arms.
Then he lifted his head, and stared down into her flushed face.
No woman manipulated him with sex, never had, never would.

'Are you sure you are too tired?' he drawled mockingly.

She looked at him for a long moment, and he could actually
see her withdrawal, the sensuality fading from her eyes,
freezing him out.

'Yes, sorry,' she apologized, and slipped out of his arms. 'But
don't let me stop you. I have it on good authority there are at
least two other women you have slept with on board. I'm sure
one will oblige. If not you could always nip ashore and pick up
a motor-racing groupie with no trouble at all.'

Anton stiffened in outrage, and for a moment he said nothing
as he fought to control the fury that surged through him at her

insult to his moral integrity, his dark eyes narrowing to slits as he took in her cool face.

'That is some opinion you have of me, Emily, and in the future I might take up your generous offer,' he drawled. 'But first I'd like to know who fed you such lies?'

'Well, I knew about Eloise, of course, but while you were doing your man thing with cars I overheard Sally Harding describing your incredible sexual skill in the bedroom, and pitying me because what man would be so crass as to invite, I believe her exact words were *at least* two of his ex-lovers on his honeymoon.'

Her explanation was delivered in such a cool, disinterested voice that Anton simply glared at her. He did not trust himself to speak—disgust and anger washing over him.

'And you believed her?' he finally demanded through gritted teeth.

She gave him a derisory glance. 'The number of women you have bedded is legendary according to the press and I don't hear you denying it.'

His reputation in the business world was first class, and he would defend it to the hilt. But he had never concerned himself with the vastly exaggerated claims the press made about the women in his life.

'I don't have to,' he snapped. 'As for Sally Harding, she is a married woman who came on to me. A woman scorned and all that.'

'If you say so.' She shrugged her shoulders and Anton saw the patent disbelief in her face as she turned and disappeared into the bathroom, slamming the door behind her.

He stepped forward, his knee-jerk reaction to go after her, convince her of the truth. Then he stopped, masculine pride coming to the fore. He had never seen the need to justify himself to a woman in his life and he was not going to start now. It smacked too much of begging…

It was another new experience for Anton. No woman had ever rejected him and *apologized*. Then insulted him so thoroughly that he was still having difficulty believing Emily…his wife of mere days…had casually suggested he seek out another woman for sex.

The anger he had held in check for so long engulfed him. A string of Spanish expletives rolled off his tongue, and in a mood as black as thunder he stalked out of the cabin and up on deck. He did not trust himself to be around Emily right now without losing control, and that was unthinkable…

When he had cooled down and returned Emily was curled up in bed fast asleep.

She was so innocent and so gullible, the Harding woman had probably known Emily was listening and had fed her a pack of lies. She was no match for some of the female sharks that moved in the circle of the super-rich, or for the news hounds that preyed on a man in his position.

Given his family background, he had learnt long ago that it was pointless issuing denials—it only added fuel to the flames of gossip. Any woman he was seen with was automatically labelled his latest mistress. Yet he had never actually kept a mistress in the true sense of the word. The knowledge of his mother's not particularly happy life spent waiting for a man to visit, a second-class lover, and for her son a virtually non-existent father, was a salutary lesson.

Sure, as a single, healthy, sexually active male, of course there had been women in his life, women he had had relationships with lasting from a few months to over a year, though he had never lived with a woman. He preferred his own space. But they were women he respected and when the inevitable parting had come, they had for the most part remained friends. In fact he could count them on his fingers, and he had only once had a one-night stand and that had been with Eloise, and a disaster. Whether Emily would believe him was questionable. But whatever her father had done to his sister, he realized, revenge and pride aside, it was up to him to reassure her. She deserved that much.

Quietly he stripped and showered, then slid into bed beside her. He looped an arm around her waist and drew her into his body. She didn't stir and for a long time he lay with Emily enfolded in his arms. She was his…and he could set her straight in the morning, was his last arrogant thought as he drifted off to sleep.

Emily stood at Anton's side as they waved farewell to the last of their guests, the picture of marital bliss, she thought, when nothing could be further from the truth.

She flinched as Anton's hands cupped her shoulders and he turned her to face him. 'So, Emily, where would you like to go? I have to be in New York next Monday, but we have a week to do what you want. We can cruise anywhere in the Mediterranean or we can go to my Greek island villa, whichever you prefer.'

She glanced up at him; his dark eyes held hers and she knew what he was thinking. She had awakened this morning wrapped in his arms, and their early morning love-making was a potent sensual memory simmering between them. No, sex session, she amended with a now familiar dull ache in the region of her heart.

Afterwards he had explained why Sally Harding had lied— apparently she had come on to him a couple of years ago and Anton had knocked her back. Her husband was a friend of his. He also told her that naturally there had been a few other women in his life. But if he had slept with the number the press accredited him with he would never have made a fortune and would have been dead from exhaustion by now. Emily had said she believed him, because lying sated beneath him she couldn't have done much else, but she noted he never said how many! He had given her a very masculine satisfied smile and a tender, but in Emily's opinion vaguely condescending, kiss.

It was amazing to her how a brilliantly clever, highly successful man in the business world could so completely separate the physical from the emotional when it came to his sex life.

She could not do it… But she was trapped, and not just by worry over her family. She was trapped by her helpless desire for him. It was like a fever in her blood. She had thought after what she had discovered yesterday that she was cured of her helpless response to him. But this morning he had proved her wrong.

He had awakened her with a kiss, she had tried to resist, she had hit out at him, and tried to wriggle from beneath him, but he had simply pinned her down with his great body and had the audacity to laugh at her feeble attempt to dislodge him. 'So you want to play rough, hmm?' he had drawled, and kissed her again, his strong hands roaming over her body, finding erogenous zones she never knew she had, until the fire in her blood overwhelmed her, and she was reaching for him…kissing him…

She knew every day she spent with him she would just fall deeper under his sensual spell. She could not resist him, and he knew it. Before she had had no idea sex could become so addictive, but she did now. She craved his touch and it filled her with shame and seriously dented her self-esteem.

Max had left earlier with the guests and, alone now apart from the crew, paradoxically the yacht seemed smaller. Spending a week with no escape from the vessel filled her with alarm. At least on land there was the possibility of walking away from Anton for a while, escaping the overwhelming physical attraction he held for her. On the yacht there was nowhere to hide…

'I suppose home is out of the question,' she said with an edge of sarcasm.

'Your home is with me. Decide or I will decide for you.'

His hands tightened on her shoulders and she saw the ruthless implacability in his dark eyes. 'In that case your villa sounds nice.'

'Good. I will inform the captain. Unfortunately I have some work that can't wait. Amuse yourself for a while, and try the pool.' He drew her to him and kissed her with a possessive passion that made her senses swim and, lifting his head, he added, 'I'll catch you later, and that is a promise.'

By the gleam of masculine anticipation in the dark eyes that met hers she knew that was one promise he would keep.

'Okay,' she murmured, and watched him stride away. Probably the only promise he ever kept where women were concerned, Emily thought sadly.

Leaning over the rail, she recalled the promise he had made in church. It seemed like a lifetime ago now. She had meant every word of her vows, but she realized they had meant nothing to him—they had simply been a means to an end. As for his excuse about his ex-lovers...if they were ex, she amended, she didn't believe him for a moment.

Anton was a man with a very high sex-drive—even she in her innocence had gathered that in the last few days. She doubted he had even noticed the difference from their wedding night, when she had loved him freely and told him so frequently, to the silent lover she had forced herself to become. If it wasn't her he was having sex with it would be some other woman.

The thought caused her pain, and with the pain came a hint of an idea, maybe a way out...

Anton was an incredibly wealthy man, and yet by some oversight he had never suggested she sign a pre-nup. Or, more likely in his conceit, his supreme confidence in his ability to keep her sexually satisfied, and with the lavish lifestyle he offered, he probably didn't think he needed one.

But the likelihood of him staying faithful to her or any woman wasn't very great. Suddenly it occurred to her all she had to do was wait. He had said she could carry on with her career, and his took him all over the world. Inevitably they would spend a lot of time apart; she could make sure of it. Once, only once, would she need to discover he had been with another woman, and she could divorce him. Then take rather a lot of his money, at least enough to make sure he could never threaten her family ever again.

It was a horrible cynical idea and not like her at all, but then living with a cynic like Anton it was hardly surprising she was learning to think like him.

In fact she could take a leaf out of his book, and spend the time on his island indulging the sexual side of her nature, a side she had never known she had before. He had said it was just lust that brought a couple together, and eventually it burnt out. Well, by the end of the week, her body sated, she might finally be rid of her helpless longing for him, or at least better able to control herself.

Yes, she decided. She would do it—make the rest of her honeymoon a sensual feast even though the marriage was a fiasco.

Washed and dressed in shorts and a tee shirt, Emily walked downstairs and out onto the veranda where breakfast was laid out. Anton had already eaten, by the look of it. He had left their bed to take an urgent call an hour or so ago. Where he was now, she didn't know.

She crossed to the balustrade and stood admiring the view. The villa was set on the top of a hill that overlooked a beautiful bay; the gardens ran down in a riot of colour almost to the beach, the white sand reaching out to the deep green sea. Around the headland she knew was a small harbour and fishing village, because that was where they had docked yesterday afternoon. But here it felt as if she were the only person in the world.

A hand wrapped around her waist and settled on her stomach, urging her back into the warmth of a large male body.

'So do you like my home?' Anton's deep voice rumbled against her ear.

'Like is too tame a word—this place is like paradise.' Or it could be under different circumstances, she silently amended.

The villa was beautiful with five bedrooms, three reception rooms, a study and a circular, elegant hall with a marble staircase. Not excessively large, but with a basement gym and games room, and fabulous terraced gardens including an infinity swimming pool. A staff of four ensured the house ran like clockwork, and a team of gardeners kept the grounds in perfect condition. The place had everything; much like the man who owned it, she thought, and inwardly sighed.

'Good. So what do you want to do today?'

'Explore, swim in the sea,' she said, wriggling around in his arms, and placing her hands firmly on his chest. 'So far I have only seen the harbour when we arrived, the house and the bedroom suite.'

'Your wish is my command.' He grinned, and half an hour later they were driving along a narrow road in an open-topped Jeep, Anton wearing the most disreputable pair of cut-off jeans that bordered on the indecent and nothing else, Emily with a baseball cap on her head at Anton's insistence, her arms and legs liberally covered in sunblock.

The Jeep screeched to an abrupt halt at the harbour, Anton leapt out and before Emily could move he had reached over and lifted her to the ground.

'First I'll take you for the best cup of coffee in the world, but don't tell my housekeeper I said that.' He chuckled, and pulled out a chair for her by a rickety table outside a small café.

Immediately the owner came out, and Emily's eyes widened in surprise as the man greeted Anton with a bear hug, and hearing Anton speaking in Greek, so obviously at home, she felt her heart squeeze a little. She was introduced to the owner, coffee was served, with small sweet-tasting cakes, and as they sat there the entire population of the village must have walked by and she was introduced to them all, old and young alike.

This was an Anton she had never seen before, laughing, chatting and totally relaxed.

'Come.' He reached down a hand to her. 'Time to explore.'

They spent the day driving around the island, which actually did not take long. They lunched on bread and cheese, high up in the centre of the island as guests of a goat-herder that Anton knew, and then spent the afternoon down on a secluded beach.

Anton stepped out of his disreputable shorts, and, totally naked, persuaded her to do the same. They swam and laughed and Emily discovered it was possible to have sex in the sea. Finally they returned to the villa as the sun was setting, Emily slightly sunburnt and covered in sand, Anton looking more bronzed and fit than ever. They shared a shower, dined on the veranda and had an early night.

It was the honeymoon she had hoped for, and, even though she knew it was a sham, Emily shed all her inhibitions and enjoyed every second. She knew she would never love another man the way she had loved Anton, and with that in mind she blocked every negative thought from her brain. One week of sensual bliss was what she had promised herself, and amazingly it was.

CHAPTER EIGHT

'SO WHAT would you like to do for your last day?' Anton asked, letting his eyes rest on Emily. She had pushed her chair back from the table, and was sitting with her long legs stretched out before her, cradling a cup of coffee in her hands, her gaze fixed on the garden and sea below.

She turned her head slightly. 'I thought I might have a swim in the pool, and then pack.'

God! But she was stunning. She positively glowed, a golden girl in every respect. The whole population of the island adored her; she was fun and friendly to everyone. She had obviously got over their argument about her father and that stupid Harding woman. But then he had always known she would after a week in his bed, he thought complacently.

Actually, he had never spent a better week in his life. She was his perfect match, in bed and out, and more than he could ever have wished for. She was wearing a flesh-coloured bikini with a fine sarong loosely draped around her and fastened with a knot between her breasts, and he felt his body stirring even though it wasn't long since they had indulged in the shower. Actually, for an innocent she had surprisingly seductive taste in lingerie, he realized, but then she was naturally sensuous, and so long as it was for his eyes only not a problem.

'Then I suppose I better make arrangements for a flight.'

Lost in contemplation of her body and what he wanted to do with it, Anton almost missed the rest of her reply. Regrouping his thoughts, he corrected her. 'No need, that is all taken care of. The helicopter will pick us up tomorrow morning and take us to Athens where my jet is waiting.'

She looked at him quizzically. 'Oh, but I thought you were going to work in New York.'

'Yes, I am.'

'Well, I have to be back in London for Tuesday. I have arranged to see some special, very fragile documents at the maritime museum to help in my research, and you did say I could carry on with my career.'

Anton's face darkened momentarily. Yes…he had said that, but that was before… Before what? Before he had developed an insatiable desire for her…

Maybe it was best he went to New York alone. He had meetings lined up all day every day and Emily was too much of a distraction. No…his nights were free and Emily could amuse herself during the day. He had never known a woman who did not love shopping and New York was a shopper's paradise.

'Yes, I did. But you have never been to my penthouse in London before. I need to accompany you the first time, clear you with Security, and introduce you to the staff,' he explained airily. 'It will be much more convenient if you reschedule your research for a later date, when we can go to London together. You will like New York, and while I work you can shop to your heart's content.'

Convenient for whom? Emily wondered dryly. He was so arrogant, so confident she would fall in with his plans like a meek little wife, and she had no intention of playing along.

She had enjoyed the week living in a fool's paradise. The

long days in the sun and the equally long steamy nights of sex—she had indulged the sensual side of her nature to the nth degree. It had not been difficult—Anton relaxed and among plain-living island people was a different person.

They had laughed and talked about anything and everything. He had told her how his Spanish Peruvian grandmother had ended up a madam in a voice filled with affection, and no re-crimination. Apparently when her lover had disappeared a few months after his mother was born, a bitter enemy of her es-tranged father had proposed an arrangement beneficial to both of them. He had needed someone to front a high-class brothel he owned, which his family had naturally known nothing about. No sex was involved, he had assured her. It had been enough for him that her father's name via his unmarried daughter was very publicly discredited twice over… She had had nothing more to lose and accepted.

To Emily, Anton's past went some way to explaining why he had been so determined she should share his name, Diaz. Polite society was hard on what was seen as immoral, most would say rightly so. Anton was a fiercely proud man and, though she knew he would never admit the past history of his family affected him in any way, deep down as a young boy in Peru he must have suffered for it. He was half Greek and yet she realized he was probably more Peruvian than anything else. He had freely admitted his work was his life and his only other great interest was breeding horses at his ranch in Peru.

They had swum naked in the sea and made love whenever the mood arose, which was pretty much constantly. But now it had to end, because underneath, in her few solitary moments, and even understanding a little better why he behaved as he did, she still could not forgive or forget the main reason he had married her, and, based on a lie, it had nothing to do with love.

'I am not keen on shopping and I can easily stay with Tom and Helen,' she finally answered.

She saw him stiffen, his darkly handsome face suddenly grim. No, he didn't like that... In his masculine conceit he thought he knew everything about her, but actually all he knew was her name and body.

'I'll be fine, and you don't need to worry,' she continued conversationally. 'I will not tell Tom and Helen the real reason you married me. There is no point in upsetting them by repeating your lies about Dad.' She rose to her feet. 'But I think I will go and book my flight before my swim.'

'No.' Anton shot up, and caught her wrist. 'I did not lie about your father, damn you, and I have a letter to prove it,' he snapped. That she could once again try to defy him after the perfect week they had shared puzzled and enraged him.

'I'll believe that when I see it,' she said with the delicate arch of one brow.

'You will—believe me,' he opined hardly.

'If you say so.' She shrugged her shoulders. 'But for all I know your sister could have lied.' She was being deliberately insulting and it pained her to do it, but she needed to make the break. She lifted wide blue eyes to his. 'After all, she was certainly no Mother Teresa, if as you say she was single and got pregnant at eighteen, a trait that seems to run in your family.' His dark eyes blazed and for a second she thought he was going to hit her.

Instead he twisted her wrist behind her back and hauled her hard against him. His mouth crashed down on hers in a deeply savage kiss that was more punishment than passion. She shuddered and he lifted his head, his dark eyes blazing down into hers.

'Hell, what's got into you? I thought...'

'What did you think?' She gasped. 'That your expertise in

the bedroom would make me forget why you married me? Well, sorry, it hasn't and it never will.' It took every shred of self-control she possessed to continue. 'You said civil and sex. And civil and sex is what you get. I need to be in London by Tuesday to continue with my career as agreed,' she reminded him emphatically.

She felt his hands tighten and then she was free. He stepped back and looked at her for a long moment with narrowed eyes, and then he gave her a dry smile.

'You're right, of course. But we will have to spend some time in the next few hours comparing schedules. I have no intention of being a celibate husband,' he drawled sardonically.

He reached out and she flinched, but all he did was tuck a stray tendril of hair behind her ear. 'And as for booking a flight, Emily—forget it.' His hand lingered for a moment on her nape. 'Go have your swim; one of the maids can pack for you. We will leave after lunch. I will see you safely settled in the London apartment and fly on to America tomorrow morning from England—it makes no difference to me.'

She looked at him quizzically. Such an about-face was unlikely from what she knew of him. But his expression was unreadable; he looked curiously detached.

'Do you really mean that?' she asked.

'Of course. Obviously the honeymoon, such as it was, is over. There is not much point in spending another night here.'

'Well, thank you.'

'You can thank me properly later. I need to call my pilot.' And, turning, he walked away.

Lunch was set out on the veranda overlooking the gardens, but there was no sign of Anton. Emily picked desultorily at a few bits of cold meat. She wasn't hungry. The maid appeared with a message from Anton. He was too busy to join her and had requested a tray in his study. He had also told her to inform Emily to be ready to leave in an hour.

Emily walked down the stairs exactly an hour later; she had changed her casual clothes for the blue suit she had worn on her wedding day. A day that seemed a lifetime ago now. Anton was standing in the hall, a laptop in one hand and a cell phone in his other pressed to his ear.

She paused halfway down. He was wearing a light business suit, immaculately tailored to his long, lithe body. He looked stunning, but she could almost feel the tension in him, could hear it in the clipped, impatient tone of his voice, and she pitied the person on the other end. He was no longer the laughing companion of the past week in disreputable shorts, but the cold, remote tycoon. Well, it was what she wanted…wasn't it?

Anton turned at the sound of heels on the marble floor, his dark eyes narrowing on his wife descending the stairs. The memory of her descending the grand old staircase of Deveral Hall on their wedding day flashed in his mind. She had been wearing the same suit, her blue eyes shining with happiness and the smile on her face enough to light up the huge hall, and it had been solely focused on him.

Suddenly he recognized the difference in her that had been niggling at the back of his mind since the arrival of the guests in Monte Carlo. The sex was great, but he had never seen the same unbridled happiness in her eyes, or heard the soft cries of love and delight she had showered him with on their wedding night. This past week on his island he had thought perfect, Emily had been enthusiastic, a truly amazing lover, but apart from a few sighs and groans a very quiet one.

Not that it mattered. She was his wife, and he had got what he wanted.

So why was he not satisfied?

'Good, you're ready.' He crossed to the foot of the stairs, and at that moment a startling idea formed in his mind, the hint of a wicked smile curving his lips… 'The helicopter is waiting.'

Emily saw his smile but did not reciprocate. She simply allowed him to lead her to the waiting helicopter. The flight to Athens was smooth and they boarded Anton's private plane for England with the minimum of communication between them.

As soon as they were airborne Anton removed himself from the seat next to her and crossed to the other side of the cabin, and, seated at a table, he opened his laptop and worked.

John the steward served coffee, and, having provided her with a handful of magazines, asked if there was anything else she wanted. He was a friendly young man and chatting to him she discovered his ambition was to travel the world and this job was one way of doing so.

As for Anton, he barely glanced at her.

She flicked through a magazine, and found an article on the discovery of a new tomb in Egypt that contained the mummy of a female pharaoh that predated all the others. She read it with interest, then, closing her eyes, she allowed her mind to drift.

Was she doing the right thing insisting on returning to England? she wondered. She wasn't ready to face Tom and Helen—they knew her too well, and would quickly realize there was something wrong with her marriage. Still, she would be staying in Anton's apartment—she could quite easily keep out of their way and a few days of her own company was exactly what she needed, she concluded, and drifted off to sleep.

When she opened her eyes, some time later, she glanced out of the window…

John appeared, quietly offering her a drink, tea or alcohol, before asking if she would like to order dinner.

It was the dinner that got her attention. 'But surely we must be landing soon.' She glanced at her wrist-watch. It was a four-hour flight, and they had been in the air almost that now.

'No, we are only about halfway.'

'Halfway!' she exclaimed. 'Halfway to where?'

'New York,' John began. 'We—'

'Shut up, John, I can take it from here.' Anton appeared and, catching her arm, he lifted her to her feet, his dark eyes gleaming with devilment. 'Time to show you around, darling.'

Flushed and almost choking with anger, she stared up at him. The filthy rotten swine had told her he would take her to London and she had actually thanked him... He had lied... The barefaced audacity of the man was unbelievable. Rotting in hell was too good for him.

'Why, you arrogant lying bast—' was as far as she got before his mouth descended on her in a kiss so deep, so passionate, she could hardly breathe, and when he finally let her come up for air she was slumped weakly against him, only his strong arms wrapped around her preventing her collapsing at his feet.

'You didn't really think I would allow you to dictate to me,' he murmured with a sardonic arch of one black brow. 'No woman ever has or ever shall.'

Speechless with rage, she gazed wildly around. Of John there was no sign. And she was stuck thirty thousand feet up over the Atlantic...

'You can't do this,' she hissed. 'It is little better than kidnapping.' His hand slipped around the nape of her neck, and he tipped her head back.

'I already have,' he drawled mockingly. 'Accept it, Emily.' Curving his arm firmly around her waist, he almost frog-marched her to the cabin at the rear that housed a double bed and a shower room.

As soon as he closed the door behind them Emily tore out of his hold and spun around. 'You rotten, lying toad,' she spat, boiling with rage. 'You said...'

He snaked an arm around her waist and hauled her back against him and she lashed out wildly with hands and feet. His other hand slipped between the lapels of her jacket and cupped her breast, and he laughed, he actually laughed as he tumbled her back on the bed.

Emily tensed, her moment of rebellion over, suddenly fiercely aware of his big body sprawled on top of her, his long fingers edging beneath the lace of her bra to pluck at her hardening nipple. She groaned almost in despair, appalled by the ease with which her body, even in anger, was incapable of resisting his slightest touch.

'Anticipation can be hell, my sweet,' he said, his sensuous lips curving in a knowing smile, and she wanted to strangle him. 'But also heaven.' He brushed his mouth against hers, and inserted a long leg between her thighs.

'We have plenty of time. How do you feel about joining the mile high club?' he asked teasingly as his fingers teased her breast.

He thought this was a huge joke...and from somewhere she got the strength to grasp his wrist and tug his hand from her breast and say, 'No.' Wriggling from beneath him, she sat up, her back to him, and adjusted her clothes with trembling hands.

She wanted to scream, rant and rave in frustration at the conniving devil that was her husband. But what was the point? It would only draw the attention of the crew, and make her look a bigger idiot than she already was.

After all, what woman in her right mind would fight with a filthy-rich handsome man who had actually done her the honour of marrying her?

She flashed a furious look back at Anton; he was sprawled

on his back, his hands behind his head. He had shed his jacket and unfastened the top three buttons of his shirt. He looked relaxed, completely unaffected by their passionate encounter, while she was still trembling.

'Feel free to change your mind any time. Long flights can be so boring.' He grinned and closed his eyes. 'Wake me when you want me.'

When hell freezes over, Emily thought, furious and frustrated.

On arrival in New York they were met by Max with a limousine and driven silently to Anton's apartment overlooking Central Park. She still had trouble believing he had actually brought her to the city against her will. But then she had very little will around him, she silently conceded.

Anton ushered her out of the car into an apartment building and straight into the elevator. He pressed the button, then leant negligently against the wall, his laptop in one hand, looking at her, a brooding expression in his dark eyes.

In the close confines of the elevator she felt the tension mounting as the silence lengthened and finally she said, 'I thought Max was coming with us?'

'No, he is parking the car, and then he will deliver your luggage and leave. He has his own place here, but he will be back tomorrow afternoon.'

'He seems to spend a lot of time with you.' She'd never really thought what Max's actual job was; she supposed he was a sort of PA. 'What exactly does he do?

'Max is the head of my security and a friend I can trust.'

'You mean a bodyguard? But that's ridiculous.'

'Not ridiculous. Inconvenient at times, but a necessity in my world. I run a highly successful business and there is always some crook wanting to make easy money or a business rival wanting to cut in on a deal. Max watches and listens out for me, ready to inform me of any danger. In fact, from the day we got engaged you have also had a bodyguard.'

'You mean I have been watched all the time?' Emily declared, appalled and furious at the thought. She felt as though her privacy had been invaded along with her body and everything else in her life since she had met Anton. 'Well, I won't have it. I will not be followed around by anyone.'

He shrugged negligently. 'Max's operatives are first class and incredibly discreet. I can guarantee you won't even notice. I am an extremely wealthy man and as my wife you could be a target for kidnappers.'

'And you would certainly know all about kidnapping,' she fumed.

'Forget it, Emily. You are here and the security is not negotiable... Understood?'

She understood just fine...but she had no intention of going along with the restriction on her privacy and she had no doubt she could slip the surveillance when she wanted to. Letting none of her feelings show, she glanced coolly up at him. 'Perfectly.'

'Good. I knew you would see reason.'

Emily almost lost it then. He had to be the most confident, arrogant, egotistical man on the planet. Instead she bit her lip and said not a word...

The elevator stopped, and Anton ushered her out with a hand at her back. Involuntarily she stiffened. His hand fell away and he cast her a sardonic smile.

'The entrance is this way.' He indicated the double doors at the end of a thickly carpeted hall and walked on, leaving her trailing in his wake.

He opened the door and stepped back. 'Your new home.' He gestured for her to enter.

He followed her and introduced her to his Spanish house-keeper, Maria, and her husband, Philip, who looked after the place for him.

'I will leave Maria to show you around. I have work to catch up on.'

'Wait…may I use your telephone?' Emily asked. 'I want to ring Helen, tell her where I am.'

Anton turned back. 'You didn't bring your cell phone with you?'

He knew she had one—he had called her frequently before they were married—and she saw the surprise in his eyes. 'Oddly enough, I did not think I needed it on my honeymoon,' she sniped.

His dark eyes shadowed. 'Okay, there is no need to labour the point, Emily. I get the message. My mistake, the honeymoon was not what you expected, but then life is rarely what we expect,' he said enigmatically. 'This is your home now; feel free to use the telephone and anything else you please. But a word of advice: there is a four-hour time difference. It will be eleven in the evening in London. I doubt Helen will appreciate the call.'

'I forgot, but I would, however, like to check my e-mails. Could I borrow a computer?'

'No need. I will have one provided for you tomorrow. As for now, Maria has prepared a meal. It is better to stay awake to avoid jet lag, though I can think of better things to do than eat, but by the look on your face I doubt if you would agree,' he drawled sardonically. 'I will see you at dinner.' And with that he left.

He had the last word as usual, Emily thought bitterly.

Maria showed her around the apartment. A huge lounge and formal dining room, a day room and study. Plus three *en suite* bedrooms and an incredible master bedroom with huge *en suite* bathroom including a wet room. The floors were polished timber, the décor traditional rather than modern, and the view over New York through a wall of glass enough to take her breath away.

She returned to the master bedroom to discover Maria had unpacked her clothes, and thoughtfully brought her a cup of coffee. 'To keep you awake after big flight,' she said in her broken English.

Showered, Emily dressed in skimpy white lace bra and briefs, white harem pants and a fitted white silk top embroidered in silver. She grimaced at her reflection; she did not have a lot to choose from. Her honeymoon wardrobe was limited, and much more revealing than the clothes she usually wore.

In her day-to-day life she preferred casual clothes, but she also kept a core wardrobe of designer clothes to suit any occasion. But taking Helen's advice she had bought her trousseau with a romantic honeymoon in mind, to please her husband. More fool her, she thought, disgusted with herself for being so stupidly trusting.

Then and now—why else was she in New York instead of London?

Dinner was a tense affair. Anton asked if the apartment was to her liking, and told her if she wanted to change anything to ask Maria. He had tomorrow morning free, and he would show her something of the city.

She looked at him across the dining table. 'There is no need. I'm sure Max will be more than enough to assure I don't get lost,' she said, still fuming at being hauled here and stuck with a bodyguard.

'Give it up, Emily,' he said, exasperation in his tone. 'Tomorrow morning I am taking you out. We are going to be here a while—you will have plenty of time to explore later.'

'Why would I want to? Especially as I did not expect to be here,' she said bluntly.

'I spend a lot of time here and as my wife so will you,' he responded curtly. 'At present I am in the process of a big takeover, and in the last stages of negotiation. I have great faith in my staff but any slip-up can cost a fortune so my personal involvement is a necessity,' he explained.

'I see. A lot more important than my research, which earns you nothing,' she said sarcastically.

'Be honest, Emily.' His dark eyes hardened on her pale face. 'Your career, though interesting, is not the major part of your life. You freelance as a marine archaeologist. I know you have been on three expeditions in the Mediterranean. But basically by far the vast majority of your time has been spent in London, researching at various libraries and museums.'

Emily sat up straighter in her chair, his disparaging but clearly informed awareness of her career enough to stiffen her spine. 'And how would you know that?' she demanded.

'I had you investigated.' He shrugged.

'Of course, silly me—what else is a prospective groom to do?' She lowered her long lashes over her eyes, and stabbed at a prawn on her plate. She was hurt that he had such a dim view of what she had worked so hard to achieve over the years. Well, what was one more hurt on all the others he had heaped on her? she thought philosophically and, picking up her wineglass, she drained it.

'Emily, ignoring reality is dangerous. You are in New York now, whether you like it or not. A place you are not familiar with and you will have protection,' Anton stated, looking directly at her. 'Especially as I do spend a good deal of time here.'

'I could not live here,' Emily said firmly. 'It is too…' She paused. She had only seen the traffic on the way from the airport and the streets teeming with people. 'Fast.'

'You won't have to all the time. My head office is here. But my home in Peru I consider my main residence,' he said smoothly. 'I think you will like it there.' And he had the gall to smile.

Not if she could help it, she thought. And she did not trust his sudden change of tone or his sensuous smile, and she recognized the darkening gleam in his eyes. Abruptly she got to her feet. 'With you there I doubt that, and I have had enough to eat,' she said curtly. 'I am going to bed…alone,' she added and turned to walk out of the room.

She had almost made it when a strong arm grabbed her around the waist.

She tried to move but his arm was like a steel band around her, and she was suddenly terribly conscious of his hard thighs against her own, and she laid a restraining hand on his broad chest.

'You are angry I brought you to New York. I understand that, Emily. But be aware my patience is not limitless.' His other hand reached up and tangled in her hair and his dark head descended, claiming her mouth with his own.

'Remember that later,' he husked when she was breathless in his arms.

She looked up into his dark, smouldering eyes, her heart racing, and she swayed slightly, then stiffened.

For heaven's sake, woman, she derided herself. The man kidnapped you, stuck you in New York—what kind of weak-willed idiot are you? And she pushed out of his arms.

CHAPTER NINE

SHE woke up alone in the big bed, only the indentation on the pillow reminding her Anton had shared it with her for the second night running without touching her. Emily told herself she was glad. She had been asleep when he had joined her the first night and she had turned her back on him when he had slid into bed last night and his mocking comment still echoed in her head.

'I often wondered what the cold shoulder meant, and now I know.' And two minutes later the even sound of his breathing had told her he was asleep.

But then yesterday morning with Anton had been a disaster, and the rest of the day not a lot better…

Like a general leading his troops, he whisked her around Manhattan. Bought her a cell phone and programmed it for her with all the numbers he thought she needed. Then he bought her a mountain of clothes, overriding all her objections. As his wife she had a position to uphold and the few clothes she had with her were not enough. Which was hardly her fault.

By the time the limousine stopped outside his office at one in the afternoon, they were barely speaking. She refused his offer to accompany him inside. Instead she had the chauffeur drive her around the main attractions. On returning to the apartment she was surprised when Maria told her her computer had arrived, and been set up in one of the spare bedrooms for her exclusive use.

She stared in disbelief at the bedroom. A computer was on an obviously new desk, a black leather chair positioned in front and the walls were lined with bookshelves—a perfect study, in fact.

She spun around on the new chair a few times, then started to work. She quickly began answering a backlog of e-mails.

One lifted her spirits no end. A confirmation that the expedition she had been researching for the last few months was definitely going ahead. All the licences and permissions had been obtained from the Venezuelan government. The expedition was to find a pirate ship sunk off the Las Rocas archipelago. She was to join the research ship in Caracas on the twentieth of September, as the onboard marine archaeologist to map out in detailed scale drawings any finds they might make on the seabed. Hopefully they would find signs of the ship and the cargo, which was reliably reported in ancient documents to include gold and treasure from all over Europe.

Hunched over the computer, she laughed out loud as she read the reply to her acceptance. Jake Hardington was a world-renowned highly successful treasure hunter and a great flirt, though Emily knew he was an extremely happy married man—his wife, Delia, was a friend of hers.

'Something has made you happy.'

She jerked her head up in surprise at the sound of Anton's voice. 'Where did you come from?'

Six feet four of arrogant male was standing looking down at her, dressed in an immaculately tailored business suit, but to her dismay the instant picture in her mind's eye was of the same body naked. His dark gaze met hers, and she fought back a blush at the thought.

'Work,' he drawled sardonically. 'And I guess I am not the cause of your good humour.'

'No. Yes…' she garbled her response. Because half the reason for the embarrassing colour tingeing her cheeks was guilt. She had no intention of telling Anton her news. His derogatory statements about her career, and the very fact she was here instead of in London, were enough to keep her lips sealed.

'I mean I was delighted.' She retrieved the moment. 'You bought me a computer and everything. Thank you.'

He bent over her and brushed a strand of hair from her brow, and ran his fingers down her cheek and around her throat to tip her head back. Nervously she licked her lips as his hooded eyes ran slowly over her, and inwardly she trembled.

'Anything you want you can have, you do know that,' he said huskily.

His mouth came down to cover hers, and as his tongue stroked against hers a familiar heat ignited deep inside her.

'Is now pay-back time?' she muttered resentfully as she remembered where she was and why, and abruptly Anton straightened.

'You disappoint me, Emily. I have never paid for a woman and you demean yourself by trying to play the whore, when we both know you are the opposite,' he said, his cold hard eyes looking down at her—in more ways than one. 'Why let resentment cloud your judgement?' He shook his dark head. 'Why deprive your body of what you so obviously want?' His dark gaze lowered to where her nipples pressed taut against the soft cotton of her top. 'You're a stubborn woman, Emily, but no match for me,' he warned and, turning on his heel, he left the room.

Inexplicably Emily had felt about two inches tall…

* * *

Thinking about it now made her grimace. Still, this morning was a new day, she told herself, a free day, and leapt out of bed. Quickly she showered and dressed in navy linen trousers and a brief self-supporting white top; she popped her cell phone in her trousers pocket for easy access in case she saw something she wanted to photograph, slung her bag over her shoulder and ventured out again into the city, a gleam of mischief in her blue eyes.

Anton was not going to have it all his own way. She dismissed the chauffeured limousine, insisting she was only going for a walk, and sauntered along the street.

At the first subway station she dashed down the stairs and squeezed on board a train that was just leaving the platform. She watched as the doors shut, and saw a look of shock on the face of a young man as he lifted a cell phone to his ear. She leapt off at the next station and dashed across the platform and jumped onto another one. She stayed for two stops, then exited the train and walked back up to the street.

She had no idea where she was and she did not care. She was free...

The street was crowded, someone bumped into her and she laughed. It was great to be one of the masses again.

Anton surveyed the six men around the boardroom table. It had taken months to get this meeting arranged and if they all agreed it was going to be one of the biggest deals Wall Street had ever seen. He was sure they would. Sitting back in his chair, he let the Texan hold the floor—the man had been his guest on his yacht and they had already worked out how to present the deal.

He felt a vibration on his chest. Damn his cell phone. He pulled it from his pocket and glanced at the screen. Then leapt to his feet.

'Sorry, I am going to have to postpone this meeting.' Angry—he was furious by the time they had all left.

He lifted his cell phone to his ear. 'What the hell happened, Max? How could you possibly lose her?' He listened, then responded with a few choice words and strict instructions to find her immediately.

Emily glanced around. The skyscrapers she had thought so great after six hours of jumping on and off underground trains and walking around now seemed threatening. She had realized when she had sat down in a restaurant for lunch, whoever had bumped into her had stolen her cell phone. But it had not bothered her because she had still had her purse and money. Except now she wanted to flag a taxi home, she had suddenly realized she had no idea of her address…except overlooking Central Park…

She did anyway, but the taxi driver didn't appear to speak very good English. She got the impression Central Park was huge and she thought he asked if she was east or west. But looking at his swarthy features half hidden by a beard and the speculative gleam in his eyes he could have said *easy* and *western*. Not wanting to risk it, she looked for a public telephone. The only one she found had been vandalized and as a last resort she walked into a nearby police station.

The policeman on the desk looked at her as if she was crazy when she explained that her cell phone had been stolen with all her contact numbers in it, and she did not know her address, and the trouble she had with trying to get a taxi. Then she finally asked if she could use their telephone to call her husband and reluctantly gave him Anton's name as she did not know his number.

He made a call and then was perfectly charming, offering her a seat and coffee. Gratefully she took the cup and gave him a brilliant smile. American policemen were really great, she thought, sipping her coffee and leaning back in the surprisingly comfortable chair he had found for her. But inside her stomach was churning. Anton would be furious. He would probably send Max for her and Max certainly would not be very happy either, she realized rather belatedly.

The door opened and the hairs on the back of her neck prickled. Slowly she looked up, her gaze riveted on the man who stood silhouetted against the opening. With the light behind him she was not able to see his face clearly, which was maybe just as well. It was Anton and her heart missed a beat; the waves of rage coming off his big tense body were intimidating enough.

He strode past her and up to the desk. 'Thank you, officer, that is indeed my wife. I will take her off your hands now. Sorry for the inconvenience.'

Emily rose to her feet. 'Hello, Anton, I didn't…' She looked at him and the words froze in her throat. His black eyes returned her look with a glittering remorseless intensity that sent a shiver down her spine. Her legs threatened to cave in beneath her, and when he wrapped his big hand around her upper arm, rather than protest, she needed the support.

'Thank you, Grant,' she threw over her shoulder at the policeman as Anton marched her out of the door.

'"Thank you, Grant."' He mimicked derisively as he shoved her into the seat of a big black Ferrari parked in a no-parking zone, and slid in beside her.

He gunned the engine and never spoke a word until they were back in the apartment.

She turned to glance warily up at him. 'I'm sorry I got lost.'

Anton stood towering over her, his eyes scathingly raking her feminine form with a blatant sexual thoroughness that brought a blush to her cheeks.

Emily could feel the unwanted flush of awareness flooding through her body at his insulting scrutiny. He looked dynamic and supremely masculine in his light grey suit jacket taut over his broad shoulders, his white shirt open at the neck, his tie hanging loose, and helplessness engulfed her as she stared at him.

Anton's grim voice broke the lengthening silence. 'You are lucky you only got lost. The desk sergeant told me about the taxi driver.' He cast her a hard, contemptuous look. 'Rather than wasting your time and talent trying to dodge Security and almost getting raped… Why don't you grow up? When are you going to get it in your damn-fool head you are no longer a foot-loose girl? Diving thirty feet off yachts and heaven knows what else. You are my wife, you are under my protection and yet you deliberately put yourself and those around you at risk. Two men lost their jobs today because of your actions, and I have probably lost the biggest deal ever as I had to walk out halfway through a meeting to find you. I hope you are proud of yourself.'

If Anton had shouted and raged at her as she had expected she could have handled it, but his contemptuous condemnation of her behaviour brought home to her how stupidly reckless she had been.

'No,' she said simply. 'I never meant anybody to lose their job. Please don't fire them.'

One dark brow arched sardonically. 'I won't…if I have your word you will stop this rebellious behaviour and start behaving as a wife should.'

'You mean bow and scrape to you,' she flared.

'Cut out the dramatics, Emily,' Anton responded and finally touched her, his hands closing over her shoulders. 'You know what I mean,' he grated, his hand sliding down her back to cup her buttocks and pull her hard against his thighs, and she trembled as the evidence of his masculine arousal pressed against her stomach.

'But, so help me God, Emily—' his black eyes burned down into hers '—if you ever put me through that again, I will lock you up and throw away the key.' She gasped, and his mouth crashed down on hers, his tongue thrusting desperately between her parted lips, passionately demanding.

She should fight, she knew she should because there was no love involved and for a million other reasons. But two long days of frustration were having a debilitating effect on her ability to resist him. Then why should she? The impish question slid into her brain.

Anton was satisfied with lust, he wanted nothing more, and, if she was honest, she finally admitted she no longer had the will or the conviction to fight the sexual attraction she felt for him. There was no point in pretending it was love even to herself…

She looped her arms around his neck, and felt his great body shudder and realized he really had been worried about her. It gave her a fuzzy feeling inside, and, though she was loath to admit, hope for the future. She ran her fingers through his thick black hair, and held him closer, responding with a hunger that matched his own. Later in bed two nights of abstinence took a long time to satisfy.

The next morning when she walked in the kitchen Max was seated at the table, waiting for her. 'Max, I might have guessed. Anton told you.' And pulling out a chair, she sat down opposite him, and poured herself a cup of coffee. Of Maria there was no sign.

'He didn't have to tell me. My operative informed me the minute you got on the subway yesterday. You do realize, Emily, it was not skill, but blind luck you caught that train and lost him. And sheer bloody luck—' he swore '—that you were not mugged, raped or worse…'

'You are forgetting kidnapped,' she said facetiously and

smiled. She had not forgotten the reason she was here instead of London.

'You think that is funny?' he snapped. 'Well, let me tell you, Emily, I have had to tell a couple in the past that their child was found dead after having been buried alive for three days in a hole in the ground, and it is not funny.'

'Sorry.' Emily instantly sobered. Max probably did not know Anton had tricked her into coming to New York.

'So you should be. What the hell are you trying to do to Anton?' She had never seen Max so coldly angry. 'I thought when he met and married you, it was the best thing that ever happened to him. At last he had love in his life, something he has never had before, but now I am not so sure. What on earth were you playing at?' He eyed her contemptuously. 'I have never in all the years I have known him seen him so distraught. He is a wealthy, powerful man and as such has enemies, and you are his wife, and should be aware of the danger. He damn near had a heart attack yesterday when you disappeared. He is by nature a loner, a very private man, not to mention a workaholic. But yesterday he dropped everything to call out the police, anyone and everyone, even the press to try and find you. The man worships the ground you walk on, and you repay him with a childish trick. Well, not any more. One of my top operatives will be arriving any minute now, and I want your word you will not try to give her the slip…understood? The alternative is I stick to you as well.'

Reeling under the verbal tongue-bashing, and amazed Max actually thought Anton adored her and was distraught she had gone missing, Emily meekly agreed.

Mercedes arrived moments later. She was a little older than Emily, and after half an hour of conversation over coffee Emily liked her. She had a wealth of experience of life in New York and a great sense of humour. From that day on she arrived every morning and accompanied Emily on visits to museums, art galleries. She showed her the best places to shop—not that Emily found herself actually enjoying her time in New York.

On a Friday night two weeks later Emily stood in front of the mirror and hardly recognized herself. Her blonde hair was swept up in an intricate twist. The black dress was strapless and clung to her every curve, one of Anton's purchases, as was the diamond necklace she fastened around her throat. He had arrived back from the office ten minutes ago and dropped the necklace he had first given her on the yacht on the dresser as he headed for the bathroom shedding his clothes, with instructions that she wear it tonight.

Their relationship had developed since Emily had got lost. She had quit sniping at him, and begun to accept his perception of marriage, and it seemed to work. The sex was great and, if sometimes she wished for the love she had dreamt of, she told herself no one could have everything. But what she had with Anton came close.

She had spent the last two weeks exploring New York with Mercedes when she was not sitting at her computer working. Which was just as well, because apart from a few social dinner engagements Anton said they were obliged to attend, she did not see a lot of him.

Max was right about him; he was a workaholic. He left for the office at six in the morning and rarely returned before eight, they dined and went to bed and the passion between them flared as white-hot as ever.

Civil and sex was easy under the circumstances and she could understand why it appealed to Anton. He had no time for anything else…

The only reason he had returned by seven tonight was because they were attending the opening of an exhibition of Peruvian art, as guests of the Peruvian ambassador to the USA, and they had thirty minutes to get there.

She heard the shower switch off, and, with one last look at her reflection, walked out of the bedroom and into the lounge. She stood looking out of the huge window, wondering how her life had come to this, waiting for Anton...

'The necklace looks good.' She turned. Anton, wearing a dark evening suit and snowy white pleated shirt, was standing a few feet away.

'How did—?'

'The reflection in the glass.' He read her mind.

He looked strikingly attractive and it wasn't just the suit. Tall and brutally handsome, he exuded an aura of strength and power and tightly leashed sexuality that took her breath away.

'We should leave; we are going to be late,' Emily said coolly. And he nodded his dark head in agreement and took her arm.

Slowly it had dawned on Emily that outside the bedroom Anton had an air of detachment about him that rather confirmed Max's comment that he was a loner. And the longer they stayed in New York, the more she began to accept that this was the real Anton. Not the deceitful seducer or the fun-loving companion he had been on the island. But the one hundred per cent seriously focused international tycoon. His work was his life; everything else was peripheral.

In a way it made life easier, she thought as they entered the Prestige's art gallery half an hour later.

Anton was a man with little or no emotion; even his revenge had lost its flavour for him, after he had revealed it to her. She remembered his dismissal of it with why spoil their marriage as the two people concerned were dead. She should have realized then… The death of his mother was probably the only event that had touched his heart in any way. Everything else was business.

'Emily. You seem miles away.'

She cast him a sidelong glance and a smile. 'No, I'm fine.' She glanced around the vast room. The walls were hung with paintings, sculptures stood on podiums, and a grand staircase led to another level and more paintings. All New York's élite seemed to be present. Waiters with loaded trays of champagne moved smoothly through the crowd, others with loaded trays of canapés circled non-stop. 'This looks very nice.'

'Damned with faint praise,' Anton murmured against her ear. And then she was being introduced to the Peruvian ambassador and his wife, and his beautiful daughter Lucita.

She was small and voluptuous with huge sultry eyes. She gave Emily a saccharine smile before turning to gush all over Anton.

Not another one… Emily thought, and found herself standing alone as Lucita wrapped her arms around Anton's neck and made to kiss him. He subtly averted his head so she caught his cheek instead of his mouth. But Emily knew… She saw it in the spiteful glance Lucita gave her, when Anton caught her shoulders and put her back at arm's length.

'So you are his wife. We were all surprised when we heard Anton had married. Have you known each other long?'

Emily opened her mouth to reply, but Anton's arm slipped around her waist and he pulled her lightly against him and answered for her.

'Long enough to know Emily was the only woman for me.'

Congratulations were offered, but Emily could sense the underlining hostility. She glanced up at Anton and caught the savage satisfaction in his expression as he smiled and they moved on.

'What was that all about?' she demanded. 'I thought the ambassador was a friend of yours.'

Something moved in the dark depths of his eyes. 'Not really. I have very few friends—plenty of business acquaintances, though,' he said, leading her slowly towards a wall to view the artwork. 'As for the ambassador, he has to appear to be my friend or lose his job, and that is what gets his goat,' he drawled mockingly.

'Are you really that powerful?' she asked.

'Yes.' One word and he took two glasses of champagne from a passing waiter and handed her one and slipped his arm around her again.

For a moment Emily looked at him. 'Is that all?'

'I sponsored the exhibition, and I also sponsor the artists.' He gestured with his glass to a huge abstract painting, all red, green and black. 'What do you think of that?'

'I'm amazed.'

'You like it?' His dark brows rose quizzically.

'No, I hate it,' she answered honestly. 'But I'm amazed you sponsored the event and the artists. I wouldn't have thought you had time.'

Anton chuckled, a low husky sound, his arm tightening around her. 'Your honest opinion is charming, though I doubt the artist would appreciate it. As for my sponsoring the event, it does not take time, just rather a lot of money.'

'I'm impressed all the same,' Emily declared as he propelled her further around the room. 'I am also hungry,' she murmured and took a canapé from a passing waiter and popped it in her mouth.

At just that moment someone spoke to Anton, she swallowed the food, and was introduced to an eminent banker and his wife.

For the next hour they circled the gallery. Anton was greeted by a host of people, and Emily shook hands and smiled in between sipping champagne and popping canapés in her mouth.

As for the paintings, two she really liked. A somewhat abstract landscape of the Andes with mist swirling that looked almost mystical, and a small painting of a little Indian boy squatting on the ground and laughing, with what was obviously his father's big black hat on his head.

Anton bought both.

'You didn't have to do that.'

'I wanted to.' He pulled her close and led her through the crowd towards the exit. 'And if I had given you the choice we would never get out of here—women take a notoriously long time to make a decision, and we are going to dinner. I am hungry.'

Emily gave him a dazzling smile. 'Anton, that is a terrible chauvinistic comment, even for you.'

'So? I want you…out of here.' His dark eyes held hers and she was captivated by the amusement, the sensual warmth in the inky depths. For a second she was back on his Greek island, and her pulse began to race, and anticipation shivered through her. Was he aware of it?

'We're leaving,' he rasped and she knew he was as they made for the exit.

'Going?' Lucita with three friends stopped them as they reached the foyer.

'Why don't you join us, Anton? We are going on to a supper club.' She spoke solely to Anton, ignoring Emily.

'No, Lucita,' he said in a voice that held an edge of steel. 'I have better things to do,' and with that parting shot he urged Emily outside.

But the moment was broken for Emily. 'That was a bit brutal—you obviously know the lady very well,' she said, moving out of his protective arm. 'And I saw the look on your face when you spoke to the ambassador, and it wasn't very edifying.'

'Edifying?' He raised an eyebrow. 'You are *so* English, Emily.'

He ushered her into the back seat of the limousine without saying another word, and slid in beside her. He closed the glass partition, and then turned to look at her.

'Yes, I know Lucita well, but not as well as you imagine. I knew her brother a lot better.' His face, shadowed in the dim light, was hard. 'Do you want to know the truth, or do you want to mark her down as another woman I have slept with? You seem to be under the impression I have slept with hundreds, which I have not. I would not even make double figures, but my reputation goes against me. Something you could not begin to understand, given the charmed life you have led.'

'I wouldn't say—'

'Say nothing and listen for a change. I was twelve when my mother brought me back to Peru to live with my grandmother. At first I went to the local school, but at fourteen I was sent to the best boarding school in the country, and that is where I met Lucita's brother. We became friends, because he was bullied unmercifully by the other boys and I stood up for him. Unfortunately for Pedro, he took after his mother, who, you might have noticed, is a small, quiet lady who I have great respect and sympathy for, but she is and always has been completely under her husband's thumb.

'Pedro and I studied together; we visited each other's home in the holidays, and played football, badly.' He grimaced. 'He had an artistic soul, and for two years we were friends, Lucita as well, until his father discovered my parentage. They were forbidden to see me again. And the man did his damnedest to get me thrown out of school.'

'Oh, Anton….' She couldn't imagine how he must have felt. He had made light of his parentage, but now she realized for a young boy it must have been hard.

'Don't worry. He was a minor government official at the time and he did not succeed. But he ruined his son's life, he sent him to another school, where apparently he was bullied again, and twelve months later Pedro committed suicide. I stood in the background at his funeral, the only teenage friend there.'

No wonder Anton had been distraught discovering his sister had committed suicide; his childhood friend had done the same.

'So you see why it gives me great satisfaction to watch the man having to be polite to me now, and I am not going to apologize for that. As for his daughter, she is just like him— the only difference is she would have me in a heartbeat simply because I am wealthy.'

'I'm sorry. I had no idea.'

He sat back in the seat. 'I told you the first time we met. I just knew you would feel sorry for me, and your sympathy is misplaced. You're too naive for your own good, Emily.' But the indulgent smile he gave her took the sting out of his words.

'I might be naive…' she looked at him curiously, a sudden thought occurring to her '…but answer me this. Why didn't you marry Lucita to get back at her father? Rather than waiting to marry me to get back at mine?'

He stilled. 'The idea never entered my head.' He shook his head, his dark eyes widening on her, and then he burst out laughing. 'Oh, Emily, I might have a vengeful streak, but I am not a masochist. You are delightful and drop-dead gorgeous and Lucita is an evil witch in comparison.'

Emily stared at him in shock. Was that a compliment? She did not know what to think…and, taking full advantage, Anton leant forward and kissed her.

The limousine stopped and Anton helped her out. 'I thought we were going to eat out,' she said as he led her into their apartment.

He smiled a soft, slow curl of his firm lips, and moved his hand from her arm to snake around her shoulders, staring into her eyes from mere inches away. 'I am still hungry, *niña*,' he said softly, his slight accent more pronounced than usual, 'but the food can wait till later.' His dark eyes smouldered as he held her and he bent closer and she felt the hard warmth of his mouth brush against her parted lips.

Far into the night Emily made love with Anton with a long, slow tenderness, a passion that brought tears to her eyes because she knew to Anton it was still just sex…

CHAPTER TEN

ANTON snapped shut his laptop, and fastened his seat belt.

They would be landing in ten minutes, and it could not be too soon. He had clinched a major deal and cleared his work schedule for the next month.

He had not seen Emily in weeks, it was becoming ridiculous and he was determined to do something about the situation. A frown crossed his broad brow. They had been married three months, the sex was great and he should be satisfied. Yet the amount of time they had spent with each other was limited.

After three weeks in New York they had returned to London. Emily had caught up with her research. But he had been obliged to travel to the Middle East. In July they had returned to Greece, but he had taken frequent trips to Athens and Moscow.

The beginning of August Emily was supposed to have accompanied him to Australia. But Helen had given birth to a baby boy and Emily had gone back to England to help look after the mother and Anton could hardly object.

But after almost two weeks on his own he had called her last night and told her to be packed—they were going to Peru tomorrow. Which gave him time to kiss the baby's head and leave. It was time they had a baby of their own; in fact Emily might already be pregnant. Not that she had said anything during their telephone calls, but then she never said much anyway...

A frustrating hour later, after discovering she was not at their apartment, he stopped the Bentley outside the Fairfax home in Kensington.

Mindy, the housekeeper, showed him into the drawing room.

Emily was sitting on a low chair, the rays of the afternoon sun shining through the window casting a golden halo around her head, and in her arms she held a baby.

She was totally oblivious of his arrival, her whole attention on the tiny infant, her beautiful face wreathed in smiles. 'You are a beautiful little boy.' She chuckled. 'Yes—yes, you are, and your aunty Emily loves you.' And as he watched she kissed the baby's cheek.

He choked...and felt an unfamiliar stab of something like emotion in the region of his heart. 'Emily.' She turned her head to look at him.

'Anton, I never heard you arrive.' Slowly rising to her feet, cradling the baby, she walked across to him. 'Look, isn't he gorgeous?'

She was gorgeous. Her hair was parted in the middle and tucked behind her delicate ears to fall in a silken mass down her back. She was wearing blue jeans that clung to her slim hips and long legs, and a soft white sweater.

He looked at the child. The baby was snuggled against her breast, and he wished it were him...

'Yes, wonderful.' He reached a finger to touch the baby's cheek.

'Helen and Tom have decided to call him Charles after our father.'

Anton looked down into her blue eyes and saw the flash of defiance she made no attempt to hide, and his mouth tightened. She was an exquisitely beautiful but wilful woman and she was never going to accept the truth about her father. As for him, he didn't care any more…

'A solid name. I like it,' he said smoothly.

'Charles Thomas.' Helen, coming in, moved to take the child from Emily's arms. 'Anton, good to see you—now, would you mind taking your wife back home, before she takes over my baby completely, and try making one of your own?' She laughed.

They all laughed but he noticed Emily avoided his gaze.

'I intend to do just that.' Anton reached for Emily and drew her into his arms, his dark eyes searching her guarded blue. 'This is a brief visit, Helen,' he said without taking his eyes off his wife. 'We are flying out to my place in Peru tomorrow.'

Just seeing Anton walk in the door had made Emily's heart lurch. It had taken all her self-control to walk slowly towards him and show him the baby, and now, held in his arms, she felt a bittersweet longing shudder through her. When he kissed her the warmth of his lips, the scent of him, aroused her in a second.

'We are leaving.' Anton lifted his head and she looked up into his dark eyes, and saw the promise of passion, and knew hers showed the same.

'Get out of here, you two,' Helen said with a chuckle. 'You're embarrassing the baby.'

As soon as they entered the penthouse Anton slid an arm around Emily's waist and pulled her towards him.

'I have waited two long weeks for this,' he husked.

'Why? Were there no willing women in Australia?' And Emily was only half teasing. She knew in her heart of hearts she loved him, yet she could not let herself trust him, and the green-eyed monster haunted her thoughts when he was gone. Not something she was proud of.

'Plenty willing but none that looked like you.' His brilliant eyes gleamed as he bent his head and covered her mouth with his.

So he had been looking, was Emily's last thought as, helplessly, her eyelids fluttered down and she raised her slender arms to wrap around his broad shoulders, her body arching into his.

His kiss possessive, his tongue traced the roof of her mouth and curled with hers, and her blood flowed like liquid heat through her veins. His hand slipped up beneath her sweater and trailed up her spine, making her shudder as he opened her bra. Then his hand stroked around to slip up beneath the front of her sweater to find the thrusting swell of her breasts.

'You are wearing far too many clothes,' he rasped, and suddenly she was swept up into his arms, his mouth desperately claiming hers again as, with more haste than finesse, he carried her to the bedroom and dropped her on the bed. 'Get them off.'

Her eyes opened and her gaze fixed on Anton ripping off his clothes like a man possessed. Naked, he was masculine perfection. Tall and broad, his muscular chest rising not quite steadily and his lean hips and thighs cradling the virile power of his fully aroused sex.

'You want me to do it for you.' He chuckled, a deep sexy sound that vibrated across her nerve endings, and, leaning over her, he stripped her jeans and briefs from her legs, before just as efficiently dispensing with her sweater and bra.

His hands cupped her naked breasts and her nipples hardened beneath his skilful touch.

'Missed me…?' He looked deep into her eyes, and she could not lie.

'Yes,' she sighed and reached for him. But inside her heart cried for what might have been. She could have been the happiest woman alive, a loving wife, but Anton had destroyed that dream with his revelation about his real motivation for marrying her.

The really soul-destroying part was that Anton didn't even see it. He was perfectly content so long as the sex was good.

Angry with herself for loving him, she reared up and, pushing him down, straddled his thighs, determined to drive him mad with desire. Why should she be the only one?

'You are eager—maybe I should stay away more often,' he said with a husky amusement in his tone, his great body stretched hard beneath her.

'Maybe you should.' She stared down into his brutally handsome face. He was watching her, a sensual gleam in his night-black eyes. He reached out a hand and captured her breast, his long fingers tweaking a pouting nipple. She jerked back, heat flooding from her breast to her thighs, but she would not be deterred from her mission to make him squirm for a change. She wrapped her fingers around his aroused manhood and lowered her head, her long hair brushing the length of his torso, and tasted him.

His great body bucked and she heard him groan, she felt his tension, and she shook with the effort it took to control her own heightened desire for him. She continued until he was straining for release, then stopped.

She raised her head. His eyes were smouldering like the depths of hell, his face taut, and she closed her fingers gently around him.

'Not yet,' she murmured. Running her tongue around her full lips, she saw the fiery passion burn brighter in his eyes. Deliberately she leant forward and trailed a row of kisses from his belly up the centre of his chest, straying once to tongue a small male nipple before moving on to finally cover his mouth with her own, her hand stroking lower to cup the essence of the man. Suddenly he was lifting her, impaling her on his fiercely erect manhood.

Wild and wanton, she rode him, his body arching up as he filled her to the hilt with increasingly powerful thrusts. His hands gripped her waist, making her move, twisting, turning her where he desired, as they duelled for sexual supremacy. She cried out at the tug of his mouth on her rigid nipples, and arched back, fighting for control.

Emily succumbed first, convulsing around him. She was mindless in her ecstasy, clenching him with every spasm in a ferociously prolonged orgasm. She heard him cry her name and his body shuddered as he joined her in a climax that finally stopped her breath. The little death.

Some time later she opened her eyes to find Anton staring down at her. 'That was some welcome home, Emily,' he said, curving her into the side of his body. She brushed a few tendrils of damp hair from her face, smoothing the long length over one shoulder and down to her breast, where his hand lingered.

'Yes, well…' It was what he expected, she thought, suddenly feeling cold inside. 'Two weeks without sex is not good for anyone,' she threw out. And saw a flicker of some emotion she could not put a name to in the depths of his dark eyes.

'Tell me about it,' he said dryly, and then added, 'It must be tough for Helen—no sex for a few weeks after the birth, I believe.'

'I doubt if Helen minds. She has a beautiful little boy to love.'

'And would you mind, if you were pregnant? You could be.'

The question blind-sided her. No, she couldn't be, but, seeing Helen with her baby for the last two weeks, it had brought home to her how much she would have loved to have Anton's child if only he had loved her… But there was no future in thinking like that. Anton did not believe in love and was therefore incapable of loving anyone; he had told her so quite emphatically.

Whereas she had been a trusting soul all her life and Anton had destroyed that part of her nature with a few words, and if he ever found out she loved him it would destroy her completely; all she had left was her pride.

'I have never thought about it, and I am not in any hurry to find out,' she lied and moved along the bed, away from the warmth of his big body.

He caught her chin between his finger and thumb and turned her head back so she had no choice but to look at him. 'Seeing you with the baby today I realized you are a natural, Emily. You will make a wonderful mother.'

A tender, caring Anton was the last thing she needed. She felt guilty enough as it was, though she had no need to be. He had deceived her into marrying him; her deceit was nothing in comparison.

'Maybe.' She shook her head, dislodging his hand, and tried a smile but suddenly a thought hit her… And, jumping off the bed in a show of bravado, she stood up totally naked and stared down at him. 'But we have only been married a few months, and, let's face it, we hardly have a marriage made in heaven. A bit of time to adjust to each other before having to adjust to a baby is no bad thing,' she offered and, turning, she walked quickly into the bathroom. She had just remembered she hadn't taken her pill the last two nights, because she had spent the weekend with Tom and Helen…

She snagged a large towel from the rail and tucked it around her body sarong-style. Then found the packet in the back of the bathroom cabinet where she had carelessly left it while Anton was away.

She took two out… Was it dangerous to take two? She had a feeling it was. She scanned the packet, but it didn't say. She placed the packet on the back of the vanity unit and popped one pill in her mouth and dropped one in the basin. Then, filling a glass with water, she swallowed it down, and let the water run to wash away the other.

'Headache?' She heard his voice and spun around to see Anton naked and leaning against the bathroom door. 'So soon?'

'Kind of,' she murmured.

Something predatory and ruthless glinted in his dark eyes as he strolled towards her and reached over the basin to where the packet lay and picked it up. 'A contraceptive pill that doubles as a headache cure. How convenient.' She saw the banked-down anger in his black eyes and was afraid.

A naked man should not be able to look threatening, she thought distractedly, but Anton did. As though sensing her thoughts, he grabbed a towel and wrapped it around his hips.

'What—no response, Emily?' he drawled, closing in on her, and she took a few steps back until she met the wall. 'No excuse, you devious little bitch?'

She sucked in a furious breath. 'That is rich coming from you,' she threw at him, her eyes flashing. He was not going to intimidate her, and she would not allow it. 'As for an excuse, I don't need one. Yes, I am on the pill—so what?' she challenged him, her anger laced with scorn. 'My body is my own—you borrow it for sex. Nothing more and, may I point out—' and she poked him in the chest with her finger '—it was your own idea; love does not come into the equation.'

Emily was on a roll and could not stop. She didn't notice the sudden narrowing of his eyes or the tension in his great body. She was too overcome with emotion—something he knew nothing about. 'Do you honestly think I would bring a baby into the world without love, just to fulfil some dynastic craving of yours? You must be joking.'

For over three months she had fought to keep control of her

emotions around Anton, but now her composure was beginning to shatter.

'Nothing to say?' she demanded into the lengthening silence, and dragged an angry if slightly unsteady breath into her suddenly oxygen-starved lungs. 'Why am I not surprised? You are so damned sure of yourself, with your limitless wealth and arrogance, it is probably the first time in years you have found something you can't buy…a baby.'

She shook her head despairingly. Was it possible to love and hate someone at the same time? she wondered. Because right at this moment, with Anton standing half naked, bristling with rage, her stupid heart still ached for him, and yet her head hated him. She tried to walk past him. What was the point in arguing?

Anton had kept control on his temper by a thread and now it broke. Ice-cold fury glittered in his eyes as he looked at her. 'That's right. I bought you,' he stated coldly. 'And nobody does me out of a deal. Certainly not you, my wilful little wife.'

He wanted to tear her limb from limb as she stood there, her long hair falling around her shoulders in golden disarray, the expression on her beautiful face one of contempt. Yet she had been deceiving him for weeks, possibly months.

'How long—how long have you been taking the pill?' he demanded, and, grasping a handful of her hair, he twisted it around his wrist and pulled her head back, the better to look into her deceitful eyes.

'Since the week after we met,' Emily shot back and told him the truth. 'When I was foolish enough to think you and I might have an affair. After all, that is what you are renowned for and that was all I expected.' She trembled at the rage in the depths of his eyes, but refused to back down. 'Imagine my surprise when you proposed marriage. And, idiot that I was, I accepted, labouring in the misguided notion that I loved you. But you soon put me right on that score, Anton. Lucky for me I already had the pills.'

Anton stared down into her blazing blue eyes fiercely battling the urge to cover her mouth with his and drive her hate-filled words down her throat. Emily had quite confidently expected to be his mistress, going so far as taking the pill in preparation. But he had surprised her with offering marriage. There was only one conclusion he could draw—she thought she was too good to have his child.

'Did you ever intend to tell me?' he demanded. 'Or was I to remain in ignorance for years?'

'Oh, I doubt it would be for more than two at the very most,' she drawled scathingly. 'You said yourself lust burns out and, for a man with your sexual appetite, I know I will not have to wait long before you are unfaithful, and then I can divorce you and you can't do a damn thing about it. Except pay up… But I'm not greedy, just enough to make sure Fairfax Engineering is totally free from you. Your one mistake was not asking me to sign a pre-nup. I would have done—I would have done anything you wanted until you revealed your real reason for marrying me. Well, you should be proud, Anton. You taught me well.' As Emily watched a shuttered expression came over his face, and his hand fell from her hair and he moved back from her.

'Too well, it would seem.' Reaching, he tugged the towel from her slender form. His rapier-like glance raked her from head to toe as though he had never seen her before, and she trembled.

'You are beautiful, but you have just proved you are a Fairfax just like your father, and now I find I would not have you as the mother of my child if you paid me,' he drawled derisively, and with a shrug he turned and strode out of the bathroom.

She watched him warily for a moment; there was a defeated look to the curve of his broad shoulders as he walked towards the bed. He ran a hand distractedly through his black hair, and then he straightened. Emily picked up the towel and wrapped it around her shivering body and took a hesitant step towards the open door, concerned. She must have made some sound because Anton spun around.

'No need to be wary. I am not going to jump you.' He smiled a bitter twist of his sensuous lips. 'The bedroom is yours, but be aware a divorce is not, unless I choose.'

She must have rocks in her head, worrying about him, Emily thought, advancing into the room.

A hand on her shoulder woke her from a restless sleep; she blinked and opened her eyes. And found Anton standing over her, dressed in a black shirt, black trousers and a black leather jacket, a mug of coffee in his hand. 'Drink this and hurry up and dress. You can have breakfast on board—we are leaving in less than an hour.'

She pulled the sheet over her breasts. 'Leaving…going where?' She was confused. 'I don't understand…I thought after last night…'

'That I would leave you? No, Emily, not yet. You are coming to Peru with me. I promised to prove to you what a stuck-up degenerate your father was. Unlike you, I keep my promises.'

She looked at him. His face was hard, his eyes cold and dead. He caught her shoulders and hauled her into a sitting position. 'After that you can go where the hell you like,' he said with icy finality in his tone.

For Emily the flight to Peru was horrendous. Twelve hours of Anton being scrupulously polite when the steward was around, and ignoring her the rest of the time. Unfortunately the atmosphere gave her plenty of time to think, and she didn't like her thoughts. She was in love with Anton, always was and always would be, and there was absolutely no future in it. Their marriage had ended the day after the wedding…

Even now Anton was still sticking to his ridiculous story about her father. Yet at one time he had told her to forget it as the people concerned were dead. Memories of the past few months flooded her mind. Their battles at the beginning, and then, after her disappearance in New York, the passionate way they made up and Max's certainty that Anton cared for her. The art gallery where she got a better understanding of why he was as he was… After that night, if she was honest, they had got along rather well. Anton had come back to London with her while she did her research. The next time in New York they had had a weekend in the Hamptons with a stockbroker and his wife and, apart from discussing business with their host one night, they had had a wonderful relaxing weekend.

She glanced at him. He was seated at the opposite side of the plane as far away from her as he could get, his dark head bent as he concentrated on the article he was reading in a financial magazine. He had shed his jacket and the dark sweater he wore stretched across his wide shoulders. As she watched he flicked a hand through his black hair, sweeping it from his broad brow. Something she had seen him do a hundred times when he was concentrating, which she found oddly endearing.

No, not endearing—she must not think like that. Their marriage was ending, and this was the last act. Only the formalities of a divorce lay ahead. She had no illusions left, and maybe that was no bad thing.

Anton had told her once to grow up…well, now she had.

Emily stared down fascinated as the helicopter transported them from the Lima airport to Anton's ranch high up into the Andes.

The fertile plains on the coast gave way to a rocky terrain and ever larger majestic hills and mountains, but with miles of jungle-like vegetation, and amazing half-hidden valleys.

The whirring blades slowed as the helicopter descended into one such huge valley. Her eyes widened at the sight of an enormous sprawling house with castellated turrets that seemed to cover half an acre, with smaller buildings, and a road surrounding it. The place was a village all on its own. Lush green paddocks and cultivated fields gave way to the natural rolling hills rising ever higher in the far distance.

'Is this it?' she asked, glancing at Anton as he removed his headphones.

'Welcome to Casa Diaz,' he said and, leaping out of the helicopter, he came around and took her hand and helped her down. He kept a hold of it as they ducked beneath the whirling blades and dropped it when they straightened up. A battered Jeep was waiting for them.

The driver, wearing a big sombrero and an even bigger smile, leapt out. 'Welcome, boss and Señora Diaz.' Sweeping off his sombrero, he bowed and ushered them into the Jeep. A moment later her suitcase was dropped in the back, and they were off.

The next half-hour was a blur to Emily. All the staff were lined up in the hall to meet her and Anton made the introductions, then requested the housekeeper serve them coffee.

Emily was intensely conscious of his hand on her bare arm, and the tension in his long body, as he led her through wide double doors set to one side of the massive marble staircase that dominated the huge hall and into a room that had to be at least forty feet long. She pulled her arm free and glanced around.

Her eyes widened in awe and for a while she forgot his icy, intimidating presence. A vaulted ceiling, heavy dark timbers, white walls, almost completely obliterated by paintings and artifacts. The place was like a museum, and she was fascinated. Spanish and Indian art and sculptures were displayed together, some really ancient, and very probably original.

She walked slowly around the room, lost to everything as she examined paintings, pictures and sepia snapshots of family with avid interest.

CHAPTER ELEVEN

THE HOUSEKEEPER arrived with a tray bearing coffee and delicate little cakes. 'Your favourite, señor.' She smiled and placed the tray on a beautifully carved antique occasional table, set between three large sofas.

'I had no idea your home was so old,' Emily finally said, turning to Anton as the housekeeper left.

He quirked an eyebrow as much as to say *So what*? but actually said, 'Sit down and pour the coffee.'

She bristled at the brisk command, but did as he said. Automatically she spooned sugar into his, black and sweet just how he liked it, and grimaced. She knew the little things about him, but not the big, she realized sadly, and never would now. She added milk to hers, and held his out to him as he sat down on the sofa adjacent to her.

'To answer your question—' he drained his coffee-cup, placed it back on the table '—the Diaz family has lived on this land since the first Sebastian Emanuel Diaz arrived in South America with the conquistadores,' he said flatly. Rising to his feet, he walked across the room to the fireplace.

'But you told me your grandmother was disowned,' she said, her eyes following him as he leant negligently against the ornate wood-carved mantelpiece. 'How did you get it back?' she asked, tearing her gaze from his impressive form. Then she realized the stupidity of her question. 'Stupid question—you probably made the owner an offer they could not refuse.' She raised her eyes to his and answered for him, sarcasm tingeing her tone. He was a ruthless devil. What Anton wanted Anton got, and it would suit his sense of justice to retrieve the family home.

'No, I did not.' His firm lips quirked in the ghost of a smile, a reminiscent gleam in the dark eyes that met hers. 'My grandmother did, thirty years after being thrown out by her father, and a few years after he died. By then her older brother had managed to bankrupt the family. My grandmother stepped in, bought the place, and spent many happy years here with her own mother. A beautiful but weak woman, and of the old school who obeyed her husband in everything, but she died happy with her daughter at her bedside. Then for the last ten years of my grandmother's life my mother and I lived here.'

'Your grandmother must have been an amazing woman,' Emily exclaimed. To go from the disowned daughter and owner of a brothel to a landowner again was an enormous leap.

'She was a true descendant of the original Diaz with all the courage that entailed,' Anton responded, one dark brow arching sardonically. 'Unfortunately my mother and sister, though kind, loving women, did not inherit her strength of character.'

'I never realized—' Emily began.

'You never realized that my family was a lot older than yours, even though it is the illegitimate side that flourished,' he drawled mockingly. 'But then life is full of little surprises.' Straightening up, he moved towards her.

She glanced up. He was towering over her, his face hard, his eyes as black as jet. In that moment she could see him as a conquistador, ruthless and cruel as they swept through South America centuries ago, and a shiver of fear snaked up her spine.

'Now is the time for your surprise. Come. What I wish to show you is in my study.

'Sit down.' He gestured to a deep buttoned leather Chesterfield, placed a few feet away from a massive leather-topped desk in the wood-panelled room. He then walked behind the desk, and, taking a key from his pocket, he opened one of the drawers and withdrew an envelope. He looked at it for a moment, and she felt the tension in the room, the tension in Anton as he walked back towards her.

'Read this.' He held out the battered envelope, a gleam of mocking triumph in his dark eyes. 'Then call me a liar if you dare.'

Reluctantly she took the envelope by one corner, avoiding touching his hand. The postmark was English. Slowly, with a hand that trembled, she withdrew the folded notepaper, and opened it. A gasp of surprise escaped her. The return address was their family home in Kensington. No, it could not be... Then she began to read.

Two minutes later Emily carefully folded the letter and placed it back in the envelope and rose gracefully to her feet. 'Very interesting,' she said and forced a smile to her stiff lips. 'But would you mind if I studied this in my room?' she asked. 'I am exhausted after all the travelling. We can discuss this at dinner.'

'Still in denial,' he mocked, but rang a bell fitted in the wall. 'It never ceases to amaze me the lengths that the female of the species will go to, to avoid facing an unpleasant truth,' he drawled cynically. 'But as you wish—dinner will be early, at seven, to accommodate your exhaustion!'

A maid arrived at his call to show Emily out of the room.

Anton watched them leave, a frown creasing his broad brow. Emily had surprised him. He had thought she would be devastated seeing the proof of her father's deceit, but instead she had smiled coolly and asked for time to study the letter. But then why was he surprised? Once he had regretted telling her about her father, but not any more. Once he had thought that was the only stumbling block to a long and successful marriage, but that was before last night when he had realized she never had any intention of being his wife or having his children. She would have been quite happy to be his mistress, but when it came to anything else she was just as big a snob as her father.

He had dealt with slurs on his upbringing all his life, and they did not bother him. But the least one expected from a wife was respect. He would be well rid of her. A wayward thought slid into his cool mind…

Why not keep her as a mistress until he tired of her luscious body? Let her earn the divorce she wanted on her back.

No, he immediately dismissed the notion because his pride would not let him. Bottom line, for all her innocence she had used him as nothing more than a stud. Nobody ever used Anton Diaz.

He left to check his horses—at least they were honest.

Emily followed the maid up the grand staircase along a wide corridor and into a lovely bedroom. Definitely feminine in white and with the occasional touch of pink. A lace coverlet with a pink satin trim running through it graced a four-poster bed delicately draped in white muslin, the tie-backs pink satin to match. Definitely not the master suite, Emily concluded, and, casually dropping the letter onto a frill-trimmed dressing table, she looked for her suitcase. A shower and change and dinner.

The last supper, she thought, and opened a wardrobe door to find her clothes had already been unpacked. Walking into the *en suite*, she glanced at the free-standing bath, but opted for a shower. She really was tired after a sleepless night, followed a long-haul flight almost halfway around the globe, followed by the helicopter flight and, although because of the time zone it was late afternoon, she had been awake for over thirty-six hours.

Stripping off the trousers and blouse she had travelled in plus her underwear, she stepped into the shower.

Emily looked at her reflection in the mirror. She had left her hair loose, simply tucked it behind her ears, but she had taken care with her make-up, subtly shading her eyelids to emphasize the blue of her eyes, with a light coating of mascara on her long lashes. Her full lips she coated in a rose gloss. And the slightest trace of blusher accentuated her cheekbones.

She needed all the help she could get. She was no actress, but she was not about to let Anton see how much leaving him was going to hurt her. She loved him, but she had too much character to live life on his terms, knowing it would eventually destroy her.

The dress she wore was a pale blue crêpe sheath with small sleeves and a square-cut neck that just revealed the upper curves of her breasts and ended a few inches above her knees. She slipped silver sandals on her feet, and fastened the diamond and sapphire locket around her neck and the matching bracelet on her wrist, but left off her engagement ring. Let Anton make of that what he will, she thought bitterly. He would anyway—but he was in for a rude awakening…

She walked down the staircase at five to seven, and stood at the bottom of the stairs looking around. She had no idea where the dining room was.

'Señora, this way—the master, he wait.' The housekeeper appeared and beckoned her to follow. Taking a deep breath, Emily entered the room. Anton was standing at the head of a long table set with the finest linen, china and crystal.

He was wearing a dark evening suit and looked every inch the Spanish grandee: arrogant, remote but devastatingly attractive. The breath caught in her throat. His dark head lifted, his black eyes roaming over her. She saw the moment he recognized her jewellery and watched him stiffen.

They were like two strangers staring at each other across a room.

Then for one tense moment their eyes fused. Emily imagined she saw a flicker of some emotion in his before his hooded lids lowered slightly, masking his expression, and he spoke.

'Emily, you look lovely as always. Please be seated,' he offered, and pulled out a chair.

She smoothed suddenly damp palms down her thighs as she walked towards him and sat down. She picked up a napkin and folded it on her lap—anything rather than look at him again, until she got her breathing under control.

The hour that followed was surreal.

The housekeeper served the food course after course, and Anton ate everything with obvious enjoyment. His conversation was icily polite, restricted to each dish and the ingredients involved, and the relative merits of the red and white wine that was served.

While Emily had a problem swallowing anything, and her replies were verging on the monosyllabic.

'Excellent meal,' he complimented the housekeeper as she served the coffee, smiled and left.

'You did not seem to eat much, Emily.' He straightened back in his chair and fixed her with black gimlet eyes. 'Something not to your liking or has something given you indigestion—or someone…like your father?'

The gloves were off with a vengeance, and actually Emily felt relieved. But before she could respond he continued.

'Not very pleasant, is it, when you find out someone you love deceived you, as I discovered last night. And you have discovered tonight.' It was then she saw the tightly leashed anger in his black eyes.

And what did he mean…someone he loved deceived him…? He had never loved her, and the only reason his nose was out of joint was because she was not the brood mare he had been hoping for.

'Not at all,' she said smoothly. She was not going to respond to his taunts. Cool, calm and collected—that was her strategy. 'In fact I am greatly relieved. I have read the letter you gave me, and, true, it is disgraceful, the sentiments expressed disgusting and totally unacceptable. Please accept I deeply regret what happened to your sister.' She was painstakingly polite. 'The poor girl must have been heartbroken.'

'Deeply regret?' he snarled. 'Is that all you have to say?'

'No.' Emily had given a lot of thought to the people and circumstances surrounding the letter after reading it and she was curious, and wanted to delve a little deeper. 'Tell me, Anton, did you see much of your father?'

'Not a lot, but what the hell has that got to do with anything?'

'Humour me. Did he treat your half-sister like his own child? Was he older than your mother?'

'No…and thirty years older.' He rattled off the answers.

'Then that might explain it.'

'Explain what—that your father seduced my sister? Don't even try to make excuses.'

'Okay, I won't.' She sat up straighter in her chair. 'My father never wrote that letter. You were wrong.' His face went dark with rage, the veins at his temples standing out so prominently she thought he was going to burst a blood vessel. 'But you were also right,' she got in quickly. 'The writing is that of my grandfather, Charles Fairfax, who had to be over fifty when he had an affair with your sister, which I suppose, in a way, makes it worse.'

Anton's black eyes flared in shocked disbelief. 'Your grandfather.'

She had been wrong, Emily thought, seeing the horror in his eyes. Anton was capable of emotion, but not one she envied him. 'Yes. My grandfather,' she said bluntly. 'An easy mistake to make,' she offered to soften the blow. 'Charles is a family name—the eldest son is always called Charles until my brother Thomas. Because my father was never on good terms with his own father so was never going to name his own son after him.'

'I cannot believe Suki…' Anton began and stopped.

He looked shell-shocked—a first for her arrogant husband, Emily was sure. 'It is true,' she continued. 'My father and aunt Lisa were horrified by the behaviour of their father when they were old enough to realize what he was really like. He was an out-and-out womanizer, a complete waster, the black sheep of the family. My grandfather and grandmother led completely separate lives but divorce was never an option. They shared the same house—you have seen my family home, it is more than big enough,' she said dryly. 'After he died when I was about seven, his name was never mentioned again. He was a horrible man and the whole family was disgusted by him,' she said flatly. 'Did you never wonder why Uncle James, an in-law, is Chairman of the Board?'

Anton listened in growing horror as Emily continued.

'Aunt Lisa worked in the offices of Fairfax as a girl. She met and married James, who was employed as the manager at the time and was actually responsible for keeping the firm viable. Grandfather Fairfax had no head for business and spent a fortune on his women. When my father was old enough to join the firm it was James who taught him the ropes and he was twenty-eight when he took over. As a result when my father died it was James he named as Chairman until Tom reaches the age of twenty-eight.'

Emily really was exhausted and, pushing back her chair, she rose to her feet, still holding her napkin. 'So now you know the truth. I am no psychiatrist, but what I was trying to say before was maybe your mother and sister were looking for a father-figure—maybe that's why they behaved the way they did. Who knows?' She shrugged. 'It is amazing how some things affect people. Look at my uncle Clive. You know why he dresses so outrageously and encourages me to?' She smiled. 'Remember the silver lamé?' Then wished she had not said it as she saw Anton grimace in disgust and, nervously twisting the napkin in her hands, she finished. 'Well, Uncle Clive is of the opinion my father and Tom have gone too far the other way. Too conservative, too strait-laced, too frightened of turning out like Grandfather Fairfax, so need shocking once in a while. Maybe he is right. I don't know.'

'Emily.' Anton rose to his feet, and reached out to her, but she took a few hasty steps back.

She didn't want him to touch her; she just wanted the whole sorry mess over with. 'But what I do know is Grandfather Fairfax instead of my father changes nothing. Though I am surprised. You're usually so thorough with your security, your investigators and everything. Why, you never noticed the letter read "*even if I were free which I am not*". That should have given you a clue—when it was written my parents were not even engaged at the time.'

'Emily. I don't know what to say.' Anton reached for her again but she shook off his hand.

'There is nothing to say.' She tilted back her head and looked straight up into his brutally handsome face. 'The truth is out; you were wrong, but right in a way. As usual for you, Anton, you always end up the winner.'

'No, Emily.' He grabbed her by the shoulders. 'I can't tell

you how sorry I am I mixed up your father with your grandfather. I would never have upset you that day on the yacht if I had known. Let me make it up to you somehow. Tell me what you want and it is yours.'

She wanted his love, but he did not have it to give. Sadly she shook her head. 'You don't get it, Anton. Whether it was my father or grandfather does not matter a damn. Nothing has changed—you married me to get back at a Fairfax. And then you wondered why I kept taking the pill. You broke my trust. Can you give that back? I don't think so. Now, if you don't mind I am going to bed and I would like to leave in the morning.' And, turning on her heel, she walked out.

Anton was waiting for her the next morning when she walked downstairs, and simply said, 'The helicopter is here, and my jet is on standby at Lima to take you anywhere you want to go. The apartment in London is yours. I will not be using it again and you have nothing to fear in regard to Fairfax Engineering—I am no longer interested.'

'That is very generous of you,' Emily said, looking up at his expressionless face. Willing him to show the slightest weakness, a gesture he cared. But the black eyes that met hers were cold and hard.

'No doubt we will have to meet again some day, but if you are hoping for a quick divorce, forget it. As far as I am concerned it will not be any time soon. Now, if you will excuse me I have my horses to attend to. I expect you to be gone when I return.'

'Be assured of it,' Emily said coolly. 'As for the divorce, I don't much care when. After this I am not likely to get married again in a hurry. But to ease your mind I don't want a penny of your money. I don't want anything from you, except you keep your promise via a written guarantee you will not interfere in any detrimental way whatsoever with Fairfax Engineering.'

'You will have it,' he snapped, and she watched as he swung on his heel and walked out. She told herself it was for the best, it was what she wanted, and kept telling herself, all the long flight back to London. Then cried herself to sleep in the bed they had shared.

CHAPTER TWELVE

EMILY leant on the rail of the ship, her friend Delia by her side, watching the dinghy taking the divers closer into one of the tiny rocky islands that formed the Las Rocas archipelago off the coast of Venezuela.

'Do you think we will strike lucky this time?' Emily asked.

Delia, older and wiser, grimaced. 'I hope so. It is over a week since we left Caracas, and this is the fourth set of coordinates we have tried, and I don't think we have much more time. I have been checking the weather forecast on the radio and there is a report of a hurricane heading for Florida and on down over the Caribbean islands. It is expected to hit Jamaica, which is not far from us, in three days.'

Emily managed a grin. 'Thanks for the positive report, pal. I think I'll go and check out the computer. It looks like they are ready to dive.' And she went below.

Jake, the head of the expedition, was one of the divers on the dive boat, wanting to explore at close hand the seabed for himself, but his second in command, Marco, was hovering over the bank of computers.

'Anything yet?' she asked.

'No. They have only just reached the site.'

Emily slid into a chair and watched the divers exploring the seabed on the computer screen. Looking for maybe a shape of the prow of a sailing ship or just wood. Or better still the shape of a cannon. After three hundred years anything down there would be buried under sand and encrusted with sea life. Vague silhouettes in the ocean bed could give up the secret of a shipwreck.

It was Emily's job to map the position on the seabed and discern what any find was from the film sent back to the computer by the diver's cameras. She loved her job, and this was the most exciting expedition she had been on so far. Yet somehow, in the five weeks since she had left Peru, she had difficulty getting excited about anything.

She tried not to think of Anton. But he haunted her thoughts day and night. Especially at night as she lay in the bed they had shared. She had yet to tell Helen and Tom that Anton and she had parted. But she knew she was going to have to after this trip. Helen had already started asking pointed questions regarding Anton's whereabouts before Emily left.

Straightening up, Emily fixed her attention on the computer screen. Her marriage was over, done with, and she had to move on. This expedition was the beginning of the rest of her life, she vowed. No more regrets...

Anton steadied the horse between his thighs as the sound of a helicopter disturbed the morning air. Max again...

Two weeks ago Max had found him drunk, and they had had a furious row. Max had told him he was heading for disaster. He had let his wife walk out, a wonderful woman who, if he had any guts, he would be fighting to win back. He was letting his business slide, and ignoring the few friends he had.

Anton had told him to get lost, he knew nothing. But after Max left he had stopped drinking. He had made a few calls consolidating his business interests and delegated the work that could not be avoided to his senior managers. He had no desire to go back to his old life flying around the world. In fact he had no desire for anything with one exception: Emily.

He rode back to the stables and dismounted and handed the reins to the groom. 'Give him a rubdown.' With a pat of the stallion's neck, he walked up to the hacienda.

Max was waiting, a deep frown on his craggy face. 'Why the hell haven't you answered your phone or e-mails?' he demanded. 'I have been trying to get in touch with you since yesterday morning.'

'Hello to you too, Max.'

'At least you look better than the last time I saw you.'

'Yes, well, fresh air and no booze help,' Anton admitted wryly.

'And help is why I am here,' Max said, following Anton into the large hall. 'It's Emily.'

Anton spun around. 'What about her?' he demanded.

'We kept a watch on her, as you said. She stayed in your apartment until ten days ago, when she flew to Caracas.'

'What? Caracas…in Venezuela…?'

'Yes,' Max said with a grimace. 'I know—not the safest place in the world.'

'Was she alone?'

'Yes.' Max nodded.

'Now I need a drink.' Anton strode through into the living room and poured a stiff whisky into a crystal glass and offered one to Max. He shook his head. The thought of a woman like Emily wandering around Venezuela on her own didn't bear thinking about. 'Why, for God's sake?'

'She has joined an expedition led by Jake Hardington and his wife, Delia, friends of Emily's from her university days, apparently. You might have heard of him—the treasure seeker. They hope to find a pirate ship supposedly sunk off the Las

Rocas archipelago by the French navy three hundred years ago. Emily is the marine archaeologist on board.'

Anton stared at his old friend as if he had taken leave of his senses. 'You are telling me that Emily has seriously gone looking for a pirate ship with a bunch of treasure hunters.'

'I know, boss. Strange, but true.'

'Actually, it is not strange.' Anton drained his glass and slammed it down on the counter. 'It is just the damn-fool sort of thing she would do. Why the hell didn't you stop her?'

'You told me to keep a watching brief, nothing more, and get in touch with you if I thought it necessary. I tried to telephone when she left London but you were not answering. I figured, well, it is her line of work, and had my man in Venezuela keep tabs on her. She joined the ship and they set sail on the twentieth, eight days ago. They are at present anchored off a reef. I might add it is not very easy to keep track of them. Treasure seekers are notoriously secretive—they up anchor and move without warning.'

'So why are you here now?'

'Because yesterday there was a hurricane warning. It is heading across the Caribbean and the treasure seekers are not that far from its predicted path. I thought you needed to know. I have hired a high-speed—'

Anton cut him off. 'Five minutes and we leave.'

Emily stood at the rail and watched anxiously as the divers' dinghy ploughed through the heavy waves and finally came alongside. The weather was getting worse by the minute. The wind had risen and the torrential rain had soaked her to the skin. The ship was rolling from side to side making her feel sick. Which was worrying enough in itself, as she had never suffered from seasickness before, but then she had never experienced gale-force winds at sea before.

Everything on board was done at high speed as the threat of drifting onto the reef was imminent. The anchor was lifted, the engines roared and the ship turned to head further out to sea.

Only to see two high-speed Venezuelan navy frigates heading towards them. A loud hailer was utilized demanding they stop, and to everyone's stunned amazement a group of gun-toting sailors boarded them. The ship was seized and ordered back to port and they were all under arrest. Jake tried to ask why but was met by a wall of silence.

Darkness was falling when the ship berthed, not at a commercial port but at a naval base.

Wearing only a cotton tee shirt and shorts, and with her hair and clothes plastered to her body, Emily was beginning to feel afraid as she was led with the others at gunpoint off the vessel.

In the fading light she saw a towering figure approaching. The naval guards parted and her mouth fell open in shock as Anton, ignoring everyone else, strode up to her.

His black eyes were sunken deep and burned like coals of fire in a face that was thinner than she remembered. She had never seen him so angry. Livid…

'That is it, Emily,' he raged, grasping her by the shoulders, his fingers digging into her flesh through the damp cotton. 'What are you trying to do—drive me out of my mind?'

Held close to him, the heat of his body reaching out to her, she shuddered in the old familiar way, though she guessed the heat he generated was more rage than anything else.

'You go off looking for some damn-fool pirate ship in the middle of a hurricane. Well, no more…I have had as much as I am going to take from you. You are coming home with me and that is final. You are not safe to be let out on your own. And I will not be responsible for your death. Hell, even Max can't keep tabs on you.'

'Emily, is this man bothering you?' Jake Hardington asked, moving to face Anton even as recognition of whom he was challenging hit him.

'Bothering her?' Anton snarled. 'I should have talked some sense into her months ago. As for you—how dare you take my wife on your idiotic expedition? I shouldn't have just had you arrested, I should have had you shot.'

'Anton!' Emily exclaimed, finally finding her voice.

'You're his wife?' Jake asked, turning to Emily. 'Anton Diaz's wife?'

'Yes,' she confessed.

Jake looked at Emily and at the man holding her, and whatever he saw made him smile and shake his head. 'You're on your own, Emily.' And stepped back to watch.

'So now you remember you are my wife,' Anton snarled. 'Why the hell could you not have remembered that before you went on this mad adventure? What is it with you? Is it your mission in life to scare me half to death?'

In a state of shock Emily simply let Anton rant on—not that she could have stopped him. He was like a man possessed.

'Why can't you be happy like other women with diamonds and designer clothes and living in the lap of luxury? But no…I had to call out the police force in New York to find you and drop the biggest deal of my life. I had to negotiate with the Venezuelan government to call out the navy to rescue you. Have you the slightest idea what you do to me? You terrify me, Emily, *madre Dios*! Loving you is liable to kill me if you do not bankrupt me first.'

Loving—had Anton said he loved her? And deep down inside a tiny flicker of something very like hope unfurled. Then she stopped thinking as his arms wrapped fiercely around her, moulding her to his hard body, and his mouth crashed down on hers.

The rain poured down on them but Emily was oblivious to everything but Anton. His mouth ravaged hers with a passion that bordered on violence and she clung to him, her hands linking behind his neck, and returned his kiss with a hunger, a desperate need she could not deny.

She moved restlessly against him, her wet clothing and his accentuating the hard pressure of his arousal against her belly.

'Hell, Emily, you could have died.' He groaned and buried his head in her throat, sucking on the pulse that beat madly there, his hands feverishly roaming up and down her body. 'Are you sure you are all right?' He groaned again and lifted his head, his hair plastered like a black skullcap to his scalp, and to Emily he had never looked better.

'Did you say you loved me?' was the only question in her mind.

'Love you...' He paused, and glanced away to the people surrounding them. His dark eyes returned to her upraised face, and, in a curiously reverent gesture, he pressed a kiss to her brow, each soft cheek. 'Yes, I love you, Emily Diaz.' And his lips curved in a wry smile. 'Why else would I be standing here making a complete and utter fool of myself in front of all these people?'

Emily had spent too long mistrusting him and thinking he was not capable of loving anyone to immediately believe him. Her blue eyes, wide and wary, searched his haggard features, looking for some sign that would convince her.

'Damn it, Emily,' Jake Hardington cut in. 'The man loves you, tell him you love him, and let us get out of here. In case you have not noticed, the rest of us are still standing here with guns pointed at us and Diaz is the only one who can set us free.'

Startled, Emily looked at Jake and back at Anton. 'Is that right?'

'Right that I love you, and right I can set them free. The other is up to you.' And she saw a hint of vulnerability in his eyes and her own softened as the hope inside her burst into flame.

They had a lot to sort out, she knew, but she had to take the risk and tell him she loved him if they were to have a future together. But she never got the chance to speak.

'But either way I am not setting you free,' Anton added, his arms tightening around her.

Emily burst out laughing. That was *so* Anton—vulnerable for seconds but quickly as arrogant and indomitable as ever. 'Oh, Anton, I do love you.' And, reaching up, she kissed him as a round of applause broke out.

'At last, Emily, and now you have got your husband in a good mood, get him to sponsor my next expedition,' Jake Hardington called out. 'Because he wrecked this one.'

Anton looked at Jake. 'Hardington, you are pushing your luck.' But he smiled, taking the sting out of his words, and, sweeping Emily up in his arms with a few instructions to the officer in charge, he carried her away.

The hotel was luxurious and Anton paced the sitting room of the two-bedroomed suite listening to the sound of the bath running. Emily was in there, and he ached to join her. But, instead, on arriving he had told her to go ahead and have a bath and he would order dinner from room service. He had done it though he had never felt less like eating in his life. He had quickly showered in the *en suite* of the other bedroom and was now wearing a white towelling robe courtesy of the hotel, pacing the floor like an idiot.

For some bizarre reason he was ridiculously nervous. This love thing was a whole lot harder than he had ever imagined— not that he ever had imagined, he admitted self-derisively. With damp palms, a pounding heart and a churning stomach, he had a whole new respect for love.

Emily had said she loved him, but it had been with an audience urging her on. She had said she loved him on their wedding night, but the next day, when he had made the catastrophic mistake about her father, she had changed her mind. How could he know she was certain she loved him now?

It was his own fault and he had spent what seemed like ages running over and over in his head what he would say to her. How he would apologize to her for his past mistakes. Straightening his shoulders, he walked into the bedroom. He had it all planned in his head. All he needed was Emily.

Emily slipped on the hotel's towelling robe and, barefoot, exited the bathroom happier than she had ever been. Anton was standing in the middle of the room, a serious expression on his handsome face. 'Anton,' she said rather shyly, 'did you order dinner?'

His dark head lifted. 'Yes.' And in two lithe strides he was beside her. '*Dio!* Emily, how can you ever forgive me?' Anton groaned. 'When I think what I have said and done since we met I cringe.' And placing an arm around her, he pulled her close. 'That first day on the boat you called me dumb and I was…' He curved a strong hand around the nape of her neck and tilted her head up to his. 'My only excuse is I didn't know if I was on my head or my heels.'

'It does not matter now, Anton,' Emily said softly. 'The past is behind us. People say the first six months of marriage are the worst, so we have two more to go,' she tried to joke.

'I could not stand another two minutes, never mind months, at odds with you.' He lifted her and laid her gently on the bed and stretched his long length out next to her. 'I need to tell you this, Emily. To confess, if you like,' he said, his dark eyes serious as, propped on one arm, he looked down at her.

'Couldn't it wait?' She smiled impishly up at him. His robe had fallen open and she rested her hand lightly on his broad chest.

'No.' He caught her hand in his and linked their fingers. His dark gaze lingered on the gold band on her finger for a moment. 'I have done a lot of soul-searching over the last few weeks, and I want you to hear me out and make you understand why I behaved as I did.'

'Do I have to? I can think of better things to do.' She grinned.

'Yes,' Anton said sternly, if a little regretfully. 'After my mother died, naturally I was upset, and finding out about Suki only made me worse. I am not good with emotions and my grief turned to anger and I vented my fury on the Fairfax family. But if you believe nothing else, believe this—from the minute I saw you I fell in love with you. I know that now, but at the time I would not admit it even to myself.'

He paused for a moment, looking deep into her eyes, willing her to believe in him, and then continued at breakneck speed. 'I did not believe in love because I had seen what it did to my mother and sister. But with hindsight, much as I loved them they were basically weak, not like my grandmother. The day I proposed to you I was mad with jealousy because I thought you had dressed so strikingly for another man. The day you walked down the aisle in church I knew the image of you would be etched on my brain for ever. Watching you sleep on the jet, I decided I was not going to tell you about your father.

'Our wedding night was the most amazing night of my life. You were everything and more than I could ever have imagined, your husky words of love much more than I deserved, which in my arrogance I took as my due.' He gave her a rueful grin. 'But you know what happened the next day—I lost my temper when you mentioned your parents and told you anyway about your father. But the truth was I was feeling as guilty as hell. I couldn't believe I had been dumb enough to think for a minute my yearly trip to Monte Carlo was suitable as a honeymoon. At one point I considered just telling the captain to set sail and leave everyone behind, but it was too late.

'Then the whole weekend went from bad to worse. I behaved like an arrogant swine. You nearly gave me a heart attack diving off the yacht and that damn Harding woman filled your head with lies about me.'

'It really does not matter,' Emily said, lifting a hand to stroke his lean cheek. Though his revelations filled her heart to overflowing with love.

'Yes, it does to me. When you told me to find another woman for the night, it gutted me. I spent hours pacing the deck before returning to bed, and realizing it wasn't your fault. You were angry and had every right to be.

'Then in Greece in my conceit I thought everything was wonderful. It wasn't until we were due to leave when I saw you walking down the stairs in the suit you had worn after our wedding that I recognized what was missing. You had looked at me with such joy, such love, when you walked towards me when we were about to leave Deveral Hall that day, but not any more. And I saw the difference. We made love but you never said the word. You never said much at all. I told myself it didn't matter. But on the spur of the moment I crazily decided to take you to New York instead of London. I could not leave you without trying to change things, though I had no idea how.'

'You were actually going to take me to London and instead you kidnapped me.' Emily chuckled. 'All because of a blue suit.'

'Yes. But then you got lost and as I stormed out of a meeting without a second thought I knew I was in serious trouble, but I was still in denial about my true feelings.'

'You were angry, and did seem a little upset when we got back to the apartment. I actually wondered if you cared.'

'Cared.' He grimaced. 'Oh, I cared. But the real clincher, the moment it hit me right between the eyes, was in the limousine on the way back from the exhibition of Peruvian art, when you asked me why had I not married Lucita to get back at her father. I realized it had never occurred to me, and it wouldn't have done in a million years, and yet the two cases were in a way similar. Then I had to ask myself why you?

'It was a completely outlandish idea. I had been a bachelor for thirty-seven years and no woman had even tempted me to get married before. So why was I so determined to marry you? I am not proud of the fact, but I could have ruined your family business, but I think it was grief that fuelled my vengeance more than anything else. I needed someone to blame. But by the time I met Tom and James I was already losing enthusiasm for the project, because there was nothing to dislike about them. Quite the reverse—I had a grudging respect for them, and then I met you, Emily…

'To be totally frank, I took one look at you and could not stop myself flirting with you rather crudely.' He grimaced again. 'Then I saw you dancing with Max, and that was it.'

Anton dropped her hand and lifted a finger to her lips and gently outlined the contours of her mouth. 'All I could think of was your lithesome body under mine. You were the most sensuous woman I had ever seen. But at the time I thought anyone who danced like you must have had a few lovers and I was going to be one of them.'

'What exactly did you intend to do?' Emily asked. 'Make me your mistress?'

'No. I decided before the music ended, I was going to marry you. Your effect on me was that instant. In my arrogance I decided you would make a wonderful wife and mother.' His expression darkened. 'It was you who thought I wanted a mistress, as I found out just before we parted.' His dark eyes held hers, intent and oddly resigned. 'I know I had no right, but I was outraged to discover you were taking the pill without telling me. I felt used like some stud to perform in bed and nothing more. Not good enough to be the father of your children.'

'Oh, Anton.' Emily looped her arms around his neck and looked deep into his eyes. 'I never thought that for a second. I loved you even when I didn't want to. But you told me you did not believe in love, civil and sex you said, and I did not think our marriage could possibly last. I did not think you could stay faithful; I was green with jealousy thinking about all your other women, and knowing you did not love me made it worse.'

'I am sorry, Emily, so sorry.' He groaned. 'I never intended to hurt you. I love you, and if you don't want children that is okay by me, but I cannot let you go. I love you so much it hurts,' he declared, and she was stunned by the flicker of pain in the dark depth of his eyes that he could not hide.

Emily was shocked that he really thought she did not want his baby. Shocked that such a strong, wonderful man, a man she had thought without emotion, could be so emotionally vulnerable. She was suddenly conscious of the heavy pounding of her heart and his, the lengthening silence and his stillness... He was afraid... Surely not.

She slipped her hands up and around his neck, and smiled brilliantly up at him. 'How about you stop talking and show me some of this love you talk about?'

'You mean that—you really do love me?' Anton asked, his dark eyes gleaming down into hers, and she urged him closer.

'Yes,' she breathed. 'But as for a baby...' She felt him

stiffen. 'I think you might be too late—I am already almost four weeks late.'

Anton's brutally handsome features clenched in a frown. 'What…? How…? When…?' He loved Emily, but she had an amazing ability to confuse his normally needle-sharp brain without even trying.

'The how you know.' She laughed up at him. 'The when and where are the last time we were in London. I had forgotten to take my pills for the two days I stayed at Helen's—when you found me I was trying to catch up…'

'Do you mind?' he asked, tension in every line of his great body.

'No—if I am right, I am delighted. I would love to have your baby, but right now I would love to have you,' she said boldly, her sparkling blue eyes lit with amusement and something more fixed on his, one long leg wrapping over his as she turned into him.

Anton's arms wrapped around her convulsively as the import of her words sank in. He almost yelled what the hell was she doing on the damn-fool expedition then? But stopped in time. She was Emily. Beautiful, wonderful, wilful, but his Emily and he would not have her any other way.

'Thank the Lord.' He groaned, his heart in his eyes as he bent his head and kissed her with all the tender passion and love in his soul.

Dinner was delivered; the waiter called out, and was met with a particularly appropriate Spanish expletive. He smiled. He was a man and he had been in service long enough to recognize it was a different appetite on the occupant's mind, and left the trolley in the sitting room and tiptoed out.

The Venadicci
Marriage Vengeance

Melanie
MILBURNE

Melanie Milburne says: 'I am married to a surgeon, Steve, and have two gorgeous sons, Paul and Phil. I live in Hobart, Tasmania, where I enjoy an active life as a long-distance runner and a nationally ranked top ten Master's swimmer. I also have a Master's Degree in Education, but my children totally turned me off the idea of teaching! When not running or swimming I write, and when I'm not doing all of the above I'm reading. And if someone could invent a way for me to read during a four-kilometre swim I'd be even happier!'

To Lorraine Bleasby, Dot Armstrong and Denise Monks—my three past and present helpers who free up my time so I can write. How can I thank you for all you do and have done for me and my family? This book is dedicated to you with much love and appreciation. I want the world to know what truly special women you are.

CHAPTER ONE

'MR VENADICCI has magnanimously offered to squeeze you in between appointments,' the receptionist informed Gabby with crisp, cool politeness. 'But he only has ten minutes available for you.'

Gabby schooled her features into impassivity, even though inside she was fuming and had been for the last hour, as Vinn Venadicci took his time about whether he would respond to her urgent request to see him. 'Thank you,' she said. 'I will try not to take up too much of his precious time.'

No matter how galling it would be to see Vinn again, Gabby determined she would be calm and in control at all times and under all circumstances. Too much was at stake for her to jeopardise things with a show of temper or a tirade of insults, as she would have done without hesitation seven years ago. A lot of water had flowed under the bridge since then, but she was not going to tell him just how dirty some of it had been. That would be conceding defeat, and in spite of everything that had happened she wasn't quite ready to shelve all of her pride where Vinn Venadicci was concerned.

His plush suite of offices in the heart of the finan-

cial district in Sydney was a reflection of his meteoric
rise to fame in the property investment industry. From
his humble beginnings as the born-out-of-wedlock
bad-boy son of the St Clair family's Italian-born
house-cleaner Rose, he had surprised everyone—
except Gabby's father, who had always seen Vinn's potential and had done what he could to give him the
leg-up he needed.

Thinking of her father was just the boost to her
resolve Gabby needed right now. Henry St Clair was
in frail health after a serious heart attack, which meant
a lot of the responsibility to keep things running
smoothly while he went through the arduous process
of triple bypass surgery and rehabilitation had fallen
on her shoulders, with her mother standing stalwartly
and rather stoically by her father's side.

This hiccup to do with the family business had come
out of the blue—and if her father got wind of it, it was
just the thing that could set off another heart attack.
Gabby would walk across hot coals to avoid that—
even meet face to face with Vinn Venadicci.

She raised her hand to the door marked with Vinn's
name and gave it a quick two-hit tattoo, her stomach
twisting with the prickly sensation she always felt
when she was within striking distance of him.

'Come.'

She straightened her shoulders and opened the door,
her chin at a proud height as she took the ridiculously
long journey to his desk, where he was seated. That he
didn't rise to his feet was the sort of veiled insult she
more or less expected from him. He had always had
an insolent air about him, even when he had lived on

and off with his mother, in a servants' cottage at the St Clair Point Piper mansion.

In that nanosecond before he spoke Gabby quickly drank in his image, her heart giving a little jerk inside her chest in spite of all of her efforts to control it. Even when he was seated his height was intimidating, and the black raven's wing of his hair caught the light coming in from the windows, giving it a glossy sheen that made her fingers itch to reach out and touch it. His nose was crooked from one too many of the brawls he had been involved in during his youth, but—unlike many other high-profile businessmen, who would have sought surgical correction by now—Vinn wore his war wounds like a medal. Just like the scar that interrupted his left eyebrow, giving him a dangerous don't-mess-with-me look that was disturbingly attractive.

'So how is the Merry Widow?' he said with a mocking glint in his eyes as they ran over her lazily. 'Long time no see. What is it now…? One year or is it two? You look like grief suits you, Gabriella. I have never seen you looking more beautiful.'

Gabby felt her spine go rigid at his sardonic taunt. Tristan Glendenning had been dead for just over two years, and yet Vinn never failed to refer to him in that unmistakably scathing manner whenever their paths crossed. She felt each and every reference to her late husband like a hard slap across the face—not that she would ever admit that to Vinn.

She pulled her temper back into line with an effort. 'May I sit down?'

He waved a hand in a careless manner. 'Put your cute little bottom down on that chair. But only for

ten minutes,' he said. 'I have back-to-back commit-
ments today.'

Gabby sat down on the edge of the chair, hating that
his words had summoned such a hot flush to her
cheeks. He had the most annoying habit of unnerving
her with personal comments that made her aware of
her body in a way no one else could.

'So,' he said, leaning back in his chair with a squeak
of very expensive leather, 'what can I do for you,
Gabriella?'

She silently ground her teeth. No one else called her
by her full name. Only him. She knew he did it deliberately. He had done it since she was fourteen, when
his mother had been hired as the resident cleaner,
bringing her brooding eighteen-year-old son with her.
Although Gabby had to grudgingly admit that the way
he said her name was quite unlike anyone else. He had
been born in Australia but, because he had been fluent
in Italian from a very young age, he made her name
sound faintly foreign and exotic. The four distinct syl-
lables coming out of his sensually sculptured mouth
always made the hairs on the back of her neck stand
to attention like tiny soldiers.

'I am here to discuss a little problem that's come
up,' she said, hoping he couldn't see how she was tying
her hands into knots in her lap. 'With my father out of
action at present, I would appreciate your advice on
how to handle it.'

He sat watching her in that musing way of his,
clicking and releasing his gold ballpoint pen with me-
ticulously timed precision: on, off, on, off, as if he
was timing his own slow and steady heartbeat.

'How is your father this morning?' he asked. 'I saw him last night in Intensive Care. He was looking a little worse for wear, but that's to be expected, I suppose.'

Gabby was well aware of Vinn's regular visits to her father's bedside, and had deliberately avoided being there at the same time. 'He's doing OK,' she said. 'His surgery is scheduled for some time next week. I think they've been waiting for him to stabilise first.'

'Yes, of course,' he said putting the pen to one side. 'But the doctors are hopeful of a full recovery, are they not?'

Gabby tried not to look at his hands, but for some reason her eyes drifted back to where they were now lying palm down on the smoothly polished desk. He had broad, square-shaped hands, with long fingers, and the dusting of masculine hair was enough to remind her of his virility as a full-blooded male of thirty-two.

He was no longer the youth of the past. His skin was clear and cleanly shaven, and at six foot four he carried not a gram of excess flesh; every toned and taut muscle spoke of his punishing physical regime. It made Gabby's ad hoc attempts at regular exercise with a set of free weights and a home DVD look rather pathetic in comparison.

'Gabriella?'

Gabby gave herself a mental shake and dragged her eyes back to his. He had such amazing eyes. And his ink-black hair and deeply olive skin made the smoky grey colour of them all the more striking.

She had never been told the details of his father, and she had never really bothered to ask Vinn directly—

although she assumed his father wasn't Italian, like his mother. Gabby had heard one or two whispers as she was growing up, which had seemed to suggest Vinn's mother found the subject painful and refused ever to speak of it.

'Um…I'm not really sure,' she said, in answer to his question regarding her father's recovery. 'I haven't really spoken with his doctors.'

As soon as she said the words she realised how disengaged and uncaring they made her sound—as if her father's health was not a top priority for her, when nothing could be further from the truth. She wouldn't be here now if it wasn't for her love and concern for both of her parents. She would never have dreamed of asking for Vinn's help if desperation hadn't shoved her head-first through his door.

'I take it this unprecedented visit to my lair is about the takeover bid for the St Clair Island Resort?' he said into the ringing silence.

Gabby had trouble disguising her reaction. She had only just become aware of it herself. How on earth had he found out about it?

'Um…yes, it is actually,' she said, shifting restlessly in her seat. 'As you probably know, my father took out a substantial loan for the refurbishment of the resort about a year and a half ago. But late yesterday I was informed there's been a call. If we don't pay the loan back the takeover bid will go through uncontested. I can't allow that to happen.'

'Have you spoken to your accountants about it?' he asked.

Gabby felt another layer of her professional armour

dissolve without trace. 'They said there is no way that amount of money can be raised in twenty-four hours,' she said, lowering her gaze a fraction.

He began his on-off click with his pen once more, a little faster now, as if in time with his sharp intelligence as he mulled over what strategy to adopt.

'I don't suppose you've mentioned it to your father,' he said, phrasing it as neither a question nor a statement.

'No…' she said, still not quite able to hold his gaze. 'I didn't want to stress him. I'm frightened the news could trigger another heart attack.'

'What about the on-site resort managers?' he asked. 'Do they know anything about this?'

Gabby rolled her lips together as she brought her gaze back to his. 'I spoke to Judy and Garry Foster last night. They are concerned for their jobs, of course, but I tried to reassure them I would sort things out this end.'

'Have you brought all the relevant documentation with you?' he asked after a short pause.

'Um…no… I thought I would run it by you first.' Gabby knew it was the wrong answer. She could see it in his incisive grey-blue eyes as they quietly assessed her.

She felt so incompetent—like a child playing with oversized clothes in a dress-up box. The shoes she had put on were too big. She had always known it, but hadn't had the courage to say it out loud to her parents, who had held such high hopes for her after her older brother Blair's tragic death. The giant hole he had left in their lives had made her all the more determined to fill in where she could. But she still felt as if the shoes were too big, too ungainly for her—even though she had trudged in them with gritted teeth for the last seven and a half years.

Vinn leaned back in his seat, his eyes still centred on hers. 'So you have less than twenty-four hours to come up with the funds otherwise the takeover bid goes through unchallenged?' he summated.

Gabby ran the tip of her tongue across lips dryer than ancient parchment. 'That's right,' she said, doing her level best to quell her dread at the thought of such an outcome. 'If it goes through our family will be left with only a thirty-five percent share in the resort. I'm not sure what you can do, but I know my father. If he wasn't so unwell he would probably have run it by you first, to see if there's anything we can do to avoid losing the major sharehold.'

His eyes were still locked on hers, unblinking almost, which unsettled Gabby more than she wanted it to.

'Do you know who is behind the takeover?' he asked.

She shook her head and allowed a tiny sigh to escape. 'I've asked around, but no one seems to know anything about the company that's behind it.'

'How much is the margin call?'

Gabby took an uneven breath, her stomach feeling as if a nest of hungry bull ants were eating their way out. 'Two point four million dollars.'

His dark brows lifted a fraction. 'Not exactly an amount you would have sitting around in petty cash,' he commented wryly.

'It's not an amount that is sitting *anywhere* in any of the St Clair accounts,' she said, running her tongue over her lips again, as if to wipe away the residue of panic that seemed to have permanently settled there. 'I'm sure my father never expected anything like this to happen—or at least not before we had time to recoup on the investment. The markets have been unstable for several months now. We wouldn't be the first to have redeveloped at the wrong time.'

'True.'

Gabby shifted in her chair again. 'So…I was wondering what you suggest we do…' She sucked in a tiny breath, her heart thumping so loudly she could feel a roaring in her ears. 'I…I know it's a bit of an imposition, but my father respects your judgment. That's basically why I am here.'

Vinn gave a deep and utterly masculine rumble of laughter. 'Yes, well, I can't imagine you pressing for an audience with me to share your observations on the day's weather,' he said. And then, with a little sneering quirk of his mouth, he added, 'You have five minutes left, by the way.'

Gabby pursed her lips as she fought her temper down. 'I think you know what I'm asking you to do,' she said tightly. 'Don't make me spell it out just to bolster your already monumental ego.'

A flicker of heat made his eyes look like the centre of a flame as he leaned forward across the desk. 'You want me to pay off the loan, is that it?' he said, searing her gaze with his.

'My father has done a lot for you—' she launched into the speech she had hastily prepared in the middle of the night '—he paid bail for that stolen car charge you were on when you were eighteen, not long after you came to live with us. And he gave you your very first loan for university. You wouldn't be where you are today without his mentorship and his belief in you.'

He leaned back in his chair, his demeanour casual as

you please. He picked up his pen again, but this time rolled it between two of his long fingers. 'Two point four million dollars is a lot of money, Gabriella,' he said. 'If I were to hand over such an amount I would want something in return. Something I could depend on to cover my losses if things were to take a sudden downturn.'

Gabby felt a prickle of alarm lift the surface of her skin. 'You mean like a guarantee or something?' she asked. 'W-we can have something drawn up with the lawyers. A repayment plan over…say five years, with fixed interest. How does that sound?'

He gave a smile that wasn't reflected in those unreadable eyes of his. 'It sounds risky,' he said. 'I would want a better guarantee than something written on paper.'

She looked at him in confusion. 'I'm not sure what you mean… Are you asking for more collateral? There's the house but Mum and Dad will need somewhere to—'

'I don't want their house,' he said, his eyes still burning like fire into hers.

Gabby ran her tongue over her lips again, her stomach doing another nervous shuffling movement. 'Then…then what do you want?' she asked, annoyed with herself at how whispery and frightened her voice sounded.

The silence became charged with something she couldn't quite identify. The air was thick—so thick she could scarcely breathe without feeling as if her chest was being pressed down with a weight far too heavy for her finely boned ribcage. Apprehension slowly but stealthily crept up her spine, with tiptoeing, ice-cold steps, disturbing each and every fine hair on the back of her neck.

Vinn's eyes were fathomless pools of murky shadows as they held onto hers. 'How do you feel about stepping up to the plate as guarantor?' he asked.

Gabby frowned. 'I don't have anything like that amount at my disposal,' she said, her heart starting to race. 'I have a small income I draw from the company for my immediate needs, but nothing that would cover that amount at short notice.'

He tilted one of his dark brows ironically. 'So I take it your late husband didn't leave you in the manner to which you have been accustomed for all of your silver-spooned life?' he said.

Gabby lowered her gaze and looked at her knotted hands rather than see the I-told-you-so gleam in his eyes. 'Tristan's finances were in a bit of a mess when he died so suddenly. There were debts and…so many things to see to…' *And so many secrets to keep*, she thought grimly.

A three-beat pause passed.

'I will give you the money,' Vinn said at last. 'I can have it in your father's business account with a few clicks of my computer mouse. Your little problem will be solved before you catch the lift down to the ground floor of this building.'

Gabby could sense a 'but' coming, and waited with bated breath for him to deliver it. She knew him too well to expect him to hand over that amount of money without some sort of condition on the deal. Sure, he admired and respected her father, he even tolerated her mother to some degree, but he had every reason to hate Gabby, and she couldn't imagine him missing a golden opportunity like this to demonstrate how deep his loathing of her ran.

'But of course there will be some conditions on the deal,' he inserted into the silence.

Gabby felt her heart skip a beat when she saw the determined glint in his gaze. 'W-what sort of conditions?' she asked.

'I am surprised you haven't already guessed,' he remarked, with an inscrutable smile playing with the sensual line of his mouth, giving him a devilishly ruthless look.

Gabby felt another shiver of apprehension pass through her. 'I—I have no idea what you're talking about,' she said, her nails scoring into her palms as she tightened her fists in her lap.

'Ah, but I think you do,' he said. 'Remember the night before your wedding?'

She forced herself to hold his gaze, even though she could feel a bloom of guilty colour staining her cheeks. The memory was as clear as if it had happened yesterday. God knew she had relived that brief, fiery exchange so many times during her train wreck of a marriage, wondering how different her life might have been if she had heeded Vinn's warning…

The wedding rehearsal had been going ahead, in spite of Tristan calling at the last minute to say he had been held up in a meeting and might not make it after all, and Vinn had arrived at the church bleary-eyed and unshaven from an international flight, after spending the last six months in Italy where his terminally ill mother had asked to be taken to die.

He had leaned in that indolent way of his against one of the columns at the back of the cathedral, his strong arms folded, one ankle crossed over the other, and his eyes—those amazingly penetrating eyes—every time Gabby happened to glance his way, trained on her.

Once the minister had taken them through their paces, Gabby's mother had invited everyone present back to the St Clair house for a light supper. Gabby had secretly hoped Vinn would decline the invitation, but as she had come out of one of the upstairs bathrooms half an hour or so later, Vinn had stepped forward to block her path.

'I'd like a word with you, Gabriella,' he said. 'In private.'

'I can't imagine what you'd have to say to me,' she said coldly, as she tried to sidestep him, but he took one of her wrists in the steel bracelet of his fingers, the physical contact sending sparks of fizzing electricity up and down her arm. 'Let me go, Vinn,' she said, trying to pull away.

His hold tightened to the point of pain. 'Don't go through with it, Gabriella,' he said in a strained sort of tone she had never heard him use before. 'He's not the right man for you.'

Pride made her put her chin up. 'Let me go,' she repeated, and, using her free hand, scraped the back of his hand with her nails.

He captured her other hand and pulled her up close—closer than she had ever been to him before. It was a shock to find how hard the wall of his chest was, and the latent power of his thighs pressed against her trembling body made her spine feel loose and watery all of a sudden.

His eyes were burning as they warred with hers. 'Call it off,' he said. 'Your parents will understand. It's not too late.'

She threw him an icy glare. 'If you don't let me go this instant I'll tell everyone you tried to assault me. You'll go to jail. Tristan's father will act for me in court. You won't have a leg to stand on.'

His mouth tightened, and she saw a pulse beating like a drum in his neck. 'Glendenning is only marrying you for your money,' he ground out.

Gabby was incensed, even though a tiny pinhole of doubt had already worn through the thick veil of denial she had stitched in place over the last few weeks of her engagement. 'You don't know what you're talking about,' she spat at him. 'Tristan loves me. I know he does.'

Vinn's hands were like handcuffs on her wrists. 'If it's marriage you want, then marry me. At least you'll know what you're getting.'

Gabby laughed in his face. 'Marry *you?*' She injected as much insult as she could into her tone. 'And spend the rest of my life like your mother did, scrubbing other people's houses? Thanks, but no thanks.'

'I won't let you go through with it, Gabriella,' he warned. 'If you don't call the wedding off tonight I will stand up during the ceremony tomorrow and tell the congregation why the marriage should not go ahead.'

'You wouldn't dare!'

His eyes challenged hers. 'You just watch me, Blondie,' he said. 'Do you want the whole of Sydney to know what sort of man you are marrying?'

She threw him a look of pure venom. 'I am going to make damned sure you're not even *at* my wedding,' she spat back at him. 'I'm going to speak to the security firm Dad has organised and have you banned from entry. I'm marrying Tristan tomorrow no matter what you say. I love him.'

'You don't know who or what you want right now,' he said, with a fast-beating pulse showing at the corner of his mouth. 'Damn it, Gabriella, you're only just twenty-one. Your brother's suicide has thrown you. It's thrown all of us. Your engagement was a knee-jerk reaction. For God's sake, a blind man could see it.'

The mention of her brother and his tragic death unleashed a spurt of anger Gabby had not been able to express out of respect for her shattered parents. It rose inside her like an explosion of lava, and with the sort of strength she had no idea she possessed, she tore herself out of his hold and delivered a stinging slap to his stubbly jaw. It must have hurt him, for her hand began to throb unbearably, all the delicate bones feeling as if they had been crushed by a house brick.

Time stood still for several heart-stopping seconds.

Something dangerous flickered in his grey-blue eyes, and then with a speed that knocked the breath right out of her lungs he pulled her into his crushing embrace, his hot, angry mouth coming down on hers…

Gabby had to shake herself back to the present. She hated thinking about that kiss. She hated remembering how she had so shamelessly responded to it. And she hated recalling the bracelet of fingertip bruises she had worn on her wedding day—as if Vinn Venadicci, in spite of her covert word to Security to keep him out of the church, had vicariously come along to mock her marriage to Tristan Glendenning anyway.

'Just tell me what you want and get it over with,' she

said now, with a flash of irritation, as she continued to face him combatively across the expanse of his desk.

'I want you to be my wife.'

Gabby wasn't sure what shocked her the most: the blunt statement of his intentions or the terrifying realisation she had no choice but to agree.

'That seems rather an unusual request, given the fact we hate each other and have always done so,' she managed to say, without—she hoped—betraying the flutter of her heart.

'You don't hate me, Gabriella,' he said with a sardonic smile. 'You just hate how I make you feel. It's always been there between us, has it not? The forbidden fruit of attraction: the rich heiress and the bad boy servant's son. A potent mix, don't you think?'

Gabby sent him a withering look. 'You are delusional, Vinn,' she said. 'I have never given you any encouragement to think anything but how much I detest you.'

He got to his feet and, glancing at his designer watch, informed her dispassionately, 'Time's up, Blondie.'

She gritted her teeth. 'I need more time to consider your offer,' she bit out.

'The offer is closing in less than thirty seconds,' he said with an indomitable look. 'Take or leave it.'

Frustration pushed Gabby to her feet. 'This is my father's life's work we're talking about here,' she said, her voice rising to an almost shrill level. 'He built up the St Clair Resort from scratch after that cyclone in the seventies. How can you turn your back on him after all he's done for you? Damn it, Vinn. You would be pacing the exercise yard at Pentridge Jail if it wasn't for what our family has done for you.'

His eyes were diamond-hard, the set to his mouth like carved granite. 'That is my price, Gabriella,' he said. 'Marriage or nothing.'

She clenched her hands into fists, her whole body shaking with impotent rage. 'You know I can't say no. You know it and you want to rub it in. You're only doing this because I rejected your stupid spur of the moment proposal seven years ago.'

He leaned towards the intercom on his desk and pressing the button, said calmly, 'Rachel? Is my next client here? Mrs Glendenning is just leaving.'

Gabby could see her father's hard-earned business slipping out of his control. He would have to sell the house—the house his parents and grandparents before him had lived in. Gabby could imagine the crushing disappointment etched on his face when she told him she had failed him, that she hadn't been able to keep things afloat as her brilliantly talented brother would have done. If Blair was still alive he would have net-worked and found someone to tide him over by now. He would have had that margin call solved with a quick call to one of his well-connected mates. That was the way he had worked. He had lived on the adrenalin rush of life while she... Well, that was the problem.

She couldn't cope.

She liked to know what was going to happen and when it was going to happen. She hated the cut and thrust of business, the endless going-nowhere meetings, the tedious networking at corporate functions—not to mention the reams of pointless paperwork. And most of all she hated the rows and rows of numbers that seemed more of a blur to her than anything else.

Gabby liked to… Well, there was no point in thinking about what she liked to do, because it just wasn't going to happen. Her dreams had had to be shelved and would remain shelved—at least until her father could take up the reins again… *If* he took up the reins again, she thought, with another deep quiver of panic.

Gabby had been the last person to speak to her brother; the last person to see him alive before he ended his life with a drug overdose. Because of that she had responsibilities to face. And face them she would. Even if they were totally repugnant to her. Being forced to marry a man like Vinn Venadicci was right up there on the repugnant scale. Or maybe repugnant wasn't quite the right word, she grudgingly conceded. Vinn was hardly what any woman would describe as physically off-putting. He was downright gorgeous, when it came down to it. That long, leanly muscled frame, that silky black hair, those sensually sculptured lips and those mesmerising eyes were enough to send any woman's heart aflutter—and Gabby's was doing a whole lot more than fluttering right now at the thought of being formally tied to him.

Entering into a marriage contract with Vinn was asking for trouble—but what else could she do? Who was going to lend her that amount of money in less than twenty-four hours?

Gabby gulped as she glanced at him again. Could she do it? Could she agree to marry him even though it was madness?

Actually, it was dangerous… Yes, that was the word she had been looking for. Vinn was dangerous. He was arrogant, he was a playboy, and—even more disturbing—he had a chip on his shoulder where she was concerned.

But she had nowhere else to turn—no other solution to fix this within the narrow timeframe. It was up to her to save her family's business, even if it meant agreeing to his preposterous conditions.

'All right,' Gabby said on a whooshing breath of resignation. 'I'll do it.'

'Fine,' Vinn said, in a tone that suggested he had never had any doubt of her accepting, which somehow made it all the more galling. 'The money will be deposited within the next few minutes. I will pick you up this evening for dinner, so we can go through the wedding arrangements.'

Gabby felt herself quake with alarm. 'Couldn't we just wait a few days until I have time to—?'

His cynical laugh cut her off. 'Until you have time to think of a way out, eh, Gabriella? I don't think so, *cara*. Now I have you I am not going to let you escape.'

'What am I supposed to say to my parents?' she asked, scowling at him even as her stomach did another nosedive of dread.

He smiled. 'Why not tell them you've finally come to your senses and agreed to marry me?'

She gave him another glare that would have stripped three decades of paint off a wall. 'They will think I have taken leave of my senses.'

'Or they will think you have fallen head over heels in love,' he said. 'Which is exactly what I would prefer them to believe at this point in time. Your father's health is unstable and will be for some weeks after the surgery, I imagine. I wouldn't want him to suffer a relapse out of concern for you or for his business.'

Gabby couldn't argue with that, but she resented him using it as a lever to get her to fall meekly in with his plans. 'I was planning on going to the hospital this evening,' she said tightly. 'Will I meet you there or at the house?'

'I have a couple of meetings that might string out, so if I don't make it to the hospital I will meet you at the house around eight-thirty,' he said. 'I would like to speak to your father at some point about my intentions.'

Gabby couldn't stop her top lip from curling. 'Somehow you don't strike me as the traditional type, asking a girl's father for her hand in marriage. In fact I didn't think you were the marrying type at all. All we ever read about you in the press is how you move from one relationship to another within a matter of weeks.'

He gave her another unreadable smile. 'Variety, as they say, is the spice of life,' he said. 'But even the most restless man eventually feels the need to put down some roots.'

She eyed him warily. 'This marriage between us…it's not for the long term…is it?'

'Only for as long as it achieves its aim,' he said—which Gabby realised hadn't really answered her question.

Vinn moved past her to hold the door open for her. 'I will see you tonight,' he said. 'I'll call you if I am going to be late.'

She brushed past him, her head at a proud angle. The subtle notes of her perfume danced around his face, making his nostrils flare involuntarily. She smelt of orange blossom. Or was it honeysuckle? He couldn't quite tell. Maybe it was both. That was the thing about Gabriella—she was a combination of so many things, any one of them alone was enough to send his senses spinning. But all of them put together? Well, that was half his problem, wasn't it?

The door clicked shut behind her and Vinn released the breath he'd unconsciously been holding. 'Damn,' he said, raking a hand through his hair. 'God damn it to hell.'

'Mr Venadicci?' His receptionist's cool, crisp voice sounded over the intercom. 'Mr Winchester is here now. Shall I send him in?'

Vinn pulled in an uneven breath and released it just as raggedly. 'Yeah…' he said, dropping his hand by his side. 'I'll see him. But tell him I've only got five minutes.'

CHAPTER TWO

GABBY put on her bravest face while she visited her
father's bedside. The tubes and heart monitor leads
attached to his grey-tinged body made her stomach
churn with anguish—the very same anguish she could
see played out on her mother's face.

'How are you, Dad?' she whispered softly as she
bent down to kiss his cheek.

'Still alive and kicking,' he said, and even managed
a lopsided grin, but Gabby could see the worry and fear
in his whisky-coloured eyes.

'Have the doctors told you anything more?' she
asked, addressing both her mother and father.

'The surgery is being brought forward to tomorrow,'
Pamela St Clair answered. 'Vinn spoke to the cardiac
surgeon and organised it when he was here earlier. He
insisted your father's case be made a priority. You just
missed him, actually. It's a wonder you didn't pass him
in the corridor.'

Gabby stiffened. 'Vinn was here just now?'

'Yes, dear,' her mother said. 'He's been here every
day. But you know that.'

'Yes… It's just I was speaking to him this morning

and he said he had meetings to attend all afternoon and evening,' she said, unconsciously biting her lip.

Her mother gave her a searching look. 'I hope you're not going to be difficult about Vinn,' she said, with a hint of reproof in her tone. 'He's been nothing but supportive, and the least you could do is be civil towards him—especially now.'

Gabby could have laughed out loud at the irony of her mother's turnaround. Pamela St Clair had always been of the old school, that actively discouraged fraternisation with any of the household staff. She had barely spoken to Vinn's mother during the years Rose had worked at the St Clair estate other than to hand Rose a long list of menial tasks to get through. She had been even less friendly towards Rose's surly son during the short time he had lived there with his mother. And after he'd had that slight run-in with the law Pamela had tried to ban him from the property altogether, but Gabby's father had insisted Vinn be allowed to visit his mother as usual.

Gabby hadn't been much better towards Rose— which was something she had come to sincerely regret in the years since. She still cringed in shame at how inconsiderate she had been at times, carelessly leaving her things about, without a care for the person who had to come along behind her and pick them up.

But it was Gabby's treatment of Vinn that had been the most unforgivable. She had been absolutely appalling to him for most of her teenage years—teasing him in front of her giggling friends, talking about him in disparaging terms well within his hearing. She had flirted with him, and then turned her nose up at him with disgraceful regularity. She had no excuse for her behaviour other than that she had been an insecure teenager, privately struggling with body issues, who, in an effort to build her self-esteem, had tended to mix with a rather shallow crowd of rich-kid friends who had not learned to respect people from less affluent backgrounds.

On one distressingly memorable occasion, at the urging of her troublemaking friends, Gabby had left an outrageously seductive note for Vinn, asking him to meet her in the summerhouse that evening. But instead of turning up she had watched from one of the top windows of the mansion, laughing with her friends at how he had arrived at the summerhouse with a bunch of white roses for her. What had shamed her most had been Vinn's reaction. Instead of bawling her out, calling her any one of the despicable names she had no doubt deserved, he had said nothing. Not to her, not to her parents, and not even to her brother Blair, whom he'd spent most of his spare time with whenever he had visited the estate.

Gabby's father reached out a weak hand towards her, the slight tremble of his touch bringing her back to the present. 'Vinn is a good man,' he said. 'I know you're still grieving the loss of Tristan, but I think you should seriously consider his proposal. You could do a lot worse. I know he's had a bit of a rough start, but he's done well for himself. No one could argue with that. I always knew he had the will-power and the drive to make it once he got on the right path. I'm glad he has chosen you as his bride. He will look after you well. I know he will.'

Gabby couldn't quite disguise her surprise that Vinn had already spoken to her father. She moistened her dry lips and tried on a bright smile, but it didn't feel comfortable on her mouth. 'So he's spoken to you about our...relationship?'

Her father smiled. 'I gave him my full blessing, Gabby. I must say I wasn't the least surprised to hear the news of your engagement.'

Gabby frowned. 'You...you weren't?

He shook his head and gave her hand another light squeeze. 'You've been striking sparks off each other since you were a teenager,' he said. 'For a time there I thought... Well...Blair's accident changed everything, of course.'

Gabby felt the familiar frustration that neither of her parents had ever accepted their only son's death as suicide. They still refused to acknowledge he had been dabbling with drugs—but then stubborn denial was a St Clair trait, and she had her own fair share of it.

'I'm glad you both approve,' she said, banking down her emotion. 'We are having dinner this evening to discuss the wedding arrangements.'

'Yes, he told us it wasn't going to be a grand affair,' her mother said. 'I think that's wise, under the circumstances. After all, it's your second marriage. It seems pointless going to the same fuss as last time.'

Gabby couldn't agree more. The amount of money spent on her marriage to Tristan Glendenning had been such a waste when within hours of the ceremony and lavish reception she had realised the terrible mistake she had made.

She stretched her mouth into another staged smile

and reached across to kiss both her parents. 'I'd better get going,' she said, readjusting her handbag over her shoulder. 'Is there anything you need before I go?'

'No, dear,' her mother assured her. 'Vinn brought some fruit and a couple of novels for your father to read by that author he enjoys so much. I must say Vinn's grown into a perfect gentleman. Your father is right. You could do a lot worse—especially as you're a widow. Not many men want a woman someone else has had, so to speak.'

Gabby silently ground her teeth. If only her mother knew the truth about her ill-fated first marriage. 'I'll see you tomorrow,' she said, and with another unnatural smile left.

The St Clair mansion was situated on the waterfront in the premier harbourside suburb of Point Piper, flanked on either side by equally luxurious homes for the super-rich and famous. The views across Sydney Harbour were spectacular, and the house and grounds offered a lifestyle that was decadent to say the least.

Gabby had moved back home two years ago, after Tristan's death in a car accident, and although now and again she had toyed with the idea of finding a place of her own, so far she had done nothing about doing so. The mansion was big enough for her to have the privacy she needed, and with her finances still on the shaky side, after the trail of debts her late husband had left behind, she had decided to leave things as they were for the time being.

The doorbell sounded right on the stroke of eight-thirty and Gabby was still not ready. Her straight ash-blonde hair was in heated rollers, to give it some much needed body, and she was still in her bathrobe after a shower.

She wriggled into a black sheath of a designer dress she'd had for years, and shoved her feet into three inch heels, all the time trying not to panic as another minute passed. She slashed some lipstick across her mouth and dusted her cheeks with translucent powder, giving her lashes a quick brush with a mascara wand before tugging at the rollers. Her hair cascaded around her shoulders in springy waves, and with a quick brush she was ready—or at least as ready as she could be under the circumstances. Which wasn't saying much…

Vinn checked his watch and wondered if he should use the key Henry had insisted he keep on him at all times. But just as he was searching for it on his keyring the door opened and Gabriella was standing there, looking as if she had just stepped off the catwalk. Her perfume drifted towards him, an exotic blend of summer blooms. Her normally straight hair was bouncing freely around her bare shoulders, the black halter neck dress showing off her slim figure to maximum advantage.

It had always amazed him how someone so slim could have such generous breasts without having to resort to any sort of enhancement. The tempting shadow of her cleavage drew his eyes like a magnet, and he had to fight to keep his eyes on her toffee-brown ones. She had made them all the more noticeable with the clever use of smoky eyeshadow and eyeliner, and her full and sensual lips were a glossy pink which was the same shade as that on her fingernails.

'I'll just get my wrap and purse,' she said, leaving the door open.

Vinn watched her walk over the marbled floor of the expansive foyer on killer heels, one of her hands adjusting her earrings before she scooped up a purse and silky wrap. She turned and came back towards him, her chin at the haughty angle he had always associated with her—even when she was a sulky fourteen-year-old, with braces on her teeth and puppy fat on her body.

'Shall we get this over with?' she said, as if they were about to face a hangman.

Vinn had to suppress his desire to make her eat her carelessly slung words. She meant to insult him, and would no doubt do so at every opportunity, but he had the upper hand now and she would have to toe the line. It would bring him immense pleasure to tame her—especially after what her fiancé had done to him on the day of their wedding on her behalf. The scar over his left eyebrow was a permanent reminder of what lengths she would go to in order to have her way. But things were going to be done his way this time around, and the sooner she got used to it the better.

He led the way to his car and opened the passenger door for her, closing it once she was inside with the seatbelt in place. He waited until they were heading towards the city before he spoke.

'Your parents were surprisingly positive about our decision to marry—your mother in particular. I was expecting her to drop into a faint at the thought of her daughter hooking up with a fatherless foreigner, but she practically gushed in gratefulness that someone had put up their hand to scoop you off the shelf, so to speak.'

Gabby sent him a brittle look. 'Must you be so insulting?' she asked. 'And by the way—not that I'm splitting hairs or anything—but it wasn't exactly *our* plan to get married, it was yours.'

He gave an indifferent lift of one shoulder. 'There is no point arguing about the terms now the margin call has been dealt with,' he said. 'I have always had a lot of time for your father, but your mother has always been an out-and-out snob who thinks the measure of a man is what's in his wallet.'

'Yes, well, it's practically the only thing you've got going for *you*,' she shot back with a scowl.

He laughed as he changed gears. 'What's in my wallet has just got you and your family out of a train-load of trouble, *cara,* so don't go insulting me, hmm? I might take it upon myself to withdraw my support— and then where will you be?'

Gabby turned her head away, looking almost sightlessly at the silvery skyscrapers of the city as they flashed past. He was right of course. She would have to curb her tongue, otherwise he might renege on the deal. It would be just the kind of thing he would do, and relish every moment of doing it. Although it went against everything she believed in to pander to a man she loathed with every gram of her being, she really didn't see she had any choice in the matter. Vinn had the power to make or break her; she had to remember that.

She had never thought it was possible to hate someone so much. Her blood was thundering through her veins with the sheer force of it. He was so arrogant, so very self-assured. Against all the odds he had risen above his impoverished background and was using his new-found power to control her. But she was not going to give in without a fight. He might make her his wife, but it would be in name only.

Not that she would tell him just yet, of course. That would be the card up her sleeve she would reveal only once the ceremony was over. Vinn would be in for a surprise to find his new wife was not prepared to sleep with him. She would be a trophy wife—a gracious hostess, who would say the right things in the right places, and smile and act the role of the devoted partner in public if needed—but in private she would be the same Gabby who had left the score of her nails on the back of his hand the night before her wedding.

The restaurant he had booked was on the waterfront, and the night-time view over the harbour was even more stunning, with the twinkling of lights from the various tour ferries and floating restaurants. The evening air was sultry and warm, heavy with humidity, as if there was a storm brewing in the atmosphere.

Gabby walked stiffly by Vinn's side, suffering the light touch of his hand beneath her elbow as he escorted her inside the award-winning restaurant. The head waiter greeted Vinn with deference, before leading the way to a table in a prime position overlooking the fabulous views.

'Have you ever dined here before?' Vinn asked, once they were seated and their starched napkins were expertly draped over their laps.

Gabby shook her head and glanced at the drinks menu. 'No, I haven't been out all that much lately.'

'Have you dated anyone since your husband died?' he asked, with what appeared to be only casual interest.

She still looked at the menu rather than face his gaze. 'It's only been two years,' she said curtly. 'I'm in no hurry.'

'Do you miss him?'

Gabby put the menu down and looked at Vinn in irritation. 'What sort of a question is that?' she asked. 'We were married for five years.' *Five miserably unhappy years.* But she could hardly tell him that. She hadn't even told her parents.

She hadn't told anyone. Who was there to tell? She had never been particularly good at friendships; her few girlfriends had found Tristan boorish and overbearing, and each of them had gradually moved on, with barely an e-mail or a text to see how she was doing. Gabby knew it was mostly her fault for constantly covering for her husband's inadequacies. She had become what the experts called an enabler, a co-dependant. Tristan had been allowed to get away with his unspeakable behaviour because she had not been able to face the shame of facing up to the mistake she had made in marrying him. As a result she had become an adept liar, and, although it was painful to face it, she knew she had only herself to blame.

'You didn't have children,' Vinn inserted into the silence. 'Was that your choice or his?'

'It wasn't something we got around to discussing,' she said, as she inspected the food menu with fierce concentration.

The waiter came and took their order for drinks. Gabby chose a very rich cocktail—more for Dutch courage than anything. It was what she felt she needed just now: a thick fog of alcohol to survive an evening in Vinn's company.

Vinn, on the other hand, ordered a tall glass of iced mineral water—a well-known Italian brand, she noticed.

'You'd better go easy on that drink of yours, Gabriella,' he cautioned as she took a generous mouthful. 'Drinking on an empty stomach is not wise. Alcohol has a well-known disinhibitory effect on behaviour. You might find yourself doing things you wouldn't normally do.'

She gave him a haughty look. 'You mean like enjoying your company instead of loathing every minute of it?'

His grey-blue eyes gave a flame-like flash. 'You will enjoy a whole lot more than just my company before the ink on our marriage certificate is dry,' he said.

Gabby took another gulping swallow of her drink to disguise her discomfiture. Her stomach felt quivery all of a sudden. The thought of his hands and mouth on her body was making her feel as if she had taken on much more than she had bargained for. She had held Tristan off for years—except for that one horrible night when he had… She swallowed another mouthful of her drink, determined not to think of the degradation she had suffered at her late husband's hands.

'You have gone rather pale,' Vinn observed. 'Is the thought of sharing my bed distasteful to you?'

Gabby was glad she had her glass to hide behind, although the amount of alcohol she had consumed *had* gone alarmingly to her head. Or perhaps it was his disturbing presence. Either way, she didn't trust herself to speak and instead sent him another haughty glare.

'That kiss we shared seven years ago certainly didn't suggest you would find my lovemaking abhorrent—anything but. You were hungry for it, Gabriella. I found that rather interesting, since the following day you married another man.'

'You *forced* yourself on me,' she hissed at him in an undertone, on account of the other diners close by.

'Forced is perhaps too strong a word to use, but in any case you responded wholeheartedly,' he said. 'Not just with those soft full lips of yours, but with your tongue as well. And if I recall even your teeth got into the act at one point. I'm getting hard now, just thinking about it.'

Gabby had never felt so embarrassed in her entire life. Her face felt as if someone had aimed a blowtorch at her. But even more disturbing was the thought of his body stirring with arousal *for her*—especially with those powerful thighs of his within touching distance of hers.

'Your recollection has obviously been distorted over time, for I can barely remember it,' she said with a toss of her head.

His eyes glinted smoulderingly. 'Then perhaps I should refresh your memory,' he said. 'No doubt there will be numerous opportunities to do so once we are living together as man and wife.'

Gabby had to fight to remain calm, but it was almost impossible to control the stuttering of her heart and the flutter of panic deep and low in her belly. 'When do you plan for this ridiculous farce to commence?' she asked, with fabricated quiescence.

'Our marriage will not be a farce,' he said, with a determined set to his mouth. 'It will be real in every sense of the word.'

Her eyes widened a fraction before she could counter it. 'Is that some sort of sick habit of yours? Sleeping with someone you dislike?'

'You are a very beautiful woman, Gabriella,' he said. 'Whether I like you or not is beside the point.'

Gabby wanted to slap that supercilious smile off his face. She sat with her hands clenched in her lap, her eyes shooting sparks of fury at him. But more disturbing was the way her body was responding to his smoothly delivered sensual promises. She could feel a faint trembling between her thighs, like a tiny pulse, and her breasts felt full and tight, her nipples suddenly sensitive against the black fabric of her dress.

'I'm prepared to marry you, but that's as far as it goes,' she said with a testy look. 'It's totally barbaric of you to expect me to agree to a physical relationship with you.'

'Aren't you forgetting something?' he asked. 'Two point four million dollars is a high price for a bride, and I expect to get my money's worth.'

She sucked in a rasping breath. 'This is outrageous! It's akin to prostitution.'

'You came to me for help, Gabriella, and I gave it to you,' he said. 'I was totally up-front about the terms, so there is no point in pretending to be shocked about them now.'

'But what about the woman you were seeing a month or so ago?' Gabby asked, recalling a photograph she had seen in the 'Who's-Out-and-About?' section of one of the Sydney papers. An exquisitely beautiful woman gazing up at Vinn adoringly.

He gave her a supercilious smile. 'So you have

been keeping a close eye on my love life, have you, *mia piccola?*'

She glowered at him darkly. 'I have absolutely no interest in who you see. But if we are to suffer a short-term marriage, the very least you could do is keep your affairs out of the press.'

'I don't recall saying our marriage was going to be a short-term one,' he said with an inscrutable smile. 'Far from it.'

Gabby felt her heart give a kick-like movement against the wall of her chest. 'W-what?' she gasped.

'I have always held the opinion that marriage should be for life,' he said. 'I guess you could say it stems from my background. My mother was abandoned by the man she loved while she had a baby on the way. She had no security, no husband to provide for her, and as a result she went on to live a hard life of drudgery—cleaning other people's houses to keep food on the table and clothes on our backs. I swore from an early age that when it came time for me to settle down I would do so with permanence in mind.'

'But you don't even *like* me!' she blurted in shock. 'How could you possibly contemplate tying yourself to me for the rest of your life?'

'Haven't you got any mirrors at your house any more, *mia splendida ragazza?*' he asked, with another smouldering look. 'I do not have to like you to lust over you. And isn't that what every wife wants? A husband with an unquenchable desire for her and her alone?'

Gabby swallowed back her panic, but even so she felt as if she was choking on a thick uneven lump of it. 'You're winding me up. I know you are. This is your idea of a sick joke. And let me tell you, I am not finding it the least bit amusing.'

'I am not joking, Gabriella,' he said. 'Love is generally an overrated emotion—or at least I have found it to be so. People fall in and out of love all the time. But some of the most successful marriages I know are those built on compatibility in bed—and, believe you me, you don't need to be in love with someone to have an earth-shattering orgasm with them.'

Gabby felt her face explode with colour, and was never more grateful for the reappearance of the waiter to take their meal orders.

Hearing Vinn speak of…that word…*that experience*…made her go hot all over. She had never experienced pleasure with her late husband. The one time Tristan had taken it upon himself to assert "his manly duty", as he had euphemistically called it, he had left her not cold, but burning with pain and shame.

Once the waiter had left, Gabby drained the rest of her cocktail, beyond caring that it had made her head spin. No amount of alcohol could affect her more than Vinn had already done, she decided. Her body was tingling all over with sensation, and her mind was running off at wayward tangents, imagining what it would feel like to be crushed by the solid weight of his body, his sensual mouth locked on hers, one of his strong, hair-roughened thighs nudging hers apart to—

She jerked away from her thoughts, annoyed that she had allowed his potent brand of sensuality to get under her guard. What on earth was she thinking? He was the enemy. She knew exactly what he was doing and why. He was only marrying her to get back at her for how she had treated him in the past. He knew it would be torture for her to be tied to him. Why else would he insist on it? Never had she regretted her immature behaviour more than this moment. Why, oh why, had she been so shallow and cruel?

Gabby's older brother Blair had often pulled her up for her attitude towards Vinn, but in a way his relationship with Vinn had been a huge part of the problem. She had felt *jealous* that her adored older brother clearly preferred the company of the cleaner's son to hers. Gabby had resented the way Blair spent hours helping Vinn with his studies when he could have been spending time with her, the way he'd used to do before Vinn had arrived with his mother.

When Gabby had accidentally stumbled upon the realisation that Vinn suffered from dyslexia she had cruelly taunted him with it, mocking him for not being able to read the most basic of texts. But for some reason, just as he had when she had led him on so despicably that hot summer afternoon when she was sixteen, Vinn had never spoken to her brother or her parents about her behaviour. He had taken it on the chin, removing himself from her presence without a word, even though she had sensed the blistering anger in him, simmering just below the surface of his steely outward calm.

Gabby could sense that anger still simmering now, in the way he looked at her from beneath that slightly hooded brow. Those grey-blue eyes were like mysteriously deep mountain lakes, icy cold one minute, warm and inviting the next, and they spoke of a man who had nothing but revenge on his mind.

She had seen the way women were looking at him. He had such arrestingly handsome features, and his presence was both commanding and brooding—as if he was calculating his next move, like a champion chess player, prepared to take as long as he needed to move his king, making his opponent sit it out in gut-wrenching apprehension.

Gabby felt another shiver of unease pass through her at the thought of being married to him. He had said he expected their marriage to be permanent. That meant there were issues to consider: children, for one thing. She was twenty-eight years old, and she would be lying if she said she hadn't heard the relentless ticking of her biological clock in the two years since Tristan had died. Children had not been an option while she had been married to him. She would *never* have brought children into such a relationship. She hadn't even brought a pet into the house in case he had used it against her in one of his violent moods.

'You have gone very quiet, Gabriella,' Vinn observed. 'Is the thought of having an orgasm with me too hard for you to handle?'

She gave him a withering look. 'No, in actual fact I find it hard to believe it possible,' she said. 'I can't speak for the legion of women you've already bedded, but I personally am unable to engage in such an intimate act without some engagement of emotion.'

He gave a deep chuckle of laughter. 'How about hate?' he asked, reaching for his mineral water. 'Is that enough emotion to get you rolling?'

She put down her glass and signalled for the waiter to refill it.

'Do you think that is wise?' Vinn asked. 'The amount of alcohol in that drink is enough to cloud anyone's judgement.'

Gabby put up her chin. 'In the absence of the engagement of emotion, alcohol and a great deal of it is the next best thing,' she said.

His eyes narrowed to grey-blue stormy slits. 'If you think I will bed you while you are under the influence, think again,' he said. 'When we come together for the first time I want you stone-cold sober, so you remember every second of it.'

Gabby put her glass down with a sharp little clunk. 'I am *not* going to sleep with you, Vinn,' she said, and hoisting up her chin even higher, added imperiously, 'For *that* privilege you will have to pay double.'

Vinn smiled a victor's smile as he reached inside his jacket for his chequebook. He laid it on the table between them, and the click of his pen made Gabby's spine jerk upright, as if she had been shot with a pellet from the gold-embossed barrel.

'Double, you said?'

Gabby felt her stomach drop. Her mouth went dry and her palms moistened. 'Um…I…I'm not sure. I…this…it…I…don't…*Oh, my God…*'

He wrote the amount in his distinctive scrawl, the dark slash of his signature making Gabby's eyes almost pop out of their sockets. 'There,' he said, tearing off the cheque from the book and placing it in front of her on the table. 'Do we have a deal or not?'

CHAPTER THREE

GABBY looked at the amount written there and felt a shockwave of so many emotions rocketing through her that she felt her face fire up. Each one of them stoked the furnace, although shame had by far the most fuel. But then anger joined in; she could feel it blazing out of control, and not just on her cheeks, but deep inside, where a cauldron of heat was bubbling over, making her veins hot with rage.

Vinn had deliberately made her feel like a high-end prostitute—a woman who would do anything for a price. But Gabby wasn't going to be bought. She had been a fool before where a man was concerned, allowing duty and blinkered emotions to cloud her judgement. This time things would be different. If Vinn Venadicci thought he could lure her between the sheets of his bed with a bank vault full of dollar bills, he was in for a big surprise.

With a coolness she was nowhere near feeling, Gabby picked up the cheque and, with the tip of her tongue peeping through her lips as she concentrated, she folded it, fold by meticulous fold, until she had made a tiny origami ship. She held it in the palm of her hand for a moment as she inspected it, and once she was satisfied she had Vinn's full attention she reached for the glass of full-bodied red wine the waiter had recently set down beside him. She dropped her handiwork in, watching in satisfaction as it floated for a second or two, until the density of the wine gradually soaked through the paper and submerged it halfway below the surface.

Gabby met Vinn's grey-blue gaze across the table with an arch look. 'I was going to say you could put your cheque in your pipe and smoke it, but then I realised you don't smoke.' She smiled a cat's smile and added, *'Salute.'*

Vinn's lips twitched, but even so his eyes still burned with determination. 'You might like me to swallow my offer, but I can guarantee you are going to be the one eating your words in the not so distant future, *cara*,' he warned her silkily.

She rolled her eyes and picked up her second cocktail. 'I will go as far as marrying you to save my family's business, but I am not going to be your sex slave, Vinn. If you have the urge to satisfy your needs I am sure there are plenty of women out there who will gladly oblige. All I ask is for you to be discreet.'

He leaned back in his chair and surveyed her features for a beat or two. 'Is that the arrangement you made with your late husband?' he asked. 'Or did you see to his needs quite willingly all by yourself?'

Gabby felt her heart come to a shuddering standstill, her face heating to boiling point. 'That is none of your business,' she bit out. 'I refuse to discuss my marriage to Tristan with you, of all people.'

Vinn's top lip curled in an insolent manner. 'Did he satisfy you, Gabriella? Did he make you writhe and scream? Or did he satisfy you in other ways by lavishing you with the worldly goods women like you crave?'

Gabby's hand tightened around her cocktail glass as she fought to control the bewildering combination of shame and anger that roiled through her. She hadn't thought it possible to hate someone as much as she hated Vinn. She didn't want to examine too closely why she hated him so much, but she suspected it had something to do with the way he looked at her in that penetrating way of his. Those intelligent eyes saw things she didn't want anyone to see. He had done it all those years ago, and he was doing it now.

She forced her tense shoulders to relax and, loosening her white-knuckled grip on her glass, brought it to her mouth and took a sip. 'What about *your* love-life, Vinn?' she asked, with a pert set to her mouth. 'Who's your latest squeeze? Are you still seeing that chainstore model or has she reached her use-by date?'

Vinn used his fork to retrieve the sunken boat of his cheque out of his glass before he trained his gaze on hers. 'Have you been taking extra classes in bitchiness, Gabriella, or is it that time of the month?'

Gabby knew she shouldn't do it, but even as the mature and sensible part of her brain considered the repercussions, the outraged part had already acted.

It seemed to happen in slow motion. The strawberry daiquiri in her glass moved in a fluid arc and splashed across the front of Vinn's shirt.

Time didn't just stand still; it came to a screeching, rubber burning, tyre-balding halt.

Gabby waited for the fall-out. Her body grew tense, her blood raced, her heart thumped. But in the end all Vinn did was laugh.

'Is that the best you can do, Gabriella?' he asked, still smiling mockingly. 'To toss your drink across the table like a recalcitrant three-year-old child?'

'If you are expecting me to apologise, then forget it. Because I'm not going to,' she said with a petulant glare.

He put the soiled napkin to one side. 'No,' he said, still smiling in that enigmatic way of his that unnerved her so. 'I wasn't expecting you to apologise now. I am looking forward to making you do so later, when we are not sitting in the middle of a crowded restaurant. And believe me, Gabriella, it will be a lot of fun making you do it.'

Gabby felt a moth-like flutter of apprehension sweep over the floor of her belly. She had faced numerous rages from Tristan in the past, but for some reason Vinn's cool, calm control was far more terrifying. But then Vinn had always been cool and controlled. Even when she had taunted him in the past he had taken it on the chin, looking down at her with those unreadable grey-blue eyes. Perhaps that was why he had become so successful over the years? He knew how to play people like some people played cards, and Gabby had a feeling he had just put down a hand that was going to be impossible for her to beat.

'Is everything all right, Signor Venadicci?' The *maître d'* came bustling over.

'Everything is perfectly all right, thank you, Paolo,' Vinn said with an urbane smile. 'My fiancée had a slight accident.'

'Oh, dear,' Paolo said, and quickly tried to make amends. 'Let me get the young lady another drink—on the house, of course. And send me the bill for the cleaning of your shirt. I am sure the table is rickety, or something. I have asked my staff to check, but you know how hard it is to keep track of everyone all the time.'

'It is fine—really,' Vinn said, rising to his feet. 'We are leaving in any case.'

Gabby was half in and half out of her chair, not sure what she should do. They hadn't even been served their meals and she was starving. She had missed lunch, and already she could feel a headache pounding at the backs of her eyes.

'Leaving?' Paolo said, looking aghast. 'But what about your food?'

'I am sorry, Paolo,' Vinn said. 'Could we have our meals packaged to take back to my house instead? My fiancée has had rather a tough day, and I think she needs an early night.'

'But of course, Signor Venadicci,' Paolo said, and quickly signalled to his waiting staff to see to it straight away. 'Congratulations on your engagement,' he added, smiling widely at Gabby. 'Such wonderful news. You are a very lucky woman. Signor Venadicci is…how you say in English? A big catch?'

'Yes,' Gabby said with saccharine-sweetness. 'He is a big catch. Just like a shark.'

Vinn grasped her by the arm and practically frog-marched her out of the restaurant, only stopping long enough at the front counter to collect their take-out meals.

'You can let go of my arm now,' she said, once they were on the street outside.

Vinn kept pulling her along towards his car, not even bothering to shorten his much longer stride to accommodate hers. 'You, young lady, need a lesson in manners. You have acted like a spoilt child. You didn't just embarrass yourself, but each and every person in that restaurant—not to mention Paolo, who always bends over backwards to please his diners. You should be ashamed of yourself.'

Gabby gave him a surly look as she tugged ineffectually at his hold. 'You started it.'

He aimed a remote control at his car. 'I asked you a question about your last marriage,' he said, opening the door for her. 'A yes or no answer would have done.'

She sent him a venomous glare. 'I don't have to answer any of your stupid questions, about my marriage or any of my relationships,' she threw at him.

'I can tell you one thing, Gabriella,' he said as he wrenched the seatbelt down for her with a savagery that was unnerving. 'Once we are married you will have no other relationships. Or at least none with a male.'

Gabby sat stiffly in her seat, trying to control her sudden and totally unexpected urge to cry. She had become very good at concealing her emotions. She had never given Tristan the satisfaction of seeing her break emotionally. Why she should feel so close to the edge now was not only bewildering but terrifying.

She couldn't allow Vinn to see how undone she was. He would relish in the power he had over her. He already had too much power over her—far more than Tristan Glendenning had ever had, in spite of all she had suffered at his hands. How could she afford to let her guard down even for a second? Especially given how she had treated Vinn in the past? Vinn had every reason to bring her down, to make her grovel, to grind what was left of her pride to dust. She had just enough self-respect to keep that from happening.

Not much…but just enough.

Vinn drove his powerful car across the Harbour Bridge to the North Shore suburb of Mosman. Each thrusting gear-change he executed set Gabby's teeth on edge, and another icy shiver of unease scuttled up her spine at the thought of a showdown with him on his own territory. In the crowded restaurant it had been safe to spar with him, or so she had thought. But being alone with him was something she wasn't quite prepared for and wondered if she ever would be.

He turned the car into a beautiful tree-lined street of the sort of homes owned by people with more than just comfortable wealth. Lush gardens, harbour views and stately mansions, with the mandatory fortress-like security that ensured a private haven away from the rest of the world. They indicated Vinn had made his way in the world and wasn't ashamed about taking his place in it amongst others who had done similarly—either by sheer hard work or the inheritance of a family fortune.

The driveway he turned into after activating a remote control device revealed a modern caramel-coloured mansion with a three-tiered formal garden at the front. Gabby could see the high fence of a tennis court in the background, and heard the sound of a trickling fountain close by. The heady scent of purple wisteria was heavy in the air, and so too was the more subtle fragrance of night-scented stocks, growing in profusion in a bed that ran alongside the boundary of the property.

She breathed in the clove-like smell, wondering if Vinn had somehow remembered they were one of her favourite flowers. She loved the variety of colours, the way the thick stalks didn't always stand up straight, and how the individual clusters of blossom maintained their scent right to the last. And yet perversely, if housed in a vase indoors, the water they sat in became almost fetid, as if those stately and proud blooms resented being confined.

Vinn unlocked the front door and indicated for her to precede him, which Gabby did with an all-encompassing sweep of her gaze. The marbled foyer was not in the least as ostentatious as she had been expecting. Even the works of art on the walls spoke of individual taste rather than an attempt to belong to a particularly highbrow club of art appreciation.

One painting in particular drew her eye: it was of a small child, a boy, looking at a shell on the seashore, his tiny limbs in a crouched position, his gaze focussed on the shell in his hands as if it contained all the mysteries of the world. Gabby peered at the right-hand corner of the canvas but she couldn't make out the signature.

'You don't recognise the artist?' Vinn said from just behind her left shoulder.

Gabby shivered at his closeness, but, schooling her features, faced him impassively, taking a careful step backwards to create some distance. 'No,' she said. 'Should I?'

His gaze was trained on the canvas, his mouth set in a grim line. 'Probably not,' he said. 'He was always a little embarrassed about his desire to paint. This is the only one I managed to convince him not to destroy.' He paused for a moment before adding, 'I believe it is one of the last works he did before he died.'

'Oh…' Gabby said renewing her focus on the painting. 'Was he very old?'

'No,' Vinn said. 'But then he wasn't the first and I dare say won't be the last artist to succumb to deep-seated insecurities about his talent. It more or less comes with the territory. Being creative can be both a blessing and a burden, or so I have heard people say.'

'Yes…I suppose so…'Gabby answered, still look-ing at the painting, which for some inexplicable reason had moved her so much.

Perhaps it was because looking at that small in-nocent child made her think longingly of having her own precious baby one day, she thought. Unlike most of her peers, she had never been interested in pursuing a demanding career. For years all she had dreamed of was holding a baby of her own in her arms, watching him or her grow into teenage, and then adulthood, just as her parents had done with her and Blair.

'We have some things to discuss,' Vinn said, and gestured for her to follow him to the large lounge room off the wide hall.

Gabby took an uneven breath and followed him into a stylishly appointed room. Two large black leather sofas sat either side of a fireplace—the shiny black marble mantelpiece and surround in a smaller room would have been too much, but not in this room. An ankle-deep rug in a black and gold design softened the masculine feel, as did the vintage lamps sitting on the art deco side tables. A large ottoman doubled as a coffee table, and a state-of-the-art music and entertainment system was cleverly concealed behind a drop-down console.

'It's a nice room,' Gabby said as she perched on the edge of one of the sofas. 'In fact the whole house is lovely. Have you lived here long?'

Vinn leaned his hip against the armrest of the opposite sofa. 'Well, what do you know?' he drawled. 'A compliment from the high and mighty Gabriella St Clair.'

Gabby screwed up her mouth at him. 'Glendenning,' she corrected him, even though she loathed her married name for all it had represented. 'My surname is still Glendenning.'

Something gleamed in Vinn's eyes as they collided with hers. 'But not for much longer,' he said. 'I have already seen to the notice. Shortly we will be husband and wife and living here as such.'

Gabby got to her feet in an agitated manner. 'I don't see what the rush is for,' she said, pacing the floor. 'What are people going to think?'

'For god's sake, Gabriella,' he said, with a flash of impatience in his tone. 'You've been a widow for two years.'

She turned around to look at him. 'Yes…but to suddenly be with you seems…well, it seems…almost indecent,' she said. 'People will think it's a shotgun marriage or something.'

He came over to where she was standing with her arms folded tightly across her chest. She considered moving sideways, but as if he knew she was looking for an escape route he placed both of his hands either side of her head on the wall behind, effectively trapping her.

Gabby felt her eyes flare with panic. She wasn't used to being so close to him. This close, she could smell the tangy lemon of his aftershave. She could even see the regrowth of stubble on his jaw, making her fingers twitch to reach up and feel if it was as raspy and masculine as it looked. She could see the deep-water-blue of his eyes with their grey shadows locked on hers. The line of his mouth was firm, but soft at the same time, making her wonder if his kiss would be just as enthralling as it had been seven years ago.

'You know, Gabriella,' he said in a low velvet tone, 'we could do something about that right here and now.'

Gabby's throat tightened as his body brushed against hers. She felt the stirring of his erection, a heady reminder of all that was different between them. He was so experienced, while she was…well, perhaps not exactly inexperienced, but way out of his class. Her body was not tutored in giving and receiving pleasure. She was totally inadequate, lacking in both confidence and skill.

Gabby was in no doubt of Vinn's attraction for her. If she was honest with herself she had been aware of it for years. It was like an electric current that throbbed in the air every time they were in the same room together. She wasn't sure if other people were aware of it, although Tristan had commented on it in his scathing way more than once.

Gabby knew it was just a physical thing on Vinn's part. Men were like that. Especially men like Vinn, who were used to having any woman who took their fancy. He was only attracted to Gabby because for so many years she had been unattainable. She was the daughter of a rich man, while he was the bastard son of a strapped-for-cash house-cleaner. The only trouble was he was prepared to go to unbelievable lengths to have her, even after all this time.

And that he was determined to have her in every sense of the word was as clear as the jagged scar that interrupted the dark slash of his left eyebrow. Apparently he had received it in a drunken brawl the night before her wedding to Tristan. Though it had only been after she'd come back from their honeymoon that Gabby's mother had told her how Vinn had spent a night in hospital after becoming involved in a punch-up. Given their heated exchange that night, Gabby suspected he had gone out to get himself trashed and had ended up in a street brawl—as he had done several times during his early twenties.

'So what do you say, Gabriella?' Vinn said, one of his strong thighs nudging between hers suggestively, temptingly, and oh, so spine-tinglingly. 'We could make a baby right here and now, and then it would indeed be a shotgun marriage.'

Gabby's stomach hollowed. Her legs felt like waterlogged noodles—too soggy to keep her upright. Her heart was racing, but not with any sort of predictable rhythm. Every second beat or so felt as if it was just off the mark, making her feel light-headed. Her unruly mind was suddenly filled with images—disturbing, toe-curling images—of his body pumping with purpose into the tight cocoon of hers, nudging her womb, filling it with his life force, his cells meshing with hers to create a new life.

Somehow she managed to activate her voice, but it sounded as if it had come from somewhere deep inside

her, croaky, rusty and disjointed. 'I—I'm not interested in…having a child,' she said. 'Not with you.'

'I am not going to settle for a childless marriage,'
he said. 'I have paid a high price for you, Gabriella.
As part of that heavy financial commitment I expect a
return on my investment.'

Gabby shoved him away, both of her hands flat on
his rock-hard chest. 'Then you've bought the wrong
bride,' she flashed at him angrily. 'It's bad enough that
you want this arrangement to be permanent, but to
want children as well is nothing short of ludicrous.'

'I never said anything to suggest this wasn't going
to be a proper marriage,' he said. 'Two point four
million dollars is not pin money, Gabriella. A divorce
could turn out to be even more expensive—although I
have that covered with my legal advisors. Tomorrow
you will sign a prenuptial agreement that will ensure
the only benefit you will receive if our marriage does
for some reason fail will be an income to pay for your
manicures and the highlights in your hair.'

Gabby was almost beyond rage. Her whole body
felt as if it was going to explode with it. She wanted
to pummel him with her fists; she wanted to scratch at
his face, to make him feel some small measure of the
pain she was feeling.

Vinn made her feel like a shallow socialite who had
nothing better to do with her time that have her nails filed
and her hair bleached. But she was so much more than
that. She hadn't been before, but after the death of her
brother—not to mention the five years of her marriage
to Tristan Glendenning, had taught her how shallow her
life had been and how much she had wanted it to change.

And she *had* changed.

She had changed in so many ways. Not all of them were visible, but they were changes she was still working on daily. Taking up the reins of her father's company was something she hadn't really had much choice over, but she wasn't a quitter and would see it through—as Blair surely would have done if his personal issues hadn't got in the way.

Thinking about her brother always stirred the long-handled spoon of guilt in her stomach, its churning action making her feel sick with anguish. If only she had known about his drug use she might have been able to help him before it was too late. But he had preferred to face death than his family's disappointment, and she would always blame herself for her part in that.

She resumed her seat on the cloud-soft sofa, her trembling hands stuffed between her equally unsteady thighs, fighting not to show how close to breaking she was. No doubt Vinn would relish that. He would be silently gloating over finally breaking her spirit.

She was trapped.

The steel bars of her guilt had closed around her with a clanging, chilling finality. Vinn had all the power now, and would wield it as he saw fit. He had insisted on marriage—but not the sort of hands-off arrangement she had naively thought he'd had in mind. She had no hope of repaying the money he had put up to save her father's business. It would take her two lifetimes to scrape together even half of that amount. Vinn had known that from the very first moment she had stepped into his office. He had played her like a master, reeling her in, keeping his cards close to his chest as was his custom, revealing them only when it was too late for her to do anything to get out of the arrangement.

It *was* too late.

She was going to be Vinn Venadicci's wife; the only trouble was he had no idea what sort of bride he had just bought. He had paid a huge price, but she was going to be a disappointment.

Of that she was heart-wrenchingly sure.

CHAPTER FOUR

VINN was still leaning on the edge of the sofa, silently watching the myriad moods pass over Gabriella's face. He was well used to seeing anger, rebellion and petulance there; even the bright sheen of moisture in her toffee-brown eyes was something he was used to witnessing. But whether or not those tears were genuine was something he wasn't prepared to lay a bet on.

She was a devious little madam. He had suffered at her hands too many times to let his guard down now. He wasn't going to give an inch until the papers were signed and she was legally his wife—in name if not yet in body.

He could wait.

He had waited for seven years. He figured waiting a little longer would only increase the pleasure of finally possessing her.

As soon as he had set eyes on her all those years ago he had been struck almost dumb by how beautiful she was. He had watched her blossom from an uncertain and overweight girl of fourteen into a young woman on the threshold of full adulthood. She had grown into an exquisitely beautiful young woman by the time she was sixteen years old, with those wide Bambi eyes and her lusciously thick blonde hair a striking contrast to her darker eyebrows and sooty black lashes. Her full lips were cherry-red, and plump and soft with sensual promise. By the time she was seventeen her teasing smile and come-hither looks had tortured him by day and kept him writhing in frustration in bed at night with the thought of one day possessing her. But even though his body had throbbed with longing he had known it would take nothing short of a miracle to bring about her capitulation.

Gabriella St Clair was out of his league. Vinn had known it, although he had never really accepted it.

Blair St Clair had in his quiet, polite way gently hinted at it, and Gabriella's parents—particularly her mother, Pamela—had communicated it without pulling any punches. It had been made perfectly clear to Vinn that Gabriella's future lay with Tristan Glendenning, an up-and-coming lawyer from a long line of legal eagles, primed to be a partner in a big city firm once he settled down to marriage to his mother's best friend's daughter.

The thing that sickened Vinn the most was that he had never believed Gabriella had truly been in love with her husband—which in itself showed how shallow she was. She couldn't have been in love with Glendenning after the way she had responded to Vinn outside the bathroom the night before her wedding.

She had clung to him feverishly, her soft lips opening to the pressure of his, her tongue darting into his mouth, tasting him, teasing him, duelling with him in a totally carnal explosion of passion that had left them both panting and breathless. Vinn's hands had uncovered her breasts and shaped them worshipfully, relishing in the creamy softness of them, and she had done nothing to stop him, rather had whimpered and gasped in delight with each touch of his hands, lips and tongue.

Her hands had reached down and cupped the aching bulk of his manhood, stroking him, torturing him until he'd been fit to burst. He would have thrust her up against the nearest wall and driven into her right then and there if it hadn't been for the sound of a footfall on the staircase, and Tristan Glendenning's private academy-tutored voice calling out.

'Gabs? Are you up here? I have to get going. Sorry, babe, but I have a few things to see to before the ceremony tomorrow.'

Vinn had put Gabriella from him almost roughly, raking a hand through his hair in the hope that it would restore some sort of order to it after her fingers had clawed at him in fervent response. Although his breathing was ragged, his heart hammering and his body aching with the pressure of release denied, he had somehow held himself together—but it had taken a monumental effort on his part.

Gabriella, consummate liar and actress that she was, had simply turned with a covert straightening of her clothing and smiled sweetly at her unsuspecting fiancé, with not a single sign of what had transpired just moments ago showing anywhere on her person. Her brown eyes had been clear and steady on his, her voice smooth and even.

'You're leaving already?' she'd asked, with just the right amount of disappointment in her tone. 'But you only just got here. You missed the rehearsal and everything.'

Tristan had leaned in and lightly kissed her swollen mouth. 'I know, dearest, but I'll make it up to you on our honeymoon, I promise. Besides, it's almost midnight. Isn't it bad luck or something to see the bride before she gets to the church?'

Vinn had pushed past them, his gut churning, his fists clenched so tight he'd thought each and every one of the bones in his hands would surely crack.

'Are you off now too, Venadicci?' Tristan had asked in a condescending tone. 'No doubt you have plenty to do, helping your mother polish the silver, hey what?'

Vinn had forced his mouth into a stiff movement of his lips that was nowhere close to a smile. 'You would be amazed at how tarnished some of those St Clair silver spoons are,' he'd said, and with one last searing glance at Gabriella strode down the hall.

Gabby lifted her head after a long silence and felt her heart give a little flutter of unease when she saw Vinn's penetrating look. 'You're really serious about this, aren't you?' she asked in a voice that came out thready. 'But why, Vinn? You're a rich man now. You've made it in the world. Why insist on marrying me?'

He pushed himself away from the sofa and came and stood right in front of her, so she had to crane her neck to look up at him. 'You still don't get it, do you, Gabriella?' he said, his eyes burning into hers. 'I don't want any other woman. Not since that night when I could have taken you up against the wall outside your upstairs bathroom. You wanted it, just as much as I wanted it so don't bother insulting my intelligence by denying it.'

Shame hoisted Gabby to her feet, her eyes blazing in fury. 'That's a despicable lie! You took advantage of me,' she threw at him, knowing it wasn't strictly true but saying it anyway. 'You were always leering at me. You did it every time you visited your mother at the house.'

Vinn's mouth stretched into a sneer. 'That's how you like to recall it, isn't it, Gabriella?' he asked. 'But I seem to remember it a little differently. You liked to flirt and tease, and you used every opportunity you could to do so. You got a perverse sort of pleasure out of dangling before me what I couldn't have, like taunting a starving dog with a juicy bone. Remember all those hot afternoons by the pool, when you knew I was going to be around to mow the lawn or trim the hedges? I knew what you were up to. You wanted me to make a move on you so you could cry wolf to your father and have me and my mother evicted. That was your game, wasn't it? You didn't even want your brother spending time with me. You were jealous he'd started to prefer my company to yours.'

Gabby's face flamed as she recalled how brazen and obvious she had been. Yes, she *had* been jealous of Vinn's friendship with her brother, but it had been about much more than that. From the moment Vinn had arrived at the St Clair mansion Gabby had felt uncomfortable in a way she couldn't adequately describe. She had only just turned fourteen at the time, and certainly Vinn, although being four years older, had never given her any reason to feel under threat. He'd mostly kept to himself, keeping his eyes downcast as he went about the odd jobs Gabby's father had organised for him.

It had only been as she'd grown from a young teen into a young woman that Gabby had begun to notice the way she felt when their eyes chanced to meet. It was unlike anything she had ever felt before with anyone else—even Tristan, who everyone knew would one day be her husband.

Looking into Vinn Venadicci's startlingly attractive grey-blue eyes now was like looking into the centre of a flame. The heat came back at her, scorching her until she had to drop her gaze.

'For God's sake, Vinn, I was what? Fifteen or sixteen?' she said, in what even she realised was a pathetic attempt to belatedly right the wrongs of the past. 'Surely you're not going to hold that against me?'

He gave a coarse-sounding laugh. 'My mother was right about you,' he said, raking her with his gaze. 'She said when the highest bidder came along you would sell your soul, and that's exactly what you did. Tristan Glendenning wanted shares in your father's business, and you were the little blonde bonus thrown in for free.'

Gabby clenched her teeth, her eyes sparking with anger, her whole body shaking with it. 'That's an atrocious and totally insulting thing to say,' she tossed back. 'Tristan's mother was my mother's best friend. They were each other's bridesmaids. It was always expected Tristan and I would marry. We grew up together, and apart from when my brother and Tristan were away at boarding school we spent most of our weekends and holidays together.' She paused for a nanosecond before adding, perhaps not as convincingly as she would have liked, 'It's…it was what we both wanted.'

Vinn gave a chillingly ruthless smile. 'Did he get his money's worth, Gabriella?' he asked. 'Were you a dutiful, obedient little wife for him?'

Gabby couldn't bear to look at the unmitigated disgust on his face. It was like confronting every stupid mistake she had ever made. How had she not known what sort of husband Tristan Glendenning would turn out to be? How could she have been so blind? She had no excuse. It wasn't as if Tristan had been a perfect stranger. She had known him all her life. And yet there had been things about him she had not known until it was too late.

Gabby spun away from Vinn's harsh expression. But the too sudden movement made her stomach heave, and her face and hands became clammy as she struggled to stay upright. She reached for the nearest arm of the sofa but her hand couldn't quite connect: it flailed in mid-air, like a ghost's hand passing through solid substance, and she felt herself go down in slow motion. Her knees buckled first and then her legs folded. Her head was spinning, and her eyes were unable to stay open as the room swirled sickeningly before her…

'Gabriella?' Vinn was on his knees, cradling her head in his hands before it connected with the floor.

She made a soft sound—more like a groan than anything else. But at least it meant she was still conscious. She was like a lifeless doll—a beautiful porcelain doll with the stuffing knocked out of it. At first he wondered if she was acting. It had all seemed so staged. And yet when he placed his hand on her smooth brow it was clammy. It made him wonder if he had misjudged her. Yes, things had been stressful lately for her—the margin call and her father's illness would have knocked anyone sideways—but the Gabriella he knew from the past would have played her histrionics to the hilt. A timely swoon or faint was well within her repertoire.

'Are you all right?' he asked, frowning in spite of his lingering doubts.

'W-what happened?' she said, opening her eyes, wincing against the light.

'You fainted, apparently,' Vinn said, although he still cradled her in his arms. She was lighter than he remembered, soft and feminine, and her scent was so alluring he couldn't stop his nostrils from flaring to breathe more of her in.

She groaned again and turned her head away. 'I think I'm going to be sick…'

Vinn decided he had better not take any risks, and quickly scooped her up and took her to the closest bathroom, holding her gently as she leaned over the basin. He winced in empathy as she emptied her stomach, her slim body shuddering with each racking heave.

'Are you done?' he asked, after a moment or two of keeping her steady.

Her hands gripped the edge of the basin, her head still bent low. 'Please…leave me alone for a minute…' she said hoarsely. 'I'm not used to having an audience at times…like this.'

'I'm not leaving you until I am certain you aren't going to knock yourself out cold on the edge of the basin or on the tiled floor,' he said. 'You scared the hell out of me.'

Vinn noticed her hands tighten their hold on the basin, making her small knuckles go white. She swayed slightly again, her eyes closing against another wave of nausea. He quickly rinsed a facecloth and, lifting the curtain of her hair, dabbed it at the back of her neck, just as his mother had done whenever he was sick as a child.

Gabby finally pushed herself back from the basin. Taking the facecloth from him, she buried her face in it, conscious of Vinn's firm but gentle hand in the small of her back, moving in a circular and bone-meltingly soothing motion.

'No more cocktails for you, young lady,' he said. 'They obviously don't agree with you.'

Gabby pressed her fingers to her temples. 'Maybe you're right,' she said, turning to face him, her body suddenly feeling weak and unsupported without the touch of his warm hand on her back. 'Would you mind if I go home now? It's kind of been a long day…' She gave a jaded sigh. 'Actually, it's been a long week…'

His eyes meshed with hers for an infinitesimal moment.

'Gabriella,' he said, 'your father is going to make it. People have triple heart bypass surgery all the time, and most if not all go on to make a full recovery.'

She bit her bottom lip and lowered her eyes from his. 'I know… It's just that he's depending on me. I don't want to let him down. I can't let him know about…about…' she flapped one of her hands '…about this margin call.'

He put his hands on the tops of her shoulders. 'The resort is secure,' he said, giving her shoulders a gentle squeeze. 'After we are married I want us to go there and check out the redevelopment. People will expect us to go on a honeymoon, so it will be a perfect excuse to do both.'

He felt her tense under his hands. 'I don't want to be too far away from my parents just now,' she said, not quite holding his gaze.

'Gabriella, you have to live your own life,' he said. 'It is your mother's responsibility to support your father, not yours. You have done enough. To be quite frank, I think you've done too much.'

A glitteringly defiant light came into her eyes as they warred with his. 'I don't want to go on a honeymoon with you, Vinn,' she said. 'Do I have to spell it out any plainer than that? I'm not going to sleep with you.'

Vinn let out his breath on a long-winded stream in an effort to contain his patience, which was already fraying at the edges. 'You know something?' he said. 'As much as I would like to, I am not going to throw you onto the nearest surface and ravish you, Gabriella. I understand you will need time to adjust to our marriage. I am prepared to give you the time you need, within reason.'

She tossed her head at him. 'Oh, yes?' she said with a scathing look. 'Within reason. Whatever that might mean. What…a couple of days? A week or two? A month?'

His eyes lasered hers. 'I told you, I want our marriage to be a real one.'

She began to push past him towards the door with an embittered scowl. 'Do you even *know* what a real marriage is about? You were the child of a single mother. You have no idea how a marriage works.'

'You were married for five years,' he inserted coolly as he put his hand on the bathroom door, closing it firmly to stop her escaping. 'How about you tell *me*?'

Gabby felt as if he had kicked her in the tenderest part of her belly, where all her hurt, all her disappointment and all her guilt were contained in one gnarled mass of miserable agony. She had to fight not to double over with the pain of it. It was crippling, agonising to withstand it, but only her strength of will kept her upright.

She would *not* break in front of him.

Vengeance was his goal, but she was not going to give in to him—and certainly not with her pride as a garnish. That was what he was after. He wanted her to grovel and beg and wear a hair shirt for the rest of her life. But she was not going to allow him to humble her.

She wasn't going to do it. Not without a fight.

She stood in place, like a fountain that had suddenly been frozen. Even the bitter tears at the backs of her eyes had turned to dry ice, burning but not flowing.

'I can tell you, Vinn, that marriage takes a whole lot more work than a few fancy-sounding promises muttered in front of a minister of religion,' she said. 'What you are asking for is a commitment that no one can really guarantee, and certainly not without love. It seems to me the only motivation you have for this union of ours is vengeance.'

Vinn's top lip lifted. 'You're surely not expecting me to *love* you, Gabriella?' he asked.

Gabby briefly closed her eyes in pain, but when she opened them again she saw the same caustic bitterness glittering in his; it hadn't gone away, and it surprised her how devastated she felt to realise it was never likely to. He would always look at her with hate blazing in his eyes and revenge simmering in his blood.

'No,' she said, almost inaudibly, 'I don't expect you to love me.'

Vinn reached past her to turn on the shower head. 'Have a shower while I find something for you to sleep in tonight,' he said. 'There is no way I am going to allow you to spend the night alone at your parents' house. You can stay here with me. There are fresh towels on the heated rail.'

Gabby's hands grasped at the basin again for balance. 'I don't need a shower—and I am not sleeping in this house with—'

He ignored her and thrust a bottle of perfumed body wash into her hands. 'As much as I hate to contradict you, Gabriella,' he said, 'you have not only managed to cover yourself in your own sickness, but me as well. Now, get into that damned shower before I change my mind and get in there with you.'

Gabby threw him a fulminating glare, but she took the body wash from him with hands not quite steady. 'Has anyone ever told you what a bull-headed brute you are?' she said.

He put his hands on his hips and stared her down. 'Get in the shower, Gabriella. You're wasting water.'

Gabby stepped into the huge shower stall, clothes and all, and on an impulse she really couldn't account for lifted off the removable shower head and aimed it straight at him.

Water went everywhere—all over the marbled walls and tiled floor, but most of all on Vinn's face and upper body, before he could snatch control of it.

'Why, you little wildcat,' he growled and, stepping into the shower with her, gave her a dose of her own watery medicine.

'Stop it!' Gabby squealed as the hot fine needles of water stung her face and shoulders. 'I'm fully dressed, you idiot!'

'So you are,' he said and, hanging the shower head back up, turned off the water. 'But then so am I and these are a brand-new pair of trousers.'

Gabby stood there dripping, caught between the urge to grab back the shower head and douse him all over again, and the even more disturbing urge to pull his glistening head down so his mouth could fuse hotly with hers.

How had the atmosphere changed so rapidly? she wondered dazedly. The air was suddenly thick with sexual attraction, heavy and pulsing, especially in a silence measured through electrically charged second with a series of plops and drips that sounded like rifle-shots.

Gabby brushed a slick strand of hair off her face with a hand that shook slightly. 'I hope you're not expecting me to pay for your trousers, because I'm not going to,' she said—more for something to say to break the dangerously sensual spell.

'No,' he said, looking at her dripping mouth and chin, his own face and hair soaking wet. 'I was thinking more along the lines of you paying a penalty in another currency entirely.'

Gabby licked the droplets of water off her mouth, trying to control the hit-and-miss beat of her heart. 'I'm n-not sure what you mean…' she said, stepping back as far as the shower cubicle would allow. But it wasn't far enough. For that matter Perth, on the other side of the continent, wouldn't be far enough.

She felt the cold hard-marbled wall at her back, and when Vinn stepped closer she felt his wet shirt and trousers come into contact with her sodden black dress. Never had the expensive designer fabric of her outfit seemed so thin, Gabby thought. She could feel Vinn's belt buckle pressing into her belly, and not only his buckle but his growing erection as well. It was rock-hard, and so close to the aching pulse of her body she couldn't breathe.

'What about it, Gabriella?' he asked in a smoulder-ingly sexy tone. 'What say we strip off and finish this properly? That's the game you want to play, isn't it? It's just like the game you wanted to play in the past. Let's get Vinn all hot under the collar so he acts like a rutting animal, right? That's what you want, isn't it?'

Gabriella was shocked at how much she wanted to rise to his challenging statement. She did want to rip his shirt from his broad chest and press her mouth on each of his flat male nipples in turn. She did want to unfasten his belt and expose his engorged male flesh to the exploration of her fingers, to feel the strength and power of his blood pulsing through him. She wanted to have him press her back against the marbled wall of the shower, his hands cupping and kneading her breasts, his mouth moving moistly over each tight nipple, until every thought flew out of her head.

But that was the trouble. Her head and all the thoughts inside it. The swirling, torturous thoughts that reminded her in that taunting, unrelenting tone how useless she was at seduction. She was a novice at lovemaking. Her own husband had found her body a total turn-off, so disgusting he had sought the company of other women.

'Gabriella?' Vinn tipped up her chin, a frown bringing his brows together. 'Are you cold? I'm sorry—I didn't notice how much you were shivering. Here, let me turn the water back on.'

Gabby was shaking. Not from cold, but from the effort of keeping a lid on her emotions. Never had she felt more outmatched, outmanoeuvred and totally powerless. Vinn had her in the palm of his hand, and if she didn't find an excuse to get him out of the bathroom within the next few seconds she knew she was going to fall apart completely.

Somehow having him witness her at her lowest point was too much to bear right now. How he would gloat and mock her for all she had represented. She could hardly blame him; she had been such a fool, a silly little insecure fool, who hadn't for a moment considered his feelings. He had every right to hate her, to want to avenge all the petty wrongs of the past. That was why he was marrying her—to bring her under his control, to humble her, to gloat over his possession of her.

'N-no, I'm not c-cold,' she said, although she was shivering. 'B-but I would like to be alone.'

Vinn adjusted the water to make it slightly warmer before he stepped out of the cubicle. 'I'll get you something to wear,' he said, and reached for a towel to dry off before he left her.

He came back to stand outside the bathroom door a few minutes later, with a tracksuit which was at least four sizes too big for her. Although the shower was now turned off, he could hear the muffled sound of Gabriella sniffing, as if she had been crying. Something pulled in his chest, like a string tied to his heart, but he staunchly ignored it. Tears and tantrums were some of the many tools in Gabriella's arsenal: she used them interchangeably to get her way. How many times in the past had he been fooled by carefully orchestrated tears? He was no such lovesick fool now—no way. He had wised up and wised up well. Gabriella had a lot riding on maintaining his goodwill right now, and he was going to make the most of it.

When she finally came out, after he had handed her the tracksuit through a crack in the door, there was no sign of distress on her face. Her eyes were clear, and if anything characteristically defiant. And he had to admit, dressed as she was in his clothes, she looked like a small child. She had rolled up the arms and the legs, but with her hair still wet and hanging about her shoulders she looked tiny and fragile and totally adorable.

Vinn felt a momentary tug at his heart again, but just as quickly ignored it. This was not the time to go all soft on her. They had a deal, and he was going to make certain she fulfilled her side of it.

'Maybe I will take you home after all,' he said gruffly. 'As your father's surgery has been rescheduled for tomorrow morning. Let's get past that hurdle before we deal with the next.'

'Thanks, Vinn…' she said, in a whisper-soft voice, her eyes lowering from his. 'This has all been such a terrible shock to me…'

Vinn wanted to ask what she was referring to: his

demand for marriage or her father's health scare? But he didn't, because he already knew the answer.

The Gabriella St Clair he knew would take her father's heart attack in her stride. But being forced to marry the bastard son of the St Clair house-cleaner was something else again.

CHAPTER FIVE

GABBY chewed her nails one by one as she'd waited with her mother in the relatives' lounge for news of her father's condition. It had been a long wait, for although Henry St Clair had been first on the list, the procedure usually took anything up to three or four hours, as veins were harvested from the lower legs to relocate in the chest as heart valves.

Finally the surgeon came out with good news. Everything had gone extremely well, and Henry was in recovery. He would be there for quite some time, before being transferred to Intensive Care, and then to the high-dependency unit a few days later.

'When can we see him?' Gabby asked, holding onto her mother's hand and squeezing it tightly.

'As soon as he is transferred to the ICU I will have someone inform you,' the surgeon said. 'Try not to be too put off by all the machines and drips attached to him. It all looks a lot scarier than it really is, I can assure you. He is one of the luckier ones. He hasn't smoked in years, and his weight is within the normal range. A family history of heart disease is, of course, unfortunate, but with the right lifestyle changes he should make a very good recovery, as long as his stress levels are kept down during rehabilitation.'

Gabby couldn't have heard more convincing words. The pre-nuptial agreement papers she had signed first thing that morning sent via express courier had been worth it. She was committed to marrying Vinn Venadicci in front of a marriage celebrant in a registry office. They would be leaving for a short honeymoon at the St Clair Island Resort later the same day.

Gabby tried not to think too much about it all, and was almost glad she had her father to worry about instead. It gave her a focus, supporting her mother, who didn't cope well even with breaking a nail or her roots showing, let alone a crisis of this sort. Her mother's reaction to Blair's death had been part of the reason Gabby had agreed to marry Tristan Glendenning, even though she had been having doubts for months. Tristan had assured her a big wedding to plan was just the thing to get her mother out of bed each day, and off the strong and highly addictive sedatives the doctor had prescribed.

Gabby's concern over her mother's health and well-being had more or less sealed her own fate. She had been so distracted by her parents and their heart-wrenching grief she had more or less had to ignore her own, and in so doing had set in motion years of hell.

Now she was doing it all over again. She was marrying a man she didn't love in order to protect those she loved with all her heart.

But for some reason Gabby didn't feel Vinn would be in quite the same category of husband as Tristan. Perhaps that was why she was feeling so unsettled.

Vinn was a mystery to her. In many ways he always had been. That was what she found so intriguing about him; she didn't know him because she suspected he didn't want to be known.

Gabby didn't think he would raise a hand to her. God knew he'd had plenty of reason to in the past, but he had never struck back at her in any way at all—apart from that kiss, of course. She had always secretly admired him for his self-restraint. She had been such a bitch towards him. How he had tolerated it still amazed her. So many young men in his position would have sought their revenge at the time; instead he had waited seven long years in order to do so...

Gabby gave a shiver and turned her attention back to her mother, who was crying into yet another crumpled tissue.

'It's OK, Mum,' she said gently. 'You heard what the surgeon said. Dad's going to be just fine.'

Pamela St Clair blew her nose. 'I know, darling, but I just wish Blair was here,' she said. 'With your father out of action for God knows how long, what will happen to the business? Your father never tells me anything about what's going on. Are you sure it's all going well? You haven't said anything about it for ages, and I can't help worrying that...well, we could lose everything we've worked so hard for. If we were to lose the house... Oh, God, I just couldn't bear it!'

'Mum, stop worrying right now,' Gabby said, hugging her mother close so she couldn't see the deceit in her eyes. 'The resort is doing just fine. I spoke to the Fosters only yesterday. Everything is fine. They've had almost full occupancy for the last month. We're making a profit, just as we hoped and planned. Everything is safe and secure.'

'I'm so glad,' Pamela said, stepping back and wiping at her tears. 'I'm also glad about you marrying Vinn. I want you to know that, Gabby.'

Gabby met her mother's tawny-brown gaze. 'I always thought you didn't like him, Mum,' she said, trying not to frown. 'You always gave the impression he and his mother were beneath you.'

Pamela gave a wincing look. 'I know… It seems so…dreadfully hypocritical of me, thinking about it now,' she said. 'But I guess it was because I was so ashamed of my own background.'

Gabby allowed her frown purchase this time. 'What do you mean?'

Her mother blew her nose again and, tucking away the tissue, faced Gabby squarely. 'Darling, your father married me against his parents' wishes. We never spoke of it to you or to Blair, and thank God your grandparents when they were alive didn't mention anything either. But I was from the wrong side of the tracks, if you know what I mean.'

Gabby could barely believe her ears. She stood silently staring at her perfectly groomed mother, with her perfect diction and rounded vowels, and wondered if she had ever known her at all.

'Vinn's mother Rose reminded me of my own mother,' Pamela explained. 'She was an unwed mother too, with no skills to speak of, and at the mercy of whoever employed her. I was shunted from place to place for most of my childhood, never making friends long enough to keep them. As a result I dropped out of school and had to rely on my looks to get me where I wanted to go. I met your father at a function where I was waiting on tables. That's where I met Janice— Tristan's mother. Her parents owned the restaurant. She was so lovely to me, and we became close friends… The rest, as they say, is history.'

Gabby swallowed. 'You did love Dad when you married him, though, didn't you?' she asked, unconsciously holding her breath.

Pamela let out a long sigh and shifted her gaze. 'I didn't at first,' she confessed. 'The thing is I got pregnant with your brother. I was stupid and naive, and I didn't factor in the risks when we first started seeing each other. Your father insisted we marry, and so we did—against all the objections thrown at us.'

Gabby didn't say a word. Her voice seemed to be locked somewhere deep inside her throat.

Her mother's reddened eyes came back to hers. 'But over time I grew to love him. I don't have to tell you he is a good man, Gabby. He doesn't always get it right, any more than I do, but he's all I've got now apart from you. I just wish Blair h-hadn't…' She took a deep, uneven breath and continued, 'I just want you to be happy, Gabby. Janice, Tristan's mother, wishes it too. I was just talking to her last night. She and Gareth think the world of you. You were such a wonderful wife to their son.' She began to sob again, and buried her face into another wad of tissues.

Gabby felt sick. Guilt assailed her, almost overwhelming her already fragile control. Tristan's parents, like hers, had never known the full story. How could she have told them what had occurred behind closed doors? How could she have ruined so many lives by telling them the sordid truth?

She had felt so alone.

She *still* felt so alone.

Did anyone understand what it was like to carry such a burden of guilt and shame and regret? Would her life always be marked by the dark stains of her mistakes? How could she clear her slate and start afresh? Was it even possible?

Gabby became aware again of her mother's renewed bout of tears, and gathered her close. 'Don't cry, Mum,' she said softly. 'Things will work out. I know they will. Vinn and I will sort things out between us.'

Pamela brushed at her eyes as she removed herself from Gabby's embrace. 'Do you love him, darling?' she asked, looking at her intently.

Gabby felt her heart drop inside her chest. How could she lie to her own mother? Hadn't she already told so many lies? 'Um… Mum…' she faltered, shifting her gaze a fraction. 'What sort of question is that? Why on earth would I be marrying him if I didn't feel like…that for him?'

Her mother smiled a watery smile and, grasping Gabby's wrists, gripped them warmly. 'Then you will be a better wife to him than I was to your father in those first years of our marriage,' she said. 'At least you're not marrying Vinn because you feel you have to. You are marrying him because you love him and can't imagine living your life with anyone else. Apart from Tristan, of course. You were soul mates—everyone knows that—but life throws up other paths, which is just as well, don't you think?'

Gabby stretched her mouth into a smile that felt as if it had been stitched in place. 'Of course,' she said. 'That's exactly what I think.'

When Gabby finally got home to Point Piper, Vinn arrived within minutes. As she checked his tall figure via the security camera, she wondered if he had been parked somewhere outside waiting for her.

He had called in at the hospital briefly, halfway through the afternoon, but hadn't stayed long. Just long enough to kiss her on the lips—a soft press of warm sensual flesh against her trembling mouth—before he turned and smiled at Gabby's mother. Gabby had listened to him chat about her father's condition with one ear while her heart had skipped and hopped all over the place and she'd surreptitiously swept her tongue where his mouth had just been. She had been able to taste him—a hint of good-quality coffee, a touch of mint, and a massive dose of sexy, full-blooded male.

Her belly had given a little quiver as she'd stood close to his side, his arm slipping around her waist in a possessive but strangely protective manner. She hadn't quite been able to control the instinct to move in even closer. He had felt so tall and strong, like a fortress.

Gabby had only suddenly realised her mother had left them to return to her father's bedside in ICU, where only one visitor was allowed at any time. She'd felt Vinn's arm drop from her waist and had quickly rearranged her features so he couldn't see how he had affected her.

'Do you think that kiss was necessary?' she asked, in a deliberately testy tone, taking great care not to glance at that sensual mouth, focussing on his grey-blue eyes instead.

His eyes contained a glint of amusement. 'Actually, I was thinking about slipping my tongue inside your mouth as well, but I thought your mother might be uncomfortable with such an obvious and very public display of my affection for her daughter.'

Gabby lifted her brows in twin arcs of cynicism. 'Affection?' she said. 'Is that what you call it? It's animal attraction, and you damn well know it.' She took a little heaving breath and added, 'And it's totally disgusting.'

He gave her a lazy smile and brushed the back of his hand down the side of her face—a barely touching caress, but it set off every nerve beneath the skin of her cheek like electrodes set on full voltage. 'Ah, but you feel it too, don't you, *mia piccola?*' he said. 'And soon we will be doing something about it, hmm?'

Gabby glowered at him even as she tried to ignore the flip-flop of her heart behind her breastbone. 'Not if I can help it,' she said stiffly, and crossed her arms tightly over her chest.

His smile widened and, leaning down, he pressed a soft-as-air kiss to her forehead before she could do anything to counteract it. 'Keep stoking that fiery passion of yours,' he drawled, in a low and sexy, knee-wobbling tone. 'I get turned on by the thought of you fighting me every step of the way, even though you want what I want. It's what you've always wanted.'

'I want you to burn in hell,' she bit out, practically shaking all over with rage.

He winked at her, and without another word turned

and walked with those long easy strides of his down the corridor to the lifts.

Gabby stood watching him, annoyed with herself for doing so, but for some reason unable to get her body to move. The lift doors opened and she saw Vinn smile as two nurses came out, each one doing a swift double-take as he stepped into the lift. The doors whooshed shut behind him.

The nurses' voices carried as they came up the corridor towards Gabby. 'Wasn't that Vinn Venadicci?' the dark- haired one asked her red-headed companion. 'You know…the hotshot property investment tycoon?'

'Sure was,' the red head said. 'I heard a rumour he's just got engaged. His future father-in-law's just had open heart surgery. I wonder how long *that* marriage will last? Vinn Venadicci is a bit of a player, or so the gossip mags say.'

'I wouldn't mind a bit of a play with him,' the dark-haired nurse admitted with a grin. 'God, those eyes of his, and that smile would be enough to melt anyone's moral code.'

Gabby spun away in disgust and, pushing open the nearest female conveniences door, locked herself inside a cubicle until she was sure the nurses had moved on.

And now she had to face her nemesis all over again, Gabby thought sourly, as she opened the door of her parents' home to let Vinn in. She stepped well back, in case he took it upon himself to repeat his mode of greeting earlier that afternoon.

'Why are you here?' she asked in a clipped tone.

Vinn reached into the inside pocket of his suit jacket and handed her a black velvet box. 'This is for you,' he said, with an inscrutable expression. 'If you don't like the design you can exchange it for something else. It makes no difference to me.'

Gabby took the small box with an unsteady hand, desperately trying not to come into contact with his long fingers. But even so she felt the zap of his touch as one of her fingers brushed against one of his. She opened the lid and stared down at the classically designed solitaire diamond ring. The brilliance of the gem was absolutely breathtaking.

She looked up at him, her voice coming out slightly husky. 'It's…it's beautiful… It must have cost you a fortune.'

He gave her a wry look. 'Not quite as much as the margin call, but certainly close.'

Gabby pressed her lips together and looked at the diamond again, her mind reeling at the thought of how much he had paid for her to be his bride. Even though she had grown up with the sort of wealth and privilege most ordinary people never saw in a lifetime, she still couldn't quite believe the lengths Vinn was prepared to go to in order to secure her hand in marriage.

It made her realise yet again how difficult it was going to be for her to get out of the arrangement. She had already endured one miserable marriage, every day a torture of secrets and lies and betrayals. How would she cope with years of Vinn's philandering? He was sure to do so, since he had done little else since he had left the St Clair estate all those years ago.

'Of course you will have to remove Glendenning's rings first,' Vinn said into the silence.

Gabby looked down at her left hand, at the diamond

cluster and the wedding band she had wanted to remove so many times over the last two years since Tristan's death. She'd felt unable to face the comments from her parents if she had done so.

'Yes…yes…of course,' she said, and began to tug at them.

One of Vinn's hands closed over hers, the other taking the velvet box out of her hand and putting it on a hall table next to him. 'Allow me,' he said. And, holding her left hand in the strength and warmth of his left one, he removed each of the rings, his grey-blue gaze not once leaving her startled brown one.

Gabby could feel her heart picking up its pace, and the way her breathing was becoming shallow and uneven. Her body felt hot inside and out—especially her hand, which was still enclosed in his. She took a tiny swallow as he reached for the ring he had bought her, and then her breathing stopped altogether as he gently eased the circle of white gold with its brilliant diamond along the slim length of her finger to its final resting place.

'It is a perfect fit,' he said with an enigmatic smile. 'How about that?'

Gabby couldn't account for her scattered emotions, but she felt as close to tears as she had the previous evening. It made her feel vulnerable in a way she resented feeling in front of someone she disliked so intensely.

'A lucky guess,' she said in an off-hand tone, and stepped back from him.

A flicker of annoyance momentarily darkened the blue in his eyes. 'Are you going to invite me in for a drink to celebrate our impending marriage?' he asked.

'If so, I think I might remove my shirt right now, in case you take it upon yourself to throw the contents of your glass at me again.'

Gabby tightened her mouth like the strings of an evening purse. 'I promise not to throw anything at you if you promise to keep your insulting suppositions to yourself,' she said, with an elevation of her chin.

'And what would some of those suppositions be, I wonder?' he mused.

She stalked towards the large lounge overlooking the harbour, tossing over her shoulder, 'What would you like to drink? We have the usual spirits and mixers, wine and champagne—French, even, if you so desire it.'

'I think you know very well what I desire, Gabriella,' he said, as he came to where she was standing in front of the bar fridge and drinks servery.

Gabby sucked in a sharp little breath as his hands came down on the tops of her shoulders. The heat of his touch was like a brand, even through the layer of her cotton shirt. She felt the solid presence of him at her back, and wondered what it would feel like to lean back into his hardness, to feel the hard outline of his body against the softness of hers, to feel his hands move from her shoulders to cup her breasts, to feel the slight abrasion of his fingers skating over her erect nipples…

She might not like him, but Gabby was starting to realise she would be lying to herself if she said she didn't desire him. He had a magnetism about him that was totally enthralling. Even now she felt an overwhelming compulsion to turn around and lock gazes with him, to see if his need was anything like her own.

'What's that perfume you are wearing?' he asked, moving in a little closer.

Gabby felt her spine give a distinct wobble as his chest rumbled against her back as he spoke. 'Um…I'm not sure… I can't remember… Something I've had for ages…' She couldn't seem to get her scrambled brain to work. It seemed to be short-circuited by all her body was feeling with him so close.

'It reminds me of warm summer nights,' he said against the shell of her ear. 'Frangipani and jasmine and something else.'

Gabby wondered if the 'something else' was the scent of her desire for him. She could feel silky moisture gathering between her thighs, the secret and hollow ache making her feel even more unguarded around him. She had always been able to hold him off with her caustic tongue. That had been her protection in the past. But what if her body totally betrayed her now? Could he sense how close she was to responding to the temptation of his closeness?

Vinn turned her around to face him, his hands sliding down the length of her slender arms, his right thumb rolling over the bump of the diamond ring on her finger, back and forth, as he watched the way her expression became shuttered, as if his touch didn't affect her one iota. But he could feel the slight tremble of her hands in his, and see the flare of her pupils, making her toffee-brown eyes darken, and the way the point of her tongue darted out to deposit a fine layer of moisture over her soft lips.

He wanted to kiss her, to taste the sweetness of her, to feel her tongue war with his until he tamed it. He wanted to press her back against the nearest wall and bury himself in her, to feel his hard body surrounded by her silky warmth, to thrust himself to paradise and take her writhing and screaming with him.

But instead he released her hands and stepped back from her. 'I have changed my mind about that drink,' he said. 'I have another engagement this evening, and since I drove myself here instead of using a cab, I don't want to end up with a drink-driving charge.'

A frown pulled at her smooth brow. 'You don't have a driver?' she asked.

'Not a full-time one,' he said. 'And nor do I have a live-in housekeeper, so I hope it's not going to be a problem for you pitching in occasionally to help keep things running smoothly at home.'

Her frown deepened, and a fiery light came into her eyes as they narrowed slightly. 'Is this some sort of sick joke?' she asked.

'It's no joke, Blondie,' he said. 'I do my own cooking, and I expect you to do the same.'

'B-but you're a multi-millionaire for God's sake!' she spluttered. 'In fact, aren't you close to being a billionaire by now?'

'So?'

'So you get people to do stuff for you,' she said, flapping her hands for effect. 'It's totally crazy, spending your time on menial tasks when you could employ someone else to do it for you so you can concentrate on what you're best at doing.'

'I happen to enjoy cooking,' Vinn said, relishing every second of their exchange. She was so pampered she hadn't a clue how the real world worked, and it would do her good to learn. It would teach her to think twice about treating those less fortunate than her with her customary disdain.

'If you think for one minute I'm going to wash your socks and fold your underwear then you are even more deluded than I thought,' she tossed at him heatedly.

'The only thing I expect you to do with my underwear is peel it off me—preferably with your teeth,' he returned with a deliberately lascivious look.

Her eyes flared and he saw her hands go to tight little fists by her sides. 'I will do no such thing!'

He gave a chuckle of laughter and, before he was tempted to kiss that pouting mouth of hers, turned on his heel and left.

Gabby stormed up and down the lounge after he had driven away, her anger duelling with her disappointment that he hadn't stayed for a drink.

No, that wasn't quite the truth, she decided on her pace back towards the sofa. What she had really wanted him to do was to stay long enough to kiss her. She had been expecting him to turn her around in his arms and smother her mouth with his. Her whole body had been screaming out for it. But he had left her high and dry. She hated him for it. She hated him for toying with her like a cat with a mouse, taunting it, teasing it mercilessly, just waiting for the best moment to make that final devastating pounce.

She hated him.

OK, so that wasn't quite the truth either, Gabby thought as she scraped her fingers through her hair. That was the whole problem. She didn't know what the hell she felt for Vinn Venadicci, but one thing was certain: it was not as close to hate as she wanted and most desperately needed it to be.

CHAPTER SIX

'DARLING,' Pamela St Clair said to Gabby as soon as she arrived at the hospital the following morning. 'Please tell me this…this…' she thrust the morning's newspaper in Gabby's hands '…this scandalmongering isn't true!'

Gabby looked at the page the newspaper was folded open to and felt a knife-like pain jab through her. There was a photograph of Vinn with his arm around a young and very beautiful brunette, who was smiling up at him adoringly. The couple of paragraphs accompanying the picture declared Vinn Venadicci was rumoured to be getting married to widowed socialite Gabriella Glendenning, nee St Clair, and the journalist was quite adamant the young woman with him was not his fiancée but a mystery date he had been seen with once or twice before.

'Well?' Pamela St Clair was practically wringing her hands. 'For God's sake, Gabby, if your father hears or sees this it could cause another heart attack.'

'Mum…' Somehow Gabby located her voice, but it sounded slightly strangled. 'Of course it's not true. You know what the press are like. They make this stuff up all the time. It's probably an old photo.'

Pamela's eyes narrowed. 'Are you sure?' she asked. 'Are you absolutely sure?'

Gabby had never felt more uncertain in her life, but she was not going to admit that to her mother. With an acting skill she had no idea she had possessed until now, she relaxed her tense features into a smile and handed back the paper with a surprisingly steady hand. 'Mum,' she said, holding out her left hand, 'do you think Vinn would give me this and then go off gallivanting with someone else the very same evening?'

Her mother gasped as she held Gabby's hand up to the light. 'Oh, my God, it's gorgeous,' she said. 'It must have cost him an arm and a leg.'

Gabby took her hand back. 'Yes, it did,' she said, unconsciously fingering the diamond. 'But apparently I'm worth it.'

Pamela looked past Gabby's shoulder. 'Oh... Vinn...' She cleared her throat delicately and continued, 'We were...er...just talking about you.'

Gabby had to summon even more acting ability to face Vinn with any sense of equanimity. 'Hi,' she said, and reached up on tiptoe to plant a brief kiss on his cheek, with the intention of landing it close enough to his mouth for her mother to be fooled. However Vinn had other ideas. He took control of her mouth in a deep, bone-melting assault on her senses that left her totally out of kilter once it ended.

'Hi yourself, *cara*,' he said, before turning to face Gabby's mother, who was trying to hide the newspaper behind her back but failing miserably. 'I hope you weren't upset by that article? I have already spoken to my legal advisors about lodging a defamation claim against the journalist concerned.'

'Oh…' Pamela said, smiling broadly. 'No…no, of course not, Vinn. I wasn't upset at all, and neither was Gabby. Were you, darling?'

Gabby smiled stiffly. 'I am well used to the mud-slinging that goes on in the press, having been subjected to it myself once or twice in the past.'

Vinn smiled as if butter wouldn't melt on his skin, let alone in his mouth, Gabby thought resentfully.

'So how is Henry doing today?' he asked, addressing Pamela.

'He's resting just now, but he's had a good night,' Pamela answered with visible relief. 'The surgeon is pleased with everything so far. It's just important we keep him quiet and free from stress.'

'Yes, of course,' Vinn said, reaching for Gabby's hand and pulling her closer. 'We'll let you get back to him while we have a coffee together. Can I get you something before we go?'

Pamela blushed like a schoolgirl. 'Oh, no, I'm fine, thank you, Vinn,' she said and then started to gush like one too. 'You're so kind. You've been absolutely marvellous. Gabby's so lucky to have someone like you. I really mean it. And that ring! Why, it's practically the Hope Diamond!'

Vinn gave a low rumble of laughter. 'Not quite— but she's worth it, don't you think?'

Pamela beamed from ear to ear. 'Well, she's my daughter, so I have to agree, don't I? But she *is* worth it—although it would please me to see her smile a bit more. Come on, darling.' She swung her gaze to

Gabby. 'I must say for someone who is supposed to be madly in love you don't seem all that happy.'

'Um… I'm just worried about Dad, that's all,' Gabby faltered. 'It's been such a trying time and…'

Vinn's arm snaked around Gabby's waist. 'I promise you, Mrs St Clair, you won't know her when I bring her back from our honeymoon,' he said. 'She will be smiling from ear to ear. I guarantee it.'

Pamela blushed again. 'Oh, my, but you have turned into such a charmer, Vinn Venadicci. And you really must call me Pamela now that you're to be part of the family.'

'Thank you, Pamela,' he said, with an easygoing smile.

Gabby pulled herself out of his hold once her mother had gone back to be with her father. 'Who is she?' she threw at him icily.

'Who is who?' Vinn asked, as he began leading the way down the corridor towards the lifts.

Gabby had to trot to keep up. 'That woman in the picture,' she said, glancing around to see if anyone was listening. 'She's your mistress, isn't she?' she hissed at him in a hushed tone. 'Don't bother denying it, because I just won't believe you.'

He pressed the 'down' button. 'Then I won't waste my time denying it,' he said. 'What would be the point, if you're not going to believe me either way?'

Gabby glared at him as they stepped into the lift, but couldn't fling a retort his way due to several other passengers in the lift. She stood stiffly by his side, her anger towards him going upwards even as the floor numbers went downwards.

The lift delivered them on the ground floor, and

Vinn placed a hand beneath her elbow to guide her out of the busy hospital foyer to where his car was parked.

'Where are we going?' Gabby asked, flinging him a churlish look.

'We are going to have a coffee together,' he said, and opened the passenger door for her. 'Get in.'

She threw him another furious glare. 'Don't order me about as if I'm a child.'

'Then don't act like one,' he returned, and repeated his command, this time with an implacable edge to his tone. 'Get in the car.'

'I don't see why we have to drive somewhere to have a coffee when there's a perfectly good cafeteria back there in the hospital foyer,' she tossed back, with a shrug of her shoulders.

Vinn's eyes challenged hers. 'You know something, Blondie?' he said. 'You are really starting to annoy me—and that is not a good thing.'

'Yeah, well, you're a late starter then, because I've been annoyed with you from the moment I met you,' she threw back, her brown eyes flashing at him.

Vinn put the brakes on his temper with an effort. 'Listen,' he said, 'I have nothing against hospital food and drink, but right now I want us to be alone. We have things to discuss.'

She gave him a contentious look. 'Like your mystery lover?'

Vinn silently ground his teeth. 'She is nothing of the sort. She's a…friend.'

Her brows lifted cynically. 'A friend, huh?' she said. 'What do you take me for, Vinn? Do you think I'm so naive I would fall for that old line?'

Vinn set his mouth. 'Quite frankly, right at this minute I don't give a damn *what* you think,' he bit out. 'I have a huge list of things to see to today because I'm going to be away next week, and I can do without this infantile behaviour from you—especially considering the money I've handed over without a single word of thanks from you.'

'You expect me to *thank* you for blackmailing me into marriage?' she asked in an incredulous tone.

'If you're not happy with the conditions you can hand back the money and the ring,' he said, locking his eyes on hers. 'Right here and right now.'

Gabby tussled for a moment with his challenging and annoyingly confident look. There was no point calling his bluff because there was no way she could find an alternative source of funds to keep the resort safe. 'You know I can't do that…' she mumbled.

'Then let's go with Plan A and get on with it,' he said and nodded his head towards the passenger seat.

Gabby got in the car with uncharacteristic meekness, her spirits sagging. Her head was starting to pound from the tension in her neck and shoulders that had been building all morning. She pressed her fingers to the bridge of her nose, her eyes scrunched closed to avoid the stab of bright sunlight coming through the windscreen.

'Hey…' Vinn's deep voice was almost as soothing as the warmth of his palm at the back of her neck, the gentle massaging of his fingers untying the knots of tension like magic. 'You have a headache, yes?'

She bit her lip and gave a tiny nod. 'I didn't sleep well, and I skipped breakfast…'

She heard him mutter a curse, but his fingers didn't stop their soothing action. She rolled her head and shoulders to make the most of his touch, her breath coming out in a long, easy stream as the tension gradually eased.

'Feeling a bit better?' he asked.

She opened her eyes and turned to look at him, her heart stalling like an old engine. There was concern in his grey-blue gaze, and his mouth had lost its grim set. He was now looking as sensually tempting and irresistible as ever. She couldn't seem to stop looking at him, at the way his mouth tipped up at the corners as if he always had a smile at the ready, the fuller bottom lip hinting at the potent sensuality of his nature.

Then there was the dark stubble that peppered his jaw, in spite of his early-morning shave, making him so essentially masculine she wanted to place the palm of her hand on his face and feel the texture of his skin, feel the abrasion of it against her softer one. She could imagine herself kissing her way all over his face, over each of the dark slashes of his eyebrows, his eyelids, and down the length of his crooked patrician nose until she got to his lips.

Gabby felt her eyelids begin to lower as his mouth came inexorably closer, his head tilting to accommodate the contours of their faces. The slow-motion brush of his lips against hers was soft, like a feather floating down to land on top of a smooth surface. Her lips tingled from the brief contact, each nerve springing to life in anticipation of a follow-up kiss.

But instead he sat back in the driver's seat and started the engine with a throaty roar. Releasing the handbrake, he sent her a smile before turning back to the task of driving out of the car park.

Gabby rolled her lips together, to see if it would stop them tingling, but all it did was make her hungry for more of his drugging kisses. Was he doing it on purpose? she wondered. Day by day ramping up her desire for him, so she would not be able to resist him when he decided it was time to consummate their marriage. Her belly quivered at the thought of him making love to her, his hands on her body, touching her, stroking and caressing her until she was boneless with need.

She fidgeted in her seat, her body hot and bothered, and that secret place between her thighs pulsing and aching and moist with want.

Would she disappoint him? In spite of her marriage to Tristan she had never experienced pleasure, only pain and shame. She mentally cringed as she recalled the filthy insults her late husband had flung at her, making her feel so worthless and unattractive the little self-esteem she had possessed had been obliterated completely.

Gabby suddenly became aware of where they were heading as Vinn took the exit to Mosman off the Harbour Bridge. 'We're going to your house?' she asked, swivelling to look at him.

'Yes,' he said, concentrating on the traffic. 'We could have gone to a café in the city, but you obviously need some peace and quiet—not to mention a couple of painkillers.'

Gabby turned back to look at the road ahead, her brow creasing slightly. The caring, solicitous Vinn was a change from the teasing, taunting one, but she

wondered if he was trying to divert her attention away
from his mystery lover by acting out the role of
thoughtful fiancé. Jealousy gnawed at her insides like
hundreds of miniature hungry mouths nipping at her
tender flesh, making her feel sick with despair.

She didn't want to feel such intensity of emotion.

She didn't want to feel vulnerable.

She suddenly realised with a little jolt of surprise
she didn't want him to want anyone else. She wanted
him to want her and only her.

Vinn parked the car in the driveway and strode around
to help her out of her side. She looked pale, and there
were dark bruise-like shadows under her eyes. Her mouth
had a downward turn to it. It was obvious she was burning
the candle at both ends, spending long hours at the
hospital as well as juggling her father's business affairs.

He was all too familiar with the worry over an ill
parent. Watching his beloved mother die had been one
of the toughest things he had ever faced, made all the
harder when he had received the news of Blair St
Clair's suicide. Vinn hadn't been able to leave his
mother's bedside and travel to the other side of the
globe to attend Blair's funeral. Nor had he been able
to offer much in the way of support to Blair's parents
and Gabriella, even though he had dearly wanted to.

The news of her engagement a few weeks after
Blair's death had been another blow he had struggled
to deal with. He had never particularly liked Tristan
Glendenning; there had always been something about
him that irked Vinn the more he got to know him. He'd
been too smooth, too self-assured, and not one bit in
love with Gabriella. Of that Vinn was sure. But in spite

of his warning she had married Glendenning anyway. And the bruisers Tristan had engaged to work him over had certainly kept him away from the wedding, as Gabriella had requested. Vinn had put up a tough fight, but four against one was asking too much—even of someone with his level of physical fitness.

Vinn escorted her inside the house and straight to the kitchen, where he pulled out a stool for her. 'Sit,' he said. 'I'll make you some scrambled eggs and toast.'

For a moment or two she looked as if she was about to refuse, but then she gave a little sigh and wriggled onto the stool. 'Don't make too much,' she said. 'I'm not really very hungry.'

'When was the last time you ate?' he asked as he placed a knob of butter in the pan and set it on the cooktop.

'I don't know… I can't remember,' she said. 'Lunch yesterday?'

He rolled his eyes as he reached for a carton of eggs in the fridge. 'If you get any slimmer you'll have to wear snow skis in the shower to stop you going down the drain.'

She gave him a droll look. 'Very funny.'

Vinn cracked some eggs into a bowl and began to whisk them. 'How are you the handling work at the office since your father's been taking a break?' he asked, in a casually interested tone.

The momentary silence made him glance at her over his shoulder. 'Not so good, huh?' he said.

'What makes you think that?' she said with a defensive set to her features. 'You think I'm not capable of handling things on my own?'

He gave the eggs a good grind of pepper before responding. 'My gut feeling is you only do it because you feel you have something to prove. Your heart's not in it. It's never been in it.'

Her silence this time was a fraction longer. Vinn could almost hear the cogs of her brain ticking over, trying to find some way of justifying herself.

'It's a family business,' she said at last.

'So?'

'So family members usually take up some sort of role in the company.'

'Yes,' he said. 'But it helps if they're suited for it. And it helps even more if they enjoy it and get some sort of satisfaction out of it.'

He turned to see her slip down off the stool, her arms going across her chest in that classic defensive pose. 'I do enjoy it,' she said, but her eyes skittered away from his.

'Perhaps. But I still think there are things you would enjoy more.'

'Oh, really?' Gabby said, flashing her gaze back to his. 'Since when have you become such an expert on what would satisfy me?'

His eyes gave her that look—the look that made Gabby's legs feel weak and watery and her belly start to flutter as if tiny wings were beating with excitement inside her. And then her colour rose as she realised she could have phrased her question with perhaps a little less propensity for a double meaning.

'Because I know you, Gabriella,' he said. 'You have no head for business. And I'm not the only one who thinks so.'

Gabby stiffened as she looked at him. 'What?' she said, narrowing her eyes in suspicion. 'You mean you've been talking to someone in the company about me?'

He leaned back against the bench in an indolent manner. 'I just poured two point four million dollars into the company. Did you think I wouldn't do a bit of research before I committed myself so heavily?'

'What sort of research did you do?' Gabby asked with a guarded look. 'It's not like you had much time. I came to see you practically at the last minute, and you—' She stopped, her heart beginning to pound as the truth began to dawn. 'You went snooping around well before then, though, didn't you? My God, but you have some gall, Vinn Venadicci. How dare you undermine me like that?'

'I was concerned about your father's health way before he had the heart attack,' he said. 'I had lunch with him a couple of months ago and it became clear to me he didn't have his finger on the pulse of the business any more. He had lost that fire in his belly. Quite frankly, I think he was relieved to leave you in charge because he was feeling so worn out. It's my bet that once he recovers he'll change his mind about retiring and want to get back at the helm—which is why I have organised a business manager to take your place until he does. He starts tomorrow.'

Gabby's eyes went wide in outrage. 'You did *what*?'

'I want you to take a break from the business,' he said, dishing up the eggs. 'Take a few months to think about what you'd like to do. You might find you'd prefer not to work at all and just enjoy being a wife and mother.'

She gave him a livid glare. 'You've got it all worked

out, haven't you, Vinn? You expect me to give up everything just to be a breeding machine. God, I can't believe there are still men like you around. I thought they died out with the dinosaurs.'

He set the plate of eggs and toast on the bench between them. 'Sit down and eat that before it gets cold,' he said.

In a fit of temper Gabby shoved the plate back towards him, with more force than she had really intended. The plate slid off the bench and shattered on the floor at his feet, eggs and toast going everywhere.

Her eyes flew to his in apprehension. 'I—I'm sorry,' she said. 'I didn't mean to do that…'

'Sure you didn't.' He stepped back from the mess, his eyes hard on hers, his mouth pulled into a tight line of simmering anger.

Gabby took an unsteady step backwards. 'I'll c-clean it up,' she said, in a voice that was scratchy and uneven. 'If you'll just show me where the dustpan and broom are…'

'Leave it,' he said tersely. 'I'll see to it myself. In any case, you probably wouldn't know one end of a broom from the other.'

She compressed her lips, struggling to keep the tears back but in the end failing. One by one they slipped past the shield of her lashes and silently flowed down her cheeks.

Vinn paused on his way back from the utilities cupboard with the dustpan and broom. 'It's just a plate of eggs,' he said, his anger fading at the sight of her tears. 'It's not the end of the world.'

She choked back a sob and covered her face with

her hands, her shoulders shaking as she began to cry in earnest.

He let out a little curse, directed at himself rather than her, and, putting the pan and broom to one side, gathered her in his arms. 'Are you *sure* it's not that time of the month?' he asked.

She shook her head, buried against his chest, and sobbed and sniffled some more.

He stroked his fingers through the silky strands of her blonde hair, enjoying the feel of her soft and pliant against him. Her sobs gradually died down until she was silent, her head turned sideways, so her cheek was pressed close to his thudding heart.

His body was getting harder by the second, and the rush of blood to his groin was making him ache to grind his pelvis against hers. He could feel the softness of her breasts pressing against his chest, and her arms had somehow snaked around his waist, bringing her lower body just that little bit closer to his.

He felt a tremor of awareness go through her, like little ripples over the surface of smooth water, and then she lifted her head and met his gaze, her lips so soft and inviting that he brought his head down and covered them with his own.

CHAPTER SEVEN

GABBY totally melted under the blowtorch of his kiss. His lips were hard and then soft, firm and demanding one minute, gentle and cajoling the next. It was a heady repertoire, making all her senses shiver in response.

She returned his kiss with a level of passion that was almost frightening in its intensity. She was on fire for him, every part of her longing to feel him touch her all over, to bring her body to the highest peak of pleasure. She felt the stirring of her intimate muscles, the liquid warmth that seeped from deep inside her to prepare her for the thick invasion of his body. She could feel how aroused he was—so very hard, so intoxicatingly male.

With his mouth still locked on hers, Gabby felt his fingers working on the tiny buttons of her cotton top, undoing them one by one as his tongue danced a sexy tango with hers. He didn't bother undoing her bra; he simply shoved it out of the way and bent his mouth to her breast. She gasped in delight as his tongue circled her nipple a couple of times, before he began to suckle on her with a gentle drawing-in motion that made her knees start to buckle. He moved to her other breast, increasing the pressure of his mouth, using his teeth in tiny tug-like bites that sent shooting sparks of need right through her core. Waves of pleasure rolled over her, making her mind empty of everything but how he was making her feel.

He brought his mouth back to hers in a scorching kiss of passionate urgency, his pelvis jammed so tightly against hers she felt the throb and thunder of his blood beneath his skin.

'You taste so damned good,' he said, just above her swollen lips. 'I want to taste all of you—every beautiful inch of you.'

Gabby reconnected her mouth to his, her tongue stroking and curling around his, tasting the maleness and fiery heat of him. Her heart-rate went through the roof as he nudged her thighs apart, rubbing one of his own against her feminine mound. Her body exploded with sensation, the deep hollow ache intensifying until she was whimpering, soft little mewing sounds that came from the back of her throat.

'Come upstairs with me,' he said, lifting his mouth again to look down at her, his grey-blue eyes as dark as she had ever seen them. 'We don't have to wait until Friday. I want you now.'

Gabby felt herself wavering. Her body was tilting her one way while her brain was trying desperately to send her back the other. He had a mistress, she reminded herself. He was a playboy. He was only marrying her for revenge. There was no love in the arrangement—not even mild affection. This was about lust. He had wanted her for a long time and had gone to extraordinary lengths to have her. He would use her, and when he grew tired of her she would be left, trapped in a going-nowhere marriage, until he decided if or when it was to end.

Her body put up an equally powerful argument. It was still throbbing with need, every pore of her skin sensitised to his touch, every nerve-ending buzzing. Her lips were as swollen as the folds of her feminine cleft, the silky moisture between them making it even harder to ignore the need he had awakened in her.

'Or what about we do it here?' Vinn said, spinning her round so her back was against the kitchen bench. One of his hands lifted her skirt, his fingers searching for her moist heat.

'No!' Gabby thrust both hands against his chest.

He cocked one brow at her, his hand stilling on her thigh. 'No?'

She pressed her lips together, trying to control her breathing, trying to tame her wild needs, trying to gather some sense of decency and self-respect.

'No…' she said, releasing a tightly held breath. 'I can't…'

'You certainly weren't giving me that impression a few seconds ago,' he pointed out, with more than a hint of wryness. 'May I ask what changed your mind?'

Gabby moved out of his hold, rearranging her clothing with as much dignity as was possible, considering her breasts were bare and still damp from the ministrations of his mouth.

'I don't want to sleep with you before we get married,' she said, saying the first thing that came into her mind.

'For God's sake, Gabriella, you've been married for to another man, so it's not as if you're some sweet virgin saving yourself for your wedding night.'

Gabby could hear the frustration in his voice, and felt guilty and ashamed for allowing things to go as far as they had. 'I'm sorry… I know it's hard for you…'

He gave a rough bark of laughter. '*Hard* being the operative word.'

She felt colour storm into her cheeks and bit down on her lip. 'This is not easy for me,' she said, still fumbling with her buttons. 'It's…it's been a long time since I…you know…was intimate with…with—'

He placed a finger over her lips, his eyes a steely grey. 'Let's not keep bringing your late husband into the conversation, hmm? Every time I think of you with him I want to punch something.'

She stood there, her mouth sealed with his fingertip, the desire to push her tongue out to meet it almost overwhelming.

After a tense moment his finger dropped from her lips. 'Was he your first lover?' he asked.

Gabby gave a tiny nod, mentally grimacing as she recalled the one and only time Tristan had forced himself on her. She had never thought it would be that painful—but then he had not done anything to prepare her. She had been used like a whore and left torn apart, both physically and emotionally.

'Has there been anyone since?' Vinn asked, after another short but tense silence.

She shook her head. 'No… No one…'

He wondered whether or not to believe her. She certainly hadn't grieved the way everyone had expected her to grieve. Her husband had wrapped himself around a telegraph pole on his way home from work on the night of their fifth anniversary, dying instantly—or so the coroner had found. The press had captured Gabriella numerous times in the first few weeks after Glendenning's death, carrying on as if nothing had happened. She had shopped, got her highlights and nails done, with nary a hint of sadness etched on her beautiful face. Vinn had often wondered if the rumours he had heard around town were true. Word had it she'd had numerous affairs during her marriage, and that Glendenning had chosen to turn a blind eye rather than jeopardise the alliance of the two well-to-do family empires.

'Did you love him?' Vinn asked.

'I thought you didn't want me to talk about him?' she said, with an ironic glance over her shoulder.

'It's a simple question,' he said. 'And, like most simple questions, a yes or no will suffice.'

'Why do you want to know?' she asked, turning to face him. 'It's not as if you have any feelings for me other than lust. Or are you not telling me something I should know?'

Vinn had to admire her talent for the quick comeback. She was good at getting the focus off herself. The funny thing was, he wasn't exactly sure what he felt about her. For years he had simultaneously desired and hated her. She had been such a toffee-nosed bitch to him in the past, and while he could forgive those misdemeanours on the basis of her youth at the time, he could not forgive her for the way she still looked down her nose at him now. To her he was still the house-cleaner's son—not worthy to hold a door open for her let alone touch her until she screamed his name in ecstasy as he was so determined she would do.

'That would suit you, now, wouldn't it, Gabriella?' he said. 'To get me to confess undying love for you? Sorry to disappoint you, but my feelings are much more basic. Lust is a good word. Perhaps a little coarse for someone from your rather cosseted background, but it more or less sums it up.'

She gave him a haughty glare.

He smiled as he picked up his car keys. 'You might want to rebutton your top, Blondie, before I take you back to the hospital to see your father. The last button doesn't seem to have found its correct hole.'

Gabby looked down at her shirt and felt her face fire up. She looked as dishevelled and as ravished as she felt—but, even worse, Vinn had yet again got in the last word. She felt as if he had her pride in the palm of his hand and with just one small clench of his fist he could totally destroy it. She was going to fight tooth and nail to stop that from happening, but with each kiss he subjected her to she realised she was drifting further and further out of her depth and into totally unchartered waters.

She had always thought marrying Tristan Glendenning had been the biggest mistake of her life, but she could see now that falling in love with Vinn Venadicci would more than likely surpass it in spades.

Gabby stood by Vinn's side in front of the marriage celebrant and listened to herself mechanically repeat the vows that under the circumstances were nothing short of meaningless.

Vinn's clear and deep voice, however, made them sound much more convincing, she thought. The way he spoke with such firm conviction sounded as if he did indeed love her, and would treat her with honour and respect for the rest of their lives.

She turned when the celebrant said it was time for him to kiss the bride, and, tipping up her face, closed her eyes as Vinn's mouth sealed hers with a kiss that had a hint of possessiveness about it. Each movement of his lips on hers seemed to say, *You are mine now, body and soul.* And Gabby knew if Vinn had his way that could very well be the case within a matter of hours.

Their flights had been booked for their trip to the St Clair Island Resort, and they were due to leave within just over an hour. Their luggage was already in Vinn's car, and once the marriage certificate was signed he escorted Gabby out to where it was parked on the street outside.

Gabby found it hard to think of something to say on the way to the airport. She was conscious of Vinn's muscled arm occasionally shifting gears near her thigh. He had already taken off his jacket and peeled back his shirt cuffs due to the increase in temperature. The ink-black springy hairs on his forearms made her feel a mixture of trepidation and excitement to feel his touch on her bare skin.

There would be plenty of opportunity to do so on the tropical island resort, she reminded herself, with another little quiver of nervous anticipation. She had looked at next week's weather forecast, and with temperatures in the late twenties and low thirties predicted on the island, she knew her bikini and sarong would be the most she would be wearing during the day. She didn't dare think what she would be wearing at night. If Vinn had his way she was sure she would be naked.

'How long has it been since you were last on the island?' Vinn's voice cut across her thoughts.

Gabby had to think for a moment. 'I flew up earlier in the year,' she said. 'February, I think it was. I went up to check over the new refurbishment, but I only stayed a couple of nights.'

He didn't say anything in response, but Gabby wondered if he thought she should have visited more often, to keep a closer eye on things. The new business manager he had appointed had already found a few mistakes in her records, which had increased Gabby's feelings of incompetence, although Vinn had not made a big issue of it at the time. He had simply told Mark Vella that things had been very stressful recently. with Gabriella's father's health issues, and Gabby had found herself hoping he was doing it for the sake of her feelings. But she had realised in a saner moment he had probably been playing the part of supportive fiancé again, and her feelings had not been a consideration of his at all.

She was not quite ready to admit it to Vinn, but since she had stopped going into the office she had felt as if a huge weight had been lifted off her shoulders. Even her parents had not been the least bit concerned when she had stepped down from the board. Instead they had both communicated how much they trusted Vinn's judgement in handling the business side of things while Henry was out of action.

'Anyway,' her mother had said with a coy smile, 'it won't be long before we hear the patter of tiny feet, I am sure. Right, Gabby? After all, you are getting on for thirty. You don't want to leave it too late to have children, otherwise you might miss out altogether.'

Vinn had smiled as he'd placed his arm around Gabby's waist. 'Don't worry, Pamela,' he'd said. 'We'll get working on it right away.'

Gabby had blushed to the roots of her hair, but had forced a stiff smile to her face. She had, however, given Vinn's arm a hard pinch, and sent him a reproachful glare when her parents hadn't been looking. But all he had done was wink at her, which had made her already simmering blood start to boil.

Vinn drove into the valet parking area at the airport, and within in a few minutes they were checked in and waiting to board.

Once they were on their way the flight gave Gabby the perfect opportunity to close her eyes and feign sleep. But after what seemed just a few minutes she opened her eyes to find herself leaning against Vinn's shoulder.

She straightened and blinked a couple of times. 'Sorry…I must have fallen asleep,' she said. 'I hope I didn't crease your shirt too much.'

His smile was easy and relaxed. 'No, it's fine. I enjoyed listening to you snore, actually.'

Gabby pursed her lips. 'I do not snore.'

'How would you know?' he asked with the arch of one brow. 'You haven't had a lover since your husband passed away, or so you said.'

She frowned at him. 'Don't you believe me?'

He looked at her for a lengthy moment. 'You cannot be unaware of the rumours that circulated during your marriage.'

Gabby felt her stomach drop. 'W-what rumours?'

His gaze continued to pin hers. 'Rumours about all the lovers you took.'

Gabby felt her cheeks grow warm under his piercing scrutiny. 'I find it rather ironic that you apparently take on board everything you read in the press when you insisted that the woman you were photographed with was not your mistress when everything pointed to her being so.'

'So you are saying the rumours about you were unfounded?' he asked, still looking at her unwaveringly.

Gabby wondered if she should tell him what had really gone on during her marriage. But two things stopped her. One was the fact they were sitting on a plane surrounded by other people, and the other was her pride. Vinn had been the one to warn her not to marry Tristan, and she had ignored that warning and paid for it dearly. She couldn't risk him rubbing her nose in it every chance he could. She had suffered enough. In some ways she would always suffer for that mistake. Her life had taken on a trajectory she could never have anticipated.

'I am saying you shouldn't believe every bit of gossip you hear,' she said. 'There are always two sides to every story.'

'I have heard there are three,' he said with an enigmatic smile. 'The wife's version, the husband's version, and then there's the truth.'

Gabby was relieved when the flight attendant announced they were preparing to land at that point, so she didn't have to continue the conversation. She pushed her handbag back under the seat in front and, tightening her seatbelt, looked out of the window at the azure blue of the ocean below.

Various other tourist islands were dotted around St

Clair Island, but to Gabby none of them seemed as beautiful and tranquil. She had fond memories of coming to the island as a child. She had spent so many magical days with her brother, beachcombing, making sandcastles and sand sculptures, going for walks to all the private beaches away from the main one at the front of the resort restaurant and bar area.

A wave of nostalgia came over Gabby as the plane touched down. She felt tears spring to her eyes, and had to blink rapidly to make them go away. Blair had loved the island as much as she did. Even after all this time it was still hard to imagine he would never come here again, and walk with her along the sandy shore to pick up a shell or two to add to his collection.

Vinn's hand reached for one of hers, where it was clasped tightly in her lap, his long fingers curling around her smaller ones. 'Everything all right?' he asked.

Gabby gave him a forced smile. 'Of course. It was just a bumpy landing, that's all.'

He gave her fingers an almost imperceptible squeeze. 'I miss him too, *cara*. He was a good friend,' he said softly.

Gabby's throat thickened, but she somehow managed to speak in spite of it. 'You were like a brother to him. I was so jealous of how well you got on. It seems so petty and childish now...'

'You *were* a child,' he said, releasing her fingers. 'And a rather spoilt one at that. I am not going to hold it against you.'

Gabby surreptitiously massaged her fingers where his touch had set off a tingling reaction beneath her skin, all the time wondering if what he had said was true. Wasn't that the whole point of their marriage?

Retribution.

Revenge.

Vengeance...

She gave a little involuntary shiver as the last word and its well-worn biblical phrase reverberated in her head.

Vengeance is mine...

CHAPTER EIGHT

THE resort managers, Judy and Garry Foster, gave Vinn and Gabby a warm welcome. Garry took their luggage ahead, and, after a little tour of the resort for Vinn's benefit, Judy led the way to their deluxe penthouse-style unit overlooking its own private beach.

There was a plunge pool and a spa and sauna, and an outdoor shower with twin shower heads set in a tropical garden that was totally private. The exotic fragrance of frangipani was heavy in the warm air, and each of the bright splashes of colour from the hibiscus blooms reminded Gabby of crushed silk.

'If there is anything you need, just dial one,' Judy said as she made to leave.

'Thank you, Judy,' Vinn said with an easy smile as he held the door open for her.

The door closed once Judy had left, and Gabby felt a shiver run up her spine when Vinn's grey-blue gaze sought hers.

'How about a swim to cool off?' he asked.

'Um… OK…' She turned to where her bag was, on the luggage rest beside Vinn's, her belly a nest of nerves at the thought of sharing this penthouse with him. It was very spacious, but it was also incredibly secluded.

Not only had she never shared a bed with Tristan, she hadn't even shared a bathroom with him. He had insisted on having his own—the reason for which Gabby hadn't found out until a few months before his death. She had gone in there in search of more soap for her own bathroom and had seen the telltale traces of white powder and the rolled-up twenty-dollar bill lying on the marble benchtop.

It had not been so much of a shock to find out her husband was regularly snorting cocaine. What had been the biggest surprise was how she hadn't until then guessed it. His erratic moods, his almost manic behaviour at times and his lugubriousness at others, she'd realised in retrospect, were all signs of a drug habit slipping out of control. Just like her parents' inability to accept Blair had been struggling with an addiction, Gabby had not wanted to face the fact her husband was a drug-user. Along with his numerous affairs it had remained yet another dirty secret—another lie to live with.

'I will leave you to get changed,' Vinn said from the door. 'I'm going to have a look at the gym set-up.'

Gabby clutched a bikini and sarong against her chest as she looked at him. 'Oh…right…thanks…'

The door closed on his exit, and she let out a breath that rattled all the way past her lips.

The beach outside their apartment was about two hundred metres long, before an outcrop of rocks cut it off from the next bit of shore. Gabby swam back and forth in a leisurely fashion, enjoying the feel of the water against her skin. When she opened her eyes underwater she could see thousands of colourful tropical fish darting about beneath her. The sandy bottom made the water as clear as glass, and even when she swam out further to sea the clarity was unaffected.

She was quite far out from the shore when a dark shape appeared, seemingly out of nowhere. She gave a startled gasp, her heart pounding like a jackhammer, but then she realised it was Vinn.

'You really shouldn't come out this far without someone with you,' he said, treading water in front of her. 'It could be dangerous.'

'I'm a strong swimmer,' she said, trying not to look at the water droplets clinging to his dark lashes, making them thick and spiky.

'Strength and fitness have very little to do with safety when it comes to getting cramp or being stung by a jellyfish,' he pointed out.

'You don't seem to find it a problem, being out of your depth,' she returned with spirited defiance.

He came up closer, every now and again one of his long legs brushing against hers beneath the water. 'That's because it's rare for me to be out of my depth.' His grey-blue eyes dropped to her mouth as he added, 'In any situation.'

Gabby's tongue flicked over her lips, tasting salt, and her own need clawed at her from inside with long-taloned fingers. He was too close, but she hadn't moved away—even though she had the width of the beach to do so. The brush of his thighs stirred her blood, making it rush through her veins at breakneck speed.

When his head came down she had already lifted her face to meet his, and their lips came together in a hardened press that contained the potency of frustration, urgency and deep-seated passion.

Gabby whimpered with delight when his tongue found hers, tangling with it, seducing it, and then ruthlessly subduing it. She faintly registered she was no longer keeping herself afloat; his arms were wrapped around her, holding her so close their near-naked bodies were almost as one. She felt his erection pressing with such strength and power against her that the breath was pushed right out of her lungs. Desire licked through her, long-tongued and feverish, making every nerve in her body zing with sexual energy.

Vinn lifted his mouth from hers. 'You don't know how close I am to thrusting myself into you right here and now,' he said, in a tone gravel-rough with need.

Her caramel-brown eyes flared in excitement—the same excitement he could feel in every delicious curve of her body pressed so tightly against him. She sent her tongue out to her lips, driving him wild with longing, and her smooth legs tangled with his.

'Do you think that's such a good idea, out here in the open?' she asked in a breathless voice. 'Someone might see us.'

'Right now I couldn't care less who sees us,' he said. 'But for the sake of decency perhaps we should take this indoors.'

She shivered in his arms, but not from cold. She felt warm and vibrant, and pliable with desire. It was immensely satisfying for him to feel that from her, even if so far it had only been physical, not verbal. She wanted him as much as he wanted her. And, God, did he want her. Every throbbing part of him was aching to sink into her, to feel surrounded by her honeyed flesh. He had dreamed of it for years, hating himself for his weakness where she was concerned, but knowing he would never be truly satisfied until he had taken her. It was a fever in his blood; it ran like a turbulent flood beneath his skin, a pounding river of need, desperate to burst from its confines.

He led her out of the water, his eyes drinking in the sight of her clad only in a red string bikini. Her slim limbs were golden and smooth, her beautiful breasts protesting about the tiny triangles keeping them in place, and the shadow of her cleavage making his imagination run riot.

There were so many things he wanted to do to her, he thought as he took her hand and led her towards the penthouse apartment. He wanted to kiss every secret place, brand her as his in every position possible, so she would no longer think of anyone but him when they made love. He wanted to pump himself into her, to make her swell with his seed, to stake his claim on her in the most primal way of all—as the father of her children. She would think twice about walking away from him if they shared the bond of a child—a child he would love with his whole being, sacrificing everything for it, just as his mother had done for him.

The penthouse was blessedly cool after the heat down on the beach, but Gabby still felt as if she was on fire. As Vinn closed the door she stood before him, trembling all over with anticipation. He had stoked her desire to an unbearable level. She could no more say no to him now than walk on the water they had just left. It was an inevitable outcome of their union—something they had both wanted for longer than perhaps she was prepared to acknowledge. And his longing was more than obvious.

It might not be dressed up in pretty words, such as those said to her by Tristan Glendenning to get her to marry him, but somehow Gabby suspected Vinn Venadicci was not going to be the disappointment in bed her late husband had been.

Sexual potency practically oozed from Vinn's olive-toned pores. He had no doubt bedded many women, done things to them she had never even thought of, and yet he was here with her now, tied to her, aroused by her and reaching for her.

Her bikini top was the first thing to go. Her breasts fell free, the achingly tight nipples soon soothed by the hot, moist cavern of his mouth. It was mind-blowing to feel the rough abrasion of his jaw on her tender flesh. And it was knee-buckling to feel him reach for the strings that held her bikini bottoms in place. They fell to the floor in a silent puddle of red fabric, her body totally exposed to him in a way it had never been before.

'You are beautiful,' he said, in that same roughened tone he had used down on the beach. His gaze ran over her. 'So stunningly beautiful.'

Gabby felt her breath hitch as his eyes came back to hers. 'I want to see you too.' *Was that what she had just said?* she wondered in amazement. Had she openly admitted how much she wanted him?

He held his arms up, as if in surrender. 'I'm all yours,' he said. 'I'll give you the honours.'

Gabby needed no other inducement. She reached out with fingers not quite steady and peeled back the black Lycra covering him, her throat almost closing over as she saw how he was made. He was big, far bigger than she had expected, even though she had been pressed up against him so intimately several times. He was as nature intended him—fully male and fully aroused.

Her fingers skated over him, like a light-footed dancer going through a complicated routine, taking her time, rehearsing, going back over the same part again and again to get it right.

'God, that feels so good,' he said, as he captured her hand and held it aloft. 'But I don't want to arrive ahead of schedule.'

Gabby felt her belly quiver like a not-quite-set jelly. She was not used to this extended routine. This strung-out torture of the senses, the screaming of desires begging to be fulfilled. Her body ached for him as it had never ached before. Silky fluid moistened her intimately, swelling her feminine folds with longing. Her breasts were tight and tender at the same time, and her mouth was already missing the heat and fiery conquering of his.

So she did what any aroused woman would do under the circumstances. She pressed herself up against him, her mouth taking his in a hot, wet kiss that showed him how much she wanted him.

He responded just the way she'd wanted him to. He pressed her to the bed behind her, his weight coming over her, his body piercing her in one thick urgent thrust that should not have hurt but somehow did.

Vinn felt her flinch and stilled his movements, raising himself up on his arms to look down at her. 'Am I going too fast for you?'

She gave her head a little shake. 'No…it's just been…a long time…'

Vinn hated being reminded of who had taken her first. It made his blood almost singe his veins to think of that silver-tongued creep having her night after night, pleasuring her the way *he* wanted to pleasure her. He would make her forget him. He would do everything in his power to make her forget, to have her scream his name when he took her to paradise.

'I'll slow down,' he said, pressing a soft kiss to her bow of her mouth. 'Relax for me, *cara*, go with me, don't tense up.'

He moved slowly, relishing the tight warmth of her, but still conscious of her hesitancy. He could feel it—the way her muscles locked as if she was frightened he would hurt her.

'That's it,' he soothed as she started to pick up his slow but steady rhythm. 'You're doing great, Gabriella, just great. Come with me, nice and slow.'

Gabby started to feel the slow melt of her bones. He was so gentle, and yet so powerful. She could feel the latent strength of him sliding inside her, each slow thrust going a little bit deeper. She felt the tremors begin, but they were not enough to satisfy the ache she felt so deep inside. She writhed beneath him, desperately seeking what she was looking for—something extra, something that would tip her over the edge of oblivion and make her his for all time.

He moved his hand down between their tightly

locked bodies, searching for the tight pearl where all her need seemed to be concentrated, and began a gentle but rhythmic stroking. Sensation after sensation flowed through her. She felt herself climbing a steep cliff; she was almost there, the plunge over the edge was so close she could almost taste it, but she kept pulling back, too frightened to finally let go.

'Come for me, *cara*,' Vinn said, kissing her mouth into soft malleability. 'Don't hold back. Let yourself go.'

She concentrated, trying so hard to keep those other dark images out of her mind, her breathing coming in quick sharp bursts. 'I can't…' she gasped, almost close to tears, annoyed at herself for being such a failure. 'I'm sorry… I just can't…'

He slowed his movements, giving her a break from the caressing of his fingers as if he sensed how fragile she felt. 'It's all right,' he said softly. 'We don't have to rush this. Take your time. I can hold on. Only just, mind you, but I can hold on.'

Gabby looked at him with shame colouring her cheeks. 'I can't do this…' she said. 'I've never been able to do this…'

A frown pulled at his brow, and she felt his whole body tense above and within hers. 'What are you saying, Gabriella?' he asked in a raspy tone.

Gabby pressed her lips together, hoping she wouldn't dissolve into tears, but still perilously close all the same.

'Are you saying you have *never* had an orgasm?' he asked after a moment.

She gave a small nod, silent tears making their way down her cheeks.

Vinn recalled her hesitancy, the flinching as if she had expected him to be rough with her. His heart began to pump—hard, out-of-rhythm pumps against his breastbone—as dark thoughts assembled themselves in his head.

His one short sharp curse cut through the air like a switchblade. 'Did that bastard hurt you?' he asked.

She didn't answer, but he saw all he needed to know in the wounded caramel-brown of her eyes, in the way her bottom lip trembled ever so slightly. His gut clenched, tight fists of anguish punching at his insides, making him see red dots of rage behind his eyes.

He moved away from her as gently as he could. 'I'm sorry, Gabriella,' he said huskily. 'I would never have taken things this far and this soon if I had known.'

She reached out a soft hand and touched him on the arm. 'It's all right, Vinn,' she said. 'I want to know what it's like. I want you to pleasure me. I was so close… I'm sure I can do it…with you…'

Vinn wavered for a moment. His mind was all over the place. She had been married for five years and apparently not once experienced the ultimate pleasure of physical union. What was he to make of that? He'd already suspected she hadn't loved Glendenning, but she had responded to *him* without restraint. He didn't want to think too much about that. He wasn't prepared to examine his own feelings, much less hers.

'I don't want to hurt you,' he found himself saying, even as his body sought the silky warmth of hers, sliding back in with a shiver of goosebumps lifting the entire surface of his skin as he felt her accept him smoothly. 'Tell me how fast, how slow, what you need.'

She gripped his buttocks tightly in her hands. 'I just need you,' she said. 'No one has ever made me feel like this before.'

She gave a breathy sigh as he began to move, slowly building up the tempo, caressing her, testing how much or how little she needed, gauging her reaction by feeling the pulse of her body and watching the flitting emotions on her face.

He knew when she was coming close. He could feel it in her body, wrapped so tightly around his, and he could see it in the contortion of her features, in the agony and the ecstasy played out on her face. He felt the first ripple course through her, heard her startled cry, and then the aftershocks as wave after wave consumed her, tossing her about in his arms, triggering his own response with a force that was beyond anything he had ever experienced. He felt himself spill, and that delicious moment or two of nothing but intense pleasure. Shockwaves reverberated through him, inducing a lassitude that made him slump over her almost helplessly, like a bit of flotsam tossed up by a very rough surf to the sandy shore.

When he finally had the energy to lift himself above her, Vinn saw that she was crying. Not noisy sobs, just silent tears that tore at him like nothing else could.

He brushed the hair back from her face, his thumb lingering over the soft swell of her bottom lip that her perfect white teeth seemed so determined to savage. 'You were amazing,' he said. 'Truly amazing.'

Her eyes couldn't quite make the full distance to his. 'I didn't realise how…how intense it could be…'

He pressed a soft kiss to her brow. 'It gets better when

you know what your body needs. I am still learning about yours—how it responds, what it wants, what it doesn't like, how soft, how hard, that sort of thing.'

She looked at him with an open vulnerability he had never seen in her gaze before—or at least not to that extent. 'Did I pleasure you?'

He frowned as he saw the deep-seated insecurity in her gaze. 'How can you doubt it, *cara*?'

She began to finger the scar that slashed his left eyebrow in two. 'I've always felt such a failure… physically,' she said, her voice so soft he had to strain his ears to hear it. 'Tristan never touched me during our engagement…apart from kissing and holding hands. He told me he wanted to wait until we were married…' She took a deep breath and added, 'I didn't realise he was having affairs. They went on for most of our marriage.'

Vinn frowned as he absorbed the information. Somehow he had thought Gabriella had turned a blind eye to Glendenning's affairs for the sake of the prestige of being his wife. Had he got it wrong?

'When did you find out about it?' he asked.

Her eyes moved out of reach of his. 'Just after our wedding. I found him in a rather…er…compromising situation.'

His gut tightened. 'How compromising?'

Her cheeks were cherry-red, her voice unsteady, and still her eyes would not meet his. 'He was being…' She winced as if she didn't like using the word. 'Serviced by his secretary…'

Vinn let out another curse as he got off the bed. He whipped a towel around his waist and began to pace.

'For God's sake, Gabriella, why the hell didn't you tell anyone? The marriage could have been annulled. Even then it wouldn't have been too late.'

She swallowed tightly, her eyes glistening with tears. 'My parents had been through so much,' she said. 'I didn't want to cause another scandal. I could just imagine the scene. Mum was so proud of the wedding—how she had dragged herself out of her depression and come off the tranquilisers. How could I do that to her? They had already been through so much. I just couldn't do it.'

Vinn frowned. 'I swear to God if I had been there I would have stopped it. But you made sure I wasn't there, didn't you?'

She bit her lip. 'I didn't want a scene, Vinn,' she said. 'I didn't want Mum and Dad upset.'

His top lip curled. 'Didn't your husband tell you he was the one who gave me this?' He pointed to the slash of the scar on his eyebrow.

She went white, her mouth dropping open. 'No... *No...*'

'He got his thugs to hold me down—all three of them,' he said, bitterness heavy in his tone. 'And then he shoved the heel of his shoe on my face, telling me it was a gift from you.'

CHAPTER NINE

GABBY thought she was going to faint. In fact she felt as if the vicious assault Vinn had just described had hit *her* full in the face.

She flinched away, her shocked gasp tearing at the dry ache in her throat. She couldn't speak, no matter how hard she tried; the words were stuck behind that boulder-sized restriction in her throat. Vinn had been brutally assaulted, and for all this time he had thought *she* had orchestrated it. Yes, she had spoken to her father's security head Tony Malvern on the phone, asking him to not admit Vinn Venadicci into the church the following day. But she had not told him to use any sort of violence. Besides, Tony was not that sort of man. He was a loving husband and father—a bit tough on the outside, but never would she believe him capable of being party to such a cowardly and vicious attack on another person. All Gabby had done was to tell him to inform Vinn he wasn't welcome to attend the ceremony in case he took it upon himself to disrupt it, as he had threatened.

'N-no… *No!*' Gabby cried. 'I didn't ask anyone to

hurt you! You have to believe me, Vinn. Why would I do such a thing?'

His eyes were diamond-hard, the cast to his features as if carved from granite. 'You resented me from the moment I walked through the gates of your family estate. You looked down your nose at me with increasing disdain as the years went on. Don't you remember how much you enjoyed taunting me, Gabriella? Setting me up just so you could giggle behind the bushes with your empty-headed friends?'

Gabby could feel her shame in the slow burn of her cheeks. 'I know I was a bitch towards you,' she said. 'I've explained it already…how I was jealous of you cutting in on my relationship with Blair. He had no time for me whenever you were around.'

'You didn't seem to mind his relationship with other people,' he commented. 'Your late husband being a case in point.'

'That was different,' she said. 'Blair and Tristan had been at school together. Also, Tristan was my mother's best friend's son. He had been coming to our house even before I was born. I was used to sharing my brother with him. It was all I knew.'

His eyes were still trained on hers—hard, unreachable, and unrelentingly angry. 'Do you deny you asked Glendenning to keep me away from the wedding?' he asked.

Gabby compressed her lips, releasing them after a moment. 'Of course I deny it. I admit I spoke to Tony Malvern, my father's chief of security, but only to ask him to refuse you entry to the church. But I never said a word to Tristan about it.'

Vinn studied her for several tense moments, weighing up whether or not to believe her. Although Tony Malvern no longer worked for Henry St Clair, since taking early retirement due to a chronic health condition, Vinn had never found him to be anything other than a hard-working and decent family man, who was paid to keep an eye on the various St Clair's business properties after hours.

'Did anyone overhear your conversation with Tony?' he asked.

She gave him a flustered look. 'I don't know... I was upset. I wasn't looking around corners to see if anyone was listening.'

'No doubt your husband was.'

Her frown deepened. 'You went out drinking,' she said. 'That's what I was told when I got back from my honeymoon. They told me you got drunk, and then got into some sort of brawl and ended up in hospital. But if you were assaulted as you said by those thugs, including Tristan, why didn't you press charges?'

'And drag your parents through a very public scandal, with their beloved daughter at the centre of it?' he asked with a sardonic lift of one brow. 'I might be a bit rough for your tastes, Gabriella, but I am not without feeling or a sense of honour.'

Gabby dropped her shoulders, her thoughts in turmoil. He had hated her for all these years for what she had supposedly done, and yet he had protected her family and therefore her as well. He had not once spoken of it to her parents, of that she was sure. Instead his anger towards her had quietly simmered in the background, as he'd waited patiently for the chance to have his revenge. By going to him for financial help that day she had unwittingly handed him one on a platter.

She brought her gaze back to his hardened one. 'That's what this marriage you've forced on me is all about, isn't it?' she said. 'You wanted to make me pay for the attack you think I ordered by locking me into a loveless marriage with you?'

His expression was unapologetic. 'I told you my reasons for wanting this marriage to take place,' he said in a gritty tone.

'Oh, yes,' she threw at him resentfully. 'You've been lusting after me for years and you just couldn't wait to get your hands on me.'

His eyes burned into hers, with a satirical glint lighting them from behind. 'I didn't hear you saying no just a little while ago,' he said. 'In fact I seem to recall you *begging* me to make love to you.'

Gabby swung away from him in fury, unable to bear his mockery of her desperate need of him. As angry as she was, she still felt the thrumming pulse of blood in her veins, the heady awareness of him and how he had made her feel. Her body was still damp from him. If it wasn't for the fact she was on the pill to regulate her cycle she might have even conceived the child he had bought and paid her to bear for him.

The thought of her belly ripe with his seed made her knees weaken unexpectedly. He might not have married her for the right reasons, but she had no doubt he would make a wonderful father. He had loved his mother more than any other son she had ever known, putting his own life on hold to nurse her through the last months of her too-short and too-hard life.

'Nothing to say, Gabriella?' he asked. 'No feisty comeback to insult me or put me in my place?'

Gabby let out a rattling breath and faced him. 'I'm sorry, Vinn, for what happened to you that night,' she said, taking her pride in hand. 'I know you don't believe me…might never believe me…but I had nothing to do with it. Tristan may have overheard my conversation with Tony, but even if he didn't he had good enough reason to stop you from coming to the wedding.'

'What was that?' he asked, holding her gaze with steely intent.

Gabby chewed at her lip, her eyes falling away from his. 'I'm not sure if he saw us kissing that night… I've often wondered…'

'He was jealous that you responded to me in a way he could never get you to respond to him,' he said. 'I don't blame him. I have revisited that kiss a thousand times in my head, and no one has come close to making me feel the way I did with your mouth on mine.'

Gabby felt warmth flow through her at his words. It was like warmed honey flowing through her veins. He had revisited that kiss so many times—as she had done over the years. What would he say if she were to tell him how often she had thought of how she had responded to him that night? How alive her senses had been, as if he had flicked a switch on in her body no one else had access to?

She had been attracted to him for so long but had stoically denied it.

She had always been in love with him, but too terrified to admit it.

Once the admission was out, Gabby felt it rush

through her like the cleansing tide of saline in grit-filled eyes.

She was in love with him.

She had felt that tug of attraction from the moment her female hormones had switched on in her youthful body. She had somehow recognised him as her match, the one person who could meet her needs, but she had pushed him away out of fear, out of insecurity, and out of misplaced pride.

Would her parents have really objected if she had told them all those years ago she loved Vinn instead of Tristan? They had lately accepted the news of her hasty marriage to Vinn without a ripple of disapproval. Even her mother, who had been so toffee-nosed towards him and his mother in the past, had practically wept as she had welcomed him into the bosom of the St Clair family…or what was left of it, Gabby thought with a painful ache, as a vision of her brother flitted into her brain.

Blair had adored Vinn. They had been mates from the word go—comrades, confidantes, all the things good friends should be.

And yet Blair had ended his life…

While his best friend was several thousand kilometres away, nursing his mother on her deathbed, Gabby realised with a stun-gun jolt of awareness.

'Is something wrong?' Vinn's voice sliced through her reverie. 'You look pale.'

'I'm fine…' she said, mentally shaking her head to get her thoughts into some sort of order. 'I'm just thinking…trying to make sense of it all…'

'What happened back then doesn't have to affect us

now,' he said. 'If you say you had nothing to do with the assault, then I will have to accept that.'

She looked at him again, swallowing against the lump of uncertainty in her throat. 'How can you ever know for sure I wasn't behind it? You don't trust me; you have no reason to trust me.'

He leaned back against the wall, his arms folded across his broad chest, his eyes still holding hers. 'As long as I am certain you were not party to it, I will be happy,' he said. 'I would not like our future children to think that at one point their mother was intent on bringing about my demise.'

Gabby felt her knees give another distinctive wobble. 'You seem in rather a hurry to land yourself an heir,' she said. 'What if I prove to be infertile?'

'Have you any reason to suspect you might be?'

'Have you any intention of releasing me from this arrangement if I am?' she countered.

His grey-blue eyes tussled with hers, bringing hers down in a submission she resented but couldn't for the life of her control. 'No,' he said. 'If you can't give me an heir naturally, then we will pursue the other options available.'

'What if I don't want to have a child right now?' Gabby asked, and then, after a carefully timed interval, added, 'What if I don't want to have children at all?'

The silence that ensued grew teeth that seemed to gnaw at the space that separated them.

'Do you have a particular aversion to motherhood?' he finally asked.

'Not really…' She waited a moment before continuing, 'I guess what I have an aversion to is being forced to deliver according to someone else's schedule, not mine.'

'Having a child should ideally be a joint decision,' he said, still honing in on her with those unreadable grey-blue eyes of his. 'If you are not ready, then we will wait until you are.'

'You don't even like me,' she said, frowning at him in irritation. 'How can you possibly think of fathering a child with me?'

His eyes ran over her sheet-wrapped form in one sweeping, all-encompassing movement that had possession and arrogant control written all over it. 'Because I have always wanted you, Gabriella,' he said. 'You are my nemesis, my other half, my completion. It was confirmed when we came together physically. I always knew it would be like that between us. I just had to wait until you were willing to see it.'

Gabby felt the need to keep some level of distance. 'What if Tristan hadn't died?' she asked. 'Would you have continued with this vendetta?'

He raised one broad shoulder in shrug. 'That would have entirely depended on you,' he said. 'I was testing the waters the night before your wedding. I was convinced you were no more in love with Glendenning than he was with you, and it seems I was right. No woman in love with another man would have responded the way you did to me.'

'So…kissing me was some sort of experiment?' Gabby asked, with reproach heavy in her tone.

'Kissing you was a temptation I could not resist,' he responded, stepping towards her, holding her in place with his hands on the tops of her shoulders. 'Like it is now, *cara*. I want to feel the tremble of your lips beneath mine, the way your tongue so shyly meets mine. I want it all, Gabriella. I want all of you.'

Gabby would have pushed him away, but he had already brought her too close to the tempting heat of his near-naked body. With only a towel loosely slung about his hips, she was left in no doubt of his arousal. Her body was just as eager behind its flimsy shroud of a sheet. Her nipples were clearly outlined, pert and aching for his touch, and her body was swaying towards him. Her mouth opened just as his was lowering to commandeer hers.

The kiss was like two combustible fuels meeting. Explosions went off in her brain, sending a fiery trail through her veins, making every nerve stand to attention. Her tongue snaked out to meet his in a sexy tangle of duelling need. Hers was igniting slowly but surely; his was at the ready, urgent, pressing, and totally, intoxicatingly, irresistibly male.

'You know I want you again, don't you?' he murmured against her mouth, as his hands skated so very skilfully over her, removing the sheet as if it was a layer of tissue wrap.

Gabby's hands had already dispensed with his towel, and were now shaping him, relishing in the tilted engorgement of him that so matched her body's intimately designed contours.

'I want you too,' she said, pressing kiss after kiss to his mouth. 'I want to feel it all again. Make me feel it all again.'

Vinn didn't need her to beg or plead. He wanted it as much as she did—the magic, the mindlessness of it, the total exhilaration of the senses that shoved aside every other rational thought. He didn't want to think just now. He wanted to feel. He had unlocked in her a treasure chest of sensuous pleasures, and he wanted to lay each and every precious piece out for his indulgence. The way she shivered when his hands touched her in the lightest of touches. The way her eyes flared when he looked at her with unwavering desire. The way her mouth softened, as if preparing for the hard descent of his, her lips parting to accept the searching thrust of his tongue.

God, had any woman done this to him in the past? With her he seemed to be always fighting for control, holding back the urge to spill, his need so great he had trouble reining it in to ensure she was not rushed, not hurt the way she had been in the past.

'Vinn?' Her soft voice was against his neck, her lips brushing his flesh.

He stroked the back of her head, his fingers splayed to feel the silky softness of her hair, to anchor him to her, to keep her where she was—close, so very close, so he could feel every beat of her heart.

'Don't talk, *mia piccola*,' he said, cupping her face to look deep into her eyes. 'Just feel.'

Gabby's eyelashes fluttered closed as his mouth came down to reclaim hers, the intimate contact so consuming she felt her mind spinning out of control. His kisses were so drugging they made her forget the past. They made her think only of the here and now, of how he made her feel, of how her body responded to him, of how it came alive in a way it had never done before. She could feel the echo of his kiss resounding in the rest of her body. It made her aching need for him all the more intense. It throbbed in her belly, low and deep, it swelled in her breasts, making them eager for his touch, and it trembled in her fingertips as she continued to explore him.

His hand pulled hers away from his hardened body, holding it above her head as he ravaged her mouth with his lips and tongue. Gabby laid her head back against the wall as he subjected her to a conflagration of the senses, her heart pounding inside her chest, her legs barely able to keep her upright.

He lifted his mouth off hers long enough to guide her back to the bed, his hands shaping her breasts, his mouth bestowing hot, sucking kisses to each one until she was twisting and turning beneath him as he pinned her with his weight.

'I have thought of doing this to you for so long,' he groaned against her right breast. 'I don't think there is a man alive who has wanted a woman more than I have wanted you.'

Gabby knew his attraction for her was only physical. He had said nothing of other feelings. At least he wasn't lying to her, as Tristan had done, but still she felt achingly disappointed her love for him was not returned. Was she destined to be tied to men who wanted to exploit her? Was she never to feel loved for who and what she was? She longed for security, for the warm protection of a love that would not die in spite of the passage of years. And yet into this loveless arrangement Vinn wanted to bring children—their children—a mingling of their blood and DNA. How could she agree to such a scheme without the assurance that he felt something for her other than lust?

'Vinn?' she said, touching his face with the flat of her palm, her fingers splaying over his stubbly jaw before she could stop them.

He turned his head and pressed a kiss into the centre of her palm. 'Do we have to talk right now, *cara?*' he asked, his eyes heavy-lidded with banked-down desire.

'Do you still hate me?'

His grey-blue eyes opened fully, and then focussed on hers. 'No,' he said on an expelled breath. 'Hate is not what I feel for you.'

Gabby drew in a ragged breath and held it. 'You…you don't?'

His eyes were unwavering on hers. 'I would not be here now, doing this to you, if I hated you, Gabriella,' he said.

'But you don't love me,' she said. And, waiting a beat, added, 'Do you?'

The distance between his brows narrowed slightly. 'That seems to me to be a rather loaded question,' he mused. 'Is that a prerequisite for allowing me access to your body? Showering you with empty words and phrases just so I can have my physical needs met?'

Gabby felt a stirring of resentment at his words. 'I am not entirely disconnected from my feelings, and I don't believe you are either,' she said. 'You make love to me as if you worship every inch of the space I take up, and yet you won't admit a modicum of affection for me. How am I supposed to make sense of it all?'

He eased himself up on his elbows, his weight still pinning her, pelvis to pelvis, stomach to stomach. 'Do you want me to tell you I love you?' he asked. 'Is that it? Is that what you want? For me to pretend to have feelings for you?'

Gabby blinked back tears. 'No, I don't want you to pretend to love me,' she said, trying to keep her voice steady. 'That's not what I want at all.' *I want you to love me for real.*

'Why is what I feel or don't feel suddenly so important to you?' he asked.

She frowned at the harshness of his tone. 'Because almost every woman wants to be assured the man she is involved with is not just using her physically. It's so degrading, so emotionless and…and dehumanising.'

He lifted himself off her, the sudden rush of cooler air on her chest and stomach making her feel not just physically abandoned, but emotionally as well.

She watched as he reached for the towel she had peeled off him just moments ago, wrapping it around himself almost savagely.

Anger flickered in his grey-blue eyes, and his body was whipcord tense as he faced her. 'Is that what you think I am doing?' he asked. 'Slaking my lust with no regard whatsoever for who you are and what you might need? Didn't the last half-hour prove *anything* to you about who I am as a person?'

Gabby pressed her lips together to keep them from trembling. 'You married me to possess me,' she said. 'I am the highly prized trophy you missed out on in the past. You know I would not have married you for any other reason than money, so you swooped as soon as the opportunity arose.'

'I am not denying I have wanted you for a very long time,' he clipped back. 'But don't let's confuse the issue with pretending things we don't feel. You have looked down your nose at me for as long as I can remember. Sure, we just had great sex—better even than I thought it would be—but that doesn't mean either of us has to pretend things we don't feel in order to feel better about the level of desire we just experienced and will no doubt continue to experience.'

Gabby pulled the sheet up to her chin. 'I don't think you would admit to loving someone even if you did,' she said. 'You wouldn't want to let anyone, particularly a woman, get the upper hand—and certainly not me.'

He gave a mocking laugh that chilled her blood. 'Is that what you think? That I've been pining away all these years with unrequited love for you, but I won't admit it in case you get the chance to use it against me in some way?'

Gabby didn't know what to think. She was confused, so very confused, and suddenly feeling more vulnerable than she wanted to be. She was making a fool of herself. She knew it, and it made her feel all the more exposed. She was practically begging him to confess feelings for her he clearly didn't have and never had. She was a fool, a romantic fool, crying for a moon that was never going to rise on her horizon.

She curled up in a tight ball on the bed, dragging the rest of the sheet over her to cover herself. 'I would like to be left alone,' she said in a toneless voice.

Vinn hesitated. He didn't really want to leave her like this, she was upset and very probably close to tears, but he just couldn't stay.

The first heady rush of love he had felt for her when she was younger had very quickly been replaced by a deep loathing for all she represented. The way she had always carried herself with that cold air of condescension, ridiculing him at every opportunity, had fuelled that hatred to boiling point. But now her adamant denial of having anything to do with his assault had made him rethink everything.

Revenge had been at the forefront of his mind for so long he needed time to re-examine his feelings. Up until a few hours ago she had hated him with an intensity that had glittered in her brown eyes every single time they clashed with his. Yet she had fallen apart in his arms, her body responding to his in a whirlwind of passion. There could be many reasons for that, he thought cynically. Two point four million of them, for starters. Anyway, she hadn't come right out and said it. She had just hinted at having feelings for him. But what if it was his wealth she was really in love with?

OK, he had saved her skin and given her a taste of what her late husband had denied her. Women were funny like that; one earth-shattering orgasm and suddenly they were madly in love with you. How many times had he heard other women say it to him, only to move on when the first wave of lust died down?

Vinn dragged on his bathers. 'I'm going for another swim,' he said. 'I guess I'll see you later.'

There was a muffled sound from beneath the tightly wrapped sheet that sounded as if she didn't care either way—which was probably no more than he deserved, Vinn thought as he softly shut the door as he left.

CHAPTER TEN

GABBY woke to semi-darkness and to a feeling that someone was in the room with her. She pushed herself upright, brushing the hair out of her eyes as she saw the shadow of Vinn's figure sitting on a chair close to the bed.

'What time is it?' she asked, trying for a cool, calm and collected tone, even though it was far from what she felt.

'Just gone nine.'

'Oh…'

'We can still have dinner in the restaurant, or order in some room service—whichever you prefer,' he said, rising to his feet and stretching.

Gabby wondered how long he had been sitting there, silently watching her. 'I need a shower,' she said. 'Do you think the restaurant will stay open long enough for me to freshen up?'

He switched on the master switch, which activated all the lamps in the suite. 'You are part-owner of this resort, Gabriella,' he reminded her. 'If you want the restaurant to remain open for you, then you only have to issue the command.'

Gabby held the sheet she had gathered around

herself up close to her chin. 'Don't mock me, Vinn,' she said. 'Please…not after this afternoon.'

'Is that what you think I'm doing?' he asked, frowning.

She gave him a surly glance. 'Look, I know I haven't got the best business head in the world, but at least I've tried my best to fill the gap my brother left.'

'Is that why you put your hand up for the job?' he asked. 'To fill in for Blair? Even though it was never what you wanted to do?'

Gabby tightened the sheet around her body rather than meet his eyes. 'We do what we do,' she said stiffly. 'There's no turning back.'

'What is that supposed to mean?'

She faced him squarely. 'My parents depend on me, Vinn,' she said. 'Do you think for a moment I would have come of my own volition to see you about the margin call? I only did it for them. I am only here now for them. I am all they have left.'

'So you sacrificed yourself?'

She lifted one shoulder. 'Your words, not mine.'

'But that's how you see it, isn't it?' he asked in an accusing tone. 'You, the Princess, have agreed to marry the peasant to save your family from financial shame.'

Gabby flinched at the weight of bitterness in his tone. 'I don't see you as a peasant, Vinn,' she said. 'I have never thought of you that way.'

His top lip curled. 'Nice try, Blondie. You nearly had me there. You sound so convincing, but we both know you will always see me as the cleaner's son. You married down, sweetheart, *way* down. How does it feel?'

Gabby held his fiery look for a beat or two before

slowly lowering her gaze. 'It certainly feels a whole lot better than my previous marriage,' she said, and then, meeting his eyes once more, added, 'That is unless you are going to add to your repertoire of accusing me of being a bitchy snob with the occasional slap or punch to bring me to heel.'

The silence began to pulse, each drawn out beat increasing the tension to snapping point.

Vinn stared at her, his eyes twin pools of stormy grey and blue. 'You mean to tell me that…he *hit* you?'

She nodded grimly. 'Not all the time, but often enough to keep me terrified he would do it again. It was a power thing. I wasn't the woman he really wanted. His parents would never have accepted any of the women he was having affairs with, so he used me as a punching bag now and again to keep me in line. I soon learned to keep my head down.'

Vinn's stomach churned. His hands felt numb even though he was clenching and unclenching them. 'Why didn't you say something?' he asked. 'For God's sake, Gabriella, you took years of that from him?'

She hugged her arms across her chest. 'I wanted to tell so many times,' she said. 'But I would have hurt people. My parents adored Tristan—he was like a second son to them. He had been so good when Blair died—he'd helped organise the funeral, and he even gave the eulogy.' She released a breathy sigh and continued. 'And then there were his parents—his well-connected parents, with a legal pedigree longer than your arm. Appearances are everything to them. How do you think they would have reacted to a spousal abuse claim against their beloved son lodged by me?'

Vinn swallowed tightly. He could see she had been in an impossible situation. The legal powerhouse the Glendenning family represented would have made anyone think twice about coming forward with such a claim against one of their blue-blooded heirs. She had gone through a living hell, each day a torture of being tied to a man who had treated her appallingly. Glendenning had even used her as a shield, making Vinn believe for all these years she was responsible for the attack on him the night before the wedding.

'I'm sorry,' Vinn said through a throat that felt as if he had swallowed a handful of razorblades. 'I wish I had known what had been going on. I wish you had felt you could have turned to me for help.'

'You were the last person I could turn to, Vinn,' she said, giving him a despondent look. 'You tried to warn me about Tristan and out of stubborn pride I refused to listen. Then, when I realised what a stupid mistake I'd made, I didn't want to hear you say *I told you so*. I just couldn't bear it.'

He scraped one of his hands down his face. 'Everyone is entitled to make a few mistakes in life,' he said. 'God knows I've made plenty. But thanks to the support and direction of people like your father I have been able to turn things around.'

'Some things can never be turned around,' she said blowing out a sigh. 'After Blair's suicide I felt so guilty... I felt like I had to do something to bring my mother out of her deep depression. My father threw himself into his work, but Mum had nothing...just me. I wanted to give her a new focus—a wedding, grand-children in the future, that sort of thing. But I didn't stop to examine how I really felt about Tristan, or—even more stupid of me—how he felt about me.'

Vinn took one of her hands and brought it up to his mouth, pressing his lips softly to the back of her knuckles. '*Cara,* don't punish yourself any more,' he said gently. 'You were in no way responsible for your brother's death. He had an addiction problem. He didn't get the help he needed. There was nothing you could have done.'

Vinn's words were like an arrow in Gabby's heart. She would always feel there was something she should have done. That was the pain she had to live with—the regret that she hadn't seen what was right under her nose.

Vinn brushed his lips over her fingers again. 'We all wish many things, Gabriella,' he said. 'Things we would have done differently if we knew then what we know now.'

Gabby felt her breathing start to shorten. 'Does that mean you want to end our marriage?' she asked.

He looked down at her for a long moment. 'Is that what you would like?' he finally asked. 'To be free?'

She couldn't hold his intense gaze, for she was sure he would see the longing and desperation reflected in hers. 'I'm not sure what the press will make of it if we end our marriage on the very day it was formalised,' she said. 'Then, of course, there are my parents to consider.'

'I was thinking the very same thing,' he said in a sombre tone. 'Your father has been through major surgery and is still a long way from being in reliable health. We can hardly fly back to Sydney and announce our separation.'

Gabby brought her eyes back to his, craning her

neck to do so. 'So…' she said, moistening her lips with the tip of her tongue. 'What do you suggest we do?'

He gave her another long, studied look. 'I told you the day you came to see me about the margin call that I believed marriage to be a permanent commitment. That has not changed.'

Gabby searched his features, hoping, praying for some clue to how he felt about her. But his expression was unfathomable. She began to toy with the idea of telling him she had fallen in love with him—openly this time, instead of hinting at it as she had done earlier. She even went as far as having the words mentally rehearsed; she could see them inside her head in capital letters: I LOVE YOU.

But something stopped her. He was still coming to terms with all he had learned about her this evening. The dark secret she had kept hidden for so long was finally out, which she could see had not only shocked him but had summoned his pity. She didn't want his pity. She wanted his love and his respect. But it would take more time to secure the latter, and the former she had no control over whatsoever.

All she knew was that he desired her, and had done for as long as she could remember. She had treated his attraction for her with disdain in the past, rejecting him in order to marry a man who had not only exploited her in the worst way possible, but orchestrated a vicious attack on Vinn that had left a lifelong scar—and not just the one on his eyebrow.

Gabby loved Vinn for who he was now just as much as she loved him for who he had been before. He had tried to rescue her from a disastrous marriage. He had done the responsible thing by coming to her as soon as he possibly could and asking her to reconsider. He had even offered himself as a substitute groom to save her pride on the day, and yet she had been too proud to listen.

Gabby thought back to that moment when Vinn's mouth had been sealed to hers. The flames of mutual desire had leapt between their bodies like an out-of-control forest fire, with every sense of hers tuned into his and his into hers, as if they had been programmed from birth to respond to each other in that heady, earth-shattering way.

Had Tristan come up the stairs just at that moment and seen them locked in such a passionate embrace? Or had he been lurking about in the shadows even earlier? Perhaps overhearing the start of Vinn's warning? Not wanting to allow Vinn the chance to besmirch him any further, he had come up in that charming, laid-back way of his and lured Vinn away from the house with a request for a private man-to-man chat that had led to Vinn spending a night in hospital, with no hope of bringing a halt to her marriage from hell?

'Gabriella?' Vinn's voice brought her thoughts back to the present moment. 'You've gone very quiet. Do you not agree we should keep our marriage as it is? For the time being at least?'

Gabby tried to smile, but it contorted her mouth, giving it an unnatural feel. 'I still can't work out why you wanted to marry me in the first place. It seems to me you have paid a heck of a lot of money for a bride who doesn't quite fit the bill of what you were expecting.' She gave him a rueful look. 'You've been short-changed, Vinn, and yet you don't seem to be the least bit annoyed about it.'

This time he took both of her hands in his, squeezing them gently. 'If I am annoyed about anything it is about my own ignorance of your circumstances.'

'It is not your fault,' Gabby said, looking up at him. 'You did the right thing by coming to me, but I was too proud to heed your advice.'

Should she tell Vinn of Tristan's cocaine addiction? Gabby wondered. The thought danced in her mind on tentative feet, like a ballerina on damaged toes, trying to convince the judges at an important audition she was worthy of the role. Every step of the process hurt unbearably, with pain and shame, and also the niggling fear that Gabby might have been partly to blame for Tristan going to such desperate measures. There had been no sign of drug use before their ill-fated marriage, but that didn't mean it hadn't been going on.

'Vinn...' she began. 'Did you know Tristan had a cocaine habit?'

'When did *that* start?' he asked, frowning heavily. 'Before or during your marriage?'

'I'm not sure,' she answered. 'I had never noticed anything untoward before, but then I didn't know he was having affairs either—so who am I to be certain one way or the other?'

'Have you considered Tristan might have been the one to get Blair involved in drugs?' he asked. 'That Tristan was perhaps his supplier?'

Gabby felt her heart slip sideways in her chest. 'Oh no...'

Vinn's expression was grim. 'You were a pawn in his game, *cara*. I am sure of it. He had to use you as a screen to keep things on the level. Especially after Blair died.'

It all made sense now Gabby thought about it. Tristan had intensified his attentions not long after her brother's suicide, insisting on their marriage even though she had been having doubts for months.

'Did you ever consider speaking to my parents the night before the wedding?' she asked.

He closed his eyes for a nanosecond. 'Yes,' he said, scoring a pathway through his hair. 'I did consider it, and I have tortured myself ever since that I didn't seek a private audience with them first. But I guess I felt at the time it was better to start with you, to somehow get you to see the mistake you were making before I approached them. After all, it was your decision. You claimed to be in love with Glendenning, and even though I doubted it I had no way of proving it either way. Other than that kiss.'

That kiss.

The kiss he had revisited so many times, Gabby thought with a delicate flutter of her insides. She looked at his mouth, at the sensual contours of it, the full lower lip her teeth longed to nibble at and her tongue longed to salve with soft moist sweeps and strokes, until he took control in that masterful but spine-loosening, gentle way of his.

His head came down and the kiss became real, exhilaratingly real, as their tongues mated, their lips suddenly hot and wet with mutual need. Gabby pressed herself closer to the turgid heat of his body, her arms going around his waist, then lower. She dug her fingers into the tautness of his buttocks to bring him up against the increasingly urgent pulse of her body.

'It's too soon,' Vinn groaned against her mouth.

'For you?' Gabby asked in mild surprise, nibbling at his lower lip, her lower body rubbing against his rock-hard erection.

'God, no.' He gave a little laugh and nibbled back. 'For you, *cara*. You will be tender inside. You were practically a virgin. You are so small, and I am—'

'So big—and I want you now,' Gabby said with a boldness she had never known she possessed. 'Right now.'

His eyes glittered with need. 'Are you sure?' he asked, stroking the side of her face with one tender hand. 'I can pleasure you instead. There are other ways of releasing the tension without hurting you.'

Gabby felt her heart swell at his concern for her. Didn't that prove he loved her? Why wouldn't he admit it? Did he think she would use it against him? Oh, how much she adored him! Why had she spurned and ridiculed him all those years ago?

'Vinn…' she said, summoning up the courage to tell him how she felt. 'There's something I want to tell you…'

Vinn kissed the side of her mouth, working slowly but steadily towards its throbbing centre. 'You have this rather endearing but no less annoying tendency to want to talk when I want you to feel,' he said. 'What could be more important right now than feeling this…?' He kissed her deeply, and then after a few breathless seconds moved his mouth to the side of her neck, making the sensitive skin there and all over her body lift in a prickly pelt of goosebumps. 'And this…?'

Gabby had no verbal answer. Everything she want-ed to say, her body said for her. She squirmed with desire in his arms, desperate to feel his electrifying touch on every part of her. Her breasts swelled with need, her nipples hard as pebbles, aching for the sweep of his tongue or the primal scrape of his teeth to soothe their ache. She pushed herself against him brazenly, throwing her head back, her insides clenching and cramping simultaneously with the anticipation of assuagement.

Vinn's mouth was on her collarbone, his tongue laving a pathway over its fragile scaffold to the sensual flesh of her breasts which he had uncovered. They seemed to swell in his hands, the softness of them like silk and cream, and the tight points of her nipples drew his mouth like a magnet, each stroke of his tongue evoking another sweet gasp of surprise and delight from her lips. She was so keen, and yet he was so hesitant. He didn't want to hurt her. And he *would* hurt her if he drove in without careful regard to her lack of experience.

He eased back, trying to control his breathing, trying to control the thundering roar of the blood in his veins, but her shy fingers searched for him and found him, the work of her fingertips sending arrows of sharp need from his groin to his toes and back, leaving him breathless and out of reach of common sense. He wanted to feel her mouth on him, the wetness and velvet softness of it taking him in, her tongue playing with him, teasing him until he exploded.

He clamped his eyes shut as his dream came alive. She was doing it by the script he had formed in his head. She was shaping him with her hands, discovering his hard length, exploring the detail of it, the moist tip of his need, the stickiness of his essence, banked up and waiting to be summoned by the honeyed grip of her body or the lick or slide of her tongue.

His back arched as he felt her soft, moist mouth close over him, and the shyness of it was part of the overwhelming allure. She didn't know what she was doing, but she was going on instinct—and everything she was doing was right. His blood surged, his pulse raced, his heart rate soared and his breathing all but stopped as she drew on him, her lips a soft but insistent caress, her tongue a teasing temptress, luring him out of the realms of control into the dark, swirling abyss of release.

Suddenly he was there, the force of it taking him by surprise. He pumped, he spilled, he shuddered—and she accepted it all, not for a moment shrinking away from the rawness of it, not for a second repulsed or shocked by how he had responded to her. Instead she smiled as she came up for air, licking her soft lips as if she had just sampled the elixir of heaven, before pressing a soft kiss to the left of his chest, right where his heart was pounding out of control.

Vinn placed his still shaking hand on the back of her silky head, stroking it absently as his breathing gradually slowed. He couldn't find the words to describe what he was feeling. She had left him stunned, not just physically but emotionally. He had had so many lovers, and not one had moved him as Gabriella had done. And not just then, but before, giving herself to him when she had been so frightened, so terrified he would use her without respect…without love.

Love was a strong word—a word he liked to shy

away from, an unfamiliar word to him. Or at least it always had been in the context of sex.

Vinn had loved his mother; he seriously doubted any son could have loved a mother more. And he loved his half-sister—not that he was at liberty to claim her as such. Lily Henderson had sought him out after an exhaustive search, trying to make sense of her place in the world as the love-child of Hugo McCready, a prominent mover and shaker in the corporate world who, even after all this time, obstinately refused to acknowledge the living, breathing harvest of the wild oats he had sowed—Vinn included.

Hugo McCready thought it his worldly privilege to seduce the young housemaids who came to clean up after him, under the nose of his long-suffering wife and three legitimate children. But Vinn suspected that, unlike him, Lily was intent on blowing McCready's cover once and for all. Vinn was primarily concerned that it would hurt her rather than their conscienceless father, and so he had done and would continue to do what he could do to protect her—even if the press consistently misinterpreted their relationship.

Paying off this loan was part of Vinn's plan to outsmart his father and his takeover bid, and it had all gone according to plan—with the added bonus, of course, of securing Gabriella St Clair as his wife. He had denied feeling anything for her but desire, but even while his body ached and throbbed for her there were other feelings he had still to make sense of in his head.

She seemed intent on prying an admission of love out of him, but he still wasn't certain of her motives. Money had a habit of inciting deep feelings in many of the women he had associated with in the past. Why else did women in their twenties marry men old enough to be their grandfathers? The press was full of such cases, where rich old men had adoring, beautiful young women draped on their arms, claiming to love them.

Gabriella St Clair had been used to a certain life-style, which she had thought was going to be ripped from beneath her, so she had laid herself at the mercy of the one man she had claimed to dislike intensely for as long as Vinn could remember. For her to suddenly turn around and claim to love him was something Vinn found a little hard to believe, even though they shared a powerful physical chemistry.

But he was starting to realise, irrespective of what she did or didn't feel for him, that perhaps Gabriella had a right to know a little more of his past than she currently did. But telling her about Lily was something he wanted to clear with his half-sister first. Lily was a very sensitive girl of just twenty. Just one year younger than Gabriella had been when she had married Tristan Glendenning. And, like Gabriella, Lily didn't know what she wanted; she was confused and looking for an anchor. Vinn was determined to be that anchor for as long as he needed to be, and to protect her from the unscrupulous man who had fathered her.

Vinn looked down at Gabriella; she was his wife now, in every sense of the word, and his blood surged at the realisation. *She was his wife.* He had made her so, not just in word and at the stroke of a pen, but in the union of their bodies—a union he could still feel buzzing in his veins.

A union he wanted again and again.

CHAPTER ELEVEN

OVER the next few days Gabby was almost able to fool herself her honeymoon with Vinn was as perfect as any other lovestruck bride's could ever be. She felt herself blooming as each lazy sun-filled day passed, with hot, sweaty nights writhing in Vinn's arms, leaving her panting and breathless and even more hopelessly in love. She spent hours watching him, her eyes drinking in every smile he cast her way, her spine melting at every light touch he gave her as they explored the various sheltered coves and beaches and rainforest walks all over the island.

Her body felt so different—so energised and alive. Which she knew had nothing to do with the light golden tan she had developed, or the delicious cuisine she had consumed, which had already gone a long way towards softening the sharp edges of her frame. It was because every nerve was tuned into him, every pore of her skin aware of him, as they lay on secluded beaches on sand as soft as finely ground sugar. He had only to look at her with those smoky grey-blue eyes of his and she would turn to him, opening her mouth for the descent of his, her legs entwining with his hair-roughened ones as he began a sensual exploration of every curve and indentation of her body until her cries of release flew up on the air like those of the wild seabirds around them.

It was the second to last day of their visit to the resort, and Gabby and Vinn had walked to the most remote part of the island, where few of the guests fancied taking a four-hour return journey to access its pristine privacy. Vinn had organised a picnic with the kitchen staff, and had carried a pack with beach towels and extra drinks for the trek back.

After a mouthwatering lunch of tandoori chicken roll-ups and a selection of cheeses and fruit, and a crisp bottle of French champagne, they had made love on the outstretched towels until every part of Gabby's body felt as if it had been refashioned into molten wax. She lay in his arms after the storm of release was over, catching her breath, her eyes closed against the sun, listening to the sound of the gentle lap of water against the shore as Vinn's fingers played idly with her hair.

Their lazy movement gradually stilled, and his breathing was so slow and even she realised he had fallen asleep. She propped herself up on one elbow and looked down at him, her heart swelling inside her chest at how magnificently male he looked, so tanned, so muscular and yet so lean.

She trailed her fingertips over the relaxed curve of his mouth, leaning forward to press a soft-as-a-breeze kiss to his mouth. His lips gave a little shifting movement, as if even in the depths of his slumber he still registered her touch.

She eased herself out of his light hold and wandered

down to the water, wading in to thigh depth before slipping under the surface and swimming out at a leisurely pace, enjoying the feel of the salt water on her sun-kissed skin. She had never skinny-dipped until now, and the freedom was totally liberating, not to mention deeply erotic. The water caressed her, making her even more aware of how much pleasure her body could give and receive.

It thrilled her how much Vinn wanted her. He might not claim to love her, but there was every indication he no longer held the angry vengeful feelings of the past. He was tender towards her, protective and considerate of her every need. At first she'd thought he was doing it for show, for the resort staff were often serving drinks by the pool and moving around the grounds, but he acted exactly the same way when they were totally alone. She liked to think he was falling in love with her, but after her mistake with Tristan she didn't trust her judgement.

When Gabby came out of the water a little while later, Vinn was sitting upright on the beach, watching her, his eyes flaring with desire as she walked towards him. She felt a delicious shiver of anticipation run up under her skin as the brush of his gaze set her alight with longing all over again.

'You look like a mermaid, *cara*,' he said as he got to his feet. 'A beautiful mermaid who has risen from the depths of the sea to seduce this mere mortal.'

Gabby's eyes were like twin magnets, drawn to his groin where his erection was already stirring in response to her. Her belly gave a little shuffle-like movement as she came up close—close enough to feel the hard ridge of him pressing against her.

'Some mermaid I must look, without any make-up on and my hair in sandy knots,' she said with a self-effacing grimace.

He smiled and brushed the wet hair back off her face with a gentle hand. 'I don't think I have ever seen you look more exquisite than right now,' he said, placing his hands on the curve of her bottom and drawing her into his heat.

She looked into his eyes and felt her insides turn over. She could feel the pulse of his blood, the thickness of him making her legs turn to water. Her breasts were crushed against his broad chest, the masculine sprinkling of hair there tickling her, tantalising her, and making her nipples tighten.

She drew in a hitching breath as his head came down, the hard urgency of his kiss in perfect tune with hers. Her hands dug into his buttocks to hold him close, her tongue tangling with his, darting and duelling, until she could think of nothing but how much she wanted him to drive deep inside her until she was shuddering and convulsing beneath him.

He pressed her back down on the towels, his mouth moving from hers to attend to each of her breasts, drawing on her until her spine was arched and her body wet and aching for the completion she knew only he could give her.

His first thrust was deep, evoking a gasping cry of delight from between her lips as her body slickly embraced him. He moved with an ever-increasing rhythm, his fingers delving between their rocking bodies to maximise her pleasure. There was no hesitancy about her responses now. Her body responded to him every time with explosive force. It felt as if every part of her shattered into a million tiny pieces for that mindless moment or two when she was tossed in the rolling waves of ecstasy, only coming back to one piece as she felt him finally lose control. She loved the feel of him at his supreme moment—the way he suddenly tensed, the way he sucked in his breath before letting it go, sometimes with a groan, other times with a harsh gasp, or, like now, with a raw, primal-sounding grunt that sent a shower of goosebumps over her skin to think she had made him experience such an intense release.

Gabby stroked her fingers up and down his back, lingering over each knob of his vertebrae, feeling his chest rise and fall against hers, his warm breath dancing against the sensitive skin of her neck.

'That feels nice,' he murmured against the tiny dip near her collarbone.

'I like touching you,' she said, still stroking him.

He propped himself up on his elbow and looked down at her. 'I like touching you too, *cara*,' he said huskily. 'I don't think I will ever get tired of doing so.'

Gabby rolled her lips together and lowered her gaze to his stubbly chin. 'So what happens if some time in the future you do?' she asked, her fingers unconsciously stilling on his back, along with her breath in her chest.

'There will be no divorce, Gabriella,' he said, forcing up her chin so she had to meet his gaze. 'You know the terms.'

She tried to push aside her resentment, but it came flooding back. 'So I suppose if I no longer please you,

you'll just hot-foot it to one of your many mistresses and let her see to your needs?'

His grey-blue eyes warred with hers. 'Is that really the sort of man you think I am?' he asked. 'Have you learned nothing about me over the last few days?'

She bit her lip, trying to rein in her emotions. 'I know you like sex, and lots of it,' she said. 'But, as you said before we were married, it is my body you want, that you lust after.'

Vinn eased himself off her and got to his feet. 'Yes, well, things are different now,' he said, turning to dust the sand off his thighs.

Gabby pulled one of the towels around her body. 'How do you mean?'

He turned to look at her, but the angle of the sun made it hard for her to see what was written in his expression. 'You are not the woman I thought you were when I married you,' he said. 'I have had to make certain adjustments since.'

Gabby moistened her mouth. 'Would one of those adjustments be learning to *like* me instead of hating me?'

'I have never hated you,' he said, and then, blowing out a breath, grudgingly admitted, 'Well, maybe I thought I did once or twice in the past, but certainly not now.'

She stayed silent, hope building a rickety scaffold around her thudding heart.

'Gabriella…' He shifted so the shadows were off his face. 'I have always kept my sex-life separate from my emotions. This is the first time I have felt something other than desire for a woman.'

'Are you telling me you…you love me?' she asked in a whisper.

He gave her a teasing smile. 'If love is an almost un-bearably tight feeling in your chest every time you see the person you are married to, then, yes, perhaps I am in love with you. Or perhaps I need to see a cardiac surgeon. What do you think?'

Gabby was up on her feet and in his arms, pressing hot, passionate kisses all over his face. 'I think you are the most wonderful person I have ever met,' she said. 'I love you so much. I didn't realise how much until just recently.'

'Enough to get rid of those contraceptive pills you've been taking?' he asked, with a distinct twinkle in his eyes.

Gabby gave him a sheepish look. 'You know about those?'

He kissed her forehead lightly. 'If you need more time, then we will wait,' he said. 'But I would like a family. It is something I have wanted for a long time. I guess growing up as an only child with a single mother has made the yearning all the greater.'

'I will throw my pills away,' she promised. 'I want to bear your children, Vinn. I want to be a wonderful wife for you, to make up for all the awful things I did to you in the past.'

He cradled her against him, resting his chin on the top of her head. 'We are different people now, Gabriella. The past should not dictate our future.'

Gabby tipped her head back to look up at him again. 'Why do you always call me Gabriella?' she asked.

His thumb rolled back and forth over the softest part of her chin, just below her bottom lip. 'It is a beauti-ful name,' he answered. 'It is also Italian. But if you would like me to call you Gabby then I will try to remember to do so.'

'No.' She smiled. 'I like the way you say my name. No one says it quite like you do. It sends shivers up my spine—always has.'

'Oh, really? Now, that *is* interesting,' he said with a smile. 'Here I was thinking for all these years you loathed the very sight of me.'

Gabby gave him a twisted smile in return. 'I think it might be true what they say about love and hate being two sides of the same coin,' she said. 'I think I was always so mean to you because I was frightened of the way you made me feel—even as young as I was when you first came to my family's home.'

He cupped her face in his hands. 'Are you still frightened of how I make you feel, *mia piccola?*'

'You make me feel safer than anyone else I know,' she said, gazing up at him devotedly. 'I never thought I would learn to trust another man after Tristan, but in these last few days you have somehow managed to sweep away every single fear I ever experienced.'

His eyes contained dark shadows of regret as they held hers. 'I wish I had been able to protect you from his hands,' he said, his jaw tightening over the words. 'If I had known what was going on I would have had him thrown in jail—but only after I gave him a dose of his own medicine. He only picked on you because he knew you couldn't defend yourself. It's a wonder he didn't…' He visibly flinched. 'God, I don't want to think about what else he could have done to you.'

Gabby pressed one of her palms to his unshaven

jaw. 'I don't see myself as a victim any more,' she said. 'I did before, but not now.'

He kissed her softly, almost worshipfully. 'We should head back,' he said as he lifted his mouth from hers. 'We have a long walk ahead, and I don't want you to be too tired for what I have in mind for later tonight.'

Gabby sent him a sultry glance as she reached for her bikini, lying on the sand next to the towels. 'You mean I have to wait until tonight to see what it is?'

He gave her a smouldering look and grabbed her by the waist, bringing her naked body up against his, turning her so his front was to her back, every plane and ridge of his body fuelling her desire like gasoline thrown on a flame.

'Maybe we could reset the timetable just a little,' he said, his teeth starting to nip at her earlobe.

'Fine by me,' Gabby said, on the tail-end of a blissful sigh as his erection probed her from behind.

Was there no end to his mind-blowingly sensual repertoire? He constantly surprised her with what he could do with his hands and mouth and body, and it constantly surprised and shocked her how hers responded. She could feel the pressure building even now, the need so insistent she thought she would die if he didn't plunge into her right there and then. But he made her wait, stringing out the torture until she was almost sobbing for the release she so desperately craved.

'Be patient, *cara*,' he said as he teased her tender, sensitised folds with the erotic promise of penetration. 'You will enjoy it much more if you have to wait for it.'

'I want it now!' Gabby said, pressing herself back into him. 'Don't make me wait any longer.'

He gave a chuckle of laughter and began to probe her—just enough to separate her, but not enough to fill her.

'Tell me what you want, Gabriella,' he growled close to her ear. 'Tell me what you want me to do to you.'

'You know what I want you to do,' she gasped, rubbing up against him wantonly.

'Do you want me to do this?' he asked, and slid inside her in one thick, slow thrust that lifted every hair on her scalp.

'Oh, God, *yes*…' She clutched blindly at his thighs, trying to keep her legs from collapsing beneath her.

'And this?' He began to move inside her, deep and far too slowly.

Gabby felt every nerve ending scream for more friction, more speed, more depth and more urgency. 'Yes…*yes*…' she let out, on a panting breath of rampant need.

He held her hips and drove deeply, gradually increasing the pace until she felt her tension building to the point of no return. She fell over the edge, freefalling into an abyss of cascading sensations, the ripples and contractions of her body sending her into a tailspin of feeling that went on and on and on.

Finally it was over, and the aftershocks like tiny rumbles deep down in her body, but then it was Vinn's turn. Gabby felt every carnal second of it—the way his legs braced themselves for the final plunge, the way his breath sucked in deep in his chest, and the way he suddenly pitched forward, the pumping motion of his body filling her, delighting her, making her feel a feminine power she had never felt before as he spilled the essence of himself into the warm cocoon of her body.

Vinn held her in place, trying to get his breathing to settle, but it was difficult. She had the amazing ability to totally unhinge him, to shatter every sense of control he had fooled himself he still possessed. He had put himself out on a limb, an unusual and totally uncharacteristic position for him, but there it was. He loved her as—he had always done.

He had been fooling himself for years that he felt otherwise, but the truth was he had always wanted only her, had only ever loved her. She was the other half he had been searching for all his life. The trouble was he had found it too early, frightening her off with his single-mindedness, virtually pitching her headlong into another man's arms because she had been scared by the intensity of what he had so clumsily communicated to her.

Vinn cupped her breasts, still reluctant to release her, his body relaxed now, but still encased in hers.

'Do you think you could find your way back in the dark?' he asked. 'You know this island better than I do.'

She slowly turned in his arms and linked her arms around his neck. 'Would it matter if we stayed out here all night?' she asked. 'I don't want this magic moment between us to end.'

He gave her a wistful smile. 'We have to fly home tomorrow, *cara*,' he reminded her. 'Back to the real world.'

'I guess… But I don't want anything to change,' she

said. 'I want to be the best wife in the world for you. I don't want to disappoint you.'

He smiled and hugged her close. 'You will not disappoint me, Gabriella,' he said. 'Of that I am sure.'

CHAPTER TWELVE

GABBY sat beside Vinn on the flight back to Sydney, her hand linked with his, her head resting against his shoulder. But her heart was still back on the island.

She had almost cried as she had packed her bag. She had wanted the magic of their honeymoon to go on and on. The blissful sense of security had settled about her shoulders like a shawl, but ever since they had got on the plane it felt as if someone had ripped it away from her, leaving her shivering in uncertainty.

Vinn was mostly silent on the journey back. He kept fidgeting with his watch, as if it was the most fascinating thing in the world, when only hours earlier Gabby's body had been his entire focus.

'Are you OK?' she asked at one point.

He turned to look at her, his expression shuttered. 'Sorry, Gabriella, did you say something?'

'I said, are you OK?' Gabby squeezed his hand but after second or two he pulled out of her hold and reached for the in-flight magazine instead.

'I'm fine,' he said, flipping a few pages, his brow furrowing.

'Have I done something wrong?' she asked after another pause.

He gave her a quick on-off smile. 'No, of course not, *cara*,' he said, patting her hand. 'I have a lot on my mind right now. Business doesn't take a holiday, I'm afraid.'

Gabby felt a twinge of remorse that she hadn't once asked him about his work. She knew so little of what he did, other than he had first made a fortune on a development project in an outlying suburb which had suddenly taken off after a change of council zoning. He had reinvested the profit into more developments, astutely keeping one step ahead of the market so he could maximise his profits.

'Is there anything I can do to help?' she asked.

He shook his head and briefly touched her nearest cheek with his fingertips. 'No, Gabriella. I want you to concentrate on producing me an heir,' he said. 'Your parents need you too, right now. Your father is doing well, but seeing you happy and contented will aid his progress like nothing else can. And a grandchild will be something wonderful for both of them to look forward to.'

Gabby settled back in her seat, smiling to herself as she thought of how she had flushed every one of her contraceptive pills down the sink at the resort apartment. Her hands crept to the flat plane of her belly, wondering what it would feel like to have Vinn's child growing there. Even though she knew it was probably unlikely, since she had only just ceased her protection, she wondered if she was already pregnant. She had been on a low-dose pill, more for convenience than contraception, and the failure rate was a lot higher than other brands…

She reached for his hand again, stroking her fingers up and down his long fingers. 'Thank you, darling, for everything you did to make the last week so special for me,' she said. 'It was a perfect honeymoon.'

He covered her hand with his and gave her another smile, but Gabby couldn't help feeling it looked forced this time. 'It was my pleasure, *cara*,' he said.

'I love you,' she said, stretching across to press her mouth against his.

'I know you do,' he said, still with that not-quite smile.

Gabby started to feel the stealthy creep of doubt; like ghostly fingers tickling the fine hairs on the back of her neck. Why, when she told him how much she loved him, did he not say he loved her too? In fact, when she backtracked through their loving exchange the afternoon before on the beach, she couldn't remember him saying he loved her at all. He had hinted at it, but not openly spoken of his feelings. But then he hadn't had to, she reminded herself ruefully. She had raced in headlong and confessed her love for him, then recklessly thrown away her pills, promising him the heir he so dearly wanted.

But what if that was all he wanted from her? What if, when she gave him the child or children he desired, he decided he no longer had a need for her in his life? He kept saying there would be no divorce, but that didn't mean he wouldn't change his mind some time in the future. After all, he had insisted she sign a pre-nuptial agreement. Didn't that suggest he had no plans or indeed no confidence that the marriage would continue indefinitely?

Everything had happened so quickly. Her father's heart attack, the takeover bid, and the sudden margin call had sent her into a tailspin, tossing her into Vinn's orbit where, two weeks later, she was still spinning.

Gabby didn't get much of a chance to speak with Vinn in private again, for as soon as they got off the plane a driver was waiting to collect them.

They called in to the hospital to see her father briefly, and then Vinn instructed the driver to drop him off at his office, before telling him to take Gabby to his house in Mosman.

Vinn gave her a brief, impersonal kiss before he got out of the car, and within moments he was striding away, his mobile phone already up to his ear.

Gabby sat back with a sigh as the driver nudged back out into the traffic. She had secretly hoped Vinn would do all the traditional things, like carry her over the threshold—perhaps carry her all the way upstairs and make love to her in the bed they would share as man and wife. But he was back to business as if the last seven days hadn't happened. He hadn't even given her a second glance as he had walked through the doors of his office block.

Gabby busied herself with unpacking once the driver had left, after carrying in the luggage for her. She put on a load of washing and while it was running wandered outside to look around the garden. The lawn had been recently mown, but there was no sign of a gardener about the place, for which she was grateful.

She needed time to settle into Vinn's house without the speculative gaze of his household staff.

Vinn had arranged the delivery of her car and her clothes on the day of their wedding. All of her things were neatly hung or folded in the walk-in wardrobe off the master bedroom—she assumed by Vinn's house-keeper, although there was no sign of anyone having been in the house for the last few days. The house was clean and tidy, certainly, but there was no fresh food in the refrigerator, so Gabby decided to drive up to the closest shops for some basic supplies.

When Gabby got back to the house Vinn was on the harbourside deck leading off the lounge, his back towards her as he spoke into his mobile phone. The hushed urgency of his tone was what made her step closer on silent feet, and her heart came to a skidding halt in her chest when she heard his words, carrying on the still afternoon air.

'No, *cara*,' he said. 'Trust me. This is not the right time to announce to the world our true relationship.'

Gabby felt as if a knife had been plunged between her ribs, but somehow she remained upright, coldly, determinedly upright, as she listened to the rest.

'I know,' he said, blowing out a sigh. 'I love you too, and I want the world to know how much you mean to me, but do you know what the press will make of this? It's too dangerous. I have a lot in the pipeline—this takeover bid for one thing. I don't want anything to jeopardise that until it is totally secure, which won't be until the end of next week at the earliest.'

There was a pause as he listened to whoever was on

the other end, and Gabby's heart thudded painfully as each second passed, in case he turned and saw her standing there, listening to every damning word.

'Look, *cara*,' Vinn went on, raking a hand through his rumpled hair, 'I spent a lot of money on securing this deal. I don't want anything to compromise it at this stage. We have to tread carefully. There are other people to consider in all of this.'

Another pause as he listened to the other person.

'I will have to tell her at some stage,' he said. 'She has a right to know. She is my wife now. But let's leave it a week or two longer, hmm? Just keep your head down, and I will send you some money to tide you over. *Ciao.*'

Vinn closed his phone and turned—to come face to face with the shell-white face of Gabriella.

'*Cara,*' he began. 'I didn't hear you come in.'

Gabby clenched her hands into fists. 'Don't you "*cara*" me, you two-timing bastard,' she bit out in blistering fury.

He took a step towards her. 'Gabriella, you don't understand. I was—'

'Oh, I know what you were doing,' Gabby shot back. 'You were talking to *her*, weren't you? Your mistress—your mystery lover. The woman you love. I heard you say it.'

'You have misinterpreted everything,' he said. 'You heard one side of the conversation and are jumping to conclusions.'

'Oh, for God's sake!' Gabby was shrieking at him and couldn't seem to stop, her voice getting shriller with each word she threw at him. 'What sort of fool do you take me for? I heard you tell her about the takeover bid. *You're* the one behind it, aren't you? You were behind it the whole time and never let on. You let me make a complete and utter fool of myself that day when I came to you for help. All the while laughing behind my back at how you'd not only got the majority share of the St Clair Resort but me as a bonus.'

He looked as if he wanted to deny it, but at the last moment changed his mind. He shoved a hand through his hair again and, tossing his phone to one of the sofas, rubbed the back of his neck with his hand, as if to release the tension there.

'There are things you don't know that I was not at liberty to tell you,' he said, in a weighted tone.

'The truth is always a good place to start,' Gabby inserted coldly.

'The truth is, Gabriella…' Vinn paused, searching for the right words. 'I have been on a vendetta of sorts, but it really has nothing to do with you.'

She gave him a flinty glare. 'Oh, please,' she said. 'Don't let the highlights fool you, Vinn. I'm not really as blonde as I look.'

'I mean it, Gabriella,' he insisted. 'The person I have been targeting is no one you know, and I would like to keep it that way. He is not the sort of person I want anyone I care deeply about coming into contact with.'

She rolled her eyes in scorn. 'So you've decided you *do* actually care about me now, have you?' she asked. 'Why? Because I've caught you out? Or because I was surprisingly good in the sack?'

'Don't cheapen yourself like that,' Vinn said, his jaw so tight his teeth ached.

'I'm hardly what you could call cheap,' she tossed back. 'Two point four million dollars is a heck of a lot of money to pay for sex. I hope you were happy with what you got, because that's all you're getting. It's over, Vinn.'

Vinn drew in a harsh breath. 'You would compromise your father's health just to spite me?'

Her eyes went wide with anger. 'You talk to me of compromising my father?' she spat. 'What gall you have! You've just done the dirtiest deed in business—swiping away his life's work behind his back.'

'It wasn't behind his back.'

Gabby stared at him, her mind reeling so much her head was starting to pound. 'W-what did you say?'

'Your father approached me about the takeover bid a couple of days before his heart attack,' he said. 'He suspected who was behind it, and he came to me for advice. I assured him I would do whatever I could to keep the St Clair Island Resort safe.'

Gabby opened and closed her mouth. Not able to speak, hardly able to think. Her father had *known*? He had already approached Vinn for help? Then why…?

'Henry was well aware of the rumours going about, and he knew he couldn't raise the funds if a margin call was activated,' Vinn said. 'I had already helped him secure the house, and—'

Her eyes went wide as she choked, 'The house? You…you own my parents' *house*?'

He pushed his hand through his hair again. 'On paper, yes, but not on principle.'

She gave him a cynical glare. 'What is that supposed to mean?'

'It means I would never take their house from them,

no matter how much money they owed me,' he said, holding her gaze.

Gabby struggled to contain her see-sawing emotions. There was so much she didn't know—*hadn't* known. She felt like a pawn in a chess game, moved about with no will or choice of her own.

'I am in no doubt that the stress of the business was what caused your father's heart attack,' Vinn continued. 'And then, of course, his worst nightmare actually did happen. The lenders suddenly wanted their money.'

Gabby swallowed a couple of times to clear her tight throat. 'So…so you had already agreed to help my father?' she said, still trying to make sense of it all.

'Of course I had,' he said. 'Your father stood by me when I was on the skids. He was the only one who ever believed I had potential. I found it hard, growing up without a father. My mother did her best, but I was heading down a pathway to disaster when your father took me aside and told me how it was up to me to turn it all around. He sponsored me through university and organised special coaching on campus to help with my dyslexia. There is no amount of money I wouldn't put out for him.'

'So…what you're saying is…the resort was never in any danger?' Gabby asked, frowning.

He met her questioning gaze without flinching. 'It was never in danger, Gabriella,' he said heavily. 'Your father is still the major shareholder, and as long as he wants to be he will remain so.'

She ran her tongue over her lips, surprised at how dry and cracked they felt. 'I'm not sure I am really following this…' she said. 'Why did you involve me? Why force me into marriage?'

He looked at her for a lengthy moment, his grey-blue eyes dark and unfathomable. 'I cannot think of a time when you were not a part of my dream for success,' he said. 'I have always wanted you. I can't explain it other than to say my life and my quest for success did not feel complete until I had you.'

'So I am some sort of status symbol, am I?' she asked churlishly. 'Like a top-model sports car to show the world you've really made it?'

'That is not quite how I would put it.'

She gave him another flinty look. 'How *would* you put it, Vinn?' she asked. 'You've already got a mistress. What on earth do you want with a wife—especially one like me?'

'I do not have a mistress,' he bit out. 'Do you really think I am that low?'

Gabby scored her fingernails into the soft bed of her palms. 'How can you stand there and lie to me like that?' she asked incredulously. 'I just heard you tell her you loved her.'

There was a long, tense silence.

Vinn let out his breath. 'All right,' he said. 'I will break my word to her and tell you.'

She arched her brows. 'What's this? A last-minute twinge of conscience, Vinn?'

He gritted his teeth and tried to be patient. 'The young woman I was talking to is not my mistress,' he said. 'She is my half-sister.'

She gave him another raised-brow look, which communicated cynicism along with disgust. 'Then why not clear up that little misunderstanding with the press?' she asked. 'Why go along with the story of her being your mystery lover?'

'I want to protect her,' he said. 'She doesn't have any idea of the sort of man her father is, or the lengths he will go to in order to keep his reputation intact.'

Gabby frowned. 'So…let me get this straight… this half-sister of yours is your father's child, not your mother's?'

'Of course she is not my mother's,' he said. 'My mother would have loved other children—she would have loved to have had a husband to bring them up with her. But the man she fell in love with was already married. He tricked her into a relationship, and then when she got pregnant put her out on the streets, threatening to destroy her if she ever told who the father of her child was. I only found out the day she died who he was. I will not rest until I bring him down for what he did to her.'

Gabby was having trouble following it all. 'Your father is a dangerous man?' she finally managed to ask.

His look was grim. 'Very,' he said. 'He has underworld connections—drugs, organised crime, that sort of thing. He found it amusing to try and swipe away your father's business because he found out about my connection to your family, but fortunately I have contacts who informed me of it so I could take evasive action.'

'Oh, Vinn…' she said. 'I don't know what to say… I feel so confused.'

He came up to her and held her by the shoulders, locking her gaze with the grey-blue intensity of his. 'Listen to me, Gabriella,' he said. 'I love you. I have loved you since the first day I set eyes on you, when you were fourteen and thinking yourself all grown up. I loved you when you *did* grow up. I even loved you when you married that scum Glendenning, because I felt deep down that one day we would be together.'

Gabby blinked back tears. 'Oh, darling, we would have been together so much earlier than this if I hadn't been too proud and stubborn to listen to you that night.'

'I blame myself,' Vinn said, dropping his hands from her shoulders as he began to pace the room. 'I handled it all wrong. I had not long landed back in the country when I heard Glendenning was playing around on you. I blame myself for Blair's death too. I should have seen that coming, but I didn't.'

Gabby shook her head and took a step towards him. 'No, no—you mustn't say that. It wasn't your fault. How can you think that?'

He gave her a grim look. 'Let me finish, *cara*, please,' he said, his voice rough with emotion. 'I was away too long. Blair had come to me for advice about his career before I left to take my mother home to Italy to die. He didn't want to take up a position in your father's business, but he was too afraid to admit it. He was ashamed of not being what your parents wanted him to be. He wanted to study art. He had a gift, a rare gift he should have felt free to explore, but he didn't want to let your parents down.'

'The painting in your foyer…' Gabby said, her heart swelling with pride and a host of other emotions she knew she would have to pick over later. 'Blair did it, didn't he?'

Vinn nodded. 'He was so talented, Gabriella. But he

didn't believe in himself. I think that's why in the end he turned to drugs. He wanted to block out the insecurities he felt—the insecurities all of us feel at times. But for him they were like demons, gnawing away at him relentlessly. I tried to help him, and I felt I was making some headway, but then my mother was diagnosed with cancer. She desperately wanted to mend the rift she had made in her family by succumbing to my father's charm and having a child out of wedlock. I felt I owed it to her to take her home, to nurse her until the day she died. It seemed fitting. She was there at the moment I drew my first breath. I was there when she drew her last.'

Gabby stumbled towards him, wrapping her arms around him, loving him, adoring him, worshipping the man he was—the man he had always been.

'I can't tell you how much I love you,' she said. 'I am not worthy of you. I don't deserve your love. I think that's why I was so reluctant to believe you actually loved me. Deep down I know I don't deserve someone as wonderful as you. But somehow you have loved me through it all.'

Vinn tucked her in close, holding her against his heart. 'You do deserve to be loved, Gabriella,' he said. 'You are more than worthy of love, and no one could love you more than me. I am sure of it.'

She looked up at him with tears of happiness shining in her eyes. 'So the honeymoon is not quite over?'

He smiled and lifted her up in his arms. 'Just as soon as I carry you out of the house and back over the threshold it is going to get a second wind—so you had better prepare yourself for it.'

'I'm prepared,' Gabby said, shivering all over in anticipation. 'Or at least I think I am.'

He gave her a smouldering look. 'Let's put that to the test, shall we?' he said, as he carried her towards the door.

And not too much later Gabby passed with flying colours.

The Blackmail Baby

Natalie
RIVERS

Natalie Rivers grew up in the Sussex countryside. As a child she always loved to lose herself in a good book or in games that gave free rein to her imagination. She went to Sheffield University, where she met her husband in the first week of term. It was love at first sight and they have been together ever since, moving to London after graduating, getting married and having two wonderful children.

After university Natalie worked in a lab at a medical research charity and later retrained to be a primary school teacher. Now she is lucky enough to be able to combine her two favourite occupations—being a full-time mum and writing passionate romances.

CHAPTER ONE

'CHLOE VALENTE, you are the most amazingly beautiful and sexy woman.'

The words were a deep, sensual purr in Chloe's ear, and a hot tingle of anticipation rippled through her body. She'd never thought of herself in that way—but as she felt Lorenzo standing close behind her, the heat of his strong body burning through her fine silk wedding gown, she knew that everything in her life had changed beyond her wildest dreams.

'Thank you for making this day so special.' She drew in a shaky breath and clung to the ornate stonework of the balcony, looking down into the fabulous ballroom, which was still buzzing with guests sipping vintage champagne. It was hard to believe that this palazzo, owned by Lorenzo's proud Venetian family for generations, was now her home. 'It's been truly wonderful. I can't imagine a more perfect wedding day.'

Venice was a magical place to be married, and a silvery dusting of snow falling from the February sky had made it seem even more enchanting and romantic. As she'd travelled back to the *palazzo* after the ceremony, reclining on velvet cushions in a sleek black gondola beside her breathtakingly handsome groom, she'd known that this was the happiest day of her life.

'The best is yet to come,' Lorenzo promised, his Italian accent purring in her ear as he traced his fingertips lightly along her collarbone. 'Let me take you to the bedroom and show you.'

Chloe closed her eyes for a moment and leant her head back against his shoulder, letting herself drift on a wave of pure pleasure. Simply knowing how much Lorenzo wanted her sent her heart racing and made butterflies of excitement flutter deep inside her.

Then the hum of conversation mixed with the clink of crystal glasses and angelic harp music floated up from the wedding reception below.

'We can't leave now.' She pushed his hands away weakly as she felt his sensual lips nuzzling her neck beneath the sleek blonde bob of her hair. 'What about all the people?'

'You always do the right thing,' Lorenzo said, sliding his hands down to her waist and turning her to face him. 'You were the perfect PA, always anticipating my needs and those of my associates. And even now you are thinking of our guests—of being the gracious hostess.'

She gazed up into his vibrant blue eyes and a familiar frisson of elation whispered through her. Just looking at him always made her feel like that. With his smouldering good looks and superb physique he was the most gorgeous man she had ever seen. It was almost impossible to believe that he was now her husband—that she was married to Lorenzo Valente.

She'd spent two years as his PA loving him from a distance, knowing that her feelings for her incredible Venetian boss could never be reciprocated. She was an ordinary English girl, and he was from one of Venice's oldest, most noble families, in addition to being an internationally respected billionaire businessman. They'd belonged to different worlds and Chloe had known they could never be together.

But then Lorenzo had asked her out on a date.

At first it had been hard to believe. Since the day Chloe had starting working in Lorenzo's London headquarters she'd seen an endless succession of highly polished society women draped on his arm— all tall, slender beauties with smoky come-to-bed eyes and flowing manes of dark, glossy hair.

They were all the complete opposite of Chloe, who was short, blonde and curvy, with a fair, freckled complexion and pale green eyes that looked ridiculously overdone if she experimented with more than a lick of mascara and the softest smudge of eyeliner.

But despite her initial doubts—how could someone as magnificent as Lorenzo be interested in someone as unremarkable as Chloe?—he had been impossible to resist. He'd swept into Chloe's personal life like a tornado, romancing her with the fast-track intensity that typified everything the passionate Italian did.

Before long all of Chloe's reservations had been blown away. She'd seen how he'd treated his previous women as passing diversions, and she knew that he was treating her very differently.

He'd never mentioned love, but Chloe realised he wasn't comfortable with sentimental displays of emotion. He had taken her to his home in Venice and he had talked about their future—and the children he hoped they would have together. To Chloe, that was the biggest sign of love and commitment she could have seen.

She'd accepted his proposal with joy in her heart, knowing that she was entering a new, wonderful chapter of her life—a chapter that she believed would last for ever.

'Come upstairs with me, and let me anticipate *your* needs, my special little Chloe,' he said huskily. 'Let me show you how pleased I am to have married you.'

Chloe looked up into his face and felt her eyes

start to grow warm with unshed tears of happiness. She had never thought of herself as special—certainly never viewed herself as sexy or beautiful. That Lorenzo had called her all those things meant more than she could say.

She gazed up at him, the love and happiness fizzing through her body more potent than the champagne she had been sipping all afternoon. And there was one wonderful thought in her head.

I love you.

Just three little words, but she'd never said them out loud. Neither of them had.

In the beginning Chloe had been too shy to admit her feelings, but now everything had changed. They were married. They'd stood up together in front of a congregation and pledged themselves to each other for the rest of their lives—and now her heart was overflowing with happiness.

Suddenly she could not help saying the words that were buzzing inside her.

'I love you.'

An immediate, terrible change came over Lorenzo—a change so profound that Chloe's words seemed to freeze and splinter in the air. Iron dread stabbed into her, and she knew that she had made a terrible mistake.

'Love?' Lorenzo's voice was hard with shock. 'Why did you say that?'

'Because…because it's true…' Chloe stammered weakly, staring at his dreadful expression.

'What game are you playing?' Lorenzo demanded, his black brows twisted incredulously. 'You know—you've always known—that's not what this is about.'

'But…' Her voice petered out and she was suddenly filled with stomach-churning anxiety. What was Lorenzo saying to her?

'You know this is a purely practical arrangement,' he bit out. 'We discussed how you would be my perfect wife. How a sensible, businesslike arrangement was far superior to an overblown emotional minefield. You always knew my feelings on the subject.'

'I don't understand.' Chloe stared at him in horrible confusion, aware that her heart had started to thump with sickening jerkiness beneath her breast.

She thought back to his proposal. It was true that he hadn't gone down on one knee to ask her to marry him, but he had taken her to Paris—the most romantic city in the world. They'd been walking along the Seine, with golden-brown autumn leaves swirling around them, when he had taken both her hands in his and asked her to be his wife.

She tried to remember his exact words—to recall how the conversation had developed. But suddenly all she was aware of was Lorenzo's angry expression as he stared down at her.

'We first discussed the matter when your mother

and sister were leaving for Australia,' he said. 'I asked about your father, and whether he was emigrating with them. You told me that you hadn't seen him since your seventh birthday.'

'But you and I weren't involved back then,' Chloe said, struggling to grasp the relevance of that past conversation. 'That was before you'd even asked me out.'

She remembered how he'd been sympathetic, and how he'd made her feel better by confiding in her that his mother had walked out when he was just five years old. It was the first time their relationship had pushed the boundaries of boss and PA. He'd even poured them a drink at the bar and told her…*told her how he believed life would be much simpler without the complications of unrealistic romantic ideals.*

Chloe pressed her hand over her mouth as she remembered what he'd said. She'd never, ever guessed that he was serious—that his cynical remark was more than a passing statement driven by unhappy childhood memories.

She stared up at him in shock, trying to recall if they'd ever discussed the subject again, but she knew that they hadn't. She would have remembered if he'd said anything to make her think his interest in her was driven by cold, practical matters.

He swore bitterly and raked rigid fingers through his short black hair. Two slashes of colour now burned on his high cheekbones and his blue eyes glittered with mounting fury.

'I thought you were different from the rest,' he said. 'Not another of those women trying to trap me into marriage with false declarations of love, and promises you had no intention of keeping. But now I see you are just like all the rest—worse even, because you've waited until now, our wedding day, to do this.'

His words sank into the turmoil of Chloe's mind and she struggled to make sense of what she was hearing. She realised she was shaking and folded her arms across her body, hugging herself tightly.

'It sounds as if you are saying you don't want to be loved.' Chloe could hear the confusion and doubt in her own voice, but she pressed on, determined to comprehend what Lorenzo was telling her. 'But I don't understand. It's natural to hope for love—and to look for it.'

'People who look for love are fools,' Lorenzo said with contempt, a vein pulsing on his temple.

'But what if you find love—even if you aren't looking for it?' Chloe asked. She'd never expected to fall in love with her boss, but his magnetic charisma and dynamic assurance had made it impossible for her not to.

'Love is an illusion—a false ideal that never holds true,' he grated, staring down at her through narrowed eyes.

'You are so harsh—so cynical,' Chloe gasped.

'Of course love exists—you can't deny what your heart feels.'

'And is your heart still telling you that you love me?' Lorenzo said derisively. 'Even now that we have revisited my feelings on the subject?'

'It's not something you can switch on or off,' Chloe said, dismayed by his attitude. She'd known he could be arrogant and overbearing at times, but she'd never thought of him as a cruel man.

It seemed there was a lot she didn't know about the man she had just married. Had she just made the worst mistake of her life?

'So you are sticking to your story?' Lorenzo asked. 'Perhaps for the sake of consistency you think it best to maintain the pretence for now?'

'What do *you* want from marriage—from your wife?' Chloe demanded, refusing to let him bully her into saying something to humiliate herself.

'I wanted someone honest and natural,' he said. 'Someone I could respect. Not another of those women whose grandiose pronouncements of love are as false as their manicured appearance.'

'I *have* been honest with you,' Chloe said, blinking furiously as she felt her eyes start to burn with tears. There was no way she was going to let herself cry in front of him, not after the way he was treating her. 'And if you can't respect that—can't respect *me*—then that's your problem.'

She lifted her chin defiantly, pressing her teeth into her lower lip to stop it quivering, and tried to push past him. But his fingers closed on her arm, biting into the flesh like a steel vice.

'Go and compose yourself,' he said, witheringly. 'But don't take too long. After all, you were the one anxious not to be rude to our wedding guests.'

Chloe drew in a startled breath, looking over her shoulder, down into the ballroom below. She had all but forgotten where she was and it was a shock to see the party still in full swing.

A wave of nausea washed through her as she wondered if anyone had seen her awful exchange with Lorenzo. But no one was looking up at them and a quick glance around assured her that they were alone on the balcony.

'There were no witnesses—which is fortunate for you—' his words were disdainful, but that did not mask the undercurrent of menace in his tone '—because I will not tolerate any further disrespect from you. Or permit you to shame me in any way.'

Chloe stared at him, suddenly unable to recognise the man she had fallen so deeply in love with. She opened her mouth to respond—to tell him that *she* wouldn't tolerate any more of *his* vile behaviour. But before she had the chance to speak he turned sharply and strode away towards his study.

She stood stock-still, watching him go—aware of

the crackling emotion storming through his tall, powerful body as his long, thrusting strides bore him swiftly along the corridor. She'd never been able to look away if Lorenzo was in the room. His presence drew her gaze like a magnet.

Even now, after everything that had just happened, she couldn't look away until he was out of sight. But, as his study door closed, she knew what she must do. She had to get herself away from him—as fast and as far as possible.

Ten minutes later Chloe hesitated by the door of her bedroom, looking down at the beautiful silk wedding gown lying on the bed. She'd felt like a princess wearing that dress. Or maybe like Cinderella going to the ball. But she'd found out in the most brutal way that Lorenzo was not Prince Charming.

She shuddered, remembering his expression when she'd declared her love for him, and pressed her hands over her face, trying to blot out the memory of the caustic look in his eyes as he'd ground her hopes and dreams into dust. He'd broken her heart and callously humiliated her in one fell swoop.

For the first time she was grateful that none of her family had made it to the wedding. Her mother and sister were too involved in their new life in Australia, and since Chloe had decided not to go with them it was almost as if they'd forgotten she existed. And of course her father was not there. She didn't even know where he was—or if he was still alive.

She drew in a deep breath and forced herself into action. She'd thought that this was the happiest day of her life, but Lorenzo had woken her up from that fairy tale with a merciless jolt. Now she'd have to hurry if she wanted to have any chance of making a clean getaway. And at that moment all she wanted was to be as far away from Lorenzo as possible.

She pulled her faux fur hat tight onto her head to completely cover her light blonde hair and obscure her face as much as she could. Then she turned up the collar of her long coat and slipped out into the corridor, heading towards the side staircase that led to the *palazzo*'s water gate.

She knew there'd be many boats at the Grand Canal entrance, waiting to ferry the wedding guests back to their hotels after the reception, and she needed transportation to get across the lagoon to the airport as quickly as possible. There wasn't much time before the last plane left the city that night.

Disguised in bulky winter layers, she didn't look anything like the petite blonde bride who had arrived that day, radiant with happiness and fresh from her wedding ceremony—and she desperately hoped that no one would recognise her. She couldn't bear it if one of Lorenzo's security staff dragged her back inside—back to Lorenzo.

She shivered as she climbed into a water taxi and gave directions for Marco Polo Airport. An icy wind that felt as if it had blown straight from the frozen spires of the Dolomites sliced right through her and started her shivering deep inside.

That afternoon the sparkling flurries of snow had seemed beautiful and romantic. Now the weather seemed unrelenting and cruel.

But at least she'd got away from the *palazzo* unchallenged, and was on her way across the dark lagoon to the airport. The windows of the boat were completely misted over so that she couldn't see anything, and the movement of the water was making her feel sick.

Suddenly the night seemed impenetrable—a swirling black and white uncertainty, with no visible landmarks. And her heart was breaking into a million tiny fragments that were no different from the icy shards of snow blowing down from the mountain peaks, to be swallowed up by the ink-black water of the lagoon.

Lorenzo stood outside on the balcony, staring into the snowstorm in a temper that was as foul as the night. The snow was falling so thickly that the lights shining from the buildings on the other side of the Grand Canal were just a dim glow, and there was no way to see any distance across the open water.

Not that there was anything to see. Chloe was gone.

She had boarded the final commercial plane to leave the city that night, and now the weather made it impossible for him to follow—even in his private jet.

He swore bitterly, gripping the balustrade with fingers that were as cold and hard as the stone beneath them.

He knew where she was almost certainly heading—to the home of her best friend, Liz, in a small village south of London. But as a precaution he had people waiting at Gatwick Airport to track her onward journey and to confirm her final destination.

It was not a long flight. In fact she was probably nearly there by now. He lifted his arm automatically to check his wristwatch, and cursed again as he saw that the face of his watch and his dark wedding suit were covered with icy white snow.

He turned abruptly and stepped into the bedroom, dashing the snow away with rough, impatient sweeps of his hands. But it was already melting with the heat of his body, so he shrugged his wet jacket off and tossed it aside.

Suddenly he froze—staring down at the wedding dress Chloe had abandoned on the bed. His heart thudded violently in his chest and he felt his blood surge angrily through his veins.

How dared she walk out on him like this?

How dared she turn tail and run away into the night?

The end of their marriage was not *her* decision to

make on a whim, simply because he had quashed her
sentimental outburst.

But that was immaterial now. He did not know or
care whether her declaration of love had been a cal-
culated ploy. Or if it had been a simple misguided
notion brought about by the grandeur of the occasion.
It made no difference now. By running away she had
sealed her fate. Their marriage was over.

He picked up the dress and found himself picturing how sexy Chloe had looked wearing it. He'd
spent most of the afternoon imagining peeling it
slowly off her delectable body.

He had truly believed that she would be a good
wife. That she would make a good mother for his heirs.

But their union had been short-lived—finished
before it had even begun.

A sudden, unwelcome memory flashed through
his mind, and he clenched his fists, unaware that he
was crushing the delicate fabric in his hands. This
was not the first time someone had walked away
from him at the *palazzo*. But no one would ever get
away with it again.

He looked down at the soft silk dress. Then, with
an abrupt, violent movement, he threw it savagely out
onto the balcony.

He stood, staring at it for a moment, forcing
himself to breathe slowly and consciously bringing
his pounding heartbeat back under his control. In the

eerie light of the storm the dress already looked in-distinguishable from the snow that had settled on the stone balcony. If the weather didn't let up, it would soon be covered.

He slammed the glass door shut. Then he turned his back and walked away.

CHAPTER TWO

Three months later.

IT WAS a beautiful day in early May. The sun was shining, the birds were singing. And Chloe stood at the graveside of her best friend, holding an orphaned baby in her arms.

It was almost impossible to believe—but it was true. Liz, baby Emma's mother, had really gone. Chloe had had three months to come to terms with the fact that her dear friend was losing her battle against cancer, but somehow her death had still come as a shock.

She'd flown from Venice on that bitter night in February and travelled straight to Liz's country village home. She'd been desperate to see her friend—partly to talk about what had happened with Lorenzo. But mostly just to seek the comfort of her company.

But when Liz had opened the door of her cottage

and beckoned her inside, Chloe had known at once that something was wrong. The cancer that they'd hoped and prayed would stay in remission had come back.

Liz had delayed telling Chloe because she didn't want to spoil what was supposed to be the happiest day of her life—her wedding day. And even more heartbreaking was the news that the disease had progressed too far for the doctors to save her.

Chloe looked down at the baby snuggled in her arms, feeling cold and empty. The May sunshine did nothing to take the chill away, and at that moment she felt as though she'd never be warm again.

'Are you all right, love?'

She recognised the concerned voice of Gladys, Liz's kindly neighbour. The old lady had been an incredible support during the past weeks. She'd helped to keep up her spirit at the bleakest of times, and offered to look after the baby, enabling Chloe to spend as much time as possible with Liz at the hospital, and then later on at the hospice.

Chloe turned and tried to make her smile convincing, although she knew Gladys was unlikely to be fooled.

'I'm fine,' she said.

'It was a lovely service,' Gladys said. 'The readings Liz asked for were beautiful.'

Chloe nodded, swallowing against the hard lump of sorrow that was constricting her throat. She had found the funeral almost unbearable. The pain of losing her best friend was still too raw. Liz had been too young to die. And baby Emma was too young to lose her mother.

'If you're sure you're all right, I'd better get back to the cottage,' Gladys said gently. 'They'll all be waiting for me by now.'

'Thank you for inviting everyone back for tea,' Chloe said gratefully. It had been thoughtful of the old lady to offer to host a small gathering after the funeral, and something Chloe just didn't feel up to.

'It's the least I could do.' Gladys brushed her thanks aside. 'You've got your hands full with little Emma. And you've already done so much.'

'I only did what anyone would have done,' Chloe said.

'No, not anyone,' Gladys said stoutly. 'You took good care of your friend during a difficult time. And now you are doing a wonderful thing—taking on her baby as your own. Liz was truly blessed to have a friend like you.'

Chloe pressed her trembling lips together and tried to smile at her. She knew Gladys meant well, but at that moment it was hard to think of Liz as blessed. She'd suffered so much, only to have her life snatched away by cancer.

'I'll see you in a little while.' Chloe gave Gladys a hug. Then, as the old lady turned to head back towards the row of terraced cottages in the village, she quietly breathed a sigh of relief. She needed to be alone for a moment.

She couldn't face being squeezed into Gladys's tiny front room with the crowd of well-meaning mourners from the village. Liz had not had any close relatives and Emma's father had never been part of the picture. From the moment he'd discovered Liz was pregnant he'd wanted nothing whatsoever to do with her, and even claimed that there was no way he could be the father.

'We'll be all right,' Chloe whispered, and kissed Emma's soft cheek. 'We've got each other.'

But as she pressed her face against Emma's wispy baby hair, she suddenly felt very alone.

She found herself thinking about Lorenzo. Three months ago she'd thought she was about to embark on the most wonderful journey of her life—marriage and children with her gorgeous Italian husband. Now everything was so different.

She had not heard a word from him since the night she left Venice, and that had hurt her more than she wanted to admit, even to herself. She'd known it was unrealistic to hope that he would follow her, saying that he'd got it wrong, and that he did love her after all.

But still, that was what she'd wished for.

She had not contacted him either. She'd been too involved with caring for Liz and Emma. And, if she was completely honest, she hadn't been able to face him.

Deep down she knew she'd behaved badly by running away without talking to him—but she'd simply reacted instinctively to the discovery that Lorenzo viewed their marriage as a loveless practicality. An overpowering need for self-preservation had kicked in, and she'd known that to protect her broken heart she had to get away from him.

But now she *had* to contact Lorenzo.

Firstly about her intention to adopt Emma. They were still officially married, and that might cause complications with the legal procedures. And secondly, about some money she'd been forced to use a couple of days earlier, from an account he'd set up in both their names before the wedding. The amount she'd taken would be nothing to a man as rich as Lorenzo, but she knew him well enough to be aware that no detail—no matter how small—ever escaped his notice.

She wanted him to know that she would pay him back as soon as she could. She had no wish to take anything from him. And the sooner she set things straight, the sooner she could put that heartbreaking episode of her life behind her, and get on with building a life for herself and Emma.

A tremble ran through her at the thought of seeing Lorenzo again, but she closed her eyes and pressed her cheek against the top of Emma's head.

'I'm not going to think about that now,' she said

to the baby. She'd promised Liz that she'd think happy thoughts, but at that moment it was a hard promise to keep.

She walked across to a wooden bench under a flowering cherry tree. The soft grass was scattered with the delicate pink blossom and it reminded Chloe of confetti.

Suddenly tears welled up in her eyes. It was the most beautiful day. But her best friend was not there to share it with her. And she never would be again.

Lorenzo Valente handled the convertible with a natural ease, shifting gears smoothly as he approached a tight bend in the winding country lane. It was a fine afternoon in May and the sun felt surprisingly warm on his shoulders as he sped along the leafy green road in rural England.

He usually enjoyed driving, but the expression on his face was far from one of pleasure—he was thinking about the latest stunt Chloe had pulled.

Very little shocked Lorenzo. He accepted the fact that being born into a wealthy family, and then multiplying that fortune by several orders of magnitude, had made him a target for various types of gold-digging parasites.

However, he'd never thought *Chloe* would steal from him. But it was just one more thing to make her pay for.

His strong fingers tightened on the steering wheel and his eyes narrowed dangerously. A minute later he reached a tiny village. He slowed the car, and took the turning that led to the church. He drove a short distance along the narrow lane and then pulled up onto the grass verge, waiting for the crowd of pedestrians leaving the church to pass.

He knew that it was the day of her friend's funeral. He'd seen to it that he had been kept very well-informed about Chloe's actions since she walked out on him.

Suddenly he caught sight of a small figure dressed in dark grey walking unsteadily across the churchyard.

It was Chloe.

A strange sensation lodged in the pit of his stomach and he felt his heart start to beat faster. He was out of the car in an instant, ignoring the curious looks he was drawing from some of the villagers. He only had eyes for Chloe.

He strode across the churchyard towards her, the soft grass muffling his footsteps. She did not see or hear him approach, and sat completely motionless on the bench beneath the flowering cherry tree, engulfed in a private moment of sorrow.

He was about to speak but he hesitated, feeling an unaccustomed stab of uncertainty. Her eyes were closed as she wept, tears sliding silently down her white cheeks as she held a baby nestled in her arms.

Her grief for her friend was so personal—he knew that his presence was an intrusion.

Suddenly she opened her eyes and stared up at him. A flash of surprise passed across her features.

'Lorenzo.' Her wide green eyes were luminous with tears in the warm afternoon sunshine, and her pale skin looked almost translucent. 'Oh, God, I can't believe you're here.'

Hearing her say his name with such feeling sent an unexpected surge of emotion powering through his veins. He wanted to reach out and smooth the moisture from her cheeks, but instead he clamped his arms stiffly by his sides.

'Really?' he said, knowing his tone was harsh, especially after witnessing the depth of her grief. But the intensity of his reaction to her had caught him off guard. He wasn't accustomed to being affected by other people's emotional displays. 'I thought that, by stealing my money, it was your intention to draw me out.'

'The money…that's why you're here?'

Chloe looked up at him, her pulse still racing from the shock of opening her eyes and seeing Lorenzo standing there. He looked so strong and vibrant— and, despite everything, he was the most welcome sight in the world.

For a moment she let herself believe that maybe he was there because he knew she needed him— knew how sad and alone she felt. She had no doubt that he was aware of everything that had happened to her since she'd left Venice. Information was another essential currency to Lorenzo.

'What other reason could there be?' he said, his piercing blue eyes boring into her.

She drew in a breath, suppressing the irrational surge of disappointment that rose up within her. But really she'd known that, if Lorenzo cared for her at all, he would have come before this.

'I'm going to pay the money back,' she said. 'I needed it urgently.'

'For what?' Lorenzo demanded. 'What was so urgent that you couldn't wait until you found some other way of paying? That you needed to take my money immediately and without permission?'

'I had to pay for this,' Chloe said, sweeping her arm around with a distracted gesture, unable to believe how cold and unfeeling he seemed. 'My savings are gone, my credit card is maxed out. I've had no income for months, but I've been looking after Liz and...'

She stopped abruptly, suddenly wishing she hadn't said so much. The state of her finances was none of Lorenzo's business.

It was a shock to find herself face to face with him again, and one heartbreaking thought kept going round in her head: he had no interest in *her*—only in what he thought she'd taken from him. Could he really have come all this way to berate her over the comparatively small amount of money she'd spent?

'I used the money to pay for the funeral,' she stated bluntly. Surely even Lorenzo wasn't so hard-hearted that he would begrudge that.

'You should have asked me,' he said coldly.

'I didn't need to ask,' she said. 'The account is in both our names. I never wanted to use a penny of that money, but I'm not going to apologise for it, because I'd do it again in a heartbeat. Liz deserved a proper funeral.'

Lorenzo stared down at Chloe, registering an undercurrent of uncertainty showing through her expression despite her continued defence of her actions. He knew she was still emotional, and he felt unwelcome feelings churn in his own stomach in response.

This was not what he had expected when he'd married Chloe—that three months after their wedding they would be meeting for the first time in an English churchyard and arguing over a stranger's funeral expenses.

He'd chosen her to be his wife because he thought she'd be reliable and stable, the way she'd been as his PA. He wanted his marriage to be straightforward and uncomplicated, not like the often hysterical and unpleasant scenarios he'd witnessed growing up as his father worked his way through a string of unsuitable wives.

But nothing had worked out the way he intended. Chloe had walked out on him. Then she'd chosen not to get in touch—even when she was in financial trouble.

'You were too proud to ask for help,' Lorenzo said. 'You'd sooner steal my money than talk to me.'

Chloe let out her breath with a resigned sigh and looked straight up into his eyes.

'I didn't think you'd let me use the money. I thought you'd freeze the account or something,' Chloe said. 'You didn't really know Liz. You only met her a couple of times.'

Lorenzo swore with sudden violence. Then frowned at the baby as she started to grizzle and fuss in Chloe's arms.

'What kind of man do you think I am?' he demanded angrily. 'You truly think I'm so petty I would not pay for a funeral?'

Chloe stared up at him with wide eyes that seemed huge in her pale face, looking as startled as the baby by his loud outburst.

'I don't know,' she said, her voice sounding shaky and uncertain. 'We might be married but it seems I don't know you at all.'

Then she looked away, down at the baby in her arms.

'I can't do this now.' She rocked Emma gently and murmured soothing words to her. 'She's probably hungry. It's been a long afternoon and I need to get her back to the cottage.'

She looked small and awkward standing there, wearing an ill-fitting charcoal-grey suit that swamped her tiny frame and was pulled out of line by the baby in her arms. The unforgiving colour drained any speck of warmth from her fair complexion and her light blonde hair hung down in a shapeless curtain nearly to her shoulders.

Next to the fresh green grass and colourful pink blossom she looked starkly monochrome, almost as if she'd stepped out of a black-and-white movie—some old-fashioned, overblown melodrama.

She didn't belong here—not like this.

The anger that had gripped Lorenzo suddenly dissipated. He had to get her away from this place. It was impossible to talk to her in the churchyard.

'We'll go together—just to pick up what you need,' he said. 'Then you're coming with me.'

Chloe stared up at him in surprise. She hadn't expected him to start issuing orders—although that was exactly how Lorenzo was used to behaving with most people in his life. And it was how he had been with her too, back before they became personally involved.

'I know you're angry with me,' she said, 'but you can't just sweep in here and boss me about. I don't work for you any more.'

'No. You're my wife,' Lorenzo grated, the tone of his voice telling her that he was far from happy about that. 'And you are coming with me.'

'But I have Emma now,' she protested, tightening her hold on the infant protectively.

'What about her father?' Lorenzo asked, studying the crying baby with a crease between his brows.

'He never wanted anything to do with her,' Chloe said. 'I'm the only one she has now.'

Lorenzo lifted his eyes to Chloe's face, and an expression she couldn't read passed across his features.

'Let's go.' He reached out and took her arm before she realised what he intended.

As his hand made contact it was as if a jolt of energy surged through Chloe. She gasped and looked down automatically, staring as his strong fingers closed around her upper arm, tanned and vital next to the dull grey fabric of her jacket.

Her heart started to beat faster, and at that moment she felt the numbness that had deadened her over recent days start to thaw.

Lorenzo was only holding her arm, but suddenly she was fully aware of him physically—aware of his sheer size and strength. And shockingly aware of the body heat radiating from his powerful, athletic form.

She found herself drawn towards him, like a flower turning towards the sun.

She'd been so cold and lonely. All at once she found herself longing to feel his strong arms around her—to press herself against the solid masculine expanse of his chest.

Suddenly she realised that Lorenzo had stopped moving. He was standing utterly still. And she knew, even without looking up at him, that he was taking in her reaction to his touch.

A flash of alarm shot through her. She couldn't let Lorenzo see how vulnerable she was feeling, how in need of physical comfort. He'd always been able to read her like a book, and right at that moment her defences were lower than normal.

'I'm not going anywhere with you,' Chloe said, trying to shrug out of his grip. But his fingers simply tightened, and with Emma in her arms it was impossible to struggle too much.

'There are matters we must discuss,' Lorenzo said, turning her round so once again they were facing each other.

Chloe shook her head, staring directly ahead—straight at his broad chest. She did not want to talk to him any more. And she definitely did not want to look into his perceptive eyes.

She had the terrible feeling she would reveal herself to him in some way—let him see how naked her emotions were, how much she craved his presence. The day had already been too painful. The thought of him driving away and leaving her alone again suddenly seemed unbearable—but there was no way she would admit that to him.

'Your desertion on our wedding day made it clear

that you are no longer happy with our arrangement,'
he said, cupping his free hand under her chin and
lifting her face to his.

Her gaze was locked to his clear blue eyes again
and the touch of his fingers against her skin made her
shiver once more.

'I didn't think we had an *arrangement*,' she
replied, feeling a chill creep back around her heart.
His words were a harsh reminder that she had been
disastrously wrong about what their marriage meant
to Lorenzo—about what *she'd* meant to him.

'Yes, we did,' Lorenzo said, 'which is why we
need to talk. There will be no further misunderstandings between us.'

CHAPTER THREE

CHLOE sat in the limousine with Lorenzo and Emma as it purred along the narrow lanes away from the village where she'd lived for the last three months. It was late in the afternoon but the sun was still shining brightly. Billowing drifts of frothy white cow parsley lined the roadside, and the hedgerows were a mass of lacy hawthorn blossom.

Chloe stared out at the passing countryside, hoping to calm her jangling nerves. She could not let herself look across at Lorenzo. She was still too unsettled and confused by her feelings towards him.

She'd spent the last few weeks desperately missing him, despite the fact that she knew she was yearning for something that did not really exist. Everything she'd believed to be true about their relationship had been false. Lorenzo did not love her. All he'd wanted was a convenient wife.

But now he had appeared out of the blue, and her

body and soul had responded to him with an intensity that had knocked her off balance. It was as if her mind had no influence over what she was feeling towards him—or even as if the heartbreaking revelation on their wedding day had never really happened.

'I gather that your friend had no immediate family.' The sound of Lorenzo's deep voice startled her. She turned to him, feeling her pulse crank up a notch once more the moment she met his steely blue gaze. 'But where are the rest of her relatives?'

'There aren't any,' she said, dragging her eyes away from his face with surprising difficulty to look down at Emma, who was asleep in the infant car seat beside her. 'That will make the adoption more straightforward. It's what Liz wanted—and what I want too.'

'Adoption is a serious commitment. And a legally binding arrangement,' Lorenzo said. 'Did you not think it would be appropriate to discuss your intention with your husband?'

His voice was level and the tone neutral, but Chloe knew it was a pointed comment. She turned back to him and saw that he was staring at Emma. There was a deep crease between his black eyebrows and Chloe realised she'd never seen him in such close proximity to a baby before.

He was looking at Emma as if she were a tiny alien who had somehow sneaked into his car.

She knew that Lorenzo wanted children—they'd

discussed it after he asked her to marry him. At the time she assumed he'd be a wonderful father. But now, judging by his expression as he studied Emma, she wasn't so sure. Perhaps he just wanted children to inherit his legacy and carry on his family name.

Chloe had always wanted to be a mother and now she had a baby to care for. It wasn't the way she would have wanted it to happen, but when she promised Liz that she would adopt Emma she'd known that the baby girl was the most precious parting gift her friend could have given her.

'There's no need for you to worry,' she said, feeling instinctively protective towards Emma. 'The adoption will not affect you.'

As soon as she'd spoken she felt his temper flare once more and a prickle passed across her skin. The limousine suddenly seemed too small, and she wished they were back in the open air again.

'We are married,' he grated. 'I imagine that the adoption courts will be interested in that—even if you think you can act as if we are not.'

'I'm not acting as if I'm not married!' she snapped, meeting his gaze straight on. 'I'm just trying to do the right thing for an orphaned baby. My promise to adopt Emma has nothing to do with you.'

His piercing gaze held hers and the air between them seemed to vibrate with sudden tension.

Chloe swallowed reflexively as she realised how

angry he was that she'd made this decision without him. He was probably thinking about how the adoption would affect him legally, and whether he would have unwanted responsibilities towards somebody else's child.

'You won't stop me doing this,' she said. 'Nothing will stop me taking care of Emma. No one will ever take this baby away from me.'

But at that moment she realised that Lorenzo *was* involved. Until they were divorced, he might have some influence over the adoption procedure.

'I *will* fight for Emma,' she added, still staring straight into his hard eyes. Her heart was beating quickly and she felt the muscles of her face grow taut as she continued to maintain eye contact. But she wouldn't look away. She couldn't cave in so easily. There was too much at stake.

'We're here.'

Lorenzo's voice broke the silence and Chloe let out a shuddering sigh, turning away to see where he'd brought them. He'd told her he had somewhere private near by where they would be able to talk, and she hadn't asked any more questions.

The idea of somewhere different, away from the cottage that held such sadness, had been very appealing. She'd quickly packed a few things, telling herself that he was right—they did still have issues that needed to be resolved. But deep down she'd known that she didn't really want to be alone at the cottage that night.

'Where are we?' she asked as they drove through an impressive brick arch. Wrought-iron gates swung silently closed behind them, then she caught her first glimpse of a sleek modern house, set in the most beautiful grounds. 'What is this place?'

If this was where Lorenzo was staying, no wonder it hadn't taken long for the limousine to come out to the village, bringing an additional driver to return with Lorenzo's convertible.

'It was your wedding present,' Lorenzo said shortly as the limo purred along the sweeping drive-way up to the front door. 'You left before I had a chance to give it to you.'

Chloe blinked in surprise, totally lost for words. She knew she ought to say something, but her mind had gone completely blank.

She realised Lorenzo was already out of the car, waiting for her to join him, so she leant across to release the safety belt that held the infant car seat securely in place. Then before she had a chance to move Lorenzo reached in and lifted the portable seat, complete with sleeping baby, out of the car.

Chloe followed him into the house with a very strange feeling running through her as she watched him carrying Emma. It was clear that he was taking care, but even so it looked more as if he were carrying a basket of groceries at the supermarket than a little baby. All of a sudden that thought struck her as absurdly funny—she just couldn't imagine Lorenzo Valente carrying a basket of food around a shop— and she bit her lip to stop herself smiling.

But then as quickly as the flash of humour had struck her, it vanished again. And she found herself trailing behind him through a beautiful house into an incredible glass-walled living room, which over-looked a stunning landscaped garden.

Lorenzo placed Emma's carrier carefully onto a cream rug and turned to speak to her.

'Chloe, this is Mrs Gill Guest, the housekeeper,' he said, gesturing a middle-aged lady forward from a doorway at the side of the room. 'Mrs Guest, I would appreciate it if you would assist my wife. Help her and the infant to settle in, and discuss any par-ticular requirements she may have, especially re-garding the baby.'

Then, without another glance in her direction, Lorenzo turned on his heel and strode out of the room, his leather-soled shoes making no sound on the natural wood floor.

Lorenzo marched through the house to his study, tension screaming in every muscle of his body. He shut the door behind him, flung off his jacket and tugged at his tie, suddenly feeling unbearably constrained.

Just a couple of hours in Chloe's company and already he was reaching the edge of his control.

He had come to England to bring his marriage to Chloe to a decisive end—but not until he'd sought retribution for what she'd done. She would not get away with walking out on him.

In theory it should be easy to take the situation back into his own hands. He'd seen how Chloe responded to him when he touched her, and he knew that she was desperate for him to give her the comfort she'd needed.

That was exactly what he intended to do. Then afterwards, once he had made her realise what she had walked away from, what could have been hers for life, he would ruthlessly sever the relationship.

His plan was perfect with its elegant simplicity.

But he had wanted her with a fierceness that had taken him by surprise—a need so overpowering that it had threatened his rational command.

Even now the fire was burning in him, making his throbbing body ache for her relentlessly, despite the fact she was now out of his sight. Three months was a long time and, although he'd considered their marriage over in all but name, he had not taken another woman to his bed.

No one had caught his eye—not one woman had stirred the same magnitude of desire within him.

When he'd looked down at her standing beside

him in the churchyard, the urge to drag her against him and crush her soft pink lips with his mouth had been almost irresistible. Passion had pulsed through his veins like molten lava, until the only thing he could think about was making love to Chloe.

He could not let it go on. He would not let his physical desire cloud his mind any longer. Chloe had already caused enough disruption in his life. He would take her to bed and get her out of his system. Once and for all.

But, deep in the dark recesses of his mind, he knew once would not be enough.

Chloe stood in the bedroom, by the floor-to-ceiling plate-glass window, staring out at the stunning view across the rolling green hills. It was a beautiful place, and exactly the type of house she'd once dreamed of living in. It reminded her of a property she'd visited and fallen in love with as a child, and she was certain that Lorenzo must remember her telling him about it.

The building was modern, with clean, simple lines and wonderful airy living spaces with masses of huge windows that made it feel continuous with the garden and the lush green countryside that surrounded the house.

It was an incredible wedding gift. Not because of its value, but because it had been chosen personally for her, in answer to a childhood dream that she'd never expected to have fulfilled.

But now she was there she almost wished Lorenzo had taken her to an impersonal country hotel, because she didn't know how to interpret his purchase of this house. It was so close to Liz's village that it could not be a coincidence. And, if he had given it to her before the wedding, she would have seen him buying a place near her best friend's home as a sign of his love. Now she was just horribly confused.

She lifted her chin and shook her hair back from her face—pushing those thoughts firmly from her mind. All she should be thinking about was how to secure her future as Emma's adoptive mother. From Lorenzo's reaction it was clear he was angry that she hadn't kept him informed about her intention. She knew that she would have to tread carefully, because she could not—*would not*—let anything stop her adopting Emma.

A gentle tap on the door pulled her out of her thoughts, and she realised it was Mrs Guest returning to babysit while she went down to talk to Lorenzo in his study. A knot of anxiety tightened in her stomach, but she did her best to ignore it and smiled at the older lady.

'Thank you for staying with Emma.' Chloe glanced over at the baby sleeping in the cot that Mrs Guest's husband had set up earlier that evening. 'She doesn't normally wake once she's down for the night, but it's such a big house I was worried I wouldn't hear her if she does.'

'It's my pleasure,' Mrs Guest said. 'The baby-monitoring equipment will be delivered tomorrow, but I'll always be happy to sit with her.'

'Thank you,' Chloe said, wondering how long Mrs Guest expected her to be staying there at that house—whether Lorenzo had given his staff any indication. 'You've been very kind.'

She left the bedroom and walked slowly down to Lorenzo's study, butterflies crashing in her stomach and her heart beating apprehensively.

In the past she'd always looked forward to seeing him. During the two years that she'd been his PA she'd eagerly awaited business arrangements that would bring him to his London offices. Then, once their relationship had moved on to a personal level, she'd spent every minute they were apart daydreaming about when they would be together again.

But now she knew he was angry with her. And the enforced wait to see him had made her nervous. She smoothed her hands down over her clothes, wishing that she hadn't changed into her jeans and a T-shirt. But the grey suit had been borrowed from Liz's wardrobe, and it had been too upsetting to wear it any longer.

She walked down the curved staircase with her gaze fixed on the open door of his study, realising that he would be able to see her coming. She started to tread as quietly as possible, thankful that her flat ballerina pumps made virtually no sound.

Suddenly Lorenzo appeared in the doorway. His blue eyes locked on to Chloe instantly, sending a rush of nerves skittering through her, which was quickly followed by a heated jolt of sensual awareness.

He looked absolutely magnificent—the epitome of masculine good looks and animal magnetism. Tall and powerfully built, his broad-shouldered athletic form would make heads turn wherever he went. But it was so much more than his physical presence that made an impact—the sheer force of his personality emanated from him, despite the fact he was standing absolutely still, wearing an unreadable expression.

Chloe took a steadying breath and forced herself to keep walking down the stairs.

'Come into my study,' Lorenzo said, standing aside just enough to let her brush past him. 'We still have a lot to discuss.'

It was another impressive glass-walled room with sliding doors that opened directly onto a wide decking area next to a large fishpond edged with a mass of flowering purple irises.

But Chloe was only conscious of Lorenzo as she slipped through the narrow gap he'd left for her, feeling the heat of his body even in the brief moment it took to slip past. She felt tiny next to him, especially in her flat shoes. For an instant she wished again she hadn't changed out of the formal grey suit—but then she pushed the thought aside.

She might be small, but she was a strong woman. She would not let herself be overwhelmed by Lorenzo. She'd been through such a lot over the last three months, and this conversation with Lorenzo was just another hurdle to get over. She might as well get on with it—on her own terms.

'I'm sorry that I didn't tell you about my intention to adopt Emma,' she said immediately, seizing the opportunity to speak first. 'I understand why you are upset about it, but it doesn't have to have any impact on you at all.'

'Of course it does,' Lorenzo said. 'Don't be so foolish—we're married.'

He stared down at her impatiently. His body was already responding to her presence—she looked as sexy as hell in her figure-hugging jeans and T-shirt. But for the first time he was struck that he hardly recognised her as the woman he'd married just three months earlier. She seemed so different.

It was clear that she hadn't had much time to spend on her appearance, but that was understandable. She looked tired and washed-out, and her freckles were more pronounced than ever against her milky complexion.

Her pale blonde hair had grown out of the sleek, tailored bob into a shapeless, uneven curtain that brushed her shoulders, with a tendency to fall forward and obscure half of her face. Her clothes were verging on scruffy and her flat shoes had seen better days.

The physical differences were distracting, but what he really found disconcerting was the change in her attitude. She had behaved badly and, even though she'd just offered him a partial apology, there was still a determined set to her shoulders and a defiant thrust to her chin.

'No, it needn't affect you—not if we hurry the divorce through before I take the adoption any further,' Chloe said.

A flash of anger surged through Lorenzo and for a moment he could not believe what he was hearing. Chloe had walked out on him on their wedding day without a backwards glance, and now she had the audacity to tell him this!

It was unacceptable—there was no way that he would tolerate Chloe telling him their marriage was over.

'No.' The word fired out of him like a bullet. 'There will be no divorce.'

'Why not?' Chloe gasped, staring at his furious face in disbelief. 'After all the things that have happened, I thought it was what you would want.'

'It is *not* what I want,' Lorenzo grated. 'A string of broken marriages is exactly what I intend to avoid.'

'One divorce is not a string of broken marriages,' Chloe said. 'Anyway, this is hardly a marriage. It was only a few hours after the ceremony when I found out that you didn't…' She hesitated, searching for words that were not too painful to say. The memory of him saying that he didn't want her love had haunted her every day for the last three months. 'I had to leave. We could probably even get an annulment if you don't want a divorce.'

As soon as she had spoken, she knew it was a mistake. A storm of powerful emotions raged across Lorenzo's face but before she had a chance to react he stepped forward and seized her upper arms, pulling her roughly towards him.

'We may not have made love on our wedding day,' he grated, lifting her onto her tiptoes and leaning down so their faces were only inches apart, 'but that doesn't mean that this union was never consummated.'

Sexual energy crackled in the air between them, making it hard to think straight. But Chloe knew that was all it was. Just sex.

'We never made *love*!' She struggled in his vice-like grip, trying to pull away—but her mind was spinning with images of the many mind-blowing nights she'd spent in his arms. 'That was the problem. I thought it meant something—that what we had was real. But it was all meaningless. You misled me into this marriage. Surely that alone is enough to make it null and void!'

'It was never meaningless,' Lorenzo said.

He glowered down at her, his expressive black eyebrows drawn low and menacing, and there was a dangerous predatory glint in his eyes. For a moment Chloe half expected him to kiss her—and to her utter confusion and shame she almost wanted him to.

'Well, it clearly didn't mean the same to you as it did to me,' she cried as she finally managed to wrench herself out of his hold.

She stood her ground and met his eyes boldly, aware that she was still easily within the reach of his strong arms. That knowledge sent a startling jolt of excitement through her, and she felt her cheeks start to burn. She lifted her chin and glared up at him, desperately trying to ignore the way her pulse rate was suddenly responding to his physical proximity.

Her body might be attuned to his—every inch of her skin tingling with a growing desire to feel his hands on her again. But it was just hormones. Emotionally he was a million miles away.

'You have no idea what our marriage meant to me,' Lorenzo said.

'No, I don't,' she agreed, remembering the confusing and heartbreaking argument they'd had on their wedding day, 'but I do know that *I* thought I'd found my soulmate—my partner for life. Instead, all I'd found was a lie!'

'I never lied to you,' Lorenzo said, 'and I thought the same thing as you—that I had found *my* partner for life.'

'How can you say that?' Chloe demanded. 'After everything you told me about not believing in love, how can you say that?'

'Because that is what I wanted,' Lorenzo said, 'and it is what you agreed to when you married me.'

'But…'

It was impossible to think with his penetrating gaze holding her captive. She sensed her body responding to him again. Her heart was racing and her skin felt hot and sensitive. She tipped her head a little further back and frowned, trying to make her gaze cold and stern—but the feel of her own hair brushing her shoulders felt like a caress, sending a ripple of sensual anticipation through her.

'Finally, a bit of colour in that face,' Lorenzo said, lifting his hand to cup her blazing cheek.

Chloe gasped as his fingers made contact, releasing another torrent of desire storming through her body.

'Don't touch me,' she said, in feeble protest.

'Why not? You want me to,' he said. 'And you still owe me our wedding night.'

'Our wedding night? You mean sex?' Her voice was no more than a startled whisper and her eyes were wide. 'After everything that has happened—everything we've said—you want sex?'

Lorenzo raised his brows and his full, sensual lips twitched into a smile that was mocking and knowing at the same time.

'Are you offering me sex?' he asked, sliding his fingers deep into her hair and pulling her close to his hard body.

CHAPTER FOUR

'You know I'm not offering you sex!' Chloe exclaimed. She tried to step back, out of his grip, but he held her firmly.

'That's what it sounded like,' Lorenzo drawled, leaning down and brushing his lips across the sensitive skin he had exposed by lifting her hair up off her neck.

A delicious shiver skittered down her spine, and he was holding her so close that she couldn't help letting him feel her very physical response to his gentle kisses. Trying to hold her body stiff and straight in denial of how she was feeling was pointless—he knew her well enough to know that she was suddenly yearning for him to make love to her.

But it was *not* love, she reminded herself. That made a difference. That *had* to make a difference.

But then why was her body slowly melting into his embrace? Why was she becoming pliable in his arms, as he arched her backwards and brought his mouth down on hers?

He kissed her with devouring heat, ignoring her feeble attempts to pull away, as he plundered her tender mouth in an overwhelmingly sexual onslaught. His body was big and strong, but it wasn't his sheer physical size and strength that overpowered her. It was the fervour of her own response to him that left her defenceless.

Her eyelids slid down and she was lost in a moment where only she and Lorenzo existed. She was aware of his potent virility with every inch of her body. His tongue moved against hers, making her want more—so much more that she trembled with pure, naked desire. Her blood was singing in her ears and her whole being was buzzing with longing.

His hands skimmed over her, then suddenly he swept her right off her feet and up into his arms.

Her eyes flew open in surprise, and her conscious mind plummeted mercilessly back to the cold light of day. Her body was still yearning for Lorenzo, muddling her grip on the situation, but she knew she had to stop him before things went any further.

Intimacy was not love. Chloe knew that she was fooling herself if she let herself believe a true connection could form between them, when Lorenzo felt no love for her.

'Put me down,' she gasped, pushing her hand against the powerful wall of his broad chest and staring up into his face.

He stood still, as solid as a rock, and held her gaze with his own. She knew what he must see in her eyes—after all, she could see the same thing glowing in his: smouldering arousal.

'On the desk—or the sofa?' he asked, his voice dangerously deep and loaded with sexual intent.

Chloe swallowed reflexively, trying to stop her mind replaying the many times they'd made love on his desk. And on various bits of furniture, and in other unusual places. During the time they'd been lovers they'd often been so wrapped up in their passion for each other that they failed to make it to the comfort of their bedroom.

At the time she'd found it thrilling. And she'd taken it as proof of the depth of his feeling for her. Now the knowledge that Lorenzo wouldn't hesitate to get physical in almost any location filled her with a mixture of excitement and panic.

'Three months is a long time,' Lorenzo said, lifting her slightly so that his face was only inches above hers. 'I've waited long enough.'

'You waited…' Chloe drew in a shaky breath and stared at him, lost for words.

Somehow, over the months they'd spent apart, it had never occurred to her to think of Lorenzo with another woman. Now that suddenly seemed naive. She knew what a hot-blooded alpha male he was, and she knew he had never spent long without a woman in his bed.

'Did you think I'd taken another lover?' he asked, his voice harsh with an emotion she couldn't identify.

'No, I…' She hesitated. 'I never thought about it until now.'

A sudden flare of anger crossed his face as he dumped her back onto her feet.

'You never thought about it!' Lorenzo exploded. 'You didn't care enough about the man you professed to love to wonder whether he'd replaced you in his bed?'

She stared up at him, suddenly feeling cold away from the warmth of his arms, despite the huge and intimidating way he loomed over her. But she realised her words had been an affront to his masculine pride.

'It wasn't like that,' Chloe said. 'You know what the last few months have been like for me.'

'No,' Lorenzo barked. 'I don't know. You walked out of my life—the life I thought we were building together—and shut me out completely.'

'What did you think I would do when you denounced my love?' Chloe cried, spiralling back to the soul-crushing moment in the *palazzo* on their wedding day. 'I opened my heart up to you—and you were angry with me! You tore my heart to pieces and shredded everything I believed in.'

'I did not expect you to turn your back on me—on our marriage—so easily,' Lorenzo replied. 'You said you loved me. Then you behaved as if I was nothing to you.'

'What was I to you?' Chloe demanded. 'Someone you tricked into marriage for your own convenience—someone you didn't care enough about to be honest with?'

'You were my wife.'

Lorenzo's voice was hard with the clipped tones of finality. He turned abruptly and strode towards the door of the study.

Chloe stared after him, feeling as if a hurricane had just ripped through the room. Her heart was racing and her scalp was prickling with the static electricity—but now that neither of them was speaking the space was filled with an unnatural silence.

Suddenly, just as his hand reached the door handle, Lorenzo turned and fixed her with his penetrating eyes.

'You are still my wife,' he said. 'And that is how it will stay.'

He closed the door behind him and Chloe sagged against the desk, feeling all the strength drain out of her body.

She'd felt as if a hurricane had torn through her, but she knew the quiet emptiness was simply the eye of the storm. It wasn't over yet. In fact it was going to get a whole lot worse before she was out the other side.

* * *

Chloe climbed back up the stairs to the bedroom where Mrs Guest was watching over Emma. Her eyes felt warm with the telltale heat of tears, but she blinked them back, refusing to let them fall. She didn't have the resilience to cope with the kindly housekeeper's sympathy. She knew her heartache was something she would have to deal with on her own.

'There you are, dear,' Mrs Guest said, smiling warmly as she walked back into the room. 'The little darling hasn't stirred since you've been gone.'

'Thank you,' Chloe said, returning the older woman's smile.

She crossed the room to look down at Emma, who was lying in exactly the same position as when she'd left her. It seemed like hours since she'd gone down to see Lorenzo, but in fact she realised only very few minutes had passed.

'You look wiped out, dear,' Mrs Guest said. 'Why don't I stay a few more minutes while you relax in the bath? You don't want to be popping your head in and out of the en suite all the time, wondering if the baby is still sleeping.'

'Thank you.' Chloe accepted the offer gratefully, suddenly desperate to lock herself safely away from the world—or, if she was completely honest with herself, away from Lorenzo. She had no idea where he was and it was perfectly possible that he could appear at any moment. She knew that he had been using this bedroom too, and right at that moment she couldn't bear the thought of coming face to face with him again. 'But actually I'll take a shower,' she added, trying to keep her voice from cracking with the wave of emotion that was rising up through her. 'I think I'm too tired for a bath.'

She locked the bathroom door and a sob broke raggedly from within her. She clamped her hand over her mouth so that Mrs Guest wouldn't hear and stumbled across the room, shedding her clothes as she went.

A moment later she turned on the shower. A torrent of warm water gushed out and she stood beneath it, finally letting go of the tears that she'd been holding back for so long. She wept with abandon, unable to control the anguished sobs that racked her slender body.

Eventually, all cried out, she leant back against the tiled wall and smoothed her hands over her hot face. Everything had come together in an unbearable build-up of misery. And at that moment it was impossible to separate her grief for her friend from her distress over the intolerable situation she'd found herself in with Lorenzo.

The water continued to pour down and she reached automatically for the shampoo. For a few minutes she would take refuge in everyday necessities and routines.

A little while later, wrapped securely in a fluffy

white bathrobe, Chloe emerged from the en suite. Mrs Guest put down her book and looked up with a smile.

'Mr Valente popped in,' she said, making a knot tighten inside Chloe's stomach. 'He said that unfortunately he had to work late. But because he knew how tired you were, he would sleep in the guest room tonight—he said he didn't want to disturb you or little Emma.'

'Thank you for telling me,' Chloe said. As Mrs Guest left, closing the door behind her, she wondered what the older lady had made of the message. While she and Lorenzo had been together they'd never slept in separate bedrooms.

Chloe crawled into bed and tried to sleep, but although she was exhausted she couldn't relax. All she could think about was Lorenzo's final comment that she would remain his wife.

She couldn't understand why he had said that. It didn't seem to make any sense. Deep in her heart she longed to stay married to Lorenzo—she still wanted everything she had wanted when she accepted his proposal to be his wife.

But the situation was completely different now. She had Emma to consider. And now she knew that he did not love her.

The following morning Chloe found herself alone in the house. Or rather, Lorenzo was not there. Mrs

Guest was in the kitchen and her husband was working in the garden.

Chloe busied herself looking after Emma, but her mind was full of confusing thoughts about the future, making it impossible for her to relax. So she carried Emma out into the garden, hoping to find a way to distract them both.

Once again she was struck by what a beautiful place Lorenzo had bought. Chloe knew he hadn't intended it to be their main home—he would never leave the grand Venetian *palazzo,* which had been in his family for generations. But this house with its clean modern lines and light, airy feel made a very pleasant comple-ment to the ornate, history-filled palace.

'Good morning!' Mr Guest appeared around the corner of the house carrying a box, which appeared to contain some kind of baby's toy.

'Hello.' Chloe smiled. It was a relief that Lorenzo had employed such a friendly, down-to-earth couple to look after the house. She'd always felt slightly uncomfortable around his formal and super-efficient staff in Venice.

'I thought the little one might like a turn in this.' He held up the box and Chloe realised that it con-tained a high-backed baby's swing seat. 'I don't know how old she is, but it says on the box that it's suitable for infants six months and up.'

'She's five and a half months now,' Chloe said,

looking down at the baby in her arms, 'but she holds herself well, and I'm sure she'd love to try it.'

She followed Mr Guest back round the corner, to a charming children's play area, complete with swings, slides, a climbing frame and a covered box that Chloe assumed was a sandpit.

'This is amazing,' she said as she watched Mr Guest attach the swing seat to the wooden frame. 'Did the previous people have children?'

'I don't think so. Mr Valente had this done when he bought the place. I know neither of you realised you'd have a little one so soon, but your husband is obviously very keen on kids. There we are,' he added, stepping back and eyeing his work to ensure the seat was hanging level. 'Give that a try.'

'Thank you,' Chloe said, as she carefully secured Emma in the seat and gave her a little push. But Mr Guest's comment about Lorenzo had taken her aback. She'd never thought of him as being keen on children. And after she'd seen him with Emma the previous day, the opposite seemed more likely to be true.

'She likes that!' Mr Guest chuckled as the baby gave a squeal of delight. 'I'll leave you to it, then. If you need anything, just give me a shout. Or call my wife—that's the back door to the kitchen right there.' He picked up the empty cardboard box and his tool bag, and headed off around the house.

Chloe glanced up and saw Mrs Guest through the

kitchen window. She lifted her hand to wave, then turned back to Emma, who was clearly having a wonderful time in the swing.

But Chloe's thoughts were on Lorenzo, and his attitude towards children.

As far as she could remember, she'd never actually seen him interact with any babies or older children—although that hadn't ever seemed unusual because no one they spent time with had a young family.

But yesterday in the limousine he'd seemed truly uncomfortable around Emma, and that had made Chloe start to wonder if he only wanted children inherit his Venetian legacy. Now she realised that *must* be the reason why he'd married—to secure himself an heir.

She pushed her hair out of her eyes, unaware of the cloudy expression on her face.

'Hello, Chloe.'

Lorenzo's deep voice startled her, and she spun round to see him standing just a few feet away. He was dressed in a dark suit, as if he'd just come from a business meeting, and his clothing seemed incongruous in the garden, especially standing next to a wooden climbing frame.

'Why did you marry me?' she suddenly blurted. 'If love didn't come into it—then why did you pick me? I'm short and ordinary-looking. I have no money or connections. You could have had anyone you wanted. Why me?'

'I already told you,' Lorenzo said, without missing a beat. 'Because I thought you'd make a good wife.'

'Don't you mean a good *mother*?' Chloe accused him, tipping her head back to shake the hair out of her eyes. 'You just married me to have children.'

'You want children too,' Lorenzo replied flatly but, despite his level tone, his gaze slid across to the baby in the swing seat. 'In the circumstances, it's fortunate that you didn't marry someone dead set against children.'

'You heartless beast!' Chloe exclaimed, snatching Emma up into her arms.

'No, I didn't mean—'

'Save your smooth-talking explanations,' Chloe cried. She held Emma high against her shoulder and she bent her head over, pressing her cheek against the baby's soft, wispy hair. 'You say you want children and that I'll be a good mother—but what about you? What kind of father will you be? All you've done is stare at Emma like she's some kind of impostor!'

She glared up at him angrily, suddenly hating how cool and controlled he looked. For the last three months her life had been horribly out of her control—it wasn't fair that he could stand there looking so calm.

'You have to give me time,' Lorenzo said. 'I have nothing against the infant, but she has arrived rather abruptly in my life.'

'She doesn't have to be in *your* life—I keep telling you that!' Chloe exclaimed, scraping her hair back from her face with a desperate gesture. 'How can you be so heartless? Her mother died!' she cried. 'My best friend died, and all you care about is my wish to adopt her baby.'

Suddenly her eyes were swimming with tears and a second later she was weeping.

Lorenzo stepped towards her immediately. Then he wrapped his arms around her sobbing body and gently drew her close. She leant into him instinctively, clinging to him, and finding solace in the familiar strength of his embrace.

She hardly noticed when Mrs Guest lifted Emma carefully out of her arms. A corner of her mind knew that the baby was safe and she closed her eyes, shutting out everything but the solid comfort of Lorenzo's body. Despite everything, he was her anchor—strong and warm, and exactly what she needed to combat the cold emptiness inside her.

A little while later, when the storm of tears had passed, Chloe opened her eyes and realised that she was cradled against Lorenzo's chest. He was holding her snugly and she was still clinging to him, her hands tangled tightly in his shirt, deep inside his open jacket. They were sitting on a bench looking away from the house, across an impressive view over the meadows.

For a moment she lay completely still, amazed at how comfortable she felt in Lorenzo's arms. But then a subtle change came over him—a slight shift in his muscles and a stiffening of his posture—and she knew that he was aware that she had roused.

She sat up slowly, suddenly feeling awkward. She had no idea how long she had wept or how long she had clung on to him. It was embarrassing to have let go of her emotions so completely in front of him.

'Emma?' she asked, her voice hoarse from crying.

'Mrs Guest has her,' Lorenzo said, realigning his jacket as she pulled away from him and sitting up straighter. 'She's fine. But how about you—do you need anything? Some water, maybe?'

Chloe nodded, suddenly realising she was really thirsty, and almost immediately Lorenzo passed her a small bottle of water. It was beaded with condensation and still cold from the fridge, and Chloe took it gratefully.

Presumably Mrs Guest had brought it out for her. It was wonderful to have someone look after her for a change. And it was even more wonderful to sit with Lorenzo, knowing that he'd been there to comfort her.

'I'm sorry,' Chloe said. 'Sorry for causing a scene like that.'

'You have nothing to apologise for,' Lorenzo said. 'Your grief is entirely natural and I don't want you to think you have to suppress it because you are here with me. I can't imagine how hard the last months have been for you.'

Chloe felt her heart turn over at his sympathetic words. She knew he was sincere, and it touched her deeply.

She turned sideways on the bench and looked at him. His arms around her had felt so natural, and now his clear blue gaze appeared completely open and understanding.

It suddenly seemed vital that they were honest with each other. After the mistrust and discord between them, she longed to find a genuine connection with him. And, as she remembered his impassioned outburst the previous evening, she realised that her actions since their marriage had left him out in the cold.

On the day of their wedding she'd been broken-hearted, and at the time she'd felt that her desperation to get away from him was justifiable. It had been devastating to be told by her new husband that he did not believe in love. But she hadn't waited for the situation to calm down. She had not given him a chance to explain.

'You upset me badly on our wedding day, but I'm sorry for how I behaved,' she found herself saying. 'For running away without telling you I was going. And for not getting in touch about Emma.'

'That's behind us now,' Lorenzo said.

His tone was clipped, and with a flash of irritation Chloe knew he was never going to admit that her behaviour had had any emotional impact on him. She'd been willing to take a step towards him—but he was not prepared to meet her in the middle.

'But we still have the future to think about,' Chloe said. 'You said last night that you want us to remain married. But, given everything you have said to me—that you don't love me, that you don't even believe in love—I don't know how I can do that.'

She paused, and looked at him utterly seriously. He appeared calm, but she could see a vein pulsing on his temple, and she knew that she was on dangerous ground. But she had to get things straightened out. Her future—and Emma's future—depended on it.

'I'm not even sure if you meant it,' she said carefully. 'Or if you were just saying it because you were angry with me again.'

Lorenzo stared at her, a spike of annoyance stabbing into his gut and a band of tension tightening across his shoulders.

Chloe was right. The previous evening he *had* reacted instinctively—striking back at her presumption that she could be the one to call an end to their marriage. But since then he had taken time to reevaluate the situation.

He had originally wanted a wife to provide him with an heir, but he had no faith in marriages based on sentiment and emotion. He wanted a stable, non-materialistic woman, who would stand by the commitment of marriage and motherhood, and not abandon her children as soon as the going got tough. Or, even more reprehensibly, sell out if she got a better offer.

Chloe had seemed to be a good candidate—until she ran out on him on their wedding day. But now things were different. She had Emma. And she had demonstrated a tenacity—a commitment to motherhood—that had made him reconsider.

'I meant it,' Lorenzo said, looking straight into her cloudy green eyes so that she would know he was sincere. 'I expect us to remain married.'

'I can't do that,' Chloe said. 'I can't stay in a loveless marriage, and I won't bring Emma up in an environment like that.'

'How will you care for her?' Lorenzo asked. 'Yesterday you pointed out that you have no job. Your savings are gone and your credit card is at its limit.'

'I'll manage,' Chloe said hotly, flashing an annoyed look in his direction. She'd known the day before that it was a mistake to let him know about her precarious financial situation—and here he was, less than twenty-four hours later, throwing it in her face.

'How?' Lorenzo pressed. 'It doesn't sound like an ideal starting point.'

'It's really none of your business,' Chloe said, but

suddenly she knew that he wouldn't care about that. As far as he was concerned he had a right to know everything—and he would keep digging until he found out. 'The rent on Liz's cottage is paid till the end of next month, and I'll get a job at a temping agency in a nearby town,' she said. 'Gladys, Liz's neighbour, will watch Emma till I can afford proper childcare. It won't be long until I'm up on my feet again.'

'It hardly sounds ideal,' Lorenzo said. 'Wouldn't you rather Emma grew up as part of a family, with you to look after her, and other children to play with?'

'Other children?' Chloe repeated, appalled by his assumption and the added barb of emotional blackmail. 'I haven't agreed to stay in this marriage, and already you have me producing children like a brood mare. Is that all I ever was to you? A convenient baby-making machine?'

'A *baby-making machine* is not a mother,' Lorenzo said harshly. 'I chose you because I knew you would be an excellent mother. You care deeply about family and about commitment. You have values that are important to me, which I consider paramount in the mother of my children. And the fact that you are willing to fight so hard for your friend's baby proves that fact.'

'How can you talk about values, when you don't even believe in love?' Chloe gasped. 'Do you expect me to give up *my* values? Give up on my right to be loved?'

'Are you going to give up on your chance for a family—on Emma's future happiness and security—to chase an illusion that doesn't exist?' he demanded.

'It does exist!' Chloe exclaimed, springing to her feet and glaring down at him.

'Really? I've never seen proof,' he said, standing up so that once again he towered over her. 'You said you loved me—then just minutes later you ran out on me. Somehow giving up on our marriage so easily doesn't seem like an expression of love.'

She stared up at him, suddenly realising that she didn't have the heart to continue arguing. She'd tried to offer him an olive branch, but all he could do was throw her love for him back in her face.

'I want a genuine commitment from you,' he said, already pushing her into a decision she wasn't ready to make. 'An absolute assurance to pledge yourself to this marriage and the family we will have together.'

Chloe blinked in surprise, almost unable to believe what she was hearing. But deep down she knew Lorenzo was serious—that he was making her a genuine proposition. It fitted completely with everything he had ever said since their terrible argument at the *palazzo* when the truth about his feelings had come out.

There was so much to think about. In her heart she longed to remain Lorenzo's wife—but at what cost? And at what cost to Emma and their future children?

Both she and Lorenzo had grown up in broken homes and she knew first-hand how devastating that could be. But would a loveless marriage be better than that—even if the parents stayed together?

Chloe did not know the answer. And she would not give in to emotional blackmail. She couldn't let Lorenzo strong-arm her into a decision that would affect the rest of her life.

'I need your answer,' he pressed, looming over her.

'Well, you can't have it,' she replied, with a voice that sounded calmer than she felt. Then she turned and headed back to the house.

Lorenzo thrust his hands into his pockets and watched Chloe walking away, feeling the muscles across his shoulders pull even tighter.

He wanted Chloe to remain his wife. Just how much he wanted it shocked him.

CHAPTER FIVE

'TAKE as much time as you need,' Mrs Guest said as she ushered Chloe out into the garden. 'It's a lovely afternoon and a bit of fresh air might make you feel more like yourself. Emma will be fine with me— she's a pleasure to look after.'

'Thank you.' Chloe smiled reassuringly at the housekeeper. She knew that she'd worried the older lady by getting so upset earlier in the day. 'I really am feeling better now. I just need a little bit of time alone, and I'd like to have a look around the garden. It truly is lovely.'

'I'll be here if you need anything,' Mrs Guest said.

The sunshine was warm as Chloe walked away from the house across the main lawn. She'd taken another shower, but when she came to get dressed again she just hadn't had the energy to be creative, so she'd simply slipped her old jeans back on with a fresh T-shirt.

Her main reason for accepting Mrs Guest's kind offer to watch Emma was that she desperately needed time alone to think. Lorenzo had given her an ultimatum: she must decide whether to stay married to him and make a true commitment to their future together—or leave him, and be left all alone with Emma.

He had been right when he'd said that Chloe was not in an ideal situation to bring up a baby on her own, but that didn't mean she couldn't do it. At least she had the type of office skills that were always in demand—and as long as she could earn sufficient money to pay the rent by the end of the month, she would have somewhere to live.

Millions of women brought up children in far less favourable circumstances—with no proper training to get a job and with no one to help out in emergencies. Gladys had been a wonderful neighbour to Liz, and Chloe knew she could count on her if she had no choice.

But should she be so quick to abandon her marriage to Lorenzo?

The flash of joy that had lightened her soul when he appeared at the churchyard the previous day had told her that her feelings still ran deep. And being held in his arms earlier had felt so right.

Now that her emotions were no longer running wild, and she had taken a moment to calm down, she knew for certain that she still loved him. Love wasn't something she could just switch on or off. It was an unfathomable, undeniable truth that filled her body and soul.

Before Liz died, Chloe had made her a promise—that she wouldn't hide herself away from life and lock up her heart because she had been hurt. But she didn't know how that promise fitted into the future Lorenzo was offering.

Should she turn her back on him and give up on the one thing she had truly wanted—marriage and a family with the man she loved? Or should she accept his offer of a secure and privileged life for herself and their children—and give up on her heart's deepest wish to experience a genuine loving relationship?

It was an impossible choice.

Lorenzo stood by the glass wall of his study and watched Chloe walking along the far edge of the pond, beside a drift of purple irises. Her head was bowed and, although her blonde hair had fallen forward to obscure her face, he knew she was deep in thought. After all, he had given her a lot to think about.

She looked tiny in her jeans and T-shirt, but Lorenzo was getting used to seeing her that way, which was nothing like the way she'd dressed when they were together. When she was his PA she had always dressed smartly for work, and, although her style had been less formal once they were personally involved, she'd always looked well-groomed.

Now the difference in her appearance seemed to underline the difference in their relationship. She looked small and fragile as she sat down on a bench, and as she lifted her head to shake her hair back from her face Lorenzo could see that she was frowning.

Her gaze drifted across the pond, then settled on the huge windows of Lorenzo's study. She was looking right at him, although he knew she couldn't see him because the glass had been treated to protect the privacy of his study. He stared back at her, feeling an unexpected jolt of irritation.

Life had been so good, with all his plans for the future falling into place nicely. Why had she gone and complicated everything? He lifted his hand abruptly and, without fully registering his intention, he hit the control that opened the large sliding doors.

Chloe was lost in her thoughts as she gazed across the pond. The sudden movement as the glass door slid silently open brought her back to her surroundings with a start. Then the sight of Lorenzo stepping purposefully onto the deck made her catch her breath in surprise.

She stared at him in shock, slowly realising that she'd foolishly sat down in view of his study. She wasn't ready to talk to him yet. She was nowhere near ready to decide what to do about his proposition.

He moved swiftly along the deck, then without breaking his stride he turned onto the gravel path that tracked the edge of the pond. He was bearing down on her so quickly that she felt her heart start to race.

She sprang up, ready to face him, although she was filled with the overwhelming urge to bolt. How had things got so difficult between them that the sight of him approaching made her want to run and hide?

She squared her shoulders and stood as tall as she could. She was *not* afraid of Lorenzo. And she would not shy away from the situation he had put her in.

'If you've come to pressure me for an answer, you're wasting your time,' she said. Her voice was clear and steady, and did not reveal how uncertain she was feeling. 'I have not reached a decision yet.'

Lorenzo came to a halt a few feet away from her— close enough for her to be reminded once again of his sheer size compared to her. But not so close that she had to crane her neck back to meet his eyes. He had discarded his jacket but he was still wearing the same white shirt as that morning.

Her eyes settled on the clusters of creases where she had balled her hands in the fabric of his shirt while she wept, and a disconcertingly vivid memory of lying with her face against his chest flashed through her mind.

'You are struggling to decide what is best for your future,' Lorenzo said, 'and I want you to understand why I believe this is the best arrangement— for everyone.'

'You already told me your reasons,' she said quietly. 'Now it's up to me to think this through. It's an important decision I need to work out for myself—decide for myself.'

'I understand that,' Lorenzo said, 'but committing to this marriage, and to raising a family with me, is a huge undertaking. I want you to make this choice with your head, not with your heart.'

Chloe frowned, trying to make sense of what Lorenzo was saying.

'But marriage is something you feel in your heart,' she said, unsettled by Lorenzo's sudden change of tack. Why was he trying to *persuade* her into this, rather than continue trying to tell her what was the right thing to do? 'When you proposed to me in Paris, I was so happy. And I truly believed you felt the same way I did.'

'I *was* happy,' Lorenzo replied. 'I thought that I had found the perfect woman to share my life with— the perfect, uncomplicated partnership based on friendship and compatibility. Not on an over-hyped emotional ideal that would inevitably disintegrate over time.'

'Not all marriages fail,' Chloe said, suddenly feeling defensive and sad at the same time. 'You shouldn't be so pessimistic—it's depressing.'

'Not pessimistic—*realistic,*' Lorenzo said. 'In my experience most marriages do fall apart, and it usually gets pretty ugly. Then the children are the ones who suffer the most.'

Lorenzo looked down at her, reading the emotion written in her expression. She was normally such a positive-thinking, forward-looking person—which was one of the attributes that had drawn him to her in the first place. It was disturbing to see her look unhappy.

'It doesn't have to be that way,' she said. 'Happy marriages and functional families do exist.'

'Neither of us experienced it as a child,' Lorenzo said, 'but that is why this arrangement can work for us. I know you want Emma, and your own children when we have them, to grow up in a stable environment.'

'I know that *I* would never abandon my children,' Chloe said. She looked up at him, the silvery green surface of the pond reflected in her eyes, 'but how do I know I can trust you?'

Lorenzo met her gaze, already knowing how intensely she was committed to motherhood. He knew how far she would go for Emma. And he knew she'd fight equally hard for her own children.

Lorenzo's mother had not bothered to fight for him. In fact she'd used him as a bargaining chip in a massive divorce settlement. What kind of mother would do something like that?

Suddenly he found his thoughts hurtling back to his childhood—to a time that he'd thought that he had blotted out of his memory. And all at once he was remembering the hurt, disappointment and confusion as acutely as the day his mother walked out.

He shook his head sharply, and focused on Chloe again. Her face was pale and worried, and he knew what she was thinking.

'I get it,' he said, his eyes boring down into hers. 'You're scared I'm going to leave you. It's happened to you before—first your father, then your mother and sister. Even…' He hesitated, reluctant to upset her more, but he had to make his point. 'Even your best friend left you.'

Chloe swallowed, the lump in her throat making it painful, and blinked back tears. How did he know her so well—yet so little at the same time?

'I'm not going to leave you,' Lorenzo said. 'That's the beauty of this arrangement.'

'But…what about when someone else catches your eye?' Chloe asked. A dark shadow moved across Lorenzo's face and she knew she had offended him with her comment, but she had to carry on—her future was at stake. 'You don't love me—what happens when you meet someone you do love?'

'Be careful what you say,' Lorenzo said through gritted teeth. 'Don't forget what happened. You are the one who left—the one who abandoned this relationship.'

'It wasn't like that,' she protested.

'Even though you *thought* you loved me,' Lorenzo

said, 'even then—with your own fear of abandonment so strong—*you* left. Not me.'

'That was different,' Chloe said. 'I'd just found out you didn't love me.'

'Do you still love me?' Lorenzo asked.

'I… No…' Chloe faltered, dropping her gaze and staring at the wide expanse of his chest. She couldn't meet his eye, or surely he would know the truth. She did still love him, but she couldn't expose her heart to him any more. It was just too painful.

'My point exactly,' Lorenzo said, his voice dripping with irony. 'You *thought* you loved me—but you were fooling yourself, living in a silly romantic dream world. It wasn't real, which is why you were able to walk out on me without a second glance.'

His fingers slipped beneath her chin and he lifted her face to look into her eyes. Chloe met his blue gaze and a frisson ran through her. The emotion she saw in the depths of his eyes was intense.

He said he didn't believe in love, but she could feel how deeply he was committed to the future he was proposing. He wanted a stable, contented family as much as she did.

'We were good together,' he said, letting his hand slip back so that he was cradling her head. 'This could be incredible. *We* could be incredible together.'

'I don't know…' Chloe started to speak, but the feel of his hand was distracting.

All she knew was she wanted to be with him. She wanted things back the way they had once been, when he made her feel special and safe at the same time.

'Make this decision with your head, not your heart,' he repeated. 'Tell me that you want to stay married to me. That you want to raise a family with me. That you want to be my wife in every way.'

'Yes,' she said. 'Yes, I do.'

But she was speaking from her heart. It was impossible to do anything else. Her heart was calling out so loudly to him that she could not have heard anything her head was saying even if she'd tried.

'You've made the right choice,' Lorenzo said, pulling her towards him.

Chloe closed her eyes as he enfolded her in his arms. It felt so good, as if she truly belonged there.

Then his hands started to move across her body, and she knew that he intended to make love to her. A quiver of apprehension mixed with anticipation tingled through her. She had just agreed to this—to be his wife in every way.

But she was suddenly nervous, as if this exact moment was the moment of no return in her life.

From this point on her future was mapped out, and before she knew it she would be a mother. She would be bound in marriage to a man who didn't love her— a man who did not even believe in love.

'What is it?' he asked, pulling back and holding her where he could meet her eyes. 'What's wrong?'

'It's too soon,' she said, tightening her fists to emphasise her words and realising to her shock that once again they were tangled in his shirt, gripping the fabric tightly. 'I'm not ready.'

'Not ready?' Lorenzo repeated. He slid his hands across her back in a way that sent shivers through her whole body. 'You know that won't be a problem for long.'

'No—I need more time to get used to this,' she said, unfurling her hands from his shirt and taking a step backwards. But his long arms were still around her, preventing her from moving very far away. 'Let me go. Let me go so I can think.'

Almost to her surprise, Lorenzo dropped his arms to his sides and stepped away, his feet crunching on the gravel path.

He stood completely still, looking down at her from beneath heavy lids. She knew how much he wanted her, and that thought sent a rush of desire storming through her.

Making love had always brought them closer, made the connection between them stronger. Surely it would do the same thing now. She had to give their new understanding a chance, but she wasn't ready to completely sign away her future.

'I'm not ready for more children,' she said.

'Everything has been so unsettled…there's Emma to consider…it's just too soon to rush into something so big.'

'I agree,' Lorenzo said, reaching into his pocket and pulling out a little foil-wrapped package. 'Making babies can wait. This, however, cannot,' he finished huskily, hauling her towards him and covering her mouth with his.

CHAPTER SIX

THE burning heat of arousal erupted through Lorenzo's body, and he dragged Chloe closer still, lifting her onto her tiptoes and bending her back to kiss her. The taste of her mouth was intoxicating, and the feel of her slender body in his arms threatened to send him over the edge.

He was holding her so close that he could feel every tremble and quake that shook her. He could tell how much she wanted him and that knowledge was setting his own senses on fire.

It was too long since he'd made love to Chloe. Too long since he'd held her naked body in his arms and brought her pleasure in every way he knew, before eventually giving in to his own explosive climax.

Now he was consumed by a sexual need so strong that he suddenly realised that he had to find somewhere private. In the past he would not have hesitated to take her right there on the bench beside the water, but he knew that this time one quick release of passion would not be enough. It would take much longer to slake the barrage of desire that stormed his body and he intended to take every ounce of satisfaction that he could.

He pulled back from his kiss and swept her up in his arms. He would take her to the pool house—they would be undisturbed there for as long as it took.

Chloe lay breathlessly in his arms, gazing up at his gorgeous face. He'd literally swept her off her feet and her heart was racing with anticipation of what was to come. Just knowing that he was carrying her away to make love to her sent a thrill of excitement skittering through her.

She had no idea where he was taking her, and she didn't care. She was only aware of the rhythmic movements of his body vibrating through her as he strode along the path away from the house. He carried her effortlessly, as if she were as light as a feather, and she revelled in his strength, remembering that he had the power to send her to unimaginable heights of ecstasy.

She hardly noticed when they reached their destination. It was only when the door clicked shut behind them that she dragged her eyes from Lorenzo's face and looked around her.

'A swimming pool,' she murmured, not really meaning to say the words out loud.

'Later.' Lorenzo's voice was thick with arousal. 'We'll swim later—now I need you naked.'

Sudden heat flared between Chloe's legs and her whole body started to quiver. She was burning up inside and she needed Lorenzo as much as he needed her.

'Put me down,' she said, wriggling in his arms. She was too restricted in his grip—she wanted to touch him, to move against him, to rip his clothes off him.

'Wait,' he commanded, striding past the pool to a lounge area beside a bar. Then finally he set her down on top of the bar, her feet swinging high off the floor.

He stood back for a moment, looking deep into her eyes, and Chloe could see that he was breathing raggedly—and she knew it had nothing to do with the effort of carrying her into the pool house. Her own heart was racing and she was trembling from head to foot.

Suddenly he stepped forward, pressing himself between her thighs, and cupped her face with his large hands. For once their mouths were the same height, and he drew closer and began to kiss her.

His tongue slid sensuously between her lips, in an erotic exploration that quickly left her breathless again. At the same time she felt him grip the hem of her T-shirt and she sat up taller, arching towards him as he peeled it off her. Her bra followed quickly, then his hands closed over her breasts, caressing and coaxing her nipples into diamond-hard points.

'Oh!' A moan of pleasure sighed out of her and

her head fell backwards. Her hands rested flat on the surface of the bar just behind her, and her arms were locked straight, stabilising her body as she thrust her breasts towards him.

His tongue flicked over one erect nipple and she trembled in response, willing him to continue. Then he sucked the whole aching peak of her breast into his mouth and worked it with his tongue. The impact was immediate and she suddenly found herself rocking her pelvis, startled by the wildfire he had ignited in an entirely different part of her body.

A low, almost feral growl rumbled out of Lorenzo, as if he was completely in tune with what she was experiencing. His hands went straight to her jeans and undid the button, then moved quickly on to the zip. He struggled for a moment, cursing her jeans as he failed to unfasten them.

'Lie back!' he commanded, and Chloe found herself obeying. A moment later Lorenzo tugged the offending garment off, removing her underwear at the same time. She was about to sit up, but then he reached out and pushed her firmly back down.

Chloe drew in a shaky breath, realising that she was lying completely naked on the bar, with Lorenzo poised intimately between her legs. His breath was hot on her exposed centre and a rush of excitement surged through her, making her start to tremble uncontrollably.

The black granite bar was cold beneath the skin,

but she was burning up with sexual anticipation. Then, when his mouth made contact with her pulsing flesh, she felt as if she'd gone up in flames.

The intensity of the sensation buzzing through her quivering body made her cry out. She could see the sky above her through the glass roof of the pool house, and it felt as if she had taken flight, spiralling up through the fluffy white clouds into the blue heavens.

She pressed her hands against the granite, trying instinctively to anchor herself, but his mouth continued to work its magic, sending her up and up, further and further out of her body. Time ceased to exist and there was nothing she could do but surrender to the incredible waves of pleasure rolling through her. Then just when she didn't know if she could bear the intensity any longer, the moment exploded into a starburst of euphoric bliss.

She lay panting on the bar, unable to move a muscle, feeling completely and utterly satisfied. Then the next thing she knew she was back in Lorenzo's arms. He carried her to the lounge area and laid her down on one of the couches.

She gazed up at him languidly, limp with the after-effects of her intense orgasm. But then, as he moved over her, a reawakened blast of sexual excitement tore through her body.

She'd never known it was possible to fly back to

such incredible heights so quickly, but as his hard, masculine length slid deep inside she cried out in pleasure.

Her whole being was suffused with glorious, undulating waves of rapture, and she closed her eyes, clinging to Lorenzo. His powerful body was hot and hard, and as he moved within her she sensed him begin to tremble and quake. Then, as he continued to thrust, driving them both on and on, they suddenly took flight together.

She felt him give one last mighty shudder as he reached his powerful climax, and at the same instant her own soul soared back into the heavens, as another explosion of ecstasy burst through her.

She cried out his name again and again, unaware that she was suddenly sobbing without restraint.

It was later that evening when Chloe drifted back to wakefulness. She was lying on the couch in the pool house, wearing a large, fluffy white robe that Lorenzo had wrapped around her after they had made love in the shower. Her body felt utterly relaxed, and was glowing with sensual fulfilment.

Her gaze settled on the dark windows and she realised with a jolt how late it was. She shot bolt upright, and saw Lorenzo coming towards her carrying a tray of food.

'Emma!' she gasped. 'What time is it?'

'She's safe with Mrs Guest,' Lorenzo said reassuringly as he put the tray on a low table and sat opposite her. 'She seems to have developed a soft spot for her. And also I believe she's already put her down for the night.'

'Oh,' Chloe said, sinking back on the couch. 'I can't believe it's so late. I must have slept a long time.'

Her hands moved instinctively to draw the robe tighter around her body. Then suddenly an unsettling wave of uncertainty washed over her as she remembered how completely she had surrendered herself to Lorenzo's lovemaking. How she had wept uncontrollably in his arms.

The whole experience had been absolutely mind-blowing—the most incredible hours of her life. Somehow she realised that everything was changed forever—that *she* was changed forever.

She was lost to Lorenzo, and she knew there was nothing she could do about it now.

'Mrs Guest sent some food over,' he said, his deep voice drawing her out of her thoughts. 'Apparently you've hardly touched your meals for the last twenty-four hours, and she wanted me to ensure that you ate something.'

Chloe gazed at him, struggling to focus on the commonplace content of his comment. Somehow it didn't seem right that they should be talking about eating after making such a life-altering decision, and sharing such an extraordinary level of intimacy.

'Are you hungry?' Lorenzo asked, leaning forward to remove the covers that were keeping the food fresh.

'I don't know,' Chloe said, gazing at the food without really seeing it.

She glanced up at him and saw that he was looking at her with a strangely intense expression on his face. Suddenly she got the impression that he knew how uncertain she was feeling. That he understood what a monumental step they had taken in their newly defined relationship.

Except he did not know how much Chloe still loved him. That was something that he couldn't—or wouldn't—understand. And something that, for the sake of her own protection, she did not want him to know.

'Start with something light,' Lorenzo said. 'Maybe some fruit.'

He leant forward to pass her a plate, then couldn't take his eyes off her as she reached out to take it.

The fluffy white sleeve of the robe fell back to reveal her slender wrist and a shot of sensual appreciation went through him.

God, he wanted her! Even after spending all afternoon revelling in her naked body—making love to her and sharing the most intimate secrets of her sexuality—just a glimpse of her wrist had him burning with desire once again.

His gaze followed her movements as she took a bite of peach, and a blast of desire shot through him as her lips closed around the fruit and the column of her throat moved as she swallowed.

But for the moment he would content himself with watching her eat. Despite the lack of inhibition in their lovemaking that afternoon, he didn't think she was ready to play erotic games with food.

She had turned away slightly, as if she was uncomfortable under his scrutiny, and abruptly stopped eating, her hand poised halfway to her mouth.

'What is it?' he asked, unsettled by the appalled look on her face.

She turned to him, wide-eyed, all the colour abruptly drained from her face.

'We're in a glass-walled building,' she said hoarsely. 'This afternoon…oh, God…anyone could have seen.'

'No one saw anything,' Lorenzo reassured her. 'It's all privacy glass; you can't see in from outside. Even now,' he added, 'even now at night time with the lights on inside. We can swim naked and no one will see.'

'Really?' she asked. 'You're not just saying that?'

'Come outside with me, and see for yourself,' he suggested. 'But finish your meal first. You need to keep up your strength.'

CHAPTER SEVEN

'DO YOU want me to take you outside to try and look through the windows?' Lorenzo asked, some time later. 'Just to prove how private it is in here?'

'No, that's all right. I believe you.' Chloe looked at him, feeling a flush of warmth on her cheeks.

'You don't sound entirely convinced,' Lorenzo said. 'Are you worried you might not like what you find?'

'No,' she said. 'I like it in here, that's all. I'm comfortable where I am.'

She was telling the truth, but in her heart she knew there was more to it than that. They'd just spent a surprisingly relaxed hour or so together, eating the delicious food Mrs Guest had provided and chatting about inconsequential topics. It had felt safe and thoroughly normal—things that had been completely lacking in her life recently. She was half-afraid if she left the pool house the spell would be broken.

'In that case, how about taking a swim?'

Lorenzo asked. 'No need to worry that you haven't got your costume.'

'I like it in my robe,' she said, ignoring the fluttering that started inside her at the thought of swimming naked in front of Lorenzo. 'I told you I was nice and comfy.'

She looked at him, letting her gaze run over his powerful body, and couldn't help smiling. He had put back on the same shirt and trousers that he'd been wearing when he found her beside the pond, but they were uncommonly crumpled for a man who usually seemed to look perfect without any effort.

'What are you smiling at?' he asked. 'I saw you giving me the once-over. Did you find something amusing?'

'You look a mess.' She laughed—then covered her mouth abruptly with her hand. It felt good to laugh, and she couldn't remember the last time she had done it.

'Hey!' Lorenzo surged off his seat and bore down on her with an indignant expression on his face, which rapidly turned blatantly sexual as he leant over her. 'At least I'm wearing my own clothes—perhaps I shouldn't have let you have that robe. I think I want it back.'

Chloe drew in a shaky breath and stared up at him with her stomach doing somersaults of anticipation. He reached for the edges of the robe, and started to pull it open. In a moment he would reveal her bare, defenceless body.

Suddenly a rush of bold, wanton confidence flooded through her.

'You can have it back,' she said, ducking beneath his arms and jumping to her feet. 'I'm going for a swim after all.'

She walked quickly to the edge of the pool, glanced over her shoulder at his startled face and smiled mischievously. Then she tossed the robe away from her.

Lorenzo stared at her, his eyes gleaming with desire as his gaze ran up and down her naked back. But then his eyes narrowed with intent and he started moving towards her.

She laughed, enjoying the freedom of the sound as it echoed off the glass walls, and dived into the clear blue pool.

The water was deliciously cool against her naked body and she glided under the surface feeling as free as a dolphin. She came up for air halfway along the pool, then continued to swim as quickly as she could to the far end. There she rolled over onto her back, pushed off the wall and kicked languorously towards her starting point, where Lorenzo was standing.

She slowed right down, trying to catch her breath, and stared up at the ceiling. Suddenly she realised that she was looking at herself reflected in the glass, so clearly that she could have been looking into an enormous overhead mirror.

It was a strange feeling gazing up at herself, her

arms and legs moving slowly, her body undulating gently in the water. She could see her breasts breaking through the surface—her nipples dark, rose-coloured buds against milky-white skin.

A wave of sexual awareness washed over her, lapping at her with the movement of the water. She knew Lorenzo was looking at her—seeing the same sight that she could see in the ceiling. Her naked limbs and exposed body—her bare breasts thrusting through the water.

The intense jolt of desire that suddenly shot through her left her light-headed with its intensity. She rolled over abruptly and stared up at Lorenzo.

He had stripped off his clothes and was standing naked beside the pool.

She gazed at him breathlessly—unable to drag her eyes away from his magnificent body. It was muscled and athletic—and entirely aroused.

The room suddenly closed in around them and she felt her pulse rate jump up another notch. Her tongue flicked out to moisten her lips and she pushed her dripping hair off her face, which suddenly felt burning hot.

Lorenzo stepped to the edge and dived in, barely making a splash. She gasped and stared down into the pool, struggling to see through the rippling surface, but almost at once he surged out of the water right in front of her. Her breath caught in her throat and a deluge of adrenaline buzzed through her veins. A millisecond later he had seized her in his arms and dragged her hard against his body.

Her feet didn't reach the floor, so she wrapped her legs instinctively around his waist. She could feel his erection nudging at her and another rush of arousal took hold of her, igniting a fire between her thighs and setting her whole body shaking.

They'd made love three times that afternoon, and each time had been as explosive and incredible as the first. It was hard to comprehend how much she still needed him—how much she wanted to feel him thrusting inside her.

She welcomed the all-encompassing, mind-blowing intensity of it, and she had no wish to take things slowly. In a shamelessly provocative movement, she clung to his shoulders to support herself, and slid her body sinuously against his, lowering herself until she felt the tip of his erection press against the pulsing centre of her desire.

A deep, almost animal sound of raw sexual need burst out of Lorenzo. She could feel his hot explosion of breath on her neck where she had bowed her head against his shoulder.

Suddenly his mouth closed bruisingly over the sensitive skin beneath her ear. He kissed her hard, working his way down the side of her neck, massaging with his tongue and nibbling with his teeth.

She closed her eyes and heard herself moaning with a build-up of raw sexual need. Her heart was racing, sending the blood pulsing through her veins, dilating her senses and making her almost unbearably aware of the silken steel of his arousal pressing against her own throbbing flesh.

She writhed against him, willing him to take her. She had to feel him inside her, filling her with hard, thrusting rapture once more. It was impossible for her to wait any longer, and she moved again, aligning herself with his erection, and pressed down onto him.

His wonderful, hard length slid deep inside her, and a moan of momentary satisfaction escaped her. But then his hands were on her waist and he was lifting her, disconnecting their bodies, pulling away and leaving her flesh empty and pulsating with unfulfilled need.

'Not yet.' The tortured sound of his voice raked across her senses, matching the level of frustration she was feeling. 'Unless you've changed your mind—we need protection.'

Understanding flashed through her mind, but she was too turned on to feel any relief. Lorenzo was already moving towards the side of the pool, carrying her with him, she still clinging to him in the same intimate position.

He sat down on the wide steps and lowered her carefully, so that she was straddling him with her knees resting on either side of him. Then he turned and reached for a condom packet, which he had left ready beside the pool.

Chloe looked down at his marvellous physique. His powerful legs were hot beneath her thighs and the muscles on his chest and stomach rippled beneath his golden skin as he moved. But her eyes were drawn to his arousal, and just looking sent another surge of excitement through her own body.

Suddenly she found herself slipping off his lap and leaning forward to take him in her mouth. She closed her lips around his powerful shaft and she sensed his body kick with pleasure. He felt smooth and hot under her tongue, and her eyelids slid down as she gave herself over entirely to the experience of bringing him pleasure.

Lorenzo stared up at the glass ceiling, almost overwhelmed by the exquisite sensations Chloe was imparting with her mouth. He could see them both reflected above, and the sight of her slender body bowed over his, her head moving in synchrony with the jolts of pleasure rocketing through his body, was almost too much.

'No more.' His voice was hoarse and nearly un-recognisable as his hands went to her shoulders to lift her away.

She raised her head shakily and he could see in her eyes that she was as turned on as he was. He reached for the foil packet with trembling hands and was glad when she took it and tore it open. Together they rolled the condom onto his erect flesh. Then, never breaking eye contact, she straddled him once more.

Chloe gazed dizzily into his eyes, gripped by a final rush of anticipation. Unable to wait another moment, she lowered herself down onto him, filling her aching body with him. Then suddenly her strength gave out and her thighs were shaking too much to hold her weight.

She closed her eyes again, revelling in the heat of him embedded deeply inside her, but desperate to feel him move. Then, as if he had read her mind, Lorenzo hauled them both out of the water as one and laid her down beside the pool. Her discarded towelling robe was beneath her, cushioning her from the hard floor, but it scarcely mattered, as all she was aware of was the glorious feel of Lorenzo thrusting inside her.

Her breath was coming in shallow gasps and the thrilling wildfire was building rapidly within her again. She could hear Lorenzo's ragged breathing, and her last coherent thought was how amazing it was that they could bring each other such extraordinary pleasure.

But then the rhythm of his fluid thrusts increased and she arched up to meet him. Every movement he made engulfed her with blazing sensation and carried her higher, up into a realm that was filled only with wave upon wave of unbelievable delight. Then when she reached a fever pitch of almost unbearable intensity, he pushed her further still, until suddenly she shot into orgasm with an unrestrained cry of rapture.

Her body convulsed with pleasure, tightening around him, driving him on to his own moment of release. Then they collapsed together, gasping for breath as they slowly drifted back down to earth.

The following morning Chloe woke up in the bedroom. At some point during the night Lorenzo must have carried her back into the house, but she had been so soundly asleep that she had not noticed.

For a moment she felt sad that the magical interlude in the pool house was over, but the next second she heard Emma stirring in her cot beside the bed. Suddenly she realised that she'd missed the baby—she'd been too distracted over the past day or so to really connect with her.

As wonderful as the hours she'd spent shut away from the world with Lorenzo had been, it was good to be back where she belonged—although as soon as that thought passed through her mind, she found herself feeling surprised at it. So much had happened in the last twenty-four hours.

'Good morning.' Lorenzo's husky voice coming from the doorway to the en suite took her by surprise.

He was already showered and dressed informally in black trousers and a grey sweater.

'Hello.' She looked up at him and smiled shyly—appreciating the gorgeous sight of him in the form-fitting sweater, but suddenly embarrassed by the complete lack of restraint she had shown the night before.

'I hope I didn't wake you,' Lorenzo said. 'I was hoping you would sleep in. I've got some arrangements I must make now, but I'd like to see you later this morning.'

He strode across to the bed and bent down to kiss her on the lips. Then he was gone.

Chloe lifted her fingers and pressed them lightly to her lips. She couldn't believe how much had changed so quickly.

Later that morning Chloe was outside with Emma. It was another fine day and the garden was lovely. As she looked around Chloe realised it was that special time of year when everything in nature was at its most verdant and fresh. The delicate new leaves had not long unfurled and the grass was a lush emerald swathe.

She felt so much better than she had the previous day. So much more hopeful for the future.

She had promised Liz that she would not batten down her heart, and she was glad that she had kept her word. Things with Lorenzo seemed wonderful. He had been considerate and caring. And he'd understood her concerns about rushing into starting a family—he'd even been the one to make them pause long enough to use protection on the occasion when Chloe had let herself get carried away on the moment.

It was true that Lorenzo continued to insist that he didn't believe in love, but Chloe found it increasingly hard to comprehend. His actions seemed loving. In fact, up until their wedding day, his actions had always seemed loving.

Chloe shook her head. She didn't understand— and she didn't want to think about it. She had promised Liz that she would think happy thoughts.

A movement caught her eye and she looked over her shoulder to see Lorenzo coming towards them across the lawn.

'Come inside and pack your bags,' he said. 'I've arranged a holiday for us. Somewhere far away with no memories or associations, where you can truly relax and recuperate.'

'Oh,' Chloe gazed at him in surprise—although it wasn't the first time he'd made a similar announcement. When they were together he was always whisking her away on exotic or romantic breaks. 'Where are we going? Is it somewhere suitable for babies—not a wooden hut on a deserted island a thousand miles from the nearest doctor?'

'Mauritius,' he said. 'Rest assured, it's perfectly civilised. We'll fly overnight and be at the hotel in time for breakfast. And, as it happens, Mrs Guest's daughter, Lucy, is a qualified nursery nurse. She'll be coming with us, to make sure you really do rest and relax.'

CHAPTER EIGHT

CHLOE sat enjoying a leisurely breakfast on their private balcony, at the exclusive hotel Lorenzo had brought them to in Mauritius. The giant suite of rooms he'd booked occupied a corner location, and in one direction she had an impressive view of the hotel's stunning gardens and in the other direction the tropical water of the Indian Ocean glittered in the bright sunshine.

She had forgotten to eat for the past few minutes, being completely captivated by the industrious efforts of a weaverbird that was building a nest not far from where she sat.

First it flew up to the palm tree right next to where Chloe was sitting. It gripped the edge of the frond in its beak and flew downwards, tearing off a strip as it did so. Then, a long ribbon of palm leaf fluttering behind it, the little bird flew to its nest, which was dangling down from a branch on another nearby tree. It was a bit too far away for Chloe to see just how it went about weaving the nest, and she was wishing she had some binoculars, when a familiar voice startled her out of her observations.

'Good morning, Chloe,' Lorenzo drawled, his voice still husky from another night of lovemaking. He pulled up a chair to join her and reached for a glass of orange juice.

'Good morning,' Chloe replied, feeling her heart skip a beat and a blush rise to her cheeks. They'd spent one night in Mauritius and it was the first time they'd made love in a bed since they'd been back together, but it had been just as incredible as all the times in the pool house. 'I've been watching a weaverbird.'

'It's the male that builds the nest, you know,' Lorenzo said, not missing a beat. 'Then he has to wait to see if the female will approve of it or destroy it.'

'Really? I've seen them on TV, but never in real life before,' Chloe said, thinking about all the effort the male had to make, never knowing if there would be a positive outcome for him.

Although it was the bird's natural instinct, she was suddenly struck by what an extraordinary act of faith that was.

It was just like life, she thought, remembering the promise she had made to Liz. There were no guarantees that things would turn out the way she hoped, but without faith and commitment she risked never finding what she searched for.

'Anyway, you'd better get ready,' Lorenzo said, taking her by surprise and standing up briskly. 'I'll be back in ten minutes. I've got a boat to take us along the coast—there's something I want to show you.'

The speedboat slowed and turned into the mouth of a wide, lazy river. Chloe had enjoyed the trip along the coast. She loved the stiff sea breeze blowing her hair and the exciting bob and bounce as the boat sped along.

The stunning beauty of the coastline had thrilled her. The pure white beaches edged with swaying palms and casuarinas, the amazing turquoise water of the lagoon and the deep blue sea out beyond the coral reef took her breath away.

At least she told herself that was the cause of her erratic heartbeat and the difficulty she was having breathing normally. It had nothing to do with Lorenzo sitting so close, his arm along the back of the seat behind her shoulders.

Emma had stayed at the hotel, with Mrs Guest's daughter, Lucy, so the only thing holding her attention was Lorenzo.

'It's so quiet,' Chloe said, pleased by how level her voice sounded. She leant forward to look over the edge of the boat. 'The river's very deep. Are those dark shadows down there rocks?'

'Yes,' Lorenzo said. 'Larger boats can't go very far upriver because of them.'

'It's incredible,' she said, looking around at the scenery. It was startlingly different from the glittering turquoise sea and white sand she had grown accustomed to back at the hotel and on their trip along the coast.

The water was very deep and flowed so slowly that the surface was smooth like a dark green mirror reflecting the lush green growth on either side of the river. The banks themselves were made of massive grey-brown boulders rising high above the water. 'I feel like I've stepped into an adventure, going up the Amazon into uncharted territory or something.'

'It is beautiful,' Lorenzo agreed, 'but hardly uncharted. We've come early to have the place to ourselves for a while.'

Chloe glanced at the driver of the boat and at Lorenzo's personal bodyguard, who was also with them. They weren't really alone, and she found herself feeling disappointed.

'What's that noise?' Chloe asked suddenly as the faint but unmistakable sound of rushing water reached her ears.

'Can you guess?' Lorenzo asked, his playful grin flashing in a way that made butterflies flutter in her stomach. It was wonderful to see him like this—it was almost as if they were back to their early days of dating, before so many horrible things had happened.

'A waterfall?' Chloe asked in delight. All her life she had loved waterfalls, being completely entranced by their beauty, power and romance.

The boat wound its way slowly up the river, the driver expertly manoeuvring between the great boulders that hid just beneath the surface.

'Wow!' Chloe breathed as the boat moved past a particularly large rock and the waterfall came into view. 'It's beautiful.'

She stared in awe at the mass of white water pouring down over a sheer drop into the river in front of them. She could feel moisture rising up from the foaming water, refreshing her warm skin.

'Come on,' Lorenzo said, holding out his hand to her as the boat pulled up to a rocky ledge. 'We can climb up and swim at the top.'

The mention of swimming sent a tingle of excitement thrilling through her. A vivid memory of the last time they swam played out in her mind.

'Is it safe?' Chloe found herself asking the first thing that came to her, although really she knew she could trust Lorenzo with her safety.

'Of course,' he said mildly.

The driver had jumped out and was holding the boat steady and Lorenzo spoke in swift Italian to his bodyguard.

'Follow me,' Lorenzo instructed. 'It's easy.'

For a moment Chloe paused, letting her eyes drink in the masculine beauty that was Lorenzo Valente—her husband. He was wearing casual shorts and a skin-tight black T-shirt that showed off his sculpted body to perfection.

His vibrant blue eyes sparkled, making the intense colour of the tropical sky fade into insignificance. And his golden skin glowed with a vitality that took her breath away and suddenly made her want to run the tip of her tongue up the strong column of his throat.

She bit her lip and ducked her head to hide her blazing cheeks. Something in his expression had made her pulse quicken—as if he was about to take her to a place where they could make love. At that moment it was exactly what she wanted him to do.

'Let's go,' she said, amazed how level she kept her voice considering the somersaults of sensual expectation her stomach was performing.

She followed Lorenzo across and up the rocks. It was an easy climb but it needed all her concentration. It would be too easy to slip. At the top she turned and realised that they were alone. Both the boat driver and the bodyguard had stayed with the boat.

'All right?' Lorenzo asked, letting his gaze linger longer than necessary on the quick rise and fall of Chloe's breasts. 'It's quite a steep climb.'

'Yes, thank you,' Chloe replied, knowing that her

rapid breathing was caused more by the realisation that she was alone with Lorenzo and the look in his eyes than by the exertion of the climb.

He led her forward onto a large flat expanse of rock. On their left they looked down at the waterfall from above, the gushing white water truly stunning with the sunlight sparkling on it.

'It's really beautiful,' Chloe said in a quiet voice, gazing at the fine mist of water droplets surrounding the waterfall and the colourful rainbows that arched around it.

'Yes, I'm still very impressed, even though I've seen it before.'

Lorenzo's voice was loaded with sexual intensity and Chloe knew he wasn't really talking about the waterfall. She held her breath and kept her face turned firmly away from him. She felt the flutter of anticipation start to rise in her stomach again and she wanted to make the moment last.

'I've always loved rivers,' she said slightly breathlessly. 'And especially waterfalls.'

'I remember,' Lorenzo said, taking her by surprise. 'You told me about that river with giant boulder stepping stones that you loved as a child when you went on holiday in Devon.'

'Oh…yes,' Chloe stammered, feeling even more shaky. She couldn't remember telling Lorenzo that, but then they had talked about so many things since she started working for him, and especially since they started dating.

'And you told me about your walking holidays in the Lake District, where you and your sister went in search of anything labelled *force*—meaning waterfall—on your map.'

'You've got a good memory,' Chloe said uncomfortably. She could have sworn she remembered every single second of their time together, remembered every single word they'd ever said to each other. It made her uneasy to realise she was mistaken.

'You don't recall our conversation,' Lorenzo said. His eyes narrowed as he studied her face.

'Of course I do.' Chloe startled herself by lying. She didn't like the sudden feeling that Lorenzo had her at a disadvantage.

'No, you don't,' Lorenzo said emphatically. A half-smile was playing at his lips but it didn't reach his eyes. 'Sit down and catch your breath.'

'I can climb up a few rocks without needing to sit down!' Chloe exclaimed.

'It doesn't matter that you can't remember.' Lorenzo's voice was quiet now, but his eyes still burned dangerously.

'Even you can't remember every single word that was said,' Chloe said huffily.

'Yes, I can,' said Lorenzo lightly, lowering himself down onto a large flat rock with a deep pool in front of it. 'Every single word. Now, sit down here with me.'

Chloe tossed her head, and looked away sideways at the rushing water of the river. She had the unnerving feeling that Lorenzo would take this as evidence that she had never paid full attention to him.

That this was the explanation behind why she had made such a terrible mistake in her expectations of their marriage.

But that was different, she told herself. Forgetting a few inconsequential conversations about family holidays, which had probably taken place during her hectic working day while she was juggling the duties of an exacting job and demanding boss, did *not* mean she would have forgotten something so important as whether he explained fully that he wanted a loveless marriage of convenience.

She took a deep breath and sat down on the rock next to Lorenzo. She'd been alone with him for no more that a few minutes and already her emotions were all over the place again. Things might be wonderful between them when they were making love— but this proved that there were still massive cracks in their relationship.

'Is that where people swim?' she asked, carefully avoiding meeting his eye. Instead she looked at the deep, inviting pool, which was in front of them, surrounded by smooth brown rocks. 'The water certainly looks cool. Does it come down from the mountains?'

'I valued every minute I spent with you,' Lorenzo said, ignoring her attempted change of subject. 'Our conversations ranged over so many topics. I was impressed by your enthusiasm for life, your honesty, the way you expressed yourself so freely and openly.'

'Is that why you tricked me into a loveless marriage?'

The words were out before Chloe fully realised what she was saying. Lorenzo had just told her something wonderful—something that should have made her heart glad. And yet she'd thrown his gesture back in his face.

A furious change came over him and he surged to his feet. Suddenly he was stripping off his T-shirt and kicking away his canvas shoes.

'I'm sorry—' she started, but the look he threw at her over his shoulder quelled her apology before she had gone any further.

'Save it!' he snapped, before turning his back on her and diving into the deep natural pool. His long, powerful strokes bore him rapidly away across the water, and Chloe knew that her unintentionally caustic comment had angered him.

She stood and stared into the water. A couple of minutes ago it had looked inviting, but now that Lorenzo was pounding his way back in her direction she found herself trembling.

'Come in with me!' he commanded, tossing his wet hair out of his eyes with a fierce gesture.

Chloe hesitated, reluctant to join him. He looked completely in his element, surrounded by the majestic power and grace of the river as it carved its way through the ancient volcanic rock. But he was emanating an untamed savage energy that suddenly frightened her as much as it excited her.

'It doesn't look safe,' she said, taking a step back from the edge. 'What stops you getting washed over the waterfall?'

'There's hardly any current this side of those big rocks,' Lorenzo said impatiently. 'As long as we stay this side it is safe. You know I wouldn't have brought you anywhere dangerous.'

Chloe drew her lower lip into her mouth, undecided. It looked like an incredible place to swim— but she was nervous both of the elemental power of the river and of Lorenzo's intense mood.

Then she remembered her promise to Liz. She might never get an opportunity like this again and she would be foolish to let it slip by. In her heart she knew Lorenzo would never put her at real risk.

She stripped off her own blouse and light summer skirt to reveal her bikini, then slid off the rock into the water. She felt herself tremble slightly and released the breath she hadn't known she'd been holding.

'Follow me,' Lorenzo said, beckoning to her as he swam away.

Chloe followed him without speaking as he led her across the pool. The water was cool, but pleasantly energising, and her body was already starting to buzz in expectation of Lorenzo's lovemaking—for she was certain that he was leading her to a place where he could make love to her.

They made their way around the bend in the river by a combination of swimming across deep water and climbing over the giant boulders that rose up beneath them. Chloe loved every minute of it. The setting was absolutely beautiful, and the knowledge that she would soon be in Lorenzo's arms heightened her pleasure.

'We're here,' Lorenzo said at last, and Chloe stopped and stared in wonder at the sight of a whole array of shallow rocky basins fed by smaller, gentler waterfalls.

'It's amazing,' she breathed, unbelievably grateful that she had followed Lorenzo and not given in to her anxieties.

'The locals come here for a water massage,' Lorenzo said, moving away from her towards one of the smaller waterfalls. 'They call it natural hydrotherapy.'

He flashed her a broad smile that showed no hint that he was still angry with her, then pushed himself backwards under the flow of a small waterfall.

Chloe stared in horrified shock as water poured down over him, plastering his black hair to his bowed head and sheeting over his body. She knew he was strong and fit, but her heart started to pound as she looked at him standing under the water.

Being pummelled by gallons of water rushing over a rocky outcrop was not her idea of a massage. It looked frankly terrifying.

'Stop it!' she shouted. 'Get out of there!' But the sound of the crashing water obliterated her cries, and Lorenzo showed no sign of moving.

She lurched forward to grab him, but water poured down over her face and into her eyes, blinding her. She flailed wildly, reaching out to him and calling his name. Then suddenly her fists came into contact with the solid muscle of his chest and she pounded him angrily—not caring whether she hurt him, just wanting him to stop his silly, dangerous game in the torrential waterfall.

The next second she felt his hands close like steel clamps on her arms, and he lifted her back out of the deluge of water.

'What are you doing?' he demanded, holding her steady as she scrubbed sodden hair out of her eyes and spat river water out of her mouth. 'This is not a leisure centre with a lifeguard watching out for us! You can't mess about like that—you must have respect for the power of natural forces.'

'I'm not the one messing about!' she cried, lashing out at him again. 'Why did you have to do that? I thought you'd brought me here to make love to me— not to scare me to death!'

Lorenzo was staring at her, clearly shocked by the vehemence of her attack on him. There was a puzzled look on his face—as if he couldn't understand what she was frightened of.

'It's all right.' He reached for her, but she stepped back out of his grasp.

'Why would you take such a risk?' she demanded. 'I couldn't bear it if—'

She stopped abruptly—suddenly not willing to reveal her feelings to him. He'd already belittled her too many times for that.

'If what?' he asked. 'What were you talking about?'

'Nothing,' she said, splashing away from him in the chest-deep water. 'I'm going back to the boat.'

'Wait.' He moved quicker than her, and the next second his hands closed around her waist. 'I thought you just said you wanted to make love.'

'Let me go!' she gasped, but he pulled her back against his body, lifting her feet off the bottom of the pool. She wriggled in his arms, but she had her back to him and there was nothing she could get hold of.

'That feels good,' he said, rocking his hips forwards so that the hard heat of his arousal nudged against the curve of her bottom. 'I like your idea to make love.'

An answering rush of desire stormed through Chloe, almost making her forget that she was angry with him. But she did not like the way he was man-handling her—even though it was turning her on faster that she would have thought possible.

'It wasn't my idea,' she said, ignoring the liquid heat that was beginning to pool deep inside her as he rocked his pelvis against her once more. 'I said that I thought that was why you'd brought me here.'

'No.' He spoke directly against her ear, his breath hot on her skin. 'I thought you'd like to see the waterfall.'

'Then why is there a condom in your pocket?' she asked in exasperation, reaching behind her to run her hand over his shorts.

It was a mistake. Her palm collided with the hard shaft of his erection straining against the fabric and another rush of arousal shot through her.

'That is for you,' he murmured throatily. 'Now, lie still and let me see what I can do to please you.'

'No…' The world formed silently on Chloe's lips, but she didn't mean it. His hands were moving over her body beneath the water, setting off a chain reaction that she was powerless to resist.

He stepped backwards through the water, pulling her with him, until he was leaning against the rock. He was firmly balanced and could support her easily while his hands ran lightly all over her body.

A deep series of tremors started to quiver through

her, and she reached out instinctively to steady herself, but there was nothing to grab on to.

'Trust me,' he murmured in her ear. 'Just let your limbs float free and trust me to hold you.'

His voice was mesmerising and Chloe found herself automatically doing as he instructed. She leant back into him so that her back was against his chest and her head was resting on his shoulder—and she let her arms and legs hover naturally in the water, finding their own balance.

He traced his hands over her body, his fingertips lightly teasing with gentle swirling patterns that echoed the gentle wash of the water over her skin. She was aware when he tugged at her bikini strings, but she didn't move, and made no effort to stop the tiny scraps of fabric floating away.

She liked feeling naked in the river pool, with his hands and the rippling water caressing every part of her body without hindrance.

Slowly he began to touch her more intimately, teasing her with a delicate touch on her breast or a gentle brush between her legs.

She began to tremble, but she trusted him completely. She knew he wouldn't let her slip, so she just floated in the water, letting the sensations ripple through her.

He started to concentrate his caresses on her breasts, and she felt her breathing deepen. Her body was rocking naturally in the water, rising slightly as she breathed in, so that her nipples broke through the surface, and sinking back down as she exhaled. The sensation it created was exquisite, almost as if his caresses were multiplied by every drop of water flowing over her skin.

'Look down at your body,' Lorenzo breathed in her ear. 'Your breasts are so beautiful.'

Obediently she opened her eyes. Her skin looked so pale in the water, and Lorenzo's hands were rich golden-brown as they moved across her body. And somehow, as she watched her body rise and fall, the sensations he was creating were enhanced.

She began to tremble harder, feeling little darts of pleasure coiling through her body from her breasts deep down through her body. His hands slid to her waist to steady her, but the next thing she knew one hand had moved straight down between her legs.

But this time he didn't brush her lightly, teasing her with delicate touches. This time his fingers went straight for the pulsing centre of her desire.

'Oh!' she cried out in startled pleasure as he began to caress her with direct intent. The games he had played earlier, teasing and tempting with gentle strokes, were over. Now he was focused on stimulating her in the most effective way he knew how.

It only took seconds before her body was writhing with overwhelming, building sensation. One hand closed over her breast, massaging and rolling her nipple, and the other stayed firmly between her legs, sending pulsing waves of sheer pleasure shooting through her entire being.

She felt as if she was taking flight. Her whole body was inflamed with pure sexual rapture. She had never reached orgasm so quickly, and a distant part of her mind could not quite believe it. But then she shot up into the heights of ecstasy like a rocket into space.

For long moments she arched back against Lorenzo, her whole body clenched in the throes of release. Then she relaxed, trembling in the glorious aftermath, and let herself continue to float.

A little while later she felt Lorenzo turning her. His arms slipped under her and he lifted her out of the water and laid her on a smooth brown rock. She sank down into the sun-warmed surface, feeling utterly spent, her arms spread wide and her legs relaxed and soft.

She was absolutely naked and lying spread out in the tropical sun without a care in the world. She closed her eyes and drifted off into a state of dreamy bliss.

Lorenzo sat beside her, looking down at her gorgeous body. She was absolutely exquisite. Her pale skin was glowing with almost ethereal beauty next to the deep brown of the rock and her hair was spread out in a golden halo around her head.

He was still so turned on that it hurt, and soon he

would rouse her again, knowing he could easily bring her back to incredible heights of pleasure, while he found his own release. But right then he couldn't get enough of simply looking at her.

He loved giving her pleasure. And he particularly loved bringing her to orgasm. Whether he took it slow, teasing out each and every nuance of her ascent, or whether he sent her sky-rocketing with a few skilled caresses, there had never been another woman in his life that he had taken so much pleasure from pleasing.

And soon he would start the process again. She was gloriously relaxed and uninhibited, which was often an incredible starting point.

He shifted his position and pulled off his shorts so that he was naked too. Then rolled a condom onto his erect penis. There would be no interruptions—this time he would take them both to the point of rapture.

CHAPTER NINE

THE sparkling azure water of the Indian Ocean stretched out in front of Chloe as far as the eye could see. In fact she knew from reading her guidebook that there were over a thousand miles of glittering ocean between the island of Mauritius, where they were staying, and the east coast of Africa.

She could hardly believe how beautiful the palm-fringed beach was. Gentle waves were lapping on the white powder sand and, out across the clear turquoise water of the lagoon, she could see a line of white water where impressive breakers were crashing into the coral reef.

She sat comfortably on her sun lounger, holding Emma on her lap while she searched through her bag looking for the sunblock.

'May I join you?' Lorenzo's silky Italian accent purred against her ear, catching her unawares, and a shiver prickled across her skin despite the heat of the tropical sun.

Her body was still humming from their amazing lovemaking at the waterfall that morning. She couldn't imagine how Lorenzo had been able to switch from that experience to spending the last couple of hours sending emails and making work phone calls.

'Of course,' she smiled, her breath catching in her throat as she turned to face him.

He looked incredible, she thought, wearing a tight black singlet that revealed altogether too much of his powerfully muscled shoulders and a pair of black shorts that showed off his strong, sexy legs.

'How is Emma?' he asked, taking the lounger next to them.

He leant back on his elbows so that his head was in the shade and stretched his long, bronzed legs out in front of him in the sun.

'Very well,' she said, looking down at him stretched out beside her. There was a funny sensation in the pit of her stomach—it was the first time he had ever asked after the baby. 'Although I can't seem to find the sunblock and I thought it was time for another coat, even though we're sitting in the shade.'

'Another pale English beauty,' he said. 'Tell me what I'm looking for, and I'll go back inside and bring you what you need.'

'Thanks, but it would be easier for me to fetch it,' Chloe said, lifting Emma up into her arms. 'I'm not entirely sure where it is. I may have lost it, in which case I'll pop to the hotel shop and buy some more.'

She tugged the baby's sunhat down snugly to shade her face, slipped her sunglasses on top of her head, and was just about to step out from under the large thatched parasol, when Lorenzo spoke.

'Then leave Emma with me,' he said.

Chloe paused, surprised by Lorenzo's suggestion. It was the first time he'd ever shown any inclination to be left alone with the baby.

Suddenly she realised she'd hesitated too long, and she glanced at him, startled to see her face reflected in the lenses of his sunglasses. She drew in a deep breath and pulled her own sunglasses down from on top of her head, hoping he had not read what was on her mind from the expression in her eyes.

Then she realised he was watching her reaction, and she felt her cheeks redden with embarrassment. The last thing she wanted was for him to think she did not trust him with the baby.

'All right,' she said, stepping back towards Lorenzo.

She started to chatter to Emma awkwardly, trying to cover up her delay in handing her over by beginning the stream of one-way conversation she usually maintained to keep the baby girl's attention.

'I'm just popping back inside,' she said to the infant. 'I won't be long. You go to Lorenzo…'

All at once her voice dried up. Calling him

Lorenzo had sounded wrong. But she couldn't call him Daddy—he was not Emma's father.

When Liz had asked Chloe to care for her daughter, she'd told her that she wanted Emma to call her Mummy, just like any other adopted child would refer to their adoptive mother. Then Chloe would use her judgement to decide when to tell her adopted daughter about her natural mother.

But Lorenzo had approached the adoption from an altogether different angle. Chloe had no idea what his thoughts on the subject were.

'Come to Daddy,' Lorenzo said, reaching out his arms to take the baby from Chloe.

'I'm sorry…' she started to say. 'I didn't know what—'

'Emma's biological father is not part of her life,' Lorenzo said flatly. 'I am the only father Emma will ever know and she will call *me* Daddy. No child growing up under my roof will be made to feel different from any other.'

A sudden swelling of emotion filled Chloe. She'd been concerned that Lorenzo had not truly accepted Emma. She believed he would always provide for her and do what he saw as the right thing. But she had worried that Emma would grow up knowing she was not the same as Lorenzo's natural children.

'That's good,' she said, knowing that it sounded inadequate in the circumstances—but she didn't want to make a big deal out of it. She was glad she was wearing sunglasses so that Lorenzo could not see the tears suddenly sparkling in her eyes. 'I know you don't want Emma to feel unloved…' She hesitated again, struggling to finish her comment smoothly. She hadn't meant to stumble into that other minefield—the discussion of love. 'I mean unwanted.'

'*Unloved* is the correct word,' Lorenzo said. 'No child growing up in my family will feel unloved.'

He reached up and took Emma decisively from Chloe's arms.

It was clear from his manner that he considered the conversation over—but Chloe did not mind. As far as she was concerned they had just made a massive step forward.

That evening Chloe and Lorenzo watched a display of the *séga,* the high-spirited and colourful national dance of Mauritius. It had been Chloe's idea—they had spent so much time alone together, mostly making love, that she was beginning to feel slightly detached from reality.

The dance was beautiful and compelling. The pulsating rhythm of the drums filled the air, and the dancers swirled and undulated without restraint. But as Chloe sat at a table with Lorenzo, watching him tap out the infectious beat with his fingers, she was beginning to think that what she really needed was to go home.

'You've had your hair cut.' He lifted his hand to touch Chloe's sleekly styled bob. 'I like it,' he added, tracing his fingers lightly over her newly exposed neck.

'Thank you.' She trembled as he caressed her sensitive skin. She was wearing a strapless dress and she felt his eyes settle on her naked shoulders.

'I don't recall noticing those freckles before,' he said, leaning closer so that she could feel his breath on the skin of her shoulders. 'Did the sun bring them out, like the ones on your face?'

'I don't know,' Chloe replied as the touch of his warm breath sent a delicious shiver quivering down her spine.

'You have beautiful skin—I adore your freckles.' He brushed his thumb lightly over her cheek.

'I ran out of foundation.' As soon as she spoke, it seemed a silly thing to say and she felt herself start to blush.

'I wondered why I noticed your freckles more,' he said, leaning forward to drop a feather-light kiss on her cheek.

'I think it's time to go home,' Chloe said, looking deep into his blue eyes.

'Of course.' He stood up immediately and led her out of the door into the hotel's lovely garden, which was their preferred route back towards their suite of rooms.

A warm, scented breeze brushed across Chloe's skin and she could hear the gentle sound of the ocean. She looked up to see the palm trees swaying against an inky black sky studded with twinkling stars. It really was a beautiful place—a true tropical paradise. But she knew Lorenzo had misunderstood her request.

'No, I mean *really* go home,' she said, turning and catching both his hands in hers. 'I'm grateful for this wonderful holiday—but it's time to go back home and get on with our lives.'

One day almost two weeks later, Chloe stood on the *palazzo*'s main balcony overlooking the Grand Canal, holding Emma in her arms. She was chatting to the baby, pointing out the various boats that went past on the water—and keeping out of Lorenzo's way.

Things between them had become strained again and, apart from at night, when they continued to make love, she'd spent very little time with him. She thought that might be part of the reason she'd found it much harder to settle in to life in Venice than she had expected.

But the main reason for her disquiet was that almost every day she had found herself thinking about the devastating argument she'd had with Lorenzo on their wedding day—and him swearing that he did not believe in love.

In fact, virtually every room in the *palazzo* held memories for her, and now as she looked back she found herself second-guessing everything that had ever been said and done between Lorenzo and herself.

If she'd been so wrong about the one thing that mattered the most—what else had not been as it seemed?

'I wonder where Daddy is now?' she said to Emma.

Since they'd been back in Venice he always seemed to be working—either at his offices or locked up in his study, or occasionally striding around the *palazzo* talking rapidly into his mobile phone, which was exactly what he was doing now.

She found it disconcerting to hear him bearing down on her while firing away in a language she still didn't fully understand—especially when spoken quickly by locals. The Venetian dialect seemed particularly impossible to learn.

She hugged Emma to her and listened carefully, trying to ascertain if Lorenzo was close. It was not that she was afraid to bump into him—it was just that she remembered from when she worked for him that if he was talking and striding like this, it probably meant he was in a bad mood.

'I'm here.' Lorenzo's deep voice coming from right behind her made her catch her breath. 'Did you want me for something?'

'Oh!' Chloe gasped, turning to see him stepping out onto the broad balcony with her. 'No, not really. I heard your voice and I was just chatting to

Emma. I've been showing her the boats on the Grand Canal.'

'Isn't she a little young for that?' Lorenzo asked, staring at her with a crease between his black brows.

'No,' Chloe responded, suppressing her irritation at the way Lorenzo was studying the baby—as if she were a strange little being of some kind. Not at all as if she was his adopted daughter. 'It's always good to chatter to babies, even if they are too young to understand. That's how they learn things.'

She pressed her teeth into her lower lip and looked at him, starting to worry that, despite his good intentions, he was having difficulty accepting another man's child into his home. The brief flash of interest he had shown in Emma that one particular afternoon on the beach in Mauritius had not been repeated, and he'd never made even the slightest effort to make a connection with the baby.

'I have something for her in my study,' he suddenly surprised Chloe by saying.

'Really?' she said, feeling a tiny spark of relief. She hoped that she'd been wrong, and that Lorenzo's aloofness had been no more than overwork. He'd taken a lot of time off to be with them, both in England and then in Mauritius. No doubt he had a good deal of work to catch up on. 'What is it?'

'I'm not entirely sure,' he said. 'Perhaps you should come with me and see for yourself.'

'That would be lovely,' Chloe said, feeling a little confused that he didn't know what the item was, but infusing her voice with warmth. If Lorenzo had made a kind gesture, she wanted him to know it was appreciated.

He set off through the *palazzo* at his usual great pace, as if he'd forgotten he was walking with Chloe, whose stride was considerably shorter. She wasn't prepared to run with the baby in her arms, so almost immediately she fell behind.

Lorenzo stopped and looked round, then glanced at his wristwatch.

'I have a conference call in a few minutes,' he said. 'Let me carry the baby, or we'll be out of time.'

Chloe handed Emma to him with a funny feeling inside. It rankled that Lorenzo only wanted to hold Emma to speed things up. But then, Chloe told herself, he had to start somewhere. If making a connection with Emma didn't come naturally for Lorenzo, then maybe it could grow from small, insignificant incidents.

He led the way to his study with Chloe half running to keep up. But when they got there he turned and abruptly passed Emma back to her.

'This is it.' He picked up a package from the floor behind his desk. 'Francesco Grazzini sent it. He's a business associate of mine,' he added, as if Chloe didn't already know that. But she held her tongue—that was not something worth starting an argument over.

'Thank you,' She smiled tightly, knowing she hadn't really managed to hide her deflated mood.

'What's wrong?' Lorenzo said, looking at her sharply.

'Nothing.' She looked back at him, biting her lip in indecision. Perhaps she should say something. But then she remembered the conference call he had mentioned—now was not the right time to get into a potentially tricky conversation with him. 'I'll leave you to your work.'

Lorenzo watched her hurry away out of his study carrying the baby in her arms. She'd forgotten to take Grazzini's package. Or maybe she'd left it deliberately—he'd seen the look on her face when he told her who it was from. Until that moment it hadn't occurred to him that she might have thought that he'd bought it.

It had seemed as if there'd been something on the tip of her tongue, something she was holding back from saying. He knew what it was about. It was clear that Chloe wanted him to show more paternal interest in Emma.

Well, he could do that—he could spend time with them and satisfy Chloe that he was making an effort with the baby. He had made a commitment that he fully intended to honour—to be a good parent and to treat the child as if she were his own. But he could not make himself have feelings that didn't come naturally. Feelings that simply weren't there.

CHAPTER TEN

'I'M SO glad you're starting to get to know Emma,' Chloe said impulsively as she watched Lorenzo playing with the baby—although *playing* wasn't really the right word to describe it. And Lorenzo didn't exactly look as if he was having fun.

Nevertheless, he was patiently handing Emma a succession of soft, colourful blocks, which she took, chewed a bit, then threw back at him. She was sitting on a rug surrounded by a circle of cushions because she wasn't very stable, and Lorenzo and Chloe were sitting facing her.

Next to the baby Lorenzo seemed huge and awkward, and Chloe found herself frowning slightly as she looked at them. It was true that he was a large, powerful man, but despite his sheer size she had never seen him move or hold himself with anything but cat-like poise. Except for when he was with Emma.

'Yes.' Lorenzo's one-word response revealed just how ill-at-ease he was feeling and Chloe found herself experiencing a hint of frustration.

She didn't know what was behind Lorenzo's lack of ease. Was he just finding the whole thing tedious? Or was he totally out of his comfort zone?

Emma was only six months old, and obviously not scintillating intellectual company. But she was fascinating and rewarding to spend time with, if you took a moment to adjust to the change of pace.

Yet Lorenzo's face was set in stone and he was not attempting to talk to her at all. Chloe wished she knew if that was just because he wasn't really interested in communicating with her, or if he felt self-conscious and unsure of what to say.

'She likes those stacking cups—the ones that are behind her,' Chloe said, wishing she could think of some way to lighten the atmosphere, but Lorenzo's oppressive silence was making her feel unsettled too.

Lorenzo didn't reply but he leant over to pick up the cups, with Emma following his movements with her bright little eyes. As he reached past her she turned her head too far and suddenly lost her balance. She rolled over sideways and knocked her head on the stack of plastic cups, and sent up a wail that echoed sharply around the room.

'Whoa!' Lorenzo said, picking her up and trying

to sit her back on her bottom, but she was wailing and arching her back, and it was clear that she would just fall over again if he let go of her.

Chloe's fingers twitched with the urge to sweep the baby up, putting both her and Lorenzo out of their misery. But at the same time she didn't want to barge in. If she always did everything it would only make things harder for Lorenzo.

He really did seem to be making an effort finally. And she'd heard the concern in his voice when Emma went over. She was unbelievably glad that he did seem to be connecting with the baby on some level—even if it was only at the most basic, simple concern over her safety.

'Here, you take her,' he said suddenly, dumping the crying baby into Chloe's arms.

'Don't worry,' Chloe said, jiggling Emma to comfort her. She couldn't help feeling disappointed that he had given up so easily. But at least he had tried, she told herself. That had to be something.

'Worry?' Lorenzo said curtly. 'Worry about what?'

'That you're not finding it easy,' Chloe said. 'That you don't know what to do right away. It will come— the important thing is that you are starting to connect with her. To feel like her father.'

'No. I'm not.'

Lorenzo's bald statement of denial sent a cold chill through Chloe, and she felt an automatic need to dispute it. Of course he was starting to feel like Emma's father—he had to be.

'I'm sure that you are,' she said gently. 'Maybe only a little. But the connection between you will grow over time.'

'I want her to be well and happy—I have made a commitment, and I fully intend to keep my word,' he said stiffly, 'but my positive intentions for the child are driven by what is the correct thing to do for her continued well-being. Not by my emotions. Not by feelings I do not have.'

Chloe stared at him, momentarily stunned by the enormity of his statement. But she could sense the frustration bubbling beneath his stern exterior—see that he was keeping something battened down inside him.

'It's understandable,' she said, treading carefully. 'She's not your flesh and blood, and she did come into your life suddenly and unexpectedly. As she gets older things will change.'

She paused, hoping for some acceptance from him. Giving him a moment to say something—anything. But he maintained an oppressive silence—a silence that Chloe felt compelled to fill. She couldn't leave things like this. She just couldn't.

'It will be different when you have your own children,' she said. 'You'll have nine months to get used to the idea of a baby. And the first time you lay eyes on it, you will love it immediately.'

'No,' Lorenzo bit out. 'There is no reason to assume I will love my children. I have told you I will do everything in my power to ensure they *feel* loved—that is the only guarantee I can make. And that is the most important thing.'

'How can you say that?' Chloe gasped. 'Of course you will love your own children. It's a natural instinct.'

'Not for everyone,' he said. 'You and I both know that to our cost. My parents did not love me—my mother sold me when I was five years old to my father as part of her divorce settlement!'

'But…but surely…at least that means your father loved you,' Chloe stumbled, horrified by Lorenzo's outburst. 'You know *he* wanted you.'

'I was nothing more than another commodity to him,' Lorenzo said bitterly.

'No.' Chloe shook her head in denial.

'Don't tell me what my childhood was like,' Lorenzo said. 'And before you start talking about natural parental instincts, perhaps you should remember how your father walked out on your seventh birthday. And your mother—she may have waited till you were grown up, but when was the last time you spoke to her?'

'Why are you being like this?' Chloe cried. 'Why would you say such horrible things?'

'To stop your unrealistic, idealised expectations,'

Lorenzo grated. 'I have given you my assurance that I will be a good father—but I can't promise to feel something that is not under my control.'

'If you don't expect to love your children—why do you even want them?' Chloe cried, jumping to her feet with Emma still in her arms and backing away from him. 'What kind of monster are you?'

Suddenly she didn't want to hear his answer—she couldn't stand to be near him a moment longer. Clutching Emma tightly, she stumbled out of the room, needing to get as far away from him as possible.

Lorenzo made no attempt to stop her leaving.

His heart was thudding violently in his chest and his palms were damp with sweat.

She had called him a monster—and maybe she was right. But all he could think about was the five-year-old boy he had once been, confused and hurting—and simply wanting his mother's warm and reassuring presence.

He didn't know anything about love. He'd never been on the receiving end of it, and he'd never felt it himself for another human being. He didn't even know if he was capable of it.

Chloe stood on the balcony that led off from the bedroom she shared with Lorenzo. It was high up on a corner of the *palazzo,* and she had a clear view out through the mouth of the Grand Canal and across the

Venetian Lagoon. It was an overcast day in June, and the calm water was a muted grey, reflecting the dull, colourless sky.

Out of nowhere she found herself remembering Lorenzo telling her about the lagoon, how the tranquil surface hid a treacherous underwater terrain of hidden channels and shifting mudflats that had protected the city against attack for centuries.

She couldn't help thinking about how that applied to Lorenzo, and how she had only just started to discover what lay beneath the surface. She'd been standing there looking out at the water for ages, while Emma took her nap, hoping the soft sea breeze would clear her head. But all she could think about was her terrible argument with him.

At first the discovery that he did not think he was capable of love had shocked and angered her. But then the more she thought about it, the more she had found herself feeling drained and heartsick. How could he have simply given up on love?

On their wedding day in February, when she'd found out that he thought marriages based on love were doomed to failure, she had been upset by how cynical he had been. But finding out that he didn't even believe that he would be able to love his own children had painted an entirely different picture.

It wasn't cynicism. It was a total lack of hope.

His life must have been so cold and empty when

he was a child, but Chloe realised she knew very little about his childhood years. He had told her so much about the wonderful city he had grown up in that she'd never noticed he talked very little about himself.

Her heart ached when she thought about it. She couldn't bear to think of him as a little boy, wandering around this *palazzo*—this huge, architectural monument to his family's great history—feeling lost and alone. And unloved.

'If you want out of this marriage, I'll understand.' Lorenzo's deep voice right behind her made her catch her breath.

'What? No…'

She spun round to face him, and was startled to see a terrible haunted look in his eyes. But then she replayed what he had just said—*if she wanted out of this marriage*…

'You made your feelings about me crystal-clear,' Lorenzo said. 'I understand if you don't want me to be the father of your children.'

'No, I…' Chloe's voice petered out as she remembered what she'd called him. 'I don't think you are a monster,' she said. 'I didn't really mean that—I've seen your good intentions towards Emma. And I know you'd only want what's best for your own children.'

'That's why I married *you*,' Lorenzo said. 'I thought *you* were best for them. I know you love

Emma as if she were your own, and that you'd love all your children just as fiercely.'

He turned away for a moment, raking his hands through his short black hair in a gesture that revealed how difficult he was finding it to talk to her. Then he turned back and looked into her eyes with his troubled gaze.

'But I know that's not enough,' he said. 'Children deserve a father who is able to love them.'

Chloe looked at him, filled with a mixture of shock and despair.

She loved Lorenzo and had committed herself to making their marriage work, despite his lack of confidence in love. But now, out of the blue, he had decided not to bother.

'Are you telling me you're not man enough to stick with this?' She did not hide the disgust from her voice. 'You're the one who pushed me into this, who told me it was for the best. And now, just like that, you're prepared to give up?'

'I'm not giving up,' Lorenzo grated, clearly angered by her words. 'I've made a considered decision. This marriage was never what you wanted—not once you knew my true feelings. Why would you fight for it now?'

'Because I don't give up that easily!' Chloe cried. 'I don't turn my back on something the moment the going gets tough.'

She pushed past him into the bedroom, intending to take Emma and go for a walk to cool off. But then she remembered what she had been thinking about when Lorenzo first came in. That his troubled, *unloved* childhood had made him lose faith in people. Had made him relinquish hope for love. Maybe that was driving his decision to give up on their marriage.

She turned back to him again, the anger that had been pulsing round her body suddenly going quiet. He had been badly hurt. Maybe he was scared that he would hurt his own children.

'I don't give up that easily,' Chloe repeated, but this time more gently. 'I know your mother's desertion hurt you and that you grew up feeling unloved. But history doesn't have to repeat itself. You have to give yourself a chance.'

She stared up into his blue eyes, which were as overcast and grey-tinged as the sky above them. She wanted to find a way to reach out to him—to help him deal with the fallout of his troubled childhood.

She took a tentative step closer and lifted her hand to touch his cheek.

His reaction was instant. It was as if steel shutters dropped down over the tiny window into his soul that she'd momentarily glimpsed, and he brushed her hand aside abruptly. His rejection of her attempt to make a connection with him was total.

'Don't touch me!' he bit out. 'I don't want your

sympathy. And I don't want to hear your amateur psychoanalysis of my life. Pack your bags—we're leaving for England tonight.'

He stormed out of the bedroom, leaving Chloe staring after him in a state of shock.

Had he just told her that he was divorcing her? That he was taking her back to England because their marriage was over?

CHAPTER ELEVEN

THE flight from Venice back to southern England was not long, but it turned out to be one of the most stressful flights Chloe could remember.

Emma, who had so far been very good on aeroplanes, started crying the minute they took off. By the time they were flying over the Alps, she was howling at the top of her lungs.

'What's wrong with her?' Lorenzo demanded loudly, staring at her with a horrified scowl on his face. 'Why is she doing that? She's always been all right before.'

'I don't know,' Chloe said in exasperation—she'd already tried everything she could think of to calm Emma down. There'd been an oppressive tension between Lorenzo and herself since their argument, but his agitation over Emma's crying was making things even more strained between them. 'I've never seen her like this.'

'Maybe it's her ears,' Lorenzo suddenly suggested. 'We're very high over the mountains—perhaps her ears are sensitive to the change of pressure.'

'It could be that.' Chloe seized on the idea hopefully. She was desperate to find a reason for the poor little thing's distress, and anxious to find a way to make her feel better. 'Could you pass me her drink, please? Maybe that will help.'

Sure enough, sucking on her drink did seem to calm Emma a little, and Chloe looked over at Lorenzo with relief.

'Maybe a doctor should examine her when we arrive,' Lorenzo suggested. 'She doesn't look quite right to me.'

'Maybe, although I don't think she has a fever.' Chloe frowned and tried to look down at Emma, but it was hard to see her properly because of the way she was positioned on her lap. She didn't want to move her and risk setting her off again. 'She's never been so upset before—but it doesn't necessarily mean it's something serious.'

She drew her lip into her mouth in consternation. She wanted to do whatever was best for Emma—only she didn't know whether she was just over-tired from travelling and needed a settled night at home. Or if there was really something wrong.

However, by the time they'd nearly reached the

glass-walled house, the decision was made for them. After falling asleep for a short while on leaving the airport, Emma had woken up fretful and hot. Then she'd starting screaming louder than anything Chloe had ever heard before.

'We're taking her to the hospital in the next town,' Lorenzo said, barking instructions to the limousine driver to change route. 'They have a children's accident and emergency unit there—it will be the quickest way to get her seen.'

Chloe tried to sooth Emma anxiously, thankful that it didn't take long to reach the hospital.

Then all of a sudden the high-pitched crying stopped, and the baby seemed to calm down. But Chloe knew it wasn't right. From screaming so energetically, Emma had quickly become listless and dopey.

'Something's wrong,' she said, startled by how loud her voice sounded in the sudden silence in the limousine. 'We'd better find a doctor.'

'This way.' Lorenzo helped Chloe out of the vehicle, and quickly scanned the hospital signs to establish where to go.

His heart had started to thud loudly in his chest, and a crushing sensation of helplessness suddenly seized him.

Emma was so tiny. It was his responsibility to take care of her—to make sure she was all right. But he did not know what to do to make her better. The only thing he could do was to take her as quickly as possible to someone who was qualified.

Her little head was resting on Chloe's shoulder, but it was rocking from side to side as Chloe walked, as if she did not have the strength to support it. He wanted to reach out and steady her, but he knew Emma was never truly comfortable whenever he tried to hold her. If he touched her, even just to support her head, it would probably just upset her again.

Frustration coiled through him, mixed with anger at his own inadequacy.

Why was he so incapable of taking care of an infant? He wanted to be able to do it—but no matter how hard he tried he always messed it up.

Suddenly he couldn't bear it any longer. He reached out and drew Chloe to his side, then cupped his large hand around Emma's head as they walked together.

He felt something warm and wet on his fingers.

'What's that?' he demanded, stopping in his tracks and studying Emma. 'It's coming from her ear!'

He swore in Italian, and reached out to take her from Chloe. Fear for the baby suddenly gripped him, and he strode through the doors of the emergency unit knowing implicitly that he would gain the doctor's attention more quickly.

'I need a doctor.' His voice cut through the background buzz of the waiting room. 'My baby is not well.'

* * *

Later that night Lorenzo watched Chloe lay Emma down to sleep in her cot in the glass-walled house. She was suffering from a nasty ear infection, and, although she probably still felt poorly, her temperature was down and the acute pain she had been experiencing had passed, since her eardrum had perforated and released the pressure.

'It must have hurt so much,' Chloe said, rubbing her hand over her own ear, as if she was suffering in sympathy.

'Yes, it must have been excruciating. And I can't believe that it could happen again,' Lorenzo replied, remembering what the doctor said about some children being prone to ear infections. 'I don't think I can stand to imagine how much pain she's in if she starts crying like that again.'

'Let's hope it's a one-off thing,' Chloe said. 'The doctor said that boys have a greater tendency to ear infections than girls.'

She sat down on the edge of the bed and looked up at him. There was an interested light in her green eyes, and suddenly he realised she was watching him pace up and down the bedroom.

He was showing a degree of agitation that she had probably never seen in him before. Hell—he'd rarely seen it in himself before.

'That was unbearable,' Lorenzo said. 'But at least if it does happen again I'll know what's going on. I have never felt so helpless and scared as when I saw that ooze coming out of her ear.'

He shuddered, scrubbing his hands over his face.

'I think you are starting to feel like a parent,' Chloe said gently.

He stopped pacing and stared down at her, thinking about what she had said. Maybe she was right.

Earlier, when he'd carried Emma into the examination room with ooze seeping from her ear, his heart had thudded painfully hard in his chest, and a terrible tightness had gripped his throat, making it hurt to speak. He'd waited in a state of agony, until the doctor had said that Emma would be all right, and explained what had happened.

Lorenzo sat down on the bed next to Chloe without speaking and looked at Emma, who was now sleeping in the cot.

'I think that maybe you are starting to love her,' Chloe added quietly, reaching out and taking his hand in both of hers.

A tremor passed through Lorenzo. And he squeezed Chloe's hands with his.

Over the next few days Chloe spent all her time caring for Emma. The antibiotics seemed to do their job and the baby quickly bounced back from her ear infection, becoming her normal sunny self in next to no time.

Unfortunately Lorenzo also reverted back to his

typical character—emotionally withdrawn and uncommunicative—leaving Chloe feeling confused and lost.

When they'd flown back from Venice, she'd been convinced that their marriage was at breaking point—that he was bringing her to England to divorce her and cut her and Emma out of his life. She was no longer worried about that, because Lorenzo finally seemed to have made a genuine connection with Emma.

The night they'd returned from the hospital and sat together holding hands, Chloe had also felt that they'd made real progress in their personal relationship. Lorenzo had begun to reveal the depth of his concern for Emma, and for the first time ever he had not rebuffed Chloe's suggestion that he was starting to experience parental feelings—and possibly even the beginnings of love for the baby.

Chloe had fallen asleep that night with a newfound hope warming her heart. Of course it was wonderful for Lorenzo and Emma, but she also dared to believe it would bring them all closer together as a family. And if Lorenzo could feel the beginnings of love for Emma—maybe there was a chance that he could grow to love her too.

But she had been mistaken.

As the days went by Lorenzo never mentioned the conversation that had given Chloe such hope again, and his taciturn mood meant she didn't dare to raise the subject. He did start spending extra time with

Emma—but his attitude towards Chloe did not appear to change at all, apart from becoming even more reticent if that was possible.

She began to feel a shadow of despair creeping over her. It was as if as soon as Lorenzo's emotional barricades had started to break down, he had deliberately set about building them up again.

Chloe spent her time wandering around the house and garden with Emma. After a while she started to feel cooped up and claustrophobic—it was a large property, but there was nowhere else for her to go. The winding country lane had no footpath beside it, and wasn't suitable for walking along, especially with a pushchair.

She began to feel her life was on hold. Lorenzo wasn't communicating with her, and she found herself seeking Mrs Guest's comforting presence more and more.

'Emma looks so much better now,' the housekeeper said, looking across from the kitchen sink, where she was preparing vegetables.

'Yes, she does,' Chloe agreed, pausing for a moment to wipe a splodge of apple purée off the baby's cheek. She had taken to giving Emma her meals in the kitchen—it made her feel less lonely.

'A much better appetite,' Mrs Guest added.

'Yes, she's nearly finished this,' Chloe said. 'Do you know if Lorenzo has any other cars here, besides the limo and the convertible?' she added, suddenly changing the subject. 'Something a bit more ordinary?'

Mrs Guest laughed.

'I don't know,' she said. 'I can ask my husband if you'd like. Are you thinking of going out on your own with Emma, and want to drive something you're more used to?'

'It was just an idea,' Chloe replied, popping the last tiny spoonful of fruit into Emma's mouth. 'There's no need for you to ask—I can do that myself.'

'I'll clean up here,' Mrs Guest said, crossing the room to wipe over the high chair. 'Why don't you take Emma out into the garden? The forecast said rain later—so you might not have a chance if you wait.'

Chloe followed Mrs Guest's suggestion, and went outside with Emma to continue their exploration of the garden. She was so grateful that it was a vibrant time of year in nature, with long daylight hours ensuring plenty of growth and changes in the garden every day. It gave her something to concentrate her attention on—and Chloe realised it was something she had missed living in the city.

The purple irises beside the pond had faded, but the water lilies had come out in a mass of impressive cream and white flowers. And the buds she'd seen on the roses climbing over the pergola had opened into full, wonderfully scented blooms.

Mr Guest had put up bird-nesting boxes in a

couple of big trees near the pond, and Chloe loved to see the acrobatic blue tit parents coming and going with a flash of blue and yellow feathers. She sat down on a bench with Emma on her lap to watch them. Mr Guest had told her he expected the young birds to fledge any day—and Chloe thought it would be amazing to catch sight of the fledglings leaving the nest box.

A few minutes later a crunch on the gravel path told her that someone was approaching. It was probably Lorenzo, because the friendly gardener usually went about his work whistling cheerfully.

Her stomach turned over with nerves, and then she looked up straight into Lorenzo's blue eyes.

'Hello,' he said, sitting down beside her and reaching for Emma. 'How is she today?' he asked, turning Emma round to face him with none of the awkwardness he'd displayed only a few days before. Then he held her standing on his knees, so she could partially take her weight with her own legs and bounce up and down, as if Lorenzo's lap was her own private trampoline.

'She's fine,' Chloe said shortly, unaccountably irritated by how natural Lorenzo now seemed with Emma.

It didn't seem fair that her stomach screwed up in knots when he approached, and yet apparently he'd completely got over his uncertain floundering with the infant.

'I have been thinking about our plan to have more children,' Lorenzo said.

'Our plan?' Chloe turned sideways on the bench and stared at him. 'I thought our plan was to wait until things are settled—until we are properly used to our new circumstances.'

Lorenzo's comment seemed to be completely out of the blue. Surely he was not about to say that he thought they should start trying for a baby. They'd only been back together for a few weeks. To Chloe it still seemed as though everything was up in the air.

'We agreed that we want children,' Lorenzo said, 'and I can't see any point in waiting. It would be better for Emma if our first biological child is as close in age to her as possible.'

'I can't believe you're serious!' Chloe gasped. 'Have you forgotten what you said to me just before we left Venice? You were ready to give up on this marriage. In fact I thought that was why you'd brought me back to England—so you could leave me here, then go and get on with your life.'

'I have not forgotten.' Lorenzo's voice was strained, as if he did not appreciate being reminded of that particular conversation. 'But things are different now.'

'No, they're not!' Chloe exclaimed. 'Just because you've had your own personal epiphany—realising you *are* capable of basic human feelings towards a baby—doesn't mean we are ready to bring more children into this marriage.'

'You are a natural mother. I thought having your own baby would give you a focus in your life. Help you move on after losing your friend,' Lorenzo said calmly, despite Chloe's rising agitation.

'Don't patronise me!' Chloe gasped. 'I've got Emma to look after. I don't need another baby to help me forget my friend.'

'I didn't mean it like that—of course I am not telling you to forget your friend. But it doesn't seem as if you have fully committed to this marriage. I thought maybe a baby—'

'No!' Chloe interrupted. 'You can't solve our problems with a baby. How can you even think of using an innocent baby like that?'

She reached across and took Emma back, then cradled her protectively in her arms.

'You knew what you were getting into when you agreed to this,' Lorenzo said harshly. 'Nothing has changed. Whatever misunderstandings we may have had in the past—*this time* you knew for certain exactly where we stood.'

'How could I have known?' Chloe cried, jumping to her feet and looking Lorenzo straight in the eye. 'I mean, really known. Until you've lived in a loveless marriage you can't know what it's like.'

'You told me to my face, the night you agreed to

stay in this marriage, that you did not love me.'
Lorenzo stood abruptly, towering over her once
more. 'Don't start this nonsense about love again.'

'It's not nonsense!' Chloe cried.

She turned away, feeling tears stinging her eyes.
She'd chosen to stay in the marriage because she loved
Lorenzo, and she couldn't imagine not being with
him. But she'd never guessed how hard it would be.

And now, knowing he loved Emma seemed to be
making it even harder. Emma wasn't his natural child,
and she'd only been in his life a few weeks, and yet
he'd already opened up his heart to her. But Chloe had
been in his life for more than two years. If he didn't
love her by now—then she knew that he never would.

'I want this marriage to work.' Lorenzo's deep
voice rumbled through her. 'But that is never going
to happen if you keep throwing obstacles in the way.'

'Love is not an obstacle!' Chloe gasped, spinning
round to face him once more. 'Most people would
think it's essential!'

She glared up at him, and saw he was looking
down at her angrily.

Suddenly she couldn't bear to talk about it any more.
There was no point. Nothing was going to change
Lorenzo's point of view and the only possible outcome
was further humiliation and heartache for herself.

'I need a car,' she said abruptly, changing the
subject completely.

'What?' Lorenzo burst out. 'What do you need a car for?'

'The same reason anyone needs a car,' she said tersely. 'I want to be able to get around the area independently.'

'The driver will take you anywhere you want to go,' Lorenzo said.

'I said *independently*,' she replied, holding his gaze crossly.

'We already have the limo and the convertible here. I can't see any need to keep another car at this property.'

'I'm not asking for anything flashy,' Chloe said, 'just a cheap second-hand car. But if you won't get me one, I can take the convertible.'

A flash of irritation passed across Lorenzo's features.

'That is a powerful vehicle—dangerous if you're not used to driving it,' he said.

'Worried I'll drive your precious car into a ditch?' she said sarcastically. 'I do know how to drive.'

'I'm not worried you'll drive into a ditch,' Lorenzo grated. 'I'm afraid you'll go right through the hedge—or wrap it around a tree.'

'Well, buy me a little run-around. I need to go back to the cottage before the lease runs out.'

'I'll take you—in fact we'll go together right now,' Lorenzo said.

'I want to go on my own,' Chloe replied, looking down at the baby in her arms. 'It's personal.'

'If you don't want *my* company, the driver will take you,' Lorenzo said stiffly. 'He will have instructions to wait for you outside until you are done.'

Then he turned and walked away along the gravel path.

The following morning Chloe stood at the window, watching the limousine drive away through the wrought-iron gates. Lorenzo had a business meeting in London, and Chloe assumed he intended to utilise the travelling time working on his laptop in the back of the limo.

She frowned, thinking that this was another day gone by when she couldn't go back to Liz's cottage. If she didn't go soon, she wouldn't have another chance. Gladys, Liz's kindly neighbour, would have had to return the keys to the letting agency.

Gladys had already been in and cleared the few remaining things that Chloe had left behind when Lorenzo whisked her away so suddenly. There had not been much to do—they'd already taken care of nearly everything in those heartbreakingly hollow days before the funeral.

But Chloe still had to pick up a box of letters and mementoes that Liz had packed for Emma before her illness had progressed too far.

'Let's go and get you some breakfast,' she said, scooping Emma up from where she was playing happily in her cot. 'Then we'll think of something to do today.'

But as soon as she'd spoken a plan was already forming in her mind. She would take the convertible and drive herself to the village. Lorenzo didn't need it that day—and, more importantly, he wasn't there to stop her going.

'Chloe!' Gladys exclaimed as she opened the front door of her cottage. 'What a lovely surprise. Oh, look how much Emma has grown! And you're looking well too. Come in—come in for a cup of tea, and tell me what you've been doing with yourself.'

'It's lovely to see you, too,' Chloe said, giving Gladys a hug. Then she followed her into her cheery front room, which was full of knick-knacks and drawings done by her many grandchildren.

'I'll put the kettle on,' Gladys said. 'Then you can tell me everything.'

Half an hour later Chloe gave the old lady another hug and stepped back out onto the street, carrying a sleeping Emma in her portable car seat.

'It's been lovely to see you,' Gladys said warmly. 'I wish we had longer to catch up, but I've got to pop out now. If I'm not back when you're ready to go—

just put the key through the letterbox. And promise to come back and see me soon.'

'I will,' Chloe assured her. 'Thank you for the tea.'

Chloe hugged the old lady one more time and went next door to Liz's cottage, carrying Emma extra-carefully to avoid waking her up. As she opened the front door the familiar scent of Liz's essential-oil burner wafted over her, sending her straight back to the time she had lived there with her friend.

She sat down on the sofa and pulled Liz's box of memories close to her. Up until that moment she hadn't had the heart to open it. But now she realised that she should do it here—where she had shared Liz's last few months.

She lifted the lid gingerly, and right on the top was an envelope addressed to her in Liz's handwriting. Her heart constricted and her hand was shaking as she lifted the letter. It was not a long letter, and the handwriting was spidery, as if Liz had struggled to find the physical strength to write it.

Dear Chloe
You have always been my best friend, and it has meant so much to me having you with me these last few months.
*   You are a wonderful person, with a kind, true heart, and I wish you only the best in life.*
*   There are no words to express what it means*

to me, knowing that Emma will be with you when I am gone. There is no one in the world I would rather bring up my precious daughter, and I trust you completely to do what is right for her.

But Chloe, promise me that you will not give up on your own happiness. I know you have been hurt in the past, but don't let that stop you taking a chance on love. I truly believe that it's better to regret the things that don't work out in the way you'd hoped, than regret not taking a chance on something that could be amazing.

Thank you from the bottom of my heart, for everything you have done for me, and will continue to do for me through Emma after I am gone. You have been the most loyal and wonderful friend anyone could ever ask for and I feel truly blessed to have had you in my life.

All my love, always.
Your best friend forever, Liz.

Chloe slipped the letter back into the envelope with a shaking hand. She didn't realise she was weeping until she saw a tear splash onto the envelope, making the blue ink start to run. She missed Liz so much, although she knew she'd always be in her heart. And she'd always cherish the memories of her friendship.

But Liz's words in the letter about taking a chance

on love had been difficult to read. That was exactly what Chloe had done by staying with Lorenzo—but it was turning out so much more painful than Chloe could have imagined.

Lorenzo gripped the steering wheel, fury eating through him as fast as the powerful limousine ate up the miles to the village.

He could not believe that Chloe had taken the convertible. He hadn't known she had it in her to show such defiance—to deliberately disobey a direct order from him. He'd only forbidden her to drive for her own safety. The roads were narrow and winding, with sudden bends that took drivers by surprise. And the convertible was an exceptionally powerful car—a steel deathtrap in inexperienced hands.

When he found Chloe he would demand an explanation. He would let her know that it was not acceptable for her to defy him—that he would not tolerate it.

Suddenly, as he approached a tight bend, a metallic shaft of light flashed in his eye. A car had driven off the road ahead of him—the driver failing to make the sharp turn in time.

'Chloe!' Her name burst from his lips and he felt his heart crash painfully against his ribs.

He slammed on the brakes, almost losing control of the limo, and pulled off the road into an entrance to a field. He was out of his seat in a second, sprinting back to where the other car had gone through the hedge.

He clambered through the broken gap in the hedgerow, oblivious to the brambles clawing at his legs, and realised that it was not the convertible. In fact it was not even the same colour or model car. He had been thinking so hard about Chloe that his mind had played a vicious trick on him.

Filled with a mixture of relief and edginess, he hurried to the vehicle, to check if anyone needed his help. The car was abandoned. The driver and any passengers had already left the scene. He laid his hand above the engine, and confirmed that the car was cold—the accident had happened some time ago.

He walked shakily back to the limo, realising he had broken out into a cold sweat. The thought of Chloe being in an accident had terrified him. He leant against the rusty five-bar gate into the field and took some deep steadying breaths.

The only other time he could remember having felt anything like it was the night of Emma's ear infection. But this time his reaction had been even more acute. He told himself that it must be because there was a car crash involved. Car crashes were sudden and violent, and were potentially fatal.

He got back into the limo and headed onwards in the direction of the village—driving much more slowly. Then, when he reached the row of cottages and saw the convertible parked at the side of the street, he felt a second, even more intense wave of relief.

Chloe had given him a nasty fright. He would make sure she never did such a thing again.

He got out of the car angrily and walked to the cottage, glancing in through the front-room window as he approached the front door. What he saw stopped him in his tracks.

Chloe was weeping. She was sitting on the sofa, with her face buried in her hands and her whole body wracked with sobs.

A pain as sharp as a knife twisted in his stomach as he watched her.

He wanted to go in and comfort her. To wrap his arms tenderly around her and take her away from whatever was causing her such distress.

But she had not wanted him there. She had made that very clear. She had told him it was personal and that she wanted to be alone.

Suddenly, he knew that he could not disturb her. His presence would make her suffering even worse.

He turned silently away. Then he repositioned the limousine further along the street so she would not see it when she left, and sat quietly waiting for her to leave. From a distance he would check she was all right. And then he would follow her home.

CHAPTER TWELVE

CHLOE stood by the floor-to-ceiling window in the bedroom, looking out over the pre-dawn landscape. It was not much past 4:00 a.m., but the dim, colourless light of dawn was creeping across the sky.

She couldn't sleep. She was thinking of the time she'd told Lorenzo about the house of her dreams—the house which she thought had been the inspiration behind the purchase of this property they were currently living in.

It was about a year after she'd started working for him, and they had driven out of London for a business meeting with a man who'd refused to leave his home in Sussex to meet with Lorenzo in London. Chloe had loved the journey, sitting next to her gorgeous boss in the front of his sports car, chattering away about inconsequential things.

Then all of a sudden something about the countryside and the narrow, twisting roads had made her remember a house she'd visited once as a child. Her aunt had worked as a housekeeper, performing a very similar role to Mrs Guest, and one summer, when the owners of the house were away travelling, she had invited Chloe, her sister and mother to visit.

Chloe had been absolutely entranced by the place. She had never seen whole walls made out of glass before—except in high-street shops—and she'd thought they were magical. Her sister had been scared of heights, and wouldn't go near the upstairs windows. But Chloe had leant spreadeagled against the glass and it felt as if she were flying over the fields.

Her mum and aunt had shooed her away, worrying about fingerprints on the window, and then Chloe had heard them talking, saying who'd want such a ridiculous amount of glass to keep clean? But Chloe hadn't cared about that—she'd simply loved the feeling of flying, and had made a wish that one day she would live in a house like that.

It was amazing that Lorenzo had remembered. And that he had taken the trouble to find this house for her as a wedding gift.

Right from the start of their relationship he had always been attentive and thoughtful. It was all those gestures that had made her believe that he loved her, even though he had never told her.

Now she didn't know what to think. How was it possible for him to pay so much attention to little things that he knew would make her happy—yet continually throw her love back in her face? Why did he act as if she were committing some terrible moral crime, simply by having feelings for him?

Chloe ran her fingers through her hair, brushing it back off her face, and sighed. A pale hint of apricot tinged the eastern sky, and she realised the sunrise was coming. The giant window would give her an amazing view.

Suddenly it occurred to her that the birds should be singing. The dawn chorus would be underway by now, but she couldn't hear a thing. The triple-glazed, reinforced glass cut out the sounds of the outside world as effectively as a sound-proofed room.

The thought upset her. At that moment it seemed like a terrible reflection of her marriage with Lorenzo. She had a perfect view—but she wasn't really living it. All the birds out there were triumphantly singing to welcome in the dawn—but she couldn't even hear the tiniest peep.

Without thinking what she was doing, she walked silently across the room to pick up her dressing gown, then went downstairs to let herself out into the garden.

But she couldn't get out. The kitchen door was locked and she couldn't remember where the key was kept.

She hurried through to the living room, to try the French windows, but when she got there she realised she had no idea how to open them. She knew they were motorised and she thought there was a remote control somewhere, or a panel on the wall, but she couldn't find anything.

Tears started to flow down her face as she stared helplessly out through the massive glass doors.

Lorenzo lay awake in bed, aware that Chloe was not beside him. He knew she hadn't been sleeping well and often rose before dawn, to stand looking out at the view over the countryside. But now he couldn't remember the last time he'd heard her moving around.

Suddenly he realised the room was extra-still. He could hear Emma snuffling in her sleep through the open door into the adjacent room. But he could not hear Chloe.

He sat up, and instantly saw she had gone.

His heart thudded and he lurched out of bed. She'd run away—walked out on their marriage again.

Then he forced himself to stay calm. He knew she would never leave Emma. She'd probably gone down to the kitchen to make herself a drink. He'd seen the half-drunk cups of chamomile tea beside her bed in the morning, and known they hadn't been there when he went to bed at night.

But that morning he sensed something was different. She'd been so upset the previous day. What if she had realised she couldn't stay in this marriage? What if she was planning to leave him?

The thought sent dread crashing through his veins once again. He pulled on his trousers and was out of the room, running down the staircase immediately.

Then he saw her. She was at the French windows, trying to find the way to open them.

'What are you doing?' he barked, his fear making his voice hard. 'Where are you going at four-thirty in the morning?'

'Nowhere.' She turned to face him and he saw that she was weeping.

A vicious spear of agony stabbed through him. She was distraught once more—and he knew it was his fault. He was incapable of making her happy, and that knowledge was killing him.

'I'm sorry,' he said, pulling her gently into his arms. He knew it wouldn't make her feel better— how could it when she was so unhappy being with him? But he didn't know what else to do.

'I couldn't open the doors.' Her voice was muffled against his chest, but Lorenzo could hear the notes of agony in it.

'If you want to leave, I won't stop you—you deserve to be happy,' he said. 'But don't run away from me again. Let me help you. Let me make sure you are all right.'

Chloe pulled away and looked up at him. His

words had startled her. It sounded as if he cared about her. But at the same time it sounded as if he was offering to help her escape from their marriage.

'I wasn't leaving,' she said, wiping the palm of her hand across her face. 'I wanted to go outside to hear the birds singing—the dawn chorus.'

'Thank God!' Lorenzo exclaimed, crushing her against him. 'I couldn't stand it—I just couldn't stand my life without you.'

Chloe drew in a shaky breath, having difficulty breathing—both from Lorenzo's lung-crushing grip and from the words he had said. Did it mean he truly wanted her in his life? That he did have feelings for her?

'No matter what—I'll never leave you.' Her voice was squeaky with breathlessness, but then he relaxed his grip slightly to look down at her.

'But you are so unhappy with me,' Lorenzo said, confusion showing on his face and in his voice.

'I'll never leave you, because I love you,' she said simply. 'I've always loved you, and it breaks my heart that you can't love me back. But I can't even imagine not being with you any more.'

A change came over Lorenzo's expression. His eyes hardened and a muscle started throbbing in his jaw. He shook his head slightly, and even shrank back a little, as if he totally denied what she had told him.

A rush of despair rose up in Chloe. It was just like the first time she had opened her heart to him on their wedding day.

'Why don't you believe me?' she cried. 'What have I ever done to make you have no trust in what I say?'

She lifted her hand to her head, suddenly feeling dizzy from lack of sleep and stress, but she stared up into Lorenzo's face. The expression of rejection she saw there cut her to the quick.

'Why can't you look into my eyes, and see that it's true?' she demanded. 'I love you so much it hurts. But all you do is look at me like that—like I'm lying.'

Lorenzo stared down at Chloe, her distraught expression making it feel as if there were a blade twisting in his guts.

Overwhelming emotion surged through his body, and he didn't know how to handle it. He looked down into her tortured face and saw how overwrought she was. *He* had done that. *He* was the reason she was so distressed.

'I'm sorry,' he said. 'I've messed everything up so badly. I don't know how I can ever put it right.'

'It's not your fault,' she said, sounding utterly dejected. 'It's not your fault you don't feel the same as I do. You can't make yourself fall in love with someone.'

There was a terrible look of despair on her face,

which intensified when Lorenzo didn't say anything. But he didn't know *how* to respond.

He had never meant to hurt Chloe, yet he had found himself doing it again and again. Why hadn't it been possible for him to find some response—any response—that would not have torn her heart apart?

Why wasn't he able to feel what she wanted him to feel?

'All I want is your happiness,' he said, reaching out to pull her into his arms. 'I don't know why it's so difficult for me to make that happen. I know I'm breaking your heart—and it's breaking my heart too.'

Chloe closed her eyes and leant against his strong body, feeling a rush of emotion rising through her as she took in Lorenzo's anguish. She had never heard him express such strong feelings before—surely it had to mean something? That perhaps he wasn't the cold, emotionally unavailable man he claimed to be?

'I'm sorry,' he gasped, letting go and holding her away from him. 'I'm suffocating you.'

'It's all right,' she wheezed. 'I like being in your arms—it feels right.'

'Yes, it does!' he exploded, raking his hands violently through his short black hair. 'It feels so right—it has always felt right. So why do I keep hurting you so badly?'

He cursed again, and Chloe could see his hands were shaking.

'You need to get away from me—so that I can't bring you any more pain.' He took a step backwards, looking down at her with wild, anguished eyes.

She stared up at him—startled by his outburst and shaken by the intensity of it, but at the same time mesmerised by his words. Had he really begun to express something she had almost stopped hoping for—something of unbelievable wonder?

'I'm sorry,' he said. 'You deserve so much more than this—you deserve to be loved. You were right about why I brought you back here. I tried to do the right thing—to let you go before I brought you any more heartache. But I just wasn't strong enough to do it. Even though I kept hurting you—I couldn't bring myself to leave you.'

'I don't want you to leave me,' Chloe said, tears sparkling in her eyes. But she held herself in check—she didn't want to do anything to send Lorenzo off the wonderful road of understanding that she hoped and prayed he was finally travelling. 'I never want you to leave me.'

'But why?' Lorenzo demanded, an agonised expression contorting his face. 'Despite my attempts to make you happy—all I've ever done is bring you misery!'

'You *know* why I don't ever want to leave you.' Chloe stepped forward and laid her hand gently on his cheek, and suddenly Lorenzo stilled—as if the fury and rage evaporated.

'I don't…I can't believe…' he stumbled, his blue eyes confused and troubled as he looked deep into hers.

'Then tell me why you have tried to make me happy,' Chloe said. She lifted her other hand and held his face, trying to give him the strength and confidence to accept what she believed to be unfolding in his heart.

'Because…' Lorenzo stared down at her with wide, glistening eyes. His emotion was so raw, so overwhelming to him that her soul ached for him.

Chloe moved her hands gently, smoothing the moisture from his cheeks. But she looked steadily into his eyes, as if she were holding his heart with her gaze.

'Because…I love you.'

Lorenzo's voice was so quiet that Chloe could barely hear him. But the heartfelt expression in his eyes told her what she had yearned to hear for so long. Her own eyes burned with joy and suddenly the tears started to fall. Her heart was overflowing with love for Lorenzo, and finally she knew that he felt the same way.

'Are they tears of happiness?' Lorenzo said gruffly, almost hesitantly, as he stared down into the face of the woman he loved—*the woman he loved*.

'Yes.' Chloe nodded, wiping her hands over her face and gazing up at him with luminous green eyes. 'Of course they are.'

A smile broke out over Lorenzo's face and he felt his heart swell to bursting.

He was in love.

In love with Chloe.

He gazed down at her, filled with the most amazing sensation of awe. How was it possible for him to feel this way?

She looked like an angel. Heavenly beauty glowed from deep within her, and Lorenzo knew he was looking at the face of love.

'I don't deserve this,' he murmured, sliding his fingers into her blonde hair and cradling her head.

'Why not?' she asked. 'Everyone deserves to love and feel loved.'

'But…it's not…' he stumbled. 'My mother…'

'The fact that your mother was a heartless witch does not mean you are like her—or that you don't have the capacity for love,' Chloe said, suddenly sounding angrier than Lorenzo had ever heard her. 'That woman trampled your heart and bound you up inside. What she did was unforgivable—but you can't let it affect your whole life.'

Lorenzo stared down at her in shock. But her impassioned outburst had struck a chord deep inside him. She knew him so well.

Another rush of emotion stormed up through him, overwhelming him once again. He cleared his throat gruffly, and stepped away to look out of the window.

'No, don't turn away from me,' Chloe said, pulling him back towards her. 'I love you—and I won't let you shut me out again.'

Lorenzo felt himself smiling.

A bubble of laughter burst out of him. He was in love with Chloe and she was taking no prisoners.

'You've been battening down your heart for too long,' she said, thumping him playfully on the chest. 'But now we've broken it free—don't think I'm going to let you get away with closing it up again.'

He caught her hands in his, and gathered them up to him, looking seriously into her eyes once more.

'I've been a fool,' he said, with heart-wrenching honesty. 'I put so much energy into convincing myself that love was a lie—that it didn't really exist. I thought I'd found another way to build my life, a practical approach that wouldn't let me down. When you said you loved me I was angry. In one fell swoop you undermined everything I had set up to be true. I think even then I knew you were telling me the truth, but I couldn't let myself believe it.'

'You believe it now,' Chloe said. 'That's the most important thing.'

'But we wasted so much time,' he said, shaking his head as he thought about the months they'd spent apart.

'It wasn't wasted,' she said earnestly. 'Not if that was what was necessary to reach through to your heart.'

Lorenzo looked down at her, feeling another wave of emotion rising through him. She was amazing.

'You are the best part of me,' he said, reaching out to her again and drawing her into his arms. 'Without you I was nothing. Don't ever leave me.'

Chloe closed her eyes and gave herself over to the awe-inspiring depth of emotion that was flowing through her body. She'd always loved him—but this was something different. Somehow knowing that her love was reciprocated had magnified the wonder of it a hundredfold.

She had never been so happy, and she had never been filled with so much hope for the future. She leant into his embrace, knowing that she had finally found what her heart had been searching for.

A few wonderful moments later, she felt herself being lifted into his arms, and he carried her back up to their bedroom. As they passed through the doorway the sound of Emma chatting to herself in her cot drifted through to her consciousness.

'I'll get her,' Lorenzo said, placing a lingering kiss on her lips before walking through the open door into Emma's nursery next to their bedroom.

Chloe watched with happiness as he carried her in. He looked so comfortable with the baby girl. He had made a true connection with her and Chloe knew truly he was ready to be her father emotionally as well as practically.

'Let's sit here a while,' he said, getting onto the bed and placing Emma on the soft cover.

Chloe smiled and picked up a handful of toys before joining them.

'You know, she can't balance very well on here,' she said, crawling into the centre of the king-sized bed to sit with them. 'It's too wobbly.'

'I'll hold her,' Lorenzo said, sitting her between his legs and gently supporting her little body. 'I just want to sit here for a while, with my family close to me.'

Chloe felt her eyes tingle with tears once again. She looked at him holding Emma and she suddenly knew she had never seen a more beautiful sight. He looked completely relaxed, sitting with his little baby daughter.

He lifted his glowing eyes and caught her gaze with his.

'Come closer,' he said, holding out his arm. 'I want both my girls close to me.'

Chloe smiled and moved across the bed, careful not to wobble Emma off balance, although she knew Lorenzo had her.

She snuggled up against him, revelling in the warm strength of his arm around her. It felt truly wonderful sitting there. Then suddenly she heard the familiar rustle of a foil packet coming from his trouser pocket as he shifted his position slightly.

At that moment she made another decision—or rather she knew that the time was right to take the next step.

She slipped her hand into his pocket and drew out the condom packet.

'Hmm.' Lorenzo made an approving sound. 'But I think it's still a bit too early to take Emma down to Mrs Guest.'

'That's OK,' Chloe said. 'We'll be alone later. But we won't be needing this.'

With that she tossed the little packet away, towards the waste-paper basket under the dressing table.

She felt a tremble pass through Lorenzo, and she looked up to see the shimmer of moisture in his eyes once more.

'I love you,' he said.

The following morning, before the cool light of dawn started to creep over the horizon, Chloe felt Lorenzo lifting her gently out of bed.

'Come with me,' he murmured in her ear, drawing her out of a deep, restful sleep. 'I have a surprise for you.'

'What is it?' Chloe asked dreamily. Her body was still fabulously relaxed, and glowing from the aftermath of the most wonderful lovemaking they had ever shared. Somehow, knowing that a new life might form inside her because of it had made it even more magical than usual. 'It's the middle of the night—where are you taking me?'

'It's not the middle of the night,' Lorenzo said, carrying her out of the bedroom, duvet and all.

He took her downstairs, then pressed a button on the concealed control panel, and the giant sliding doors in the living room glided open.

Chloe drew in a surprised breath of fresh pre-dawn air, but her body was still cosy, wrapped up snugly in the duvet.

'I've got us a front row seat,' Lorenzo said, carrying her across the glistening dew-covered lawn towards the bench that overlooked the meadow. 'With full surround sound.'

Chloe smiled—completely speechless. She couldn't believe he had planned this, woken up hours before he had to, just to bring her outside for the dawn chorus.

They sat together on the bench, watching the golden tinge in the east unfold into the most beautiful sunrise Chloe had ever seen, and listening to the sound of myriad birds greeting the new day in a truly magnificent ensemble.

'Thank you,' Chloe breathed when the symphony of birdsong had eased from its glorious crescendo.

'That was the most amazing thing anyone has ever done for me.'

'You're welcome,' Lorenzo said. 'All I want, more than anything in the world, is to make you happy.'

'All I need to make me happy is your love,' she replied, gazing up into the face of the man she adored.

'Chloe Valente, I love you,' he said, his voice vibrating with powerful, heartfelt emotion. 'I love you more than I can say. And I always will.'

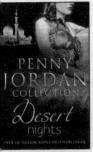
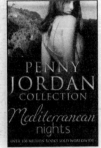
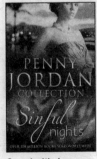

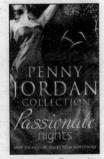

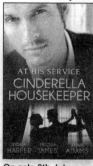